CW00522130

Other Books by Lee Winter

On the Record series

The Red Files

Under Your Skin

The Superheroine Collection

Shattered

Standalone

Breaking Character

The Brutal Truth

Requiem for Immortals

Changing the Script

LEE WINTER

Dedication

For my love. Thank you for everything you did on this book, even for the sarcasm-dipped-in-marshmallows notes. (The cartoons helped.) We got there in the end!

Acknowledgments

This book would be much poorer without the generous insights and technical expertise of film-making guru Silvia Lindner. For months, Silvia amused and educated me on everything from the subtleties between lights and lamps, PAs and ADs, O-1 and O-2 visas for working in Hollywood, and breaking down how the major studios act. Thanks. You're a legend.

Fellow Ylva author and doctor Chris Zett was as brilliant as ever in explaining all the ways my banged-up, stubborn cop would be treated and medicated. I appreciate the medical advice—even if Sam Keegan made a terrible patient!

New Zealand Police Media were so wonderful. Their job is to deal with the media, but they helped out an Australian author bobbing up with constant questions about procedure, uniforms, weapons, and response times for back-up to regional areas. They were fast and amusing. Thanks!

Also a big "cheers, mate", to Australian policewoman Darrelle Dawes for helping out with police procedure on being surrounded in a hostile environment. Great insider info!

Editors always help make a book sing, and thanks go once more to Alissa McGowan for thumping this one into shape with her usual rigor and humor. Always a fun ride.

Beta readers Diana, Donna, and Alex were invaluable. Sorry, Diana, for making you read this so many times! You're a saint. A shout-out also goes to my long-time beta, Char, who tried in vain to help once again, but the technology gods kept on intervening. Curses!

For Astrid, boss-god at Ylva, my eternal thanks for keeping the faith in me.

Lastly, to my readers, I would be nothing without you. Your love for the *Breaking Character* world is why this book now exists. I hope you enjoy this spin-off, too.

Chapter 1

Worst. Movie. Ever.

Alex Levitin had just broken the number-one rule of Hollywood. She was late. And not just a little.

Naturally her beat-up, elegantly rusting '97 Prius had chosen today of all days not to start. Then her Lyft driver had insisted on taking a "shortcut," cavalierly waving away Alex's long and exacting set of directions.

Bursting through the doors at the upmarket Lemontree Lounge and Grill, she scanned the room for the face of a film executive who was probably no longer here.

She'd researched rising-star producer Caroline Bassett in the past week and now knew about the woman's nut allergy, shoe size, and the fact that two months ago she'd left a TV soap she'd been producing to join the film studio—after a flurry of executives had been shunted out the door.

Alex's eye finally fell to an elegant, spray-tanned, sallow-cheeked woman at a corner table who appeared as though air was her favorite food group.

She waited? That was...unexpected.

Caroline Bassett wore expensive suits and ambition well. Her perfectly coiffed, highlighted blonde hair was a tribute to conservative news anchors and industrial-strength hairspray. She reclined against her white-washed wooden chair, waving around a cocktail in one hand and tapping away at an iPhone with the other.

Alex slowed her scrambling pace to a saunter, hands running down her black pants as if to erase the impossible stench of hopeless, late, and unprofessional.

glanced up, their eyes met, and her lips curved into a smile ..ight have been airbrushed on. She dropped her phone to the ..ched white tablecloth.

"Alexandra." She rose, air-kissing her.

"Ms. Bassett, good afternoon."

"Caroline, please. It's a delight to meet you."

It is? Alex was pretty sure no one at a major studio would be thrilled to meet a relative unknown like her. "I'm so sorry I'm late. My car—"

"Never mind." Caroline waved away her excuse. "My time's short, I'm afraid, so we'll have to skip the formalities." She paused, gaze darting to someone at a distant corner table. "I had *no* idea Cade was with Byron." She sounded gleefully scandalized.

Alex turned to see the A-listers in question canoodling in a small booth. "Um…"

"Did you receive our script?" Caroline asked, her tone and focus suddenly as sharp as the crisp seam on her cream silk shirt. "*Shezan: Mistress of the Forest*?" She rolled her tongue all over "mistress" as though speaking of a sexual thriller instead of a tawdry, B-grade flick that reeked worse than a gutter outside a pub on a Saturday night.

"I did. I've got to say, I was very surprised to get your message." Alex had no clue what was in her indie-filmmaker repertoire of liberal, philosophical think-pieces that made any Hollywood studio think *she* should direct this movie.

Truthfully, Alex had never seen a worse script in her life. Oh, it wasn't just the sleazy male lead character, the cheap violence, or the asinine dialog. Nor was it the excuse to have a lot of loin-cloth-wearing Amazons of color that, as a lovely bonus, added a weird racist tinge. Her biggest objection was the ending. It hooked up the unrepentant, creepy poacher with the sweet nymph who guarded the animals of her forest.

What. The. Hell? How was it even funded? By a major studio no less?

A twenty-something waitress interrupted, her ample bust straining against her blouse, a fourth, unopened button threatening to give up its day job. The nametag suggested she was called 'Desire.' Unless the restaurant had misspelt Desiree, this was undoubtedly another unemployed actress.

"May I get you a drink?" Desire's eyes lit on Alex as though she was the tastiest morsel on the specials board. "Or something to eat?" She pointed to a paper menu on the table.

Alex ran her eye down the list of exotic dishes that included eighteen-dollar raw-beet and tofu appetizers with unpronounceable garnishes.

Caroline's lips pursed.

Oh, right. Hadn't she said she was in a hurry? "I'll stick to drinks."

The tight lips instantly ceased their puckering.

"Do you have any Ethiopia Organico coffee?" Alex asked.

"We have forty-seven coffee varieties, including that one." Desire beamed.

"Good. I'll take a cup. No milk or sugar."

The waitress's gaze lingered a beat too long before she turned to Caroline. "And for you, ma'am?"

Caroline waved her away wordlessly.

The waitress nodded and disappeared.

A smirk edged Caroline's lips. "You have a fawning groupie."

"Or more likely she'll have a script she wants me to read. And a boyfriend."

"No doubt." Caroline's smile finally spread to her eyes. "I thought you English only ordered tea?"

"I've been in LA fifteen years now. I'm adapting." Alex cleared her throat. "As are you. From TV soaps to movie studios in five years. Impressive."

"Yes," Caroline agreed. Her smile became shark-like. "I am."

Alex smothered a laugh at the lack of modesty. "So about *Shezan*… My main question is, why me?"

"We've seen your work. Loved it." Caroline's smile resumed its earlier fakeness. "Especially that climate-change flick. Bold. Brilliant, darling. Art! You've turned a lot of heads."

Art? Riiight. Wasn't schmoozing supposed to be a little more subtle?

The organic coffee arrived, along with a coquettish smile before Desire departed with a jaunty swish of hips.

Definitely an actress.

Alex reached for her coffee. "Are you talking to a number of directors or just me?" She choked down a swallow of the scalding drink, wishing she could convince herself to appreciate the slightly burnt, bitter flavor. She'd read somewhere that the coffee beans deal had lifted a whole Ethiopian village out of extreme poverty so, on principle, she refused to hate it.

"You're our first choice." Caroline's words would probably have held more weight if her gaze hadn't been roaming the room restlessly, weighing up everyone in a suit.

Sure I am. Alex wondered how many others had turned this down before her. After all, *Variety*, usually the even-handed bible of the industry, had called *Shezan: Mistress of the Forest* the most toxic film ever green-lit, and had helpfully listed the assortment of directors and writers who'd said yes and later fled. No one smart would touch this dumpster fire now.

Hell, Alex was only here for the free lunch and networking. It wasn't a shrewd move to say a flat no to a powerful studio. She half listened as Caroline launched into a spirited defense of the wonders of *Shezan*. The executive dropped in carefully chosen keywords, although each came with an asterisk. Autonomy, *within reason*. Script rewrites allowed, *with studio input*. The sets had already been built and were ready, *using the previous directors' visions*. And she'd get a big say in expenditure, as long as she *stuck to the limited budget*.

"How limited?" Alex asked curiously.

Caroline mumbled a small number before throwing a gulp of neon cocktail down her throat.

Surely Alex had misheard. "Seriously?"

"Look, it's not one of our top-listed projects." Caroline dabbed her lips with a paper napkin. The crimson smear left behind looked like a blood stain. "You'd be amply compensated, of course. But due to the situation with creative people linked to the project…ah…leaving us so unexpectedly, well, we've already sunk significant funds into it that we can't get back."

"Why did the others leave?"

"Various reasons." Caroline gave a small shrug. "Who cares? They're gone, and we want you. So, bottom line, we need someone talented and dedicated, who can make something feel larger than life on a tight budget. Someone who wouldn't mind shooting in a distant location like New Zealand. That's why we cast around for a well-credentialed indie director."

Alex's bullshit detector shot up. "There are plenty of indie directors."

"Yes, but we need someone like you, who can bring to life a female-focused project, make it *worthy*." She looked as if she was debating whether to whip out a pink pussy hat to sell her point. "And we need someone who also can fix not only the film, but also the, erm, small image problem *Shezan* has at the moment." Caroline swirled her cocktail.

Small image problem? *Most toxic film ever* was not a *small* image problem.

"I'm not going to lie to you; we need your talent, your eye. You're a perfect choice for us." Naked ambition burned in Caroline's gaze. Despite Alex's years in LA, she had never gotten used to seeing this. The rawness of it was unsettling. There was a reason you shouldn't look directly into the sun.

"We can do bold things together," Caroline concluded, patting Alex's wrist with cool, spindly fingers. "And *I* want this deal." Another shark grin. "Very much."

Alex took a sip of her coffee and debated whether to be honest. Honest…in LA. "I believe you," she finally said. "So would I be right in thinking you want this deal so much because you're new to your job? You need a few quick wins? Maybe fixing the 'worst movie ever' is your play to be noticed? That's ambitious," Alex said lightly. "I'm curious…as the studio's only female executive, was it your idea to be the one to win over the gay, feminist filmmaker?"

"Hmm." Caroline's expression sharpened but her lips twitched. "You know, Alexandra, I like you. You're clever. Clever women go far in this town. Of course, they go much farther when people never realize just how clever they are."

"Ah. Did I just break the fourth wall by pointing out the game in play?" Alex's lips curled.

Caroline snorted and one immaculate eyebrow lifted. "I see your English streak's still in you after all." Her laugh was carefully curated. "You prefer to cut to the chase? All right: Tell me, shall we do this? Do you want a 'quick win,' too? One everyone will be watching? Big risk, but huge gain."

Far too big a risk. Even though Alex was between jobs, and no one in her indie world had sent her anything exciting lately, her reputation was all she had. There was nothing she'd heard today that had convinced her to put everything on the line. For all the experience she'd get in working with a major studio, there was no avoiding the fact that this film was a reputation killer.

There was no nice way to say this. "Look, Caroline, I appreciate the offer and that you thought of me, but I don't think..."

Caroline's phone jangled to life. Glancing at the name on the screen, she rose. "Excuse me, I must take this call." She left without waiting for a reply and strode into the nearby bar area.

Alex glanced around at all the networkers at adjacent tables. Then she turned her own phone off mute and scrolled through her mail. One new message made her scowl. She read her ex-girlfriend's email, stomach plummeting, then read it again, much more slowly. *Holy...*

She dialed a number she knew by heart. "Bettina!"

"Alex?" The accountant's crisp, professional voice had once made her melt into puddles. Those days were long gone.

"You... I..." she choked out. "You said my finances were 'fab.' You said you'd sorted everything for me!"

"What's wrong?" Bettina's unflappable voice asked. "Breathe and tell me."

Breathe? I'll give you 'breathe'! "You've forwarded me an IRS bill for $45,000!"

"Ah that. Yes. It seems the IRS changed a couple of components of their tax act and I wasn't aware."

"What? Isn't that your actual job?"

"Not exactly," Bettina said in a dismissive tone. "They've tightened some areas on individual deductions related to independent film companies like yours, and reallocated certain write-offs into a new category for which you don't fit the criteria anymore. No one could have predicted that."

"Predicted... Bettina, it's *$45,000*! I don't have that kind of money lying around."

"No need to get hysterical."

"Hysterical!"

"Not to mention glass half-empty. It could have been much more if I hadn't found you some new deductions. Some of my film clients were hit with much larger bills."

"Bettina, this is so damned typical. You're all front. Do you even know what you're doing?"

"If this is going to degenerate into insults, I'll hang up. I did your taxes for free, you know. I think I'll send you the bill now that we're no longer together."

"Which I will shred along with your phone number."

"*So* dramatic. You're obviously in the right line of work. And I don't have to take this abuse." The line went dead.

Alex dropped her phone back on the table and scowled. Quickly she ran through her options. She didn't own much, so there was nothing to sell. It made no sense to accumulate things given her nomadic lifestyle, shooting all over the world. Her apartment was a rental. Her bank accounts weren't bulging, either, because while her small production company's movies broke even these days, any profits were reinvested into her next project. Her Londoner parents were retirees who made do on the pension, not that she'd ask them or anyone she knew for money.

So her options had just narrowed into one. She'd do a movie so far beneath her that her tattered dignity might never recover. *Christ.*

It wasn't supposed to be like this. She'd come to Hollywood with dreams to make movies that *meant* something. What was *Shezan's* message? How to devalue near-naked women via interpretive dance? How to keep a straight face while saying lines that boiled down to, "Hark, Forest Mistress, beware the white man's fire stick"? Or was it actually some fiendishly clever metaphor about powerful, white, entitled men always winning, so don't even bother fighting the system?

Alex rubbed her head.

But what if...she did the impossible? What if she took a leaf out of Caroline's book? *Big risk, huge gain... if I succeed.*

A tiny flame of challenge curled inside. Imagine if Hollywood's much-mocked "worst script" could be turned into something good? What would *that* do for her reputation? This could make or break a career. Besides, she'd never been to New Zealand before. So maybe it'd be fun, seeing somewhere new.

On top of that, hadn't Caroline said in her email that Chloe Martin was its star? In one of those six degrees of separation things, Alex's best friend, Bess, and Chloe's best friend, Summer, were dating each other. That connection meant Alex had encountered *Shezan's* star fairly often in her social circle.

The New Zealand woman was likable, laid-back, dry, and amusing. That was a relief. Divas were a nightmare Alex could do without, especially given the drama she'd have ahead with such a low-quality script. A script she'd make sure was improved drastically if she took the project.

So...really, taking this job would be like doing her friends a favor, wouldn't it? Ensuring Chloe's role was improved, not to mention helping all those poor chilly Amazons get a better shake. Hell, Alex was practically doing a service for humanity.

Ugh. So lame. She tapped her glass with a short fingernail... Maybe if she made a list. She was good at lists.

Alex set to scribbling on a napkin.

Cons:
Crash and burn if I don't pull it off. *Everyone* will know.
Hollywood is watching closely and I may not get a second chance after this.

Pros:
Chloe is cool—no diva drama.
I'll be seen as a genius if I succeed.
Pay off the IRS...happens even if the film tanks.
~~Amazons!!!~~ (Scratch that. You are *not* fifteen.)

Her last point made her roll her eyes. That reminded her. Grabbing her phone, Alex looked up who was doing *Shezan*'s costumes. Who would she have to growl at to get something less prurient on the design board?

The name staring back at her made her do a double take. Only recently signed to the production, apparently, was one Skye Storm—the brilliant costume designer Alex had worked with on one of her first films, *Heaven's Blood.* Never a more talented, warmer, or eccentric soul had she encountered.

It was weird that Skye was doing *Shezan* when she had her pick of films these days, but Alex wasn't about to look a gift horse in the mouth. As she imagined the possibilities ahead, her stomach began to calm. Two wildly creative, un-mainstream brains working on this could actually produce something original.

Right. Alex added Skye's name to her pros list. She studied it for a moment.

Am I seriously thinking of doing this?

Caroline joined her again, looking suitably contrite. "Sorry about that. Studio VPs are like toddlers. They always want your attention *now.*" She cocked her head. "So, you were saying something about how you don't think this is the film for you?"

Alex shook her head. "I was actually saying I don't think I can see a better way to challenge myself than with *Shezan.*" She smiled. "I'm good to go. No doubts."

Caroline's eyes slid to the napkin with Alex's list scribbled over it, and her lips quirked. "Yes. I can see that."

"Well, no doubts now," she corrected with a grin.

"Excellent." Caroline signaled for the check, clearly done with the conversation, her mission accomplished. "I'll have the contract sent over in an hour. You'll need to be in New Zealand ASAP. *Shezan*'s EP, Quincy Blackman, has been down there already for a few months. He's going stir crazy without a new director to move things along. Be a dear and Skype him the good news and put him out of his misery. I'll send you his details." She rose as the check arrived. "Welcome aboard. The studio will be delighted."

Alex nodded, her stomach dropping in freefall at her fate being officially sealed, before remembering her manners. She thanked Caroline for that cup of bad, village-saving coffee and watched, numb, as the executive floated over to the counter to pay. She couldn't back out now.

Her phone beeped a reminder of an upcoming appointment. Already?

Time flies when you're selling your soul.

Alex was packing furiously early the next morning when her phone rang. She knew who it'd be without looking. Elizabeth "Bess" Thornton—Alex's best friend, fellow Brit, and formerly America's most-hated TV villain—often multi-tasked with calls at this time of day.

"Hello, Bess." Alex tossed rugged brown boots into her bag. "This is an ungodly hour, even for you."

"Did I wake you? I'm terribly sorry." Bess's voice came in tight puffs down the phone. Rhythmic footfalls on a treadmill slapped in the background.

"Not this time." Alex held up two jackets before tossing the thicker one in with her boots. "Where's the fire? It's barely six."

"I heard the news from Skye."

Already? Alex should have guessed. "Of course you heard." Skye Storm wasn't just a costume-designing genius but LA's networking queen. One of the side effects of Bess being involved with Skye's daughter, Summer, was that Bess now got all the industry gossip first.

"You didn't even think to talk to me first?" Bess asked. "Why not? Aren't we friends?!"

"Ease up, love. I only signed the contract last night!"

"Contract?" The rhythmic running ceased abruptly. "Alex? Are you directing a new film?"

"Wait, aren't you calling about *Shezan*?"

Bess's hiss at the name of the movie was probably not a good sign. "No! I called because Skye says a lot of industry people are furious with Bettina for screwing up their taxes. I assumed you were caught out, too, so I called to check. What's this about *Shezan*? Isn't that the diabolical *Tarzan/Sheena* rip-off everyone's shredding? That thing Chloe's starring in?"

Alex winced. "Well, I think it's more a 'reimagining' than a rip-off."

"Oh, yes, they're *reimaginatively* ripping off someone else's ideas and making it worse."

"It's not *that* bad."

"Not that..." Bess sucked in a deep breath. "You're saying it's not just pretty girls bouncing around in leather bikinis?"

"Well, no, not bikinis. It's more like this tiny, skinny piece of leather loin cloth—"

"And *this* is what you've signed on to? This?"

"Well." *Shit.* "Yes?"

A ragged breath followed. Then damning silence. Finally: "Good God, Alex, why?"

"It's a challenge." She hoped that sounded more convincing to Bess's ears than it did to her own. "I want to see if I can take a movie everyone is writing off and turn it into something worth watching. If I do that, everyone will be talking. Besides, I won't be alone. I'll have Skye transforming the Amazon costumes into something powerful. And it might even be fun to try something new." There, that sounded plausible, didn't it?

"Alexandra, last time I checked, you create indie masterpieces about intense emotional journeys using esoteric societal metaphors. You don't do *fun*."

The upside *and* the downside of best friends was how well they knew you. "Fine! That isn't the only reason I'm doing it."

"So Bettina did mess up your finances?"

"Yeah. And now I have a tax bill only *Shezan* can fix."

"Which is why I called. Why not come to me?" Bess sounded hurt.

Back when they'd dated, Bess sometimes got this tone to her voice, silently asking whether Alex would like any financial help. Alex's gut reaction was the same now as then.

"Look, you're my best friend. And *that's* why." Alex willed her to understand. "Money is complicated, and it creates a messed-up dynamic. People act weird. I don't want that between us."

"It doesn't have to be weird. Money's just..." Bess cast around for a word. "...a tool that can make problems disappear. I have more of it than I know what to do with now. I'd love to help you if you'll let me."

"No, Bess. It's not that I don't appreciate the offer, but it *would* be weird. For me. Every time I looked at you, I'd know that I owed you. Even if it was just a loan, still, I'd think about it all the time. I don't want that. I love us as we are—equals. I'd do a hundred *Shezans* before I took a cent from you."

"I really wish you'd let me help." Bess sighed. "But I understand."

"Thank you. And it's better this way, trust me. Besides, if my bold, insane plan comes off, and I turn this trash into something good, this could end up being the best decision of my life." She slapped on her most confident tone to sell it.

"All right. If you're sure?"

Sure? Oh hell, not even close. "Yes. Absolutely. But thanks for the thought, love."

"Well." Bess sounded mollified. "If you change your mind, I'm only a call away."

"I know. And it'll be fine. One movie and everything's solved." How simple it sounded. Life was never that easy.

"Okay then. Keep an eye on Chloe and Skye out there in the wilds. You know how close they are. Chaos will be their middle names."

"Oh lord." Alex laughed, picturing them up to mischief together. Skye had virtually adopted Chloe as another daughter. "I'll probably come back to LA having aged twenty years, with a shock of white hair." Alex ran her fingers through her short red strands.

"If anyone could pull that look off, it'd be you." Bess sounded affectionate. "I'll leave you to it." She rung off.

It was nice to have Bess's solid faith in her. *She* didn't doubt Alex's abilities to pull off this impossible plan. If only Alex could convince herself as easily.

Chapter 2

Lost in Translation

AFTER THIRTEEN EXHAUSTING HOURS SQUEEZED on a plane watching more syrupy family movies than she had the stomach for, Alex now found herself cooped up in a rental car. Not ideal given what a nervous driver she was when off the beaten track. Still, New Zealand didn't have that many people, did it? So, she'd be fine.

Thick grasses; huge, jagged ferns; and fat, towering trees crept in on either side, with moss-covered trunks as shaggy as carpet. The vegetation was so densely packed up against the road that driving felt like being shot through nature's torpedo tube. Except twistier. And much colder.

Alex hadn't anticipated the way New Zealand's icy blue fingers could somehow claw their way right inside her jacket and button-down shirt until she felt the chilled hand flat upon her chest. Even with the heater on, she was shivering. Not for the first time, she considered detouring to the nearest town to pick up some thermals. If only she had any clue where the nearest town was. On account of the fact she was a little...disoriented. Sidetracked? Okay, *fine*, she was lost.

Somehow between Auckland International Airport and here, she'd gotten all turned around. She'd given up trying to figure out the confusing GPS two minutes after leaving the airport, and when she'd stopped to fill up her car and ask for directions, she'd merely been told to turn right at a nearby dairy.

Mystifyingly, no cow-milking farms had materialized, and the only business she'd passed for miles was a cheery convenience store. The car's map book had gotten her this far, but now nothing made sense.

She glanced around again, sure she'd been past here already. The road signs looked suspiciously like ones she'd seen half an hour ago. It made no sense. Alex liked things that made perfect sense. Logic, lists, and problem-solving were her middle name. Ordinarily.

A huge, gnarled tree jutted into the ominous skies. Okay, *that* she definitely recognized. Damn it. She was going in circles.

Her gaze swept the stunning landscape. Any other day, she'd slow right down and admire the vibrant green scenery, but she had a film set to get to. Specifically, a rented farmer's paddock just outside the tiny town of Ika Whenu, near the only slightly less tiny Te Aroha. She should reach it if she ever got out of Mangatarata Forest. Which was looking like a big if. She'd have to pull over and consult the map book again.

She remembered the road suddenly widening at a clearing in the next mile or so. So she'd be able to stop there, figure out her bearings, and…

Oh bollocks. There! Right there! Alex stomped on the brakes. She'd gone right by it.

Putting her car into reverse, she backed quickly into the small clearing, then turned off the engine and exhaled. Glancing around, she noticed she was blocking a small dirt lane beyond which lay dense forest.

Suddenly, a roaring black blur burst out of a hole in the scrubby bushes. The motorcycle looked about a second away from slamming into the side of her car.

No! Alex's eyes widened, her hands frozen on the steering wheel as she gasped.

Half a second to impact.

Hunching her shoulders, Alex braced herself for the hit.

At the last moment, the motorcycle swerved sharply as its owner wrenched the machine down on its side, flattening it to just miss the nose of the car.

Even so, it was so close that one spinning, horizontal rear wheel passed under the front and came back out again. The machine continued on its trajectory, propelled along in a sickening, screeching slide across dirt and undergrowth before coming to a rest in the middle of the road in a fiery trail of sparks.

Oh fuck!

Alex flung open her door and sprinted over to the unmoving, black-leather-clad rider, who was pinned under the bike.

"I'm so sorry!" she called. "I didn't know that was an actual road." *Stupid comment.*

"Well, now you do." The reply was low, annoyed, and unmistakably female. It was accompanied by a pained grunt. "Forestry Road's where the Maramarua Forest dirt-bike trail ends." She looked past Alex to her car. "You've blocked the exit where bikes slow down before they turn onto the main road."

"Sorry, I just got here." Alex's gaze swept the downed bike and its rider. "Are you hurt?"

"I'll know when I'm vertical again." The woman tried to shift and gasped. Her face contorted under the open-faced, black, retro-style helmet. "My leg's stuck. Do you think you could make yourself useful and pull the front up a little while I…?" The woman stopped mid-sentence and peered up at Alex. "Oh. Never mind."

"What?"

"You're the size of a sparrow. It'd probably kill you. Even faster than you almost killed me."

Alex glanced down at herself. Her thin, black, tailored pants, jacket, and white shirt didn't exactly bulk out her frame. And okay, she was kind of…well…waif-ish. Genetics and all that. Her nerdy black-framed glasses didn't help her look any more solid, she supposed. But she had muscles, if you hunted for them, and…

Who am I kidding? The last time a cameraman in the field had asked her to shoulder his unit while he changed a cable, it had almost pinned her to the ground.

Adrenaline was kicking in now, though. Couldn't people do amazing acts of strength in a crisis? She'd read that somewhere. With a firm step forward, Alex grasped the handlebars, gave the woman a determined look, and said, "Don't count me out. I may surprise you. Ready?"

With a skeptical look, the woman said, "Guess I don't have much choice." She bit her lip, braced her arms against the bike, and nodded.

Alex could do this. She would! She pulled with all her might. Astonishingly, the bike shifted. And then shifted again. It moved almost a quarter of a foot.

Yes! Sparrow, my ass!

Then, to her horror, her back gave out. The handlebars started to slip. Her strength left her like a deflating balloon as the weight of the bike wrenched down on her trembling arms. "No…nononono… Bollocks! Watch out!"

The metal deadweight dropped back onto the woman's hip and thigh with a sickening thud.

Pain flared across her face, and this time her groan sounded like it had been wrenched out of her.

So much for adrenaline.

Silence descended for a few moments as they eyed each other.

"You're right," the woman finally spoke, irritation etched on her features. "That *was* surprising."

"I'm really sorry!"

"Guess I'll have to do it myself." She suddenly flung her arms up and pushed the bike hard, baring her teeth under the strain. This time the machine lifted a full foot from the ground.

Jesus. Alex jumped in to help, despite the woman's frosty glare, and between them, the chassis lifted enough for her to slide her leg out, then the rest of her.

For a moment, the woman lay there beside her bike, dazed, dragging in deep breaths, and staring at her dented machine. Then she made to stand.

"What are you doing?" Alex asked in alarm, waving her hands in frantic "stop" gestures.

"I have to get my bike off the road before it causes an accident." Her voice became dry as she added, "Well, another one." Her expression hardened. "Do you usually just fly off roads into clearings without looking? I saw you go past and thought it was clear, but the next second, you're shooting backwards like a maniac to block my path, leaving me nowhere to go." She gritted her teeth as she edged herself onto her knees.

"Um, should you be moving at all?" Alex fumbled through her pocket, digging out her phone. *Did I switch on global roaming yet?* She couldn't remember. "I should call 9-1-1."

"Fat lot of good that'll do in New Zealand." She placed one hand on the ground in front of her. "Calling 9-1-1... You're American then? You sound English."

"Born in London, now living in LA."

The woman didn't answer as she shifted her weight forward onto her hands and knees and took a deep breath. Then promptly vomited.

"Oh my God! It's...it's internal bleeding!" Alex cried out. *Isn't that what they say on TV?* "What *is* the damned emergency number around here? Or the number for the cops—they'll know what to do."

"I wouldn't bother trying the police." The woman dragged herself unsteadily to her feet and wiped her mouth with the back of her gloved hand. "They're not working today." Gingerly, she tested her weight on her leg and grimaced.

"What?" Alex looked up. *Lord.* She was so tall. Maybe five-ten or eleven? Strong shoulders, straight posture, almost a military bearing, and she didn't seem to be carrying an ounce of excess weight.

The woman took off her helmet and ran a hand through her collar-length dark-blonde hair. The sleek cut suited her chiseled face and its strong jaw and high cheekbones. She was about Alex's age, in her late thirties. Drawing her sunglasses up to sit on the top of her head revealed probing blue eyes. That intense gaze stared right into Alex, then stared some more, as though deconstructing her at the cellular level.

Alex couldn't decide exactly how intimidated to be.

The woman staggered forward with another pained wince.

Alex rushed over to put a steadying arm around her waist. "Hey, let me help. And why aren't the cops on duty?"

"The closest station is shut today." She gave Alex an impatient look and elbowed her hand away. "Don't touch. I'm all right. I just need a second to catch my breath."

"You were in an accident. You vomited!"

"And?" She drew in a deeper breath and rubbed the side of her thigh. After a moment, she looked a little stronger. Okay, maybe she really was "all right," if her definition was merely being vertical.

"Vomiting's a bad sign," Alex persisted.

"My stomach just cramped and I drank too much water at my last break. That's all. You watch too much TV."

True. Her guilty pleasure was Summer and Bess's former hospital drama, *Choosing Hope*. Addictively bad, it definitely shouldn't be forming the basis of Alex's medical conclusions. She cast around for a topic change. "It's terrible your local police station's shut."

"Is it?"

"Of course!" Was this woman nuts? "How incompetent is this place?"

"Let me guess, there are 24-7 police stations where you're from?" The woman cocked an eyebrow.

"Well, of course." Did she think criminals took the day off because the police weren't around?

"Lucky you, having all your whims fully catered to."

Whims? Alex scowled. "Being safe from criminals is hardly a *whim*."

"I guess it depends on the crimes." The woman placed her helmet on the ground and dusted down her leather pants.

"If there are no cops, shall I call an ambulance?"

"No. I'm okay."

Alex glanced back to the road, her gaze coming to rest on the downed bike. "Will that be okay, too?"

"I don't know." Agitation crossed her face. She walked carefully back to her bike, this time without the unsteadiness of earlier, and studied the damage. Annoyance replaced the fear in her expression as she lifted it gently upright and wheeled it back to the side of the road. "Do you know how long I saved up to buy this?" She shook her head. "Three years. This is a Triumph Tiger XCX. It's my…" She stopped, and her face closed over. "It's important to me."

"I'm so sorry," Alex said again. "Truly."

"So you keep saying."

"I can't help it. Apologizing is an English pastime." She offered a grin but was met with an even stare. Alex's gaze flicked over the bike. Nothing seemed to be hanging off it, and the wheels didn't seem wonky as far as she could tell, but the scrapes and chips in that sleek black paint were an eyesore. "I'll pay, of course. For repairs. I mean, I should have looked before reversing across your path."

"Damn straight you're paying." The woman's fingers shifted restlessly over the machine, cataloguing its flaws, pausing over each scratch and dent. "I'd say you're very lucky the police station's shut today. You're a textbook case of dangerous and reckless driving. That could mean a fine of thousands or up to three months jail."

The hell? "How was I to know a tiny side road in the middle of nowhere would have motorcycles spitting out of a hole like some Bat Cave!"

"Ignorance is no excuse." The woman walked around to the front of Alex's car and studied the license plate. "A rental. So who are you and where do I send the bill… Ms…?"

"Alex Levitin." Alex pulled out her ID to prove it.

The woman peered at it, as though memorizing the details, then nodded.

"And you are?"

She cocked her head. "Sam Keegan."

"Okay, Sam Keegan, you can send the bill or the insurance details to my film set. It's a bunch of trailers—what you'd call luxury caravans—parked on location at a farm, near…" She dragged her paperwork out of her pocket and had a stab at the name, Ika Whenu. "Ike-a When-oo."

"It's pronounced Icka Fenoo." Sam squinted at her. "It's disrespectful if you can't even get the name right. Locals won't be kind if you screw that up."

Alex gritted her teeth. *Lovely.* "Do you need the full address for the set?"

"No, I know where it is. Everyone does. You movie people aren't exactly subtle. And a lot of locals are starstruck that Hollywood has landed." Her tone dripped with disdain.

"Not you? What have you got against movies?"

"Nothing, usually. But this one? What could I possibly have against an exploitative flick that puts our local women in costumes that make them look cheap and feel embarrassed, and has some of our less evolved young males calling them degrading names? I have seen more pub fights start in the past three months over that demeaning movie than all other topics put together."

Oh crap. Alex squared her jaw. "Sounds like they're spending a bundle around town. Can't be all bad."

"Money isn't everything, though. Although I'm sure the entitled bastard running this show thinks it is. Would explain a lot."

Right. So…now was probably not the time mention the *she* was the entitled bastard running *Shezan*. "Look, can you just tell me where the set is from here? That's why I was pulling over—to check my map. I got so turned around. I've been trying to get there for ages."

"How long have you been trying?" Sam walked stiffly over to Alex's rental and cupped her hands against the glass, looking inside.

"Two hours. Or maybe, um, three."

Sam turned back to her with an incredulous look. "That's ridiculous. It's only a ninety-minute trip from the airport *all* the way to your set. And you have a GPS in there." She tapped the car window. "Come on"—she eyed her suspiciously—"no one's that navigationally challenged."

No kidding. "Yeah, well, I'm apparently the exception to that rule. See, I was aiming to get to Mangatarata first, which I know is a forest from all the green splotches on the map, and from there find the road to Ika Whenu. But I'm following all the local signs yet keep ending up here."

"Tourists." Sam barked out a laugh.

Alex glared and waited.

"You want to get to Mangatarata. But you've probably been going left at the sign to *Maramarua.* They're not the same names. So, at the next T-intersection, go right at the sign, not left. Left is one long loop road."

Some eye for detail she had. "The names *are* a mouthful," Alex tried. "Thanks. I'd be stuck here in the middle of nowhere forever if you hadn't come along."

The other woman's expression turned wintry. "You know, 'middle of nowhere' is still someone's home. Like mine, for instance."

"I didn't mean it like that."

"*Sure* you didn't. We're not living in Middle Earth out here. If that's what you want to see, do the Hobbiton tour at Matamata. Yes, another M-A-name. However will you find it?" Her lips tugged up at her own joke. Sam's hand suddenly reached for her hip as she winced.

"You *are* hurt! Let me drive you to the hospital."

"I'll be fine. It's nothing. I'm more worried about Tiger."

Alex frowned. "Who?"

"My bike." She picked her helmet up from the ground, slid onto the motorcycle's seat, and settled.

"Oh. Of course. There are no tigers anywhere here. I knew that, obviously. You'd need CGI if you wanted them." *Oh shit. I'm rambling.*

Sam slid her helmet back on. "Good luck with your movie." She did up her chin strap. "A word of warning? That *Variety* story's all anyone's talking about. And to save you asking, yes, we do get the internet out here, too."

That didn't bode well.

"Apparently your film is 'toxic sludge.'" Sam eyed her curiously. "You must really want the money. Is it worth it?"

Alex shot her a lethal stare, the one that made extras squeak and drop things. "Maybe I happen to think it can be turned into something good. You know, if the right people were committed to it."

"Committed's the word, all right." Sam laughed. "Actually, I bet it'll be as good as your driving."

"For the last time, that was a damned accident!" Alex shoved her hands onto her hips.

"Much like your film." Sam turned the ignition on her bike. After a sick sputter or two, it turned over. When she gave it a testing rev, it didn't sound half bad for what it had been through. It was clear by Sam's expression she thought the same. "I'd probably respect you if you turned around right now and headed back to the airport instead of working on that steaming pile of *pekapeka* droppings. That's a bat, by the way," she added in an over-bright, helpful tone. "For people who don't care about learning local names."

Right, that was it. "I'm sorry you and your bike got hurt, but you can just...get nicked now!" Alex inhaled in fury.

Sam choked out a laugh. "You know, that's the only thing you've said so far that I completely agree with." She sized Alex up, slid her sunglasses back on, then smirked. "You look so outraged. Look, tell your boss to look out for my bill. I'm sure he'll love that—how long have you been in New Zealand? Quite a record laying out a local in three seconds." She revved the bike again, waved like the fucking Queen, and roared away.

Alex was left, quite literally, eating dust.

She wished she could be completely consumed with rage. That would be so much easier if she wasn't transfixed by the sight of Batgirl flying up the road. *Sexy as hell.*

She scowled.

Chapter 3

Setting the Scene(ry)

Shezan's Executive Producer Quincy Blackman greeted Alex like a long-lost relative. He was at least fifty, and his disappearing hairline and expanding waistline had seen better days. His ruddy skin was beaten and crinkled from sun exposure, although she doubted he got much of that around here. She caught the look of desperation in Quincy's eye as he gave her a greeting hug. Yep, he was definitely going stir crazy out here.

The set was a short but muddy trek from the car park, past an enormous Maori security guard.

"The first director, Mitchell Finch, was here ten weeks before he took off over script issues," Quincy said. "The second, Bud Mackay, lasted a month and then slunk off in the middle of the night before sending me a good-bye email from his stopover in Denpasar. That was fun to wake up to. Hope the last-minute flight fees fucked him over." He shook his head. "And here we are."

A dozen trailers for crew, cast, and production facilities were parked on the farmer's property, only a few miles from the magnificent Wairere Falls, their film's main backdrop. She'd looked up the falls while she'd been waiting to board her flight; if nothing else, their scenery would be breathtaking.

"We have the influence of both former directors on our three current permanent sets—the poacher's tent, Amazons' base, and Shezan's tree hut. When Mitch was in charge, he insisted on the hero's set being built right next to Wairere Falls, which makes dealing with straying tourists and the elements tricky. Not to mention the twenty-minute hike to get there with all our lighting gear, which involves wading through mud on bad-weather days. Don't start me on how often it rains down here. We've had to invest in a ton of wet-weather gear and umbrellas."

"You're joking, right?" Alex peered at him. "You haven't built a duplicate set on a nice, dry sound stage in Auckland to shoot our close-ups in a controlled environment?"

He shrugged. "Well, we have the editing team already set up in Auckland, but Mitch was adamant about needing realism for shooting his art."

"I'm all for the natural look, but how did he keep down the wildlife sounds? The noise of the waterfall and drizzling rain? Not to mention the issue of shooting drenched actresses, which makes Wardrobe and the talent miserable?"

"Yes, well, we didn't really solve those issues before Mitch or Bud left. Anyway, I'll take you to our more distant sets tomorrow. It's too late today. Gets dark early out here."

She nodded and glanced around. The grass paddocks the production team had taken over had obviously once been used for farm animals of some sort, if all the manure she kept dodging was any indication.

"Sorry no one was able to meet you at the airport," Quincy was saying as he led her to a giant tent in the middle of a paddock. "I was interviewing some locals. And the production assistants are out, buying up all the plywood. Don't ask. Let's just say, one gale and our wildlife ranger's office set ended up halfway to Hawaii. So I couldn't spare a driver."

"That's a shame. I had a run-in with a biker on the way here." The fiery flash of a certain blond's eyes darted into her brain. "My fault. Car meets motorcycle."

Quincy stopped dead. "Tell me you didn't kill a local in your first hour in New Zealand?"

"Not *kill*. She's still breathing…and riding. She knows where I work and said she'd send my boss her bill. So look out for it, okay?"

"How bad was it?" He sounded worried.

"Bike and rider got a scraping and she only just avoided hitting me. She had to lay her bike down to prevent impact. I promised we'd pay all her damages. I tried repeatedly to get her on-scene medical attention. She wasn't interested."

"I...see." He gave a weary sigh. "So before my third director even sets foot on location, it's already a shit-show. Lord, I am being punished."

"Won't insurance cover everything?"

"Leave it to me. I'll make this all go away. You just focus on finishing this god-awful movie so I can go home to dry ground and sunshine and have a nervous breakdown in peace."

"Was that your welcoming motivational speech?

"Pretty much."

"You're really bad at them," Alex said dryly.

Quincy snorted in amusement.

They reached a tent with rigging along one side. The rustic construct was done up to look like it'd been made from leather. Not bad. Solid. A little too shiny, though.

"Poacher's tent," Quincy said. "Come in. Set Design and Props have just finished with it. They're quite proud of it."

Alex gave it a critical eye. "How long has the poacher been living here?"

"Six months or so. Maybe a little longer."

"Seems a long time for a poacher, or any kind of hunter. He's killing, moving on."

"Love makes people do illogical things?" Quincy suggested with a rueful look. "Hell if I know. I didn't write the script."

Right. "So, six months then... Might want to scuff it up a bit more. Especially the tent pegs and flap. They should have mud and dust on them."

"Mmm." Quincy called over a young woman who'd been trailing them. "Your production assistant. Give her any notes. Alex, meet Alice." He laughed. "Ah hell, that won't ever get confusing."

"Hi," Alex said and regarded the diminutive woman. She was like a tiny blonde mouse in sneakers. Only shorter. "We've met, I think."

"Yeah," she nodded. "On one of your earlier films? *Tarnished Sunshine.* It's an honor to work with you again, Ms Levitin."

"Thanks. You, too. Call me Alex."

"Right." Quincy gave them an impatient look, ushering them into the tent. "Shall we?"

Stepping inside, Alex slowly turned her head, taking it all in. A neutral blue palette had been used. Rifles leaned against packing boxes. She stepped around an old brown leather chair in front of the tent flap which faced some strung-up photos from hunts. A pair of small beds sat on opposite sides of the tent; one for the poacher, one for his nineteen-year-old daughter. A faded privacy partition was next to her bed.

"Well?" Quincy gave her a hopeful look.

"No." She inhaled. "Look, the color? It should be deep red or brown. Power. Blood. He lives on it. That chair? Shouldn't be facing that way. He's a hunter. It's innate for him, never having his back to an entrance where he could be pounced on. And those photos? Don't start me."

She pointed to one picture of the actor who played the poacher with his arm around a bright-eyed blonde woman. They wore affectionate smiles.

"Definitely not," Alex said. "He's all about trophies. He's dragged his reluctant daughter along to watch him slaughter animals so he feels powerful. You've read the script; you know the way he talks to her. She's his trophy, too. Any photo of her would be him in a dominant position, and her subordinate."

Alice scribbled furiously.

Quincy regarded her thoughtfully. "Anything else?"

"The obvious is tent size. How do you plan to get three actors, two camera guys, one hair, one make-up person, a boom op, a dolly grip, and me in one room? Why isn't one wall detachable so we can get crane cameras in and so on? Isn't that standard?"

"Well, Mitch wanted..."

"Realism." Alex sighed.

"Mmm." Quincy nodded.

She exhaled. "Well, I'd rather have access. Can we fix it, please? And given the weather conditions, can we still make it as watertight as possible?"

Quincy nodded. "Of course."

Alice wrote another note.

Gaze roaming, Alex pointed under the bed. "The screwdriver? Not a prop, I'm guessing?"

Alice rushed forward and grabbed it. "Sorry."

"Can we talk about the animal heads?" Alex said, gazing at the hanging trophies.

"You've got to admit, he'd be into collecting these," Quincy suggested.

"A giraffe, a zebra, and a...snow leopard. Care to tell me what's wrong with this picture?"

Quincy squinted at them.

"Where do they live? Not in the same place, that's for sure."

"So he travels," Quincy said. "These are from previous hunts."

"He's not going to haul that lot out with him here. He'd keep them at home. It's not practical for a man on the move. Alice, find us some more believable local carnivores, please?"

"Um, which ones?"

"Scarier the better."

"But..." Alice stopped, then shook her head. "Never mind."

Alex paused. "No, go on."

"Where is this film set exactly? There was nothing about it in the info pack we all got."

"Wait, don't you know?" Alex glanced at the executive producer. "Hasn't this been figured out two directors ago?"

Alice and Quincy exchanged loaded looks.

"Yeah, about that, no one reached agreement," Quincy scratched the back of his neck, "so we're keeping it vague...just some make-believe time and place."

"That won't work. We need to unvague it. We need to be regionally consistent or we'll be a laughingstock. Well, more of one. It'll help our costume designer, too. Cultural authenticity will help elevate us from 'toxic sludge.'"

Alice nodded, pen poised for a verdict.

"Surely we start with a country?" Alex said. "If there are Amazons, I'm guessing that narrows it down."

"The Amazons thing is just a filler name," Quincy said. "Any tribe will do."

Alex glanced between them. "Seriously?"

Quincy shrugged. "Doesn't really matter, does it? Deepest darkest jungles stuff?"

It mattered if he didn't want some weird regional Frankenstein monster. "Okay then, new project. Alice, I want you to do some research and find me a forest that most closely matches the flora you see around here. Similar trees, bushes, and so on. Okay? And when you do, *that's* where it's set. After that, find me a predator from that forest, get me a fake trophy, and toss the rest of those." She waved at the wall of trophies. "And on that note, a giraffe? How is any he-man proud to have bagged himself a skittish, vegetarian, bean pole of an animal that wouldn't hurt a fly?"

"He *is* our bad guy for a reason," Quincy suggested. "He does asshole things like that."

Alex laughed. "Sure. Nice try. Alice, ditch the giraffe, would you?"

"Okay, what else?" Quincy asked.

"Dogs. A picture of his dog somewhere. Some big brute of a thing. He's devoted."

"He is?"

"Yes." Alex grinned. "He loves his dog more than his daughter."

"*Bastard,*" Quincy drawled.

This time even the mousy assistant tittered.

"Fix the rifles, too, will you?" Alex continued. "They look like props that fell out of a mail-order box last week. Make them look used but well-polished. Only thing the man loves more than his dog is his guns." She clapped her hands. "Okay, that's it for now."

She left the tent and gave Alice the go-ahead to get started on the list.

"You have a keen eye," Quincy said as Alice disappeared.

"Serves me well. Most of the time." *When I'm not running over stray motorcyclists.* "What else is set up?"

"Around here? Only other thing we had was the ranger's office, but like I said…"

"Halfway to Hawaii." Alex sighed.

"Yes." Quincy pointed to the sheer, green, ancient mountain behind them, pushing up into white, low-lying clouds. "Up there is what will make our picture beautiful. The falls have to be seen to be believed. I've wrangled one of New Zealand's best cinematographers. He's perfect. Knows how to get the most out of low and filtered light, which you get a lot of under foliage and on a rainforest floor."

"He's available? For *Shezan*? If he's that good, why isn't he doing something…" *Worthwhile? Excellent?* "…else?"

"He's newly retired. I convinced him to do one more flick. Got lucky he was already bored out of his brain after two months at home."

"Ah."

"So the last issue is, we have an occasional tourist problem because we're shooting in a public national park. Our permit allows us to shoo away any tourists. They go away grumbling, and we have Sid for when they don't."

"Sid?"

"The man mountain you passed on the way in?"

"Okay. So how are we on the schedule? How badly behind?"

"It's bad but not atrocious. I'll leave you some of my notes. Hoping we can pick up some time now you're on deck."

"Script status?"

"Not signed off yet. Our new writer's been working on it back home. Goes by the name of Max K."

Sounded like an energy drink. And Alex didn't trust people without surnames. She'd side-eyed Cher plenty for years. "How far advanced is he?"

"That's…a tricky question."

At that moment, Alice scampered up. "I've let Props and Set Design have your notes. Oh, and the new Lighting PA, Kevin, managed to break a light."

"Damn it!" Quincy scowled. "Fire him."

"Over a dropped light?" Alex shook her head. "How new is he?"

"It's his first week," Alice said. "He's never done a movie before. He was learning how to connect it, and it slipped from the rigging."

Quincy muttered. "Figures. Look, you may as well know, the best film crews in New Zealand either passed on this production or are working on the new Peter Jackson flick in Wellington. We got what's left over, the C-team. Truth is, I only hired Kevin because he had a forklift license and we don't have anyone else with one."

Well. Alex could hardly blame the top Kiwi crews for avoiding *Shezan*. They read *Variety*, too. "Look, Quincy, don't fire the kid for one mistake. Maybe get his boss to impress on him how expensive those lights are and that if he makes a habit of it, we'll be canning his ass. Okay?"

Alice eyed Quincy, who finally sighed and nodded his approval. Alice departed to deliver the good news.

"You're too kind," Quincy said. "Although I suppose we do still need a forklift driver. All right, come on, let's sit and talk properly. The script is giving me a bug up my ass."

Yours, mine, and the universe's.

Quincy led her to Craft Services, which comprised a gleaming trailer, a bunch of trestle tables and chairs, and an awning that covered the seating and serving area. He waved her to a seat. "Coffee? Tea? Anything else?"

Glancing at her watch, which read 5:09, she joked, "I'd kill for a beer."

"I hear ya. But we don't have catered alcohol on set. We're hitting the pub a little later, though, so you can grab one then."

"The pub? Any good?" She hadn't found a decent boozer in LA. One thing she'd really missed about home.

"Te Wharariki Hotel is an acquired taste. It's a bit tired, stuck in another time period, and the only game in town. Good chow, though. Cheap, too. So much so, we pick up the tab for the non-local cast and crew to eat there nightly rather than contract Craft Services to provide our dinners." He paused and reached into a folder. "So, the script. It still needs more work."

No kidding.

He slid a copy across the table. "I've highlighted the main issue everyone has with it. And there's a reason we can't fix it."

Alex flicked to a yellow Post-It note and read the page underneath.

Exactly what she'd first thought. Why would anyone want the heroine falling in love with the creepy poacher and leaving her forest to go be with him? "Hate it." Alex dropped the script back on the table. "Both her romantic interest in him and her leaving her animals and forest to be with him."

"Agreed. Max K's giving himself an ulcer over it."

"My other issue is her leaving traps for the poacher all over the forest. And not just because it reads like *Home Alone in the Jungle*."

"That might be a catchier title," Quincy muttered.

"Because wouldn't she catch her own animals?"

"Due to the wonders of movies, she doesn't."

"Mmm. And so she snares the poacher, drags his ass back to his tent to give him an excruciating moralizing sermon, and then...she falls for his seductive, middle-aged charms... Finally, she becomes the stepmother of his bratty daughter, who's almost the same age as her."

"Yes." He ran his fingers through his balding hair. "That's essentially it."

"So the moral is, what? Poachers win in the end? Might is right?"

"I think it's supposed to be love conquers all, but yes, it's problematic."

"And the Amazons, her distant allies, throw her a going-away party. That was lovely, wasn't it?" Alex tapped the script in annoyance.

Quincy coughed.

"So tell me, why can't we change the whole sodding ending?"

"One of the studio's VPs, Richard Howard, is insisting we keep it. He won't budge on it. And he's the reason this film is even being made in the first place. He's the only one behind it."

"He knows what year it is, right? Audiences will destroy this."

"His daughter, Melody, is a budding actress and has her first role in *Shezan*. But her talent's a little too thin to be the star, even if she did have the right look, which she doesn't. So she's playing Poacher's Daughter."

Alex recalled the photo in the poacher's tent of the angelic blond.

"So if you slash most of the poacher plot, especially the bad ending, it automatically downsizes the daughter plot," Quincy finished. "Since most of her lines come from welcoming Shezan into her father's life, we can't cut any of them without the studio VP kicking up a major storm."

"So recast her as someone else. An Amazon?"

"Can't. Melody refuses point blank to play an Amazon—something about the 'objectification of women'—so there's no way around our bad ending."

"The woman has standards, and yet she's doing this movie?"

"I gather it's the only one that'll have her." He lowered his voice. "*More wooden than a pier*, the casting director's notes said."

"I want to meet her. Check out her range and see what she can do. Maybe I'll get an idea?"

"Set your bar low. And remember, Melody and her father are ninety percent why this script can't be fixed and also why it's green-lit in the first place."

"This is bollocks. Keeping that atrocious ending will hurt his daughter more by making her movie a joke."

"I know. We all know." He blew out a breath. "But now you understand all of it—the reason the film's been approved, and the reason everyone keeps heading for the hills. Directors and writers blow in, think they can rewrite that ending and the film will be saved. When they find out it can't be fixed, they bolt out again."

"Why didn't you bolt, too?"

"Alimony. Three ex-wives. Expensive business, marriage. Stay single; there's good advice for you." He gave her a rueful look. "This is one club it's better off not being a member of."

She chuckled at his expression. "Well, I'm not planning on ever getting a husband."

"Well, no wives, either. Same deal."

Ah, so he had done his research.

"So, your turn?" Quincy prodded. "Why are you involved in this *Shezan* sludge? Your credits are excellent. Better than we deserve, to be honest."

"Thanks," Alex murmured, suddenly doubting herself all over again. "I wanted to make a name for myself as the person who turned the most slammed movie into something decent. A lot of eyes are on this. Imagine pulling off the unthinkable."

Quincy blinked in surprise.

Oh. Right. A little too optimistic. "And I have a tax debt," she admitted.

"Ah. Thank God." He smiled and raised his coffee in salute. "Now it all becomes clear. I thought you were nuts for a second." He chuckled. "It's ambitious what you're planning. Most of the LA people are here for the pay day and don't care too much about the end result. And, aside from the cinematographer, the locals comprise mainly people with enthusiasm but not much experience. So we have that, a bad script, a low budget, and we can't write out the daughter plot. Thank God we have a Shezan who can act."

"Chloe's good?" That was a relief. Alex had had a sudden nightmare thought on the flight over: What if Chloe was dreadful and she had to fire a woman so close to all Alex's friends?

"She's solid. Not great, not yet, but it's her first big role. For a former model, she's pretty good. Camera loves her, too. Might even make a decent career out of acting if this film doesn't sink her for life."

"Is Chloe here yet?"

"She was, but while we've been prepping, I cleared her to visit her family for a few days in Auckland. She'll be back tomorrow. You know her, don't you? Didn't you say that in our Skype call?"

"Met her a few times. She's cool. Should be easy to work with."

"Good. I think we'll have our hands full placating the high-strung Melody Howard."

"Right." Alex yawned, and hid it behind her hand.

"Sorry. Forgot you've had a long day." Quincy stood. "Let me show you to your trailer. Maybe you'd like a rest before dinner and that beer you're holding out for."

"Good idea." Now that he said it, the fatigue started sliding in behind Alex's eyeballs.

He led the way to a bank of gleaming silver trailers and pointed. "Yours is that one. Over there's mine. Production over there, Costumes and Wardrobe there."

"Is Skye on set?"

"Yes. She's been redesigning the Amazon outfits while muttering about them being 'preposterous eye sores unfit for a porn film.'" He smiled. "It was our second director, Bud, who had the idea to give the Amazons costumes so skimpy. He argued that if we can't fix the script, why not make it so full of eye candy that people will go in spite of it?"

"There's a progressive point of view."

Quincy shrugged. "Well, he's gone, and he took his designer with him. Skye's going to fix it, so we're back on track with that, right?"

He had a point. Although the widely mocked exploitation of the Amazons had done more to harm the movie than anything else.

"And here you are." Quincy brought her up to her trailer and passed her a note. "Your pin code." He tapped the numbers in for her and opened the door.

"Right, it's just a standard-issue, film-hire trailer," he said, waving her up the stairs in front of him. "Big bed, tiny bathroom, tinier kitchenette with microwave, bar fridge down there, and tea and coffee supplies in the cupboards up there." He waved above the kitchen sink. "Also you get TV, a sofa, fold-out table, and the lasting smell of *eau de luxury trailer*." He snorted. "I'll get Sid to bring your bags in from your car so you can decompress for a bit."

"Right." Alex dragged the car keys from her pocket and tossed them to Quincy.

She looked around. It was actually far nicer accommodation than she'd become accustomed to hiring for her own movies. What a difference a studio budget makes, even a smaller one than usual.

"Bring your appetite to Te Wharariki Hotel," Quincy said. "The serving sizes are insane, even by American standards." His eyes slid down her sparse frame. "Though I'd be happy to have your leftovers," he joked, and patted his stomach. "They think everyone's in training for some rugby team. Actually half their customers look like it: huge bastards, no necks, and they blot out the sun when they walk."

Alex wondered what this movie would do to her diet. "Right," she said, her whole body flagging with exhaustion.

He gave her a wave. "I'll see about setting you up with some time with Melody tomorrow."

"Great." She watched him leave, and then stood at the top of the stairs, taking in the chaotic set in its various states of readiness.

And so it begins.

Chapter 4

Hounds of Hell

SENIOR CONSTABLE SAMANTHA KEEGAN TOSSED her backpack into the rear of her patrol car and zipped her fleece-lined black jacket higher up her neck. Five a.m. and freezing. Everything ached down her left side, thanks to her close encounter with the asphalt yesterday, and the biting temperature just made everything worse. Still, it didn't feel like anything too permanent had been done in the damage department, beyond what had happened to Tiger.

She slid inside the police vehicle with a wince, pushed the heater slider up to full, and turned on the car's ignition. As she reached for her seatbelt, a white-and-tan-colored blur outside the passenger side caught her eye.

It disappeared.

Then a plaintive yip sounded.

Bruce, her neighbor's small, old-as-the-hills Jack Russell terrier, often requested a ride-along. He enjoyed the scenery when she did her rounds. Or, more likely, he could smell the contents of her backpack.

Fine. She opened the passenger door and waited. A second later, his furry body flew inside in a scrabble of claws. He threw himself onto the seat, then her lap, in a blur of wagging tail and wet nose.

"Yeah, yeah. I'm just as exciting to smell today as I was yesterday. Now take a seat, Mister. We need to get going."

She pushed him back onto the passenger seat, where he turned in bouncy circles until he settled.

"It's far too early for this level of enthusiasm." Sam pulled his door closed. "Or any."

The sun hadn't yet risen and wouldn't for an hour yet. Bruce yipped and looked impatiently out the window.

"All right, let's get the rounds done so I can get a nice hot shower and you can sneak back in your mistress's window and pretend you haven't been cheating on her."

Sam's elderly neighbor wouldn't stir until eight, so they had time. Besides, Mrs. Fenley was probably all too aware of what her dog got up to each morning. Bruce didn't hide his enthusiasm. Plus, he'd done rounds every day with Ika Whenu's previous cop, the late Mr. Fenley.

Sam's first stop was farthest out of town and needed to be done before dawn. Her patrol car crept higher and higher into the remote foothills before she parked out of sight behind a stand of willows. It was beautiful out here, green and quiet, but desolate.

"You know the drill," she told Bruce as she grabbed her pack. "I'll be back in ten minutes. In the meantime, no barking. No running off with any passing hussies or huskies, no matter how awesome they smell. Okay? I'll leave the window down a little." She gave him a ruffle under his chin. "Back soon."

He curled into a ball and placed his head on his paws, used to her routine.

Sam slipped the backpack on her shoulders and tightened the straps. She crept around the perimeter wall of the Wild Boars' the Waikato region bikie-gang compound until she reached an old puriri tree. The gang's boss, Dino Taumata, was too damned lazy to get the shaggy green giant cut back, so a number of its long limbs hung over the brick wall.

Sam hauled herself up into the tree's fat, woody heights, wincing as her battered body protested. She slid along a hanging branch until she could drop a few feet onto the top of the ten-foot-high brick wall. The landing was jarring, and she rubbed her hip at the fresh stab of pain. *Damn it.* Maybe she should have skipped this particular stop today.

Too late now, though.

Peering into the compound below, Sam took in the familiar sight. A lone spotlight on the facing wall shone down, casting shadows over rusted-out car bodies, motorcycle engines, and empty brown beer bottles.

A corrugated iron shed on the far side housed a workshop with disintegrating posters advertising motorbikes stuck to it. A larger building nearby was where the dozen-odd gang members slept, partied, and plotted their criminal enterprises. A large sign on the clubhouse building read: *Trespassers will be shot. Survivors will be shot again.*

For about a year, Sam had strongly suspected the growing spike in drug-related crimes around her town and neighboring ones was thanks to the Boars. Whether Dino Taumata was making his own addictive crap elsewhere and storing it in that triple-locked shed or importing it from other bikie gangs and distributing it, she had no idea. And with no proof, she couldn't call in a special drug-raid team to find out, either. So all she could do was wait, surveil, and hope Dino slipped up sooner or later.

But that wasn't why she was here this morning. Today was about being prepared.

She crawled along the back wall, her black leggings, dark T-shirt, and black jacket rendering her little more than a shadow in the pre-dawn light. A charcoal-colored beanie prevented her blonde hair from being visible, too. Right now, the only way she could be spotted was by smell, but that's where the Wild Boars had a potent, lethal weapon.

Four of them, to be accurate.

Scampering sounds and a series of barks came from behind the workshop shed. Upon catching her scent, the four enormous beasts thundered around the corner and bounded over to the bottom of the wall beneath her. She could pick out each of the so-called "hounds of hell:" Killer, Hellbeast, Demon, and Brute.

The quartet of Rottweilers were lean, mean bruisers, and plenty of rumors swirled as to why they were so vicious, but without proof of abuse, Sam couldn't have them seized, either.

She lowered her torso over the lip of the wall, feet dangling, lining up her landing over a springy manuka bush directly below.

The hounds of hell circled, leaping up toward her and barking as she inched herself lower and lower, until she was hanging by her fingertips.

She let go.

The manuka bush cushioned her fall and she rolled sideways, coming up on her knees. Her body shrieked at the abuse. She crawled forward until she was hidden in the shadow of a rusted-out car body, then stood.

The Rottweilers were on her immediately, flinging their heavy black bodies at her, pinning her back to the ground.

"Hey, kids," she laughed as Killer bounced up onto her thigh, barking happily, while Hellbeast sniffed her feet with interest. "I know, I know. I brought breakfast. Give me a sec." She reached for her backpack as the animals clambered all over her in excitement.

Unwrapping a bundle of raw meat—offcuts courtesy of the local pub's kitchen—she laid it on the ground and stepped back hastily. The dogs devoured the pile ravenously.

She looked for the battered old Toyota hubcap that was around here somewhere. Finding it under a rusting car body, she hauled it out and filled it to the brim with water from a bottle in her backpack.

Killer bounded over and licked up slopping mouthfuls of water. Sam gave her an affectionate pat.

"I'm sorry your master is such an asshole," she told her softly. "I'm working on rectifying the situation. In the meantime, it's good we're all friends, right?" She scratched behind Killer's floppy black ears.

Sam glanced around, checking she was still alone. Her nose wrinkled. This smelly, run-down dump looked the same as it had four months ago when she'd first begun her pre-dawn tactical visits. Back then, she'd started by just dropping meat over the wall from a safe distance. Now, it was a full-service feed, with water and cuddles, too.

So, fine, Sam was secretly a sucker for dogs. They were beautiful, intelligent creatures that humans probably didn't deserve, especially humans like the Wild Boars.

This particular gang was a royal pain in her ass. They'd been amusing themselves for years by targeting her. They loved to deface her house with crude graffiti, slash her patrol car's tires, piss on her garden's plants to the point she hadn't bothered replacing them, and generally make nuisances of themselves.

In turn, she'd dished out speeding tickets like confetti every time they went a shade over the limit. That war had all been manageable, though. Until last year when the meth started hitting the streets, along with rumors that Dino's men were behind it.

Suddenly crime—real crime—started going up as new addicts sought ways to afford their next fix. The local pub was getting targeted regularly by thieves bashing their way in looking for cash.

On that note, she should get back, finish her rounds. Gina would be up soon, opening the pub's kitchen, and looking for Sam.

She returned to the wall. Her hands sought out the shoddy, irregular brickwork, which jutted out in places, creating a natural climbing wall. She'd gotten scaling it down to a fine art these past four months. Placing the toe of her boot on the lowest bulging brick, she propelled herself three feet up the wall, then looked to the next foothold. She was two-thirds the way up when the lumbering form of Dino Taumata exited the clubhouse.

Crap! What is he doing up at this hour?

Sam flattened herself against the wall. Her eye darted to where she'd laid out the dogs' food. *All gone.* Thank God.

As the gang boss's gaze roamed the yard, Sam sucked in a breath. Even though he knew exactly who she was, Sam wasn't in uniform or on official business and was definitely trespassing. There was nothing stopping his thugs roughing her up, claiming they were defending themselves from some anonymous intruder they didn't recognize.

Her limbs were starting to tremble from the exertion of holding her unnatural position.

Dino's back was to her now as he paused strolling. He was staring at the ground. Had he spotted the water in the hubcap? Were the dogs still drinking from it? Wait, where were the dogs, anyway?

Oh no. Killer was headed toward the bottom of the wall below Sam, tail wagging happily. Her eyes widened.

Don't bark, girl.

What was Dino doing? *Hurry up, asshole. Get your ugly bum back inside.*

Sam's arms were starting to cramp; she'd have to let go any minute. Of course, the gig would be up a lot faster if Dino turned around to see what Killer was so interested in.

Don't bark, don't bark.

Killer barked.

Fuck!

The dog jumped against the wall below her, as if this was a fun new game.

Dino's back was still to them. He fumbled with his pants, and a second later, an arc of pee shot through the air in front of him.

She used the distraction to slither the rest of the way up the wall. Sam had finally reached the top when Killer barked again, jumping even higher. Hellbeast trotted over to join the game.

Dino's neck began to crane around. The arc of urine stopped. His whole body was now shifting.

She didn't have time to check her landing on the other side. She simply rolled over, clenched her eyes, and let herself drop. As the wind whooshed past, she prayed there'd be some bushes to break her fall.

WHOOMPF!

The air slapped out of her lungs painfully as she landed on her back. No bushes. Soft ground, at least, but also one small, sharp rock. Her thump of impact was drowned out by the hounds of hell choosing that moment to bark furiously.

Sam lay frozen, waiting for sounds of Dino reacting, calling for his gang, anything.

Silence.

For several, long, agonizing minutes, all she heard was her racing heart, and Killer's occasional bark, as she struggled to get oxygen back into her lungs.

The stench of cigarette smoke wafted through the air.

Gingerly she turned over, biting back a gasp, and crawled to her knees. Using the wall to push herself up, she wobbled to her feet and then pulled herself along the bricks until she managed to make it to the road. She'd dodged a bullet, but probably cracked something in the process.

Wearily, she trudged back down the hill to her patrol car and sank with relief into her seat. Everything throbbed and ached. Bruce gave her a baleful look, no doubt smelling his canine competitors all over her.

"Yes, boy, I know, I know. I'm disloyal as hell. But it's for a good cause. Want to drive me home now? Cos I don't think I can." At that thought, she sagged against the seat.

I'll just shut my eyes for a minute, she told herself.

An hour later, Sam opened her eyes to find sunlight streaming into her car. Bruce was snoring comfortably in her lap, and her whole body felt like one giant bruise. Right. She needed to get to hospital ASAP. And on that note, there was no way she'd be able to work today. She dug out her phone and called her boss.

The answering machine kicked in at Sergeant Vaughan Peterson's home. It was just after six. She left a message and was a little surprised when he didn't pick up mid-recording. Not like Sam called her sergeant often. Or ever.

Still, she trusted he'd at least listen to the message. As the officer in charge of her station in Ika Whenu and two other small, local ones, he might even swing by for an hour or so this morning and take up some of her slack.

There was no way she'd be sharing how she got hurt, though, given anything involving the bikie gangs made him twitchier than hell.

Bruce woke, yawned, stretched, did a fresh circuit around her lap, and then headed back to his own seat. A glance out the window was followed by a pointed stare in Sam's direction. Subtle. Breakfast time, and he wanted to be home to be fed by his mistress.

Duty first. "Got to finish rounds," she told him and started the car. "Gina will wonder why her delivery hasn't turned up, and do you want her trying to go and fetch it herself? You know how she gets. And her heart is no good."

Bruce yawned again.

"Responsibilities first, then food, okay?"

His ears pricked up at the magic word, and she laughed, before instantly regretting it. *Ow, damn it.*

Gina, aka Mumma G, as everyone in Ika Whenu and beyond called her, was a sixty-seven-year-old warm, bosomy, round-faced Maori woman. She bustled to the side door of the Te Wharariki Hotel, where Sam leaned against the glass, holding up a tray of bread.

The fiercely independent Gina no longer drove, much to her frustration, so a few years ago Sam had taken it upon herself to do any delivery chores she needed each day before work. Like early-morning pick-ups from the bakery, for instance.

"You're late, bub," Gina said, worry flickering in her eyes. "I'd make some salacious remark if this was one of my boys, but you? You never get up to mischief, do you, hon?" She stepped aside and waved Sam through to the kitchen.

"No, no mischief," Sam agreed through gritted teeth, carrying the bread inside.

"What's wrong?" Gina asked, eying her. "You're walking funny."

"Funny?"

"Like you're favoring one side."

"Oh that, yeah, it's nothing. Bit stiff today." Explaining she'd hurt herself while feeding a bikie overlord's hounds wouldn't go down well with the woman who saw Sam as the daughter she'd never had.

"And why so late?" Gina barreled on. "I had a call from Mason saying you hadn't been past yet on rounds and were you okay?"

"I'm going there next." The old farmer's arthritic hands had gotten so bad that he struggled to open the heavy, complicated gates to his milking sheds. It was a small matter for her, and a huge deal for him, to just flip the catches on the way past each morning and close them again each night. Right now, the poor man was probably sitting around listening to his baleful cows complain that they hadn't been milked yet. "I'd better get right over there."

"That's good," Gina replied, but her frown hadn't disappeared.

Sam tensed for the next round of health and wellbeing questions.

Instead, Gina changed tack. "Did you hear about the trouble in here last night?" She nodded at the bar she'd run for decades with her husband before he'd passed. Gina now ran things herself.

Sam scanned the room for signs of destruction. She took in the battered, dark-timber floors and old, red-brick walls studded with fading, framed photos, including the Ika Whenu district champions rugby team from 1973 and a prize-winning cow draped in a blue ribbon. "What happened? Why didn't you call me?"

"Sid was here. Kev, too." Gina smiled, as she always did, at the mention of her two strapping adult boys. "They sorted it for me quick smart, eh. Besides, it was a scuffle more than anything."

"What happened?"

"You know Christine and Kelly? The Duncan twins?"

"Those sweet kids?" Sam folded her arms.

"Well, you know how the girls got jobs on that *Shezan* movie? The one that's shooting near Wairere Falls?"

As if there were two big Hollywood movies being shot in their district? Sam gave an impatient nod. Trust the trouble to revolve around that production, just for something completely different.

Gina leaned in. "And you know the skimpy outfits the Amazons have to wear, right?"

Everyone did. The Duncan sisters had shown photos of themselves in the costumes after their first fittings, looking awkward and humiliated. The smallest sliver of brown leather hung between their legs, and even less covered their breasts. Sam had felt terrible for them. They might be over eighteen (just barely), but still, it was so wrong.

"So in the pub last night, just before closing," Gina continued, "that hothead Fletcher grabbed Kelly's phone. Next thing, those costume photos were all over Twitter along with some very rude comments.

"Kelly's boyfriend sees the posts and races over here to find out what's going on. And then fists start flying, the boyfriend laying into Fletch till he's crawling under the tables to get away. The Duncan sisters were screaming, the old drunks at the back started laughing and catcalling and taking bets."

Sam inhaled. "And why wasn't I called?"

"Well, Sid and Kev aren't exactly small blokes, are they? They broke it up and chucked Fletch out of the pub. I've banned him for a month. The Tweet was deleted, order was restored, and I didn't need to bother you. Besides, I hate calling you in here on your downtime."

"I would've come, though." Sam worried her bottom lip. "I don't want you to ever jeopardize your safety because you think I need a break from the locals all laying their troubles on me between beers. It's what I do."

"You *do* need a proper break, though. I keep telling you this." She wagged a finger in Sam's face. "When was the last time you took a real holiday?"

"You know there's no point."

She didn't need to spell out why. This was a one-cop town. Ika Whenu, population 2,735, was too small to warrant a full-time police replacement.

So any time she booked a few weeks off from the office, stuck a sign up on the door announcing it, and made plans to relax around home, fix up her bike, or binge watch *Wellington Paranormal,* the same thing happened. Within half a day, someone would see the sign on the police station door, take twenty steps to the right, and bang on her door instead.

Always they'd be sort of sorry, but not sorry enough to respect her time off, while claiming an emergency that usually wasn't really. And they knew she couldn't say no. Besides, that was the job, wasn't it?

"So why not leave town for a break? Didn't you want to travel?" Gina asked. "I'm sure you made plans way back when, with..."

Sam narrowed her eyes, daring her to finish that sentence.

"Fine, burn yourself out and get all surly and unapproachable then." Gina huffed dramatically.

Sam grinned. "How's that any different to me at any other time?"

"I know you think you're doing your job by being all standoffish with everyone. Actually, you're only reinforcing the rumors Dino's spreading about you."

"What's he saying now?"

"You don't want to know."

"Tell me."

"Let's just say that if you get called *hukapapa*, you'll know who started it."

Great. It meant ice, snow, and frost in Maori. But the subtext was "frigid ice bitch." Probably also meant lesbian frigid ice bitch, knowing him.

"I hope you bring Dino down a peg one day. He's bad news," Gina said. "Always has been, even as a boy. I remember him back when you went to school with him."

"Me, too." How could Sam forget the number-one asshole who'd made her childhood so miserable? "And I'm working on him. I'm building my case and laying down the groundwork."

"Please just be careful? I worry about you, bub."

"I know. Thanks. I'll be fine."

"I'd give you a hug, but I know how much you squirm." Gina chuckled.

Thank God the woman was capable of occasional restraint. Sam's ribs might never recover if Gina offered one of her trademark stuffing-squeezer hugs right now.

With a deep sigh, Gina became rueful. "You're such a good girl. So loyal and dedicated." She cupped Sam's cheek before she could dodge. "I'm sorry folks don't see you for who you are. You're always so alone."

Sam shrugged. "People are naturally cautious around cops. That's life."

"But—"

"No. I'm fine with it." She was so done with this conversation. "Anyway, I'd better see to Mason and his cows, and get Bruce back to Mrs. Fenley before he eats my police scanner."

Gina laughed. "All right, I'll let you get on with your day."

A tray of apricot danishes slid out onto the counter, courtesy of the cook, who immediately retreated to the back of the kitchen. "They look great, Dutch," Sam called.

He grunted his approval.

Man of few words.

Sam reached out to snag one, but Gina's hand flashed out and slapped it away.

"No. They're for the movie people. They asked me to make them."

Sam pouted.

"Oh, don't look so put out." Gina cackled. "Come by tonight. I'll cook you something special myself. No arguments. You need to get out of that depressing house of yours."

"I get out. I hit the trails on Tiger." And she stalked the local bikie-gang elements regularly. Never let it be said she didn't have hobbies. "And I visit you."

"I meant interacting with people who aren't family." Gina tsked. "It's been a while since you had…a close friend."

"Gina…" Sam warned.

"Fine, fine. I won't push. Get on with ya. See you tonight." Gina bustled off into the kitchen, calling to Dutch that the bread had been delivered.

"About time," came his grouchy reply.

You're welcome.

With a final mournful look at Dutch's fine pastries, Sam hauled her aching body back into the street.

Chapter 5

Thorn in My Side

ALEX WAS SHUNTED OUT OF sleep by some loud thumps and her trailer rocking. Sliding up the blind shuttering her bedroom window, she looked outside. Sunlight clawed at her. Distant bird calls and sheep baaing reminded her exactly where she was. But not why she'd been jolted awake.

A grizzled, bearded male head bobbed past her window, stopped, and turned at the sight of her. "Oh, mornin'," he said, far too chirpily. "I'm Frank. Frank Buddins from You Dump, We Pump."

"What?" She rubbed the sleep out of her eyes.

"We're the number-three sewerage-removal company in all of the Waikato region."

"Number three?"

"I know! It'd be funnier if it was number one or two." He cackled.

Alex rubbed her eyes harder.

"See now, I know what you're thinking."

She was pretty sure he didn't.

"What exactly is it we do? Well, You Dump, We Pump specializes in reaming out caravans and motorhomes and the like. Which is why I'm here. Gotta clean out yer system."

"Um…"

"So could you not use the loo for a bit? Gotta do yer black water tank. Also, it could get a little whiffy. Best not to breathe in during The Process." He punched the words like they were a top-level military codename. "Well, not through your nose at least," he continued. "Also, before I forget, if you love the way we ream you out today, could you leave us a good rating on Google? Cheers!" He disappeared from view.

She stared after him.

Moments later, her entire trailer thrummed with vibration and pumping sounds that made her head hurt. That and the decree to not use the bathroom suddenly made her want to go. Sod's law.

Alex instead rose, put a mug of tea in the microwave, hating herself a little for it—her British DNA shuddered at the flagrant tea abuse—and grabbed her phone. She checked the time—6:47 a.m.—and did a quick conversion to LA. Almost midday yesterday for Bess.

She sent a flurry of texts, demanding to know whether she was completely bonkers for participating in a certain cinematic cluster-fuck.

Bess replied almost immediately.

You have exactly the same quotient of bonkers as you've always had. 73%.

A pause. Then…

Okay, Summer thinks I'm being a bit unkind. So, you're only 71% bonkers. But remember, it takes some degree of crazy to pull off what you have in mind. Therefore, you're exactly the right person for the job. You CAN do this. And if all else fails, Skye will help make it a beautiful-looking cluster-fuck. Oh, btw, Rowan has asked if you could take copious notes? He needs more material for his new comedy show.

Alex rolled her eyes and typed a reply. *Ha-ha. Glad my nightmare exists to be fodder for our friends.*

I don't make the rules.

Alex smiled at that. Bess's next text landed a second later.

If you're really worried, I could call?

Nah, I'll be fine.

That's the spirit.

She could almost see Bess's wry smile as they said good-bye.

Next she texted her old Cambridge friend, Rowan, whose long-faced comedy routines were well received in clubs around LA for their general "being pathetic at success and adulting" themes. It was a troubling sign he suddenly wanted to borrow from her experiences.

No, Mr Blagge, you can't use my sad life in your stand-up. Nice try.

"Hold on," Frank called. "Just gotta jiggle you a bit, make sure there's no sediment sticking to your bottom."

My bottom. Right. She resumed writing as the vehicle began shuddering a little.

Isnt yor claim to comedy fame being pethetic yoursefl, anywat? :)

Christ! Her phone beeped.

Sorry?

The microwave pinged. Her bladder complained. And...Alex realized she'd accidentally sent the text to Alice, her production assistant.

Great.

That kicked off a frantic day of catch-up. Paperwork piled up, studio calls were made, and notes were compiled to understand what she'd been left to deal with.

Alice appeared mid-morning to explain excitedly how there was only one forest anywhere which might support an indigenous tribe of female warriors that also had flora matching New Zealand.

"Valdivian Temperate Rainforest," the bright-eyed assistant said. "It's in South America, partly in Chile and Argentina. All the ferns and moss and trees look like you're in New Zealand. It's uncanny."

"Excellent."

"It's much cooler than most. I mean, it's the only rainforest on earth which includes glaciers. But, um, there's one problem." Alice opened her iPad. "These are the main creatures that live there."

Taking the device, Alex scanned it. Her eyes widened at the adorable fawns, frogs, otters, owls… "Where are my damned predators!"

"I know. Everything seems miniature there. Smallest deer. Smallest cat. Cute frogs, too."

"Jesus, it's like Bambi's forest. Why even give our Amazons weapons if this is what they're up against? Our warriors could just tickle their furry little bellies and send them on their way."

"Well, we could cheat?" Alice suggested. "There are pumas in the closest forests. Wolves, too. Maybe some of them got…lost?"

Alex snorted. "God knows the domesticated varieties love to wander. Well, since we'll be inventing a fictional name for our movie forest, we may as well value-add some carnivores, too. So find me a waylaid puma for the poacher's wall of shame. Oh, and get all the rainforest's flora and fauna details to Skye. And thanks for your work."

Alice shot her a brilliant smile and disappeared.

One irritation solved, a thousand more outstanding. Alex headed over to Production to tackle whatever fresh hell was waiting.

Quincy proved helpful as the morning dragged into lunch, but Alex could see it in his eyes: The mountain of work wasn't going to get any smaller.

Just after lunch, her executive producer, assistant director, and half a dozen crew escorted her to the two forest sets. The photos didn't do them justice. They were breathtaking. Wild, beautiful, otherworldly.

Shezan's tree house was an exceptional piece of engineering. Bamboo hid its steel construction, and the rigging on one side would allow the cameras to clip on and focus on the star as she slept, ate, petted the animals, and whatever else Mistresses of the Forest got up to. All this with a stunning waterfall crashing into a lagoon framed over her shoulder. So, it all looked the part. Director One had been right. It would be a crime not to use this glorious natural backdrop. And the sets *had* already been built. But…

Shooting in the forest sets would be a technical nightmare. It wasn't like they could just turn down the volume on the waterfall. So much sound looping would be required to fix the audio in the studio later. And then there was the constant rain, the mud, and the leeches.

Alex's afternoon slithered downhill after that, landing at rock bottom thanks to a strange meeting with actress Melody Howard. The woman lived down to her reputation as a spoiled young woman whose mediocrity was the only thing greater than her over-confidence. Really, she should be in middle management.

Melody was sitting opposite Alex in the deserted Craft Services area. Aged twenty-four, she had glorious, long blonde hair and perfect eyebrows that probably had their own Instagram page. Everyone was beneath her. That apparently included Alex, who had gently tried to coax an impromptu acting performance out of her, hoping to showcase Melody's abilities and thereby find some inspiration.

"No." Melody eyed her. "No way."

"No?"

"I am not going to *re*-audition for you. It's not my fault an earlier director approved my hiring. Deal with it."

Deal with it?

"And I won't be singled out for discrimination. I notice you haven't asked anyone else to comply with this..." she whirled her finger between them, "irregular process."

Alex peered at her in surprise. She'd yet to meet a performer who didn't love to show off a little. And exactly what "discrimination" was she experiencing here? Were entitled, white, rich divas suffering somehow and Alex hadn't been informed?

"It's not a re-audition."

Melody gave a withering stare.

"I'm trying to find your strengths so I can work with you to bring them out on film."

"*Sure*." Melody folded her arms. "And no."

This attitude would get most actors fired, but Melody clearly knew she was bullet-proof. Alex's head started pounding again. "Well, how about we rehearse the Poacher's Daughter's lines a little?"

Melody tilted her head. "I can do that."

Thank God.

"On the condition that you rename my character from Anna to Jennifer."

"Why?" Not that Alex cared. What was one bland name over another?

"It's in honor of my good friend Jennifer Aniston." Melody shook her hair back. "She's *completely* underrated."

"Underrated."

"And a dear, dear friend." Melody smiled beatifically. "Do it, and I'll even tweet about my part. I have eighty-seven thousand followers. I'm a social media influencer."

Alex was doubtful that Melody, despite her father's connections, was best friends with any A-lister. In her experience, name droppers rarely had famous friends for long.

Gritting her teeth, Alex said, "Jennifer it is." Sliding a copy of the script across the table, she added, "Begin from 'Father, I don't know why we have to stay out here so long. It's so wild and strange and I just want to go home.'"

It soon became apparent that Quincy had actually understated Melody's lack of talent.

Melody's range never got above the level of a read-through. She punched all the wrong words, inserted unexpected pauses mid-sentence, and her gaze roamed so much that Alex started to wonder if she had an eye condition.

After the fourth awful run-through, Alex put down her own copy of the script and asked: "Why are you doing this? *Shezan*, I mean?"

"My father thinks it would be a good fit to showcase me."

"Your father? Not you?"

She shrugged. "My boyfriend thinks so, too. How hard can it be?" Melody reached for her phone and started scrolling through it. "Acting's not exactly rocket science, is it?"

Just perfect.

The rest of the day involved a blurring montage of paperwork, inspecting crew builds, and placating tearful twin sisters. Apparently some local had tormented them the previous night over their Amazon costumes. That had taken time to deal with. She'd sat down with them, handed over a box of tissues, told them the outfits were changing, and explained, amid hand pats, that certain obnoxious men could be trash and not to take their attitude on board, because it was about those men, not them.

"Not *all* men," Christine helpfully added between great gulping sobs.

"Right," Alex replied dryly. "Thanks for that always-forgotten clarification."

After Alex recruited Skye to help explain about the empowering new outfits she was making, the twins left looking happier.

Alex collapsed into her chair. The emotional heavy lifting of being responsible for so many people was exhausting. These kinds of spot fires were usually handled by assistants, but Alex wasn't quite sure she agreed with outsourcing upset people to others, even if she could. She retreated to her trailer to try to figure out the main logistical issues without people talking at her constantly. She'd lost track of time when a knock sounded.

"Seven o'clock, Alex," came Alice's voice. "Everyone's leaving for the pub now. Want to come?"

Slapping down the notes that were starting to blur, she sighed. Food sounded like a perfect distraction. She'd begged off last night due to jet lag and was looking forward to seeing the heart of Ika Whenu's social scene.

Chapter 6

Beers, Bribes, and Brawls

Te Wharariki Hotel was loud, old, drafty in the corners and smelled, unsurprisingly, of stale beer. The atmosphere, though, was jovial, with bubbles of laughter from dozens of groups sitting around low wood tables. Easy-listening pub-rock music pumped through the aged speakers near the ceiling.

Alex fell into step with Sid, the set's security guard.

"Grub's ordered over there." Sid pointed to a counter and a till. "Mum's the cool chick in the green cardie behind the counter. This is her place, eh. Her name's Gina Mahuta, but everyone calls her Mumma G."

"Okay." Alex took in the wide-smiling woman bending an ear to one of the patrons at the bar. A large Maori woman in her late sixties, 'Mumma G' had bushy, gray-streaked black hair and bright fashion tastes that ran to a green cardigan and an orange sundress. "Right. What do you recommend on the menu?" Alex asked, following him to the counter.

"Anything's good but the schnitzel's a real treat. Trout's choice, too. It's caught locally every day on Lake Tarawera."

"Choice, huh?" She smiled. "Chloe says that a lot."

"I do." Chloe slapped Alex on the shoulder, coming up behind her. "Old habits die hard."

Alex was pleased that *Shezan*'s star was looking so refreshed and relaxed after her trip home.

"By the way, the salad's decent, too," Chloe continued. "If you're not into inhaling half a cow."

"That sounds more my speed. Can you order me one? I need a quick pit stop."

Alex found the Ladies and headed inside, praying the facilities were empty, because the hubbub outside was starting to give her a headache.

No such luck. The stalls were empty, but someone was at the sinks. The woman had her shirt pulled up in front of the mirror, twisting to prod a dark shadow on her back. A well-muscled, smooth back.

Hot.

Wait... "Geez! How did you get that bruise?" Alex gasped. "It's huge."

The woman lurched around, wrenching her shirt down, and glowered.

Alex found herself in the familiar glare of the woman she'd almost flattened yesterday. "Oh. Right."

With an annoyed look, Sam flattened the wrinkles out of her T-shirt and reached for her jacket's zip.

"Did you get a doctor to look at that?" Alex asked.

"It's nothing. Don't worry, your money's safe, in case you're afraid I'm going to sue."

"That wasn't—" Alex started to protest. "Wait, *have* you been thinking of suing us?" She pictured '*Shezan* Director Almost Kills Local' headlines in the mix of atrocious press they'd already had.

"And there it is." Sam washed her hands. "Knew it." She was leaning over the sink too carefully.

"Are you hurt anywhere else?"

"No." Sam met her eyes in the mirror. Her words were cool.

"Okay, let me know if there's anything I can do."

Sam took a step toward her.

Awkward silence grew as Alex felt the heat being radiated off Sam. She was so damned near, right inside Alex's space. *Why?*

"You could get out of my way." An impatient look flitted across Sam's face, and that cool gaze darted to the door.

Which Alex was blocking. *Oh! Oh shit.*

"Right, yep." Alex gave a tight nod. "Got it. I'll just...y'know." She jerked her thumb at a toilet stall. "Get out of your hair. Let you poke over your war wounds or whatever." She shut the stall door behind her. As she undid her belt, she couldn't resist calling out: "But you've got to get that checked out, okay?"

No reply. A moment later, the bathroom's main door opened and closed noisily.

"Bye," Alex said to herself since the woman had plainly left. "Christ, it's people being so cheerful that keeps me going." Sam probably thought Alex was the weirdest, nosiest chick around. She could hardly blame her.

The tips of two black boots briefly came into view beneath the door.

Oh fuck. So... not *gone then?* Someone else must have come in instead.

This time, when the main door opened and shut, Alex didn't say a peep.

"I like cheerful people, too, darling," came Skye's amused voice from near the sinks. "Now then, who was that tower of broodiness who just left? And how many of her kittens did you run over?"

Alex sighed. "Not sure, but I think it was a lot."

As she washed up a few minutes later, she chose not to dwell on why Sam's opinion of her even mattered in the first place. Or why she suddenly wanted to fix it. Either way, if they were going to be bumping into each other on the regular, some positive PR might be the go.

Sam was ready to bail. It'd been stupid to agree to come to the pub tonight anyway, but Gina had been so insistent that morning. And if she'd said no, she'd have had to explain why she was in no fit state to be sociable.

She had slept most of the day, woken up late in the afternoon, taken some pain killers, and headed for Te Wharariki Hotel. She'd even felt okay through most of Gina's sublime Garlic Crumbed Trout Special.

But between being polite with the locals and ignoring the entire *Shezan* crew that had just poured through the door, the dull ache in her side turned into raw pain.

Retreating to the bathroom for a quiet look at her injuries, she wound up with Alex Levitin in her face instead. Her concern over Sam's injuries was obviously all about the size of the insurance bill.

Strange woman.

Sam left the bathroom, ready to call it a night. She'd done her duty and put in enough of an appearance to get Gina off her back about her lack of socializing.

"Leaving so soon?" Sid blocked the pub's rear exit. "Ain't even seven-thirty."

"You sound way too perky. And I'm tired."

"Pity. I was gonna introduce you to *Shezan*'s new boss. They got their asses one cool director now. Hell, *Shezan* mightn't end up so bad, eh?"

"Don't hold your breath. Anyway, I don't care. I'm heading off."

"Nah, stay! Come on, Sam. I might even break out the guitar tonight! Get the place jumping?"

"If that's the best you can offer, I'm definitely leaving," she deadpanned.

"You love my singing." He feigned a hurt look.

"I love my bed more."

"Kev said you once called my voice smoother than molten caramel." He showed all his gleaming white teeth in a charming grin.

"I had no idea your little brother was suffering from delusions. Tell him to get that checked out. Speaking of Kevin, where's he been hiding? I haven't seen him around."

"He got a new job." Sid shifted uneasily.

"Oh great." She exhaled. "A *job*?"

"No, not like that. It's legit." Sid's eyes darted about.

"If it's legit, then why didn't I hear about it on GNN?" Gina's informal gossip network was legion, after all.

Sid smirked. "Because he hasn't told Mum yet. He doesn't want to jinx it."

"Oh sure, that's why." Sam slapped his enormous barrel chest. "Come on, that boy's got stickier fingers than a lizard. Spent half my life hauling his ass out of trouble, and you know it."

"But—"

"Mac's Three Wolves Pale Ale," a voice said near Sam's ear, followed by the appearance of a large, frothy beer. "That's your drink, right?" Alex Levitin's hopeful face greeted her.

Sid embraced the interruption. "Right-ho, I'll leave you guys to catch up!" He made good his escape before she could argue.

"I asked Gina what you like," Alex said. "Did you know she knows *every* single type of drink you love? That's amazing."

"You think so?"

"Well, sure. It's a level of customer service I've never seen."

Sam eyed her cautiously, wondering what the catch was.

"So?" Alex said, arm still holding out the now-wobbling drink. "I think we've already established that I'm a weakling, unable to shift large motorcycles from desperate damsels. And this glass is huge and heavy." She quirked her lips. "So…"

"I don't recall ever being a desperate damsel. In fact, I seem to recall rescuing myself." Sam reluctantly relieved Alex of the beer. With a sigh, she said, "Can we just say I accept your apology for everything you've ever done to me and leave it at that? You don't need to bribe me."

"It's not a bribe. It's a 'Hey, look at this beer I found, I better get it to its rightful owner' thing." She grinned.

"Uh-huh." Sam became aware of several locals watching them, curiosity burning in their expressions. Her gaze slid about the pub. A table at the back corner between the fire escape exit and the dart board seemed deserted. Maybe she could dispense with the pleasantries and this persistent woman out of the line of sight of the other patrons.

"Great idea." Alex nodded and started heading for the corner table.

"No, it's not! I did not suggest—" Sam couldn't help but notice her feet were following.

"Didn't have to." Alex slid into the chair and waved Sam closer. "Sit." She smiled. "Come on, one drink."

Sam slid slowly into the seat opposite. One drink wouldn't kill her, she conceded.

"Why did you choose this table?" Alex asked curiously. "Is it because you don't like being the center of attention?"

Am I that obvious? Sam took a sip of her beer before answering. "I suppose."

"Do you know you're rare as hen's teeth in my world?"

"I am?"

"Everyone I meet in LA's dying to get noticed. Makes for a long day."

Sam scowled at the reminder of the woman's work on *Shezan*. "What do you do in the movies? What's your job, exactly?"

"Ah, there you are!" Gina bustled over to Alex. "Thought I'd lost you." She slapped a small bottle of beer in front of her, along with a clean glass and a salad.

"Um, I didn't order this." Alex pointed to the beer.

"It's on the house. Your friend Skye—lovely woman, by the way—tells me this is your second-favorite beer, but we don't have your favorite. Stay long enough, though, and maybe I'll order some in." She beamed, pouring amber fluid into the glass, the frothy white head a perfect inch at the top. "Enjoy." She took off again, her wide arms pumping.

"I dread to ask what I did to deserve this from the pub owner." Alex took a sip.

"You prevented me from fleeing tonight. Gina's mighty grateful," Sam drawled.

"Why does she care what you do?"

"She's called Mumma G for a reason. She fusses over everyone."

"She worries about you especially. The way she talks about you is filled with affection."

How...perceptive. But to hell Sam was going to explain that Gina had raised her for six years with her own family. "That's just Gina. So this month she's decided I should get out more. So what?"

"Oh, right." Alex grinned. She lifted her glass. "Well, cheers."

Sam couldn't bring herself to clink glasses, even for politeness. She was worn out. Why was she even here, enduring this stranger and her third degree?

"So..." Alex took another sip of beer, watching her. "She thinks you don't get out much?"

"Of course I do!" What an idea.

"No argument from me. We met because you *do* get out, didn't we?"

"True." Sam suppressed her annoyance at the reminder. Roger at A1 Mechanics still hadn't been able to give her a date for getting her bike back. He'd finished writing her up a quote, though. When he'd told her the amount, she'd almost choked on all the zeroes. "Special custom paint had to be ordered in," he'd explained. Good thing she wasn't paying.

"Tell me about your beloved Tiger. Had it long?"

"Three years."

"It's a passion for you, trail-bike riding?"

"Yes."

"Do you go out often? Is it always the same trails?"

"It varies."

"Which is your favorite?"

"Why? You're not planning on riding the trails, are you?"

"Oh God, no. That's not my thing," Alex said. "Besides, if I went down, unlike you, I'd stay pinned." She laughed.

Sam was inclined to agree. There wasn't much to her; a sparrow was right. She studied her glass. Three more gulps and she could thank Alex for the beer and leave. Actually, why had she even agreed to sit with this annoying woman?

"Have you always lived in Ika Whenu?"

Sam shrugged in response, sighed, then took a great gulp of beer until the glass was almost drained. Sooner this was over, the better.

"Okay, easier one. What do you do for a living?" Alex asked.

She finished the beer. "I'm surprised the locals haven't filled you in by now." She really was. Sam banged her now empty glass on the table.

"I never asked. Should I have? This sounds interesting."

Sam studied her glass, white foam remnants sliding down the inside. People never found the answer to that question interesting. They clammed up, stepped back, got guarded, and then the awkward jokes started. *Don't arrest me, okay?* Her jaw tightened.

"Hmm, no comment, huh?" Alex studied her. "Okay then, let me guess." Her gaze slipped appreciatively over Sam's figure. "Personal trainer?"

"Out here? People would laugh if a gym ever opened up."

"Army drill sergeant?" Alex's eyes glittered. "You know, running a soft bunch of recruits into the ground, screaming out orders."

"People who have to scream to get respect have already lost it."

"Deep." Alex's eyes sparkled. "Lumberjack, fire fighter, construction worker, oil rigger, or mountain climber?"

"I'm sensing a theme." Sam almost smiled. "And no."

"Well then, that just leaves Amazon."

"Excuse me?"

"You look like an Amazon. So...what other conclusion do I have left?" She gave her an innocent look. "Want to come audition to be an Amazon extra?"

Distaste coated her tongue. "Hell. No."

Alex burst out laughing. "How did I know you were going to say that?"

"I hide my love for your film so well." Sam firmly repressed a lip twitch. She absolutely was not amused. No, siree.

"So what *do* you do? And if you refuse to answer again, I'll be pretty disappointed." Her smile was wide and a little infectious.

Sam resisted her charms. Typical Hollywood schmoozing, no doubt. But she wasn't easily buttered up by a cute face or a cheeky smile… She blinked. *Not that Alex Levitin is cute or cheeky.* Alex was a manipulator, and Sam didn't owe anyone explanations. "Feel free to leave if you don't like the company. I won't be offended," she said indifferently and waved at the Exit door near them.

Alex put her elbow on the table, formed a fist and rested her chin on it, and sized her up. "Nope. I like a challenge."

"Or you just like badgering strangers."

"That, too." Alex's roaming gaze settled on the dart board. "Do you play 'martial arts?'"

Sam blinked.

"Darts? Do you play?"

Many hours of her misspent youth had been in here with that dart board. There wasn't a lot to do in Ika Whenu as a kid, so, by fifteen, she'd become the best player in town. "Some."

"So I have a challenge then: We do the best of three rounds. And if I win, you answer my question in *no less* than fifty words. None of these monosyllabic, too-cool-for-this-conversation answers."

Surely Sam's job wasn't *that* interesting to Alex? "And what do I get if I win?"

"Name it." Alex grinned.

That was a tempting prospect. "If I win, you stop this." Sam waved her hand between them.

"Stop what?"

"Badgering me."

"No one forced you to sit with me." Alex's shoulders tensed. Her brows drew together. "Is that really how you see this?"

Was it? Sam was no longer entirely certain. It was true she had sat down here under her own steam. Probably just needed a break after her damned ribs had started aching again. That's all it was. And it certainly didn't mean she wanted this…peculiar, persistent woman all up in her face. "I meant stop trying to *know* me. I don't like it when people do that."

"You don't like when people try to make friends with you?" Alex's eyes widened in surprise.

Sam shook her head. "It's when they grill me to figure out what makes me tick. I'm not a science project. People only ever want to know me because they're nosy. Then they get their answers and fixate on someone else. That's life in a small town. Don't need it from strangers, too." She shrugged as if to say, *This doesn't bother me one bit.*

It did, though. Always had. She was only ever interesting until people got to know her. Then they got bored because she wasn't what they wanted her to be. She'd never be much of a conversationalist, for instance. She'd always been too introspective, too brooding, too tough, too tall, too closed off. And she'd never be the life of a party. If you wanted someone to singlehandedly kick out a dozen rowdy gatecrashers, though, Sam was your gal.

"I'm not *people*," Alex protested. "I'm genuinely trying to find out more about you. You're interesting to me."

"Or, more likely, I'm some curious itch to be scratched." Sam rolled her eyes. "I'll agree to your challenge, but only one round."

"Two rounds," Alex said. "And I'm interested in people."

"Well, there's a depressing hobby if ever I heard one. In my experience, people tend to disappoint." Sam finished the last of her beer. "And only one round."

"As if you could ever disappoint," Alex scoffed, mischief in her eye.

Is she...flirting? Sam started. *No. Surely not.*

"Two rounds," Alex continued. "Non-negotiable. And before you say no, imagine winning. You'll finally be rid of me."

"Good point." Sam rose instantly.

"Wow, you agreed to that pretty fast. Should I be offended?" Alex's eyes teased her.

"Probably." This time, Sam allowed a small smile. "I'll get the darts."

Returning a few minutes later, she laid out a tray of three darts, then pointed behind her. "See where that rug ends? That's what we use as the toe line. Want to go first?"

"It's been years since I tossed a dart. I'll probably nail one into the brick work. Why don't you start?" Alex pushed the darts Sam's way. "Show me how it's done."

"I haven't played in years, either." *But it's like riding a bike.* Sam rose, fingers stroking the familiar roughness of the knurling pattern on the grip. To her surprise, she felt a little skip of excitement as she headed for the line.

Aiming, she tossed the first dart. A little off target, it embedded in the twenty wedge. Pain shot up her side. *Damn it.*

She surreptitiously rubbed her side, then threw the second dart. It shot a little left and hit the five. *Rusty.* Also, that really hurt. Biting hard on her lip, she tried again.

Her third dart dug into the outer ring of the bullseye. Not quite on target, but satisfyingly close. She extracted the darts and glanced back at Alex, who was watching with an inscrutable expression.

"Pretty good for someone who hasn't played in years." Alex sounded amused. "You're not pulling a con on me, are you?"

"Don't believe in cons."

"Interesting to know." Alex waved at the dart board. "Have your second round. I want to try this salad first." She picked up the fork, spearing lettuce and tomato.

Sam returned her attention to the cork circle in front of her, rubbed at the pain in her ribs with her left arm, and threw her first dart. This time it was just shy of the inner ring. *Much better.*

"Nice one," Alex said, then pointed a fork at her food. "Hey, this salad's really good."

"Of course it is. Everything's grown fresh. No pollution, nothing's being rammed into trucks for transport."

Alex laughed.

"What?"

"I love how proud you are of all things local. Throw again. Not *too* straight, though. I have a lot riding on this."

"Finding out my occupation is hardly 'a lot'."

Alex offered a mysterious grin.

Sam tossed the second dart. *Yes!* Like the old days.

"Bullseye," Alex murmured, tone approving. "Can you do it twice? Even more centered than that one?"

More *centered*? *Who plans to have it dead center?* Sam threw her third dart. This one landed back on the outer circle. Damn. Not quite.

"So close." Alex put down her fork. Her expression was admiring.

Hmm. Sam collected the darts and walked back to drop them on the table. "You're up."

Alex snagged them and sauntered over to the toe line, getting into position. She was relaxed, and her head became very still.

The first dart jagged to the right of center in the one wedge. She looked unconcerned. "Oh well." Her eyes sparkled.

Those eyes are pretty.

Um, what?

Alex tossed the next dart, and this one embedded itself beside the first. Without comment, Alex immediately let her third dart fly. And it, too, was placed beside its brothers in a neat, tight, line of three. All exactly, evenly spaced.

"Oh look," she said, "three ones. A Bag of Nails. Or the Eric Bristow, if you want to get technical."

She knew the jargon? Sam moved to stand beside her and examined that perfectly positioned trio. Not a random placement. "Maybe one of us *does* believe in cons?" she murmured. "I'm curious as to what your next trick will be."

Alex walked to the board and plucked the darts out but made no comment. After returning to the toe line, she paused and said, "Maybe I should make it a fairer contest?" She gave Sam a cheeky grin and stepped back five more paces. Then she turned, and in three blurred, rapid throws, nailed three bullseyes. It was seamless.

Holy… Sam couldn't hide her astonishment. "How did you do that?"

"Dad taught me." Alex headed back for the board and retrieved the darts. "He worships darts. Maybe a little too much."

"Too much?"

"You've heard of a card shark?"

Sam nodded.

"My old man's a darts shark. Every now and then, if someone comes into his local pub and is being a real prat, Dad'll become their best mate, buy them a few beers, and then fleece them at darts faster than anything. He's not a crook, though," Alex added quickly. "He has a strict code: Only assholes are targeted. And he never tries it on anyone who can't afford to lose the dough."

Did he want a medal for income-testing his marks? Surely Alex didn't support this, did she? Was she *proud* of her father for his illegal endeavors? Well, if so, the woman wouldn't be the first family member to enable the black sheep in the family.

Sam sighed. How was she any better? She'd spent years kicking Kevin's sorry butt, hoping he'd get a clue before he went too far and did something for which she had to put him behind bars. Was that protecting him from himself or enabling him? She was no longer sure.

Alex smiled widely. "So about my prize..."

"I hardly think learning what my job is was worth the effort of your... artful con."

"Ahh, but I never said what question I'd ask you." Alex tsked. "Why would I waste my win on something I could easily find out from asking anyone in here?"

Sam's heart started pounding. "What?"

"Don't look so stricken. I'm not about to ask anything embarrassing. Promise."

"What do you want to know?" Sam pushed the words out as a litany of personal questions invaded her mind. She braced herself.

Alex stared at her in astonishment. "What *are* you imagining?"

"Just ask." Sam gritted her teeth. She was an honorable woman, so she'd answer and do so honestly. And then she'd simply avoid this woman for the remaining few months Alex was here.

"Why Ika Whenu? From what I've seen, you seem smart, strong, and capable. You could go anywhere, do anything. But here you are."

Sam debated how to answer. "It's...complicated."

"So are my taxes. Trust me." Alex's smile was gentle. "And you can do better than that. Remember, no less than fifty words."

A bang near the nearby fire-escape door startled them, and they turned as it began to open. A familiar-looking young man with a bowed head encased in a beanie headed for the bar.

Sam watched him closely, trying to place him.

He reached the patrons waiting to be served. To squeeze past the first young woman, he placed his hands on her waist, muttered "'Scuse me," and physically shifted her to one side to get past.

That voice. *Fletcher bloody Norton.*

"Ugh," Alex said in disgust. "I hate it when guys do that. And they only do it to women, especially women my size." She looked indignant.

Sam said grimly, "He shouldn't even be in here. He's banned."

Fletcher came up to a tiny, brightly dressed older woman with gray-blonde hair. One of the *Shezan* people. He attempted his waist-grabbing-and-relocating maneuver on her, and his hand slid across her backside when he was done. The woman's head snapped around to glare at him, as she jerked away from him.

"The hell!" Alex's infuriated voice said. "Did you see what he did to Skye? That's assault."

"I'll deal with it," Sam said, rising. "Gina already has him on her blacklist for some trouble he started last night over two local girls."

"Wait! Do you mean the Duncan sisters?"

Sam paused. "Yes?"

"Is he that reprobate who was terrorizing them all over social media?"

"That's the one." She strode toward him. "Fletcher Norton!" she ordered sharply.

He turned, caught sight of her, and quailed.

"A quiet word, if you please." Sam crooked her finger and angled her head toward the corner of the room.

"Or a loud one," Alex interjected, behind her. She called out, "Like, keep your bloody groping mitts to yourself."

Sam grabbed Fletcher by the rugby jersey and pulled him out of the crowd at the bar. "This way, Mr. Norton."

"Hey, I didn't do nothin'! I just came to apologize to Christine and Kelly," he whined.

"Then you probably should have picked a time when they were actually in attendance and a place that didn't involve your being banned," Sam said curtly. "Move it." She tugged him again. "We're going to have a chat about how you treat women."

Alex's eyes narrowed. "A chat? This knuckle-dragger had two of our *Shezan* cast in tears today! And he grabbed Skye's ass! He needs a lot more than a polite word asking him to pretty please be a good boy. Bollocks! He needs a kick in the damned pants!"

Fletcher's shocked expression at being shredded by a furious woman half his size set the entire room tittering.

Sam let go of him and rounded on Alex. "This is not your concern. Let me deal with this matter."

"Or, hey, much better idea, let *me* deal with it. He's messed with my people, so I have the responsibility, not you."

"It was just a bit of fun," Fletcher complained. "And they got all offended."

So much for claiming he was here to apologize. Sam scowled. The idiot was just sorry he couldn't get a beer with his friends.

"Here's a pro tip," Alex shot at him, "a joke involves laughter."

Sam's voice hardened. "Alex, I need you to step back and let me do my job."

Frowning, Alex opened her mouth to protest.

"Um, hey, Alex?" Sid called out helpfully. "Mad respect and all, like, serious props, but I think 'cop' trumps 'director.' Y'know?"

Alex's wide eyes met Sam's. "Cop?"

Director? Sam sucked in a shocked breath. *Alex is that crappy movie's director? She's behind all this?*

The room exploded into laughter.

"Oh, didn't you know, love?" Gina's voice carried cheerfully across the ruckus. "Senior Constable Keegan is our town's cop. And a mighty fine one at that."

Sam blocked out the howls of mirth. "You are the director of that…? You have to be kidding me."

"Why so shocked?" Alex folded her arms.

"You have to ask?" Was she serious? "Because *Shezan* is such a B-grade, misogynistic pile of crap."

A hard glint appeared in Alex's eyes.

Sam couldn't care less. She had to understand what she'd done. "Our local women shouldn't be forced to parade around in next to nothing to be mocked by idiots like Fletch."

"Hey!" Fletcher protested.

"Shut up!" Sam and Alex snapped simultaneously.

He inched away from them. "Okay, so if you two don't need me anymore, I'll just…" He jerked his thumb behind him toward the exit.

"No. Stay. I'm not done with you," Sam ordered. Eyeballing Alex, she said, "Look, the fact is you and this film are the reason the Duncan sisters copped abuse in the first place. Those obscene costumes alone—"

"Are you for real? I'm to blame for *his* bad behavior? Are you going to let him off the hook? My people deserve respect, not abuse, damn it!"

A few whistles and claps from the cast and crew reverberated.

"I agree!" Sam threw her hands up in frustration. "*I'm* the one who's been defending them."

"Actually all you're doing is making shitty assumptions. We've been working on addressing the film's issues, such as costumes, which you'd know if you had asked any of us. But my main problem is that the message you're sending to everyone here is that cowards like Fletcher aren't responsible for trolling and hurting young women because a *movie* made him do it!"

"I..." *Hell!* Sam's brain stuttered to a halt. Was that really what she was saying? No! She'd been protecting her town! She knew that, but did everyone here think she'd been giving Fletch a free pass? Heat from anger and embarrassment started creeping up Sam's neck as Alex regarded her evenly, waiting for an answer.

Fletcher took advantage of the stand-off. "Crazy bitches," he muttered, before shoving Sam out of the way to sprint back out the fire-escape door.

The hard slam of his hands caught the worst point of Sam's abused ribs. Agony seared her like slicing knives. "Oh fuck," she gasped out, clutching her side. She folded like a deck chair and dropped to her knees.

"No!" Gina rushed over, pushing aside customers in her haste.

"Sam!" Alex said at the same time.

Sid bolted after Fletcher, shouting, "I'll get the bastard! No one hurts my sister!"

"*Sister*?" Alex peered after him in puzzlement.

All Sam knew was pain. "Ahh." The word came out small and pathetic. *Shit.*

"I'll get you to the doctor," Alex said. "Who's closest?"

"I'll be okay. Gimme a minute," Sam ground out. *Damn, damn, damn.* Now Dino's gang would know within the hour that Ika Whenu's cop was out of action. They'd probably be selling meth outside the high school by morning. Well, probably not, but they *could*. And who would stop them?

"You're not okay!" Alex snapped. "Stop saying you are."

"What's happened?" Gina bent down beside her. "Oh bub, I knew this morning you weren't yourself. How'd you hurt yourself this time?"

"It's nothing," Sam hissed. "I'm going home to rest. But I just...I need a minute."

"I'll make sure you get there," Alex said firmly. "Where's home?"

"Next to the police station." Gina gave her an approving look. "On Main Street."

"Right." Alex nodded. "I know where it is."

"No!" Sam barked. "Both of you, stop it! I don't need help." She glared at Alex. "And this wouldn't have happened if you'd let me do my job. Now, back off! I. Am. Fine."

With that, she pushed off the ground, burying a groan of pain, and shoved open the exit door. She did it with all the force of her rising fury, hoping she wouldn't look as weak as she felt, and regretted it instantly. The jarring sensation shuddered up and down her body.

Glancing back, she caught Gina's worried frown in a sea of curious faces...and Alex.

Alex's expression was hooded and dark. Concern mingled with irritation in that gaze, and suddenly, more than anything, Sam wished she'd never clapped eyes on her.

Alex was maddening, nosy, bossy, and worse. Much worse: She was the person behind *that* terrible movie.

Sam injected so much anger and frustration into her parting glare that it should have melted the Under-18s netball trophy on the shelf above the juke box.

Alex simply met her stare evenly. Then, like she wasn't even the least bit intimidated, she pointed at Sam's side and mouthed: "Get that looked at."

Chapter 7

Loyalties and Lies

What Sam appreciated most about Te Aroha & District Community Hospital was that it was just far enough away from Ika Whenu that she could hunker down into her hoodie and be ignored and anonymous. Not that she could entirely relax here, though. Hospitals—or the smell of them—reminded her of visiting her mother. To this day, harsh disinfectants always made her a little nauseous.

"Nothing broken," Dr. Sue-Yin Linn told her when the scans and X-rays came back, "despite the extensive bruising. Although there's one hair-line fractured rib on the left side."

That explained the pain. Splatting off walls only worked out for cartoon coyotes, it seemed.

"Why did you delay treatment?" Dr. Linn continued. "Concussions can kill, young lady. Well, the subdural hematoma can, if you want to get specific."

Young lady? Sam was thirty-six and had shouldered more responsibilities before age twelve than most people would ever know.

"I can see by your face you want to say some things to me." Dr. Linn smiled. "Go right ahead. Get it off your chest."

"No thanks." Sam scowled and zipped her hoodie back up. "I'll leave it to your imagination."

"Clever." Dr. Linn sighed. "Listen, Senior Constable, it's not my place, but you really do need to have some sort of a buddy system. I've been complaining about these solo police stations for years. It's a research project of mine. And I often write to the Letters to the Editor column of the *Herald*, pointing out their pitfalls. Does anyone listen? No."

Yes, Sam knew about the doctor's one-woman campaign. It was one of the things she appreciated about her. Not that she'd ever say.

"So if New Zealand Police can't provide you with adequate ongoing backup, can you at least tell a trusted family member or friend when you're about to do something monumentally..." Dr. Linn paused. "Risky."

Risky? Not stupid? Sam admired her restraint. "I'll take that under advisement."

"Which means you'll ignore me till the next time you're in here. Look, it's your life, but you're too young to die."

Die? Sam's head snapped up. "I fell off a ten-foot wall. That's hardly life threatening."

"This time. And what about next time?" She faded out at Sam's back-off glare. "All right, fine. Be all brave then. And I'll be here waiting when your luck runs out. In the meantime, I might write another scathing letter to the *Herald* complaining about the risks of understaffed regional stations."

"You do that." Sam stood. "Is that everything?"

Dr. Linn huffed out a breath. "Apparently." She slid some paperwork across the desk. "Your painkillers. Ibuprofen, 800mg, three times a day. Can I convince you not to go back to work for a few days?" Her expression was resigned.

"I think you know the answer. Ika Whenu relies on me. I can't just not be there for days on end. As it is, I've already been off duty too long."

"That's not how injuries work, but I had a feeling you'd say that. Desk work only for a fortnight. Okay? Nothing vigorous outside of work, either."

Sam opened her mouth to protest.

"No, I mean it. Sit your pretty butt at your desk for a full two weeks. No..." she checked her notes, "daily jogs or scaling walls. Failure to get adequate rest will only prolong recovery. It'll mean you won't be able to get on that motorcycle of yours for even longer."

Sam's eyebrows lifted. "I never mentioned my bike."

"You didn't have to. You think I don't see you roar through town on your way to the trails once a week? You're hard to miss." Dr. Linn cocked her head. "Remember two months ago, when you got written up in the newspaper for finding that marijuana crop? You arrested the Brady brothers...all four of them? Amazing, given they're all bigger than my car."

"What do you drive?" Sam drawled. "Because that might not be too impressive."

"Well, it impressed the hell out of my intern, who has a huge crush on you. I get regular reports whenever you fly through our neck of the woods on that shiny black bike."

"Great." Sam rammed her hands in her hoodie pockets. "Send him my regrets."

"Her."

Sam paused, intrigued for half a second at the possibilities, before remembering all the reasons complications were not for her. "Her then."

Dr. Linn's smile became rueful. "Lord knows I tried." She tapped the paperwork. "Go. Take your meds. Behave. Stay off high walls. Live to fight another day."

"Yes, Doc."

An hour later, with the written quote from Roger's A1 Mechanics in her pocket, Sam, now dressed in jeans, a white T-shirt, and leather jacket, pulled her patrol car into Joe's sheep farm, where *Shezan: Mistress of Exploitation* was being filmed. Far catchier title, in her opinion.

A large shadowed form skulked near the gates as she parked her car. As she got out, Sam wondered if she'd cross paths with *Shezan*'s bossy director today. And how she'd feel about it if she did.

She was still torn over the events of last night. On the one hand, Alex Levitin had been...well...amusing, in some ways. She was the chatty type, with a lot of opinions. She was also cute in a nerdy-glasses kind of way. Different. You didn't get much different out here.

But whatever else Alex was, she'd also humiliated Sam in public, made her look weak and ineffectual.

It didn't help that Alex had said some things that maybe weren't *entirely* wrong. Sam might have let her anger toward a shitty, misogynistic movie affect how she'd treated Fletch, half excusing him for being an asshole. That was unacceptable. She'd correct it when he resurfaced. Sid hadn't caught him last night. Didn't matter. The little punk would turn up again soon.

She locked up and glanced at the guard.

Oh, no way.

"Seriously, Sid? This is the security job you got? Why didn't you tell me?"

"I know what you think of the movie." He gave her a sheepish look. "You haven't exactly been subtle."

"Well, just make sure they're paying you right. No funny business."

"Yeah, nah, they're not like that. Pay's choice."

"Glad to hear they're good for something." She pointed past the gate. "Let me in? I've gotta talk to whoever takes care of the bills around here."

"Quincy Blackman, the executive producer, does the money stuff. He's in the production trailer." He pointed to a sea of silver motorhomes. "Last one down the end. Sign's on the door. I'll call for an assistant to take you there." He reached for the walkie talkie on his hip.

"No need."

"Sis, you can't just wander around a set. It's against the rules."

"Watch me." She straightened. "I'll be in and out before they know it."

He frowned. "If it was anyone else..." Sid sighed and stepped back. "Hey, did you go to the hospital? What's the verdict?"

"That's filed under none of your business, little bro." Sam smiled.

"No worries. I'll just ask GNN." He cackled.

"Course you will." She rolled her eyes. "But Gina's only a reliable source *if* I tell her anything." Sam grinned, then strode off across the paddock toward the production trailer.

A pair of nuggety Maori stuntees crashed through a jumble of fake trees and bushes to her right, skidding and bouncing to a halt in front of her. She leaped away, only just avoiding them.

"Oh fuck, sorry, lady." The first one dusted himself off, bounding to his feet. "Bloody stunt rehearsal got away from us."

"Bro, that's the local copper, right?" the second one said, clipping him lightly around the earhole. "Show some respect, eh?"

"Shit, didn't recognize you without the uniform," the first one said, shooting her a cheeky grin. "Sorry."

They loped back to where they'd come from.

She peered after them, seeing rigging poles holding up lights, a crane with an unmanned camera on the end, gymnast mats, and several brawling figures practicing a scene with a leotard-wearing female in the middle.

"No!" a burly man shouted, his accent all LA, as he bellowed, "Do it again, and try not to dislocate Kiri's shoulder this time."

Behind them she could see the lithe forms of about six women learning moves that could be a dance or a fight. A male choreographer, all elegance and leonine grace, was demonstrating a rhythmic action that they were copying.

"Make way!" A man hauling a ladder intersected her view of the women. He wore a red Budweiser cap, a black T-shirt that said "Shezan Rulez," and a worn baseball jacket with a Dodgers logo. "And you're late." He pointed at the rehearsing women. "Amazon training started half an hour ago. Better get changed. Can't work out in that." He shook his head. "Didn't you pay attention in the briefing? Whatever.. Move it!"

"I'm not a..."

He was gone before she could protest.

She left the buzzing action and continued toward the trailers, crossing paths with a familiar sight.

Kevin. Sid's skinnier, younger, light-fingered brother blanched at the sight of her. He wore a red "Shezan Rulez" cap.

Jesus, he works here, too? Sid had left some things out.

"Got my eye on you, Kev," she told him solemnly. Okay, so she wasn't above a little tree shaking to see what fell out. Sometimes the best confessions came from a good bluff.

He swallowed, eyes bulging. "I'm working in the lighting department here. I swear I'm on the up and up. Sid got me the job. You can check with him."

"Mmm. They must be giving lighting jobs to anyone then," she teased, "since you never managed to turn the lights off once at home when we were kids."

Kevin cackled at that, shoulders relaxing. "Yair." He always stretched out the word "yeah" until it was something else entirely. "Pretty much."

She smiled. The Mahutas were good people to grow up with. Even Kev, when he wasn't nicking everything that wasn't nailed down—although she really wished he'd stop doing that.

Alex rounded the corner, deep in discussion with a man wearing a battered tool belt.

Kev took that as his cue and scrammed.

"Because the platform has to be that wide," Alex was saying, "or we can't support the weight of the cameraman and gaffer. It's simple physics. What's there isn't adequate."

"But the ground's so muddy with last night's rain, the struts keep slipping," the builder said. "Can't we just move a few meters over to more solid ground? There are rocks that would be so easy to—"

"Absolutely not. The sight lines are perfect as is. The waterfall's right over Shezan's shoulder, the Kauri tree will frame it. And there's all that weird moss growing there. Never seen anything like it."

"Pahau-kakapo? Giant moss?" the builder suggested.

"Whatever it is, I want it in the shot, too, which won't happen if you move the rig even three feet. So if the ground's too unstable, why can't you forget the struts and build a platform on the ground first? Put the rigging on that? Come on, didn't you used to build houses? You didn't move a house because of mud, did you?" She pinned him with a penetrating gaze.

Oh, nice argument. Sam almost felt sorry for the man.

"Um, no."

"Right. Good…look into it. I have to…" She glanced up and spotted Sam. Surprise crossed her face. "…Go." Alex left the builder and walked over. "Senior Constable Keegan. I didn't expect to see you. What brings you to my world?" Her smile was tentative.

"Apparently I'm auditioning to be an Amazon," Sam deadpanned.

"You're a shoo-in." Alex's eyes crinkled.

"I don't know." Sam touched her abused ribs. "I've been benched by my doc."

"We could prop you up against a tree." Alex paused. "Are you any better?"

"My X-rays say I'm okay. More or less."

"Thank God." Alex's expression became guarded. "Look, I'd like to talk to you about last night, but I can't right now. I think…maybe things were said that…" She inhaled. "Weren't said in the best way."

Not an apology, but more a regret for her delivery? Before Sam could answer, a woman's voice shouted from the distance: "Alex! Phone call from LA! Mr. Howard's on line two. Urgent!"

"Damn." Alex took off at a jog, calling over her shoulder, "Sorry. Later! It's madness around here."

Sam watched her retreating form for a few moments, then made her way up the steps to the silver motorhome marked Production.

As she was about to knock, a man in his fifties came stomping out, a disgruntled look tugging at his hairy lips. His shirt read: *You Dump, We Pump.*

"Careful. Bloody viper pit in there, lady," he grumbled. "They just canceled me contract. My brother-in-law's gonna be so pissed at me." He blinked. "Pissed? Ha. That's funny." He grinned.

If he says so. Sam stepped around him and knocked on the door.

"No, Frank, fired is fired," came a masculine voice within. "You almost shook our people out of their beds. Bother someone else."

She opened the door. "I'm not Frank."

A balding man in a thick corduroy jacket, burgundy turtleneck, and black jeans snapped his head up from the paperwork. "No, you're not." He studied her. "Ah, yes, the police officer. I recognize you from last night's little contretemps at the pub. Sit." With a wary look, he pointed her to a plastic chair.

Contretemps? Who speaks like that? Sam ignored the chair and stood in front of him. "I'm Sam Keegan," she said. "You're *Shezan*'s producer? Quincy Blackman?"

"Executive Producer. What can I do for you? If this is about you apologizing to my director for your behavior last night, I'm more than happy to arrange it." His gaze sharpened.

Apologize? The hell she would! "That was a private matter. So, no."

"Sounded pretty public to me. You told the entire pub that we're producing a B-grade, misogynistic pile of crap. Did I get the quote right?"

He had her there. She cleared her throat. "Did Alex...Ms. Levitin... mention anything about an incident involving her vehicle pulling into my path, stopping suddenly, almost impacting my motorcycle, causing it significant damage? I've brought the repair bill. She said the studio would pay, which I believe makes this yours." She placed the quote on his desk.

He barely flicked a glance at it before raking her with a dissecting gaze. "Look, when my director first explained the incident to me, I made inquiries with our insurer. They won't pay because Alex didn't touch you or your bike. If you couldn't slow down in time to avoid a *parked* vehicle, you were speeding. The fault is yours."

"She reversed suddenly across my path. I had no time to slow down!"

"She didn't hit you, though. Our insurer isn't liable for a cent. And before you ask, no, the studio won't be making any payout out of its own pocket, either."

Sam folded her arms. "Come on, a company like yours could pay this out of petty cash."

Quincy nudged the quote. "Some reason you won't ask your own insurer to pay?"

Yes, she could put in an insurance claim. Problem was, given Tiger had been customized a lot, her insurance excess was almost six hundred dollars on any claim made. She didn't have that sort of spare cash. Besides, why should she pay anything?

Squaring her shoulders, Sam said: "Out here we do things informally. Handshake agreements are rock solid. It means less paperwork, and no one gets their insurance premiums jacked up. That's why I haven't spoken to my insurer, because it wasn't my fault *and* Ms. Levitin admitted liability and promised to pay."

"Fault has not been proven. In fact, I think you're just hoping the rich movie studio will foot the bill. No thanks. We'll pass."

Sam stared at him. "If I was trying to screw over the 'rich studio,' wouldn't I be suing you for pain and suffering, too? Wouldn't my lawyer be in here? Hell, I can still do all that."

Quincy didn't look the least bit perturbed. "Know what I love about small towns? You hear a lot of things around the local drinking establishment. And oh how they love talking about their aloof town cop."

Hardly a news flash. Sam ground her jaw.

"I heard, for instance, Senior Constable Keegan, that you're always doing reckless stuff. Dirt-bike riding. Stunt-jumping creeks. Waging a war on bikers. That all sounds mighty dangerous. Who knows how you really hurt yourself? On top of that, I now have a pub full of witnesses who saw an assailant injure you last night."

"That just aggravated the existing injury from the incident involving your director."

"According to you." Quincy gave her a long look. "So in sum, the only thing we know for sure is that *you* hurt your motorbike. And *you* have somehow hurt yourself, probably more than once, including last night, which is unfortunate but not our fault. Now if you want to make a civil claim for damages, that's your call. Just know that the studio has fancy lawyers and deep pockets to drag this case out for months if we thought we'd win. Which we would."

Sam's throat went dry. "And does your director agree with how you're handling this?"

"Alex knows exactly how the film biz works. She left it to me. Join the dots."

She knew? How could Alex joke with Sam just ten minutes ago, knowing Quincy was about to shaft her? Talk about two-faced.

"If you'd like to stop by Craft Services, they have raspberry muffins this morning. Freshly baked from that lovely local pub of yours. Help yourself on the way out." He turned back to his desk.

Sam snatched up her paperwork and slammed the door on her way out.

Ten feet away she spotted Alex, talking to the builder again. Sam's eyes narrowed, and she made a beeline.

The builder took one look at her, clutched his tool belt, and said, "I have to be…um, somewhere else." He disappeared in a pounding of black boots.

Alex turned. "Sam? Are you okay? You look—"

"I just spoke to your boss."

She paused. "Quincy? Is this about your bike? I'm glad he's sorted it out."

Sorted it out? "You *approve* of this?"

"Sure." Alex's expression was puzzled.

"So you're just like your father, after all," Sam said, voice low. "You really stuck to his playbook: Buy them drinks, befriend them, then play them for a sucker."

The smile fell off Alex's face. "*Excuse* me? You're insulting my dad? How dare—"

"Forget it. I'm done." She stalked away. *Shezan* and Alex Levitin could both go to hell.

Back home at last, Sam changed into her police uniform, trying to ignore the mounting fear that it was going to take forever to get her bike back. She slammed her front door, locked it, and headed next door to her station only to find it already open.

"Well, look who the *pekapeka* dragged in," came a deep male voice.

"I think the saying's cat, not bat," Sam said. "And what are you doing here?"

"Why so surprised?" Sergeant Vaughan Peterson asked. "I *am* the officer in charge of your little armpit of a station." He offered his best 'just kidding' expression, but she knew he meant it.

"You didn't have to come."

"It's not every day I find out one of my most dedicated officers has been almost hit by a car and yet failed to file an incident report. Why is that?"

"I can't file a report. Didn't see who did it." Of course, it'd be tempting as hell to sling Alex Levitin with dangerous and reckless driving charges. Hell, the karma would be a bitch. But Sam was neither dishonest nor vindictive. "It was so fast. They were gone before I knew what happened."

"Not like you. You're usually so good with details." He gave her a sharp look. "So what happened?"

"Minor fender bender. Damage was all at my end."

"Mmm." He considered that. "So are you better now? Don't say you are if you aren't. I don't need the paperwork if you cark it."

Charming. "Hospital wants to see me again in a few weeks to make sure nothing's worse, but for now I can do desk work."

"Okay. Are the Boars are giving you any trouble lately?"

"Nothing new, beyond their little drug couriers being sighted all over town. I collared Don Mathers a few days ago, trying to solicit new buyers. That was in my daily report. He had no meth on him that time, but I got him on 'possession of an instrument for the purpose of taking drugs.' Meanwhile, I'm watching. Building a case against the Boars."

"Watching is one thing, but tackling a gang direct without my approval or back-up could get you fired for recklessness. Understood?"

Christ, typical. Had her boss ever taken a risk a day in his life? Sam folded her arms. "Yeah. That everything?"

He cleared his throat.

Sam waited.

"So about Mr. Mathers..." He glanced away. "I'm dropping the charges."

"What?" Sam blinked. "He's trying to drum up meth customers."

"A lot of speculation there. No evidence. Did he have any drugs on him?"

"Only an old bong with marijuana residue. But the witnesses I interviewed said he told them—"

"So no *direct* evidence he was dealing. Maybe he was just big-noting himself? Maybe he was doped up and didn't know what he was promising them? Who knows? So I've determined I won't be pursuing the matter at this time."

"Why?"

He straightened. "Mathers is low-hanging fruit. I have operational matters ongoing elsewhere."

"Such as?"

"Need-to-know basis."

Oh for God's... "Look, I know Mathers. There is nothing whirling around in that idiot's head beyond getting cash for weed. He's of no use as an informant. He has a memory like a sieve and the brains of a glow worm."

"That's your opinion. It was my duty to let you know I'm not proceeding. I've done that. So...consider yourself informed. Okay, Senior *Constable*?"

Why did she bother putting the squeeze on these little bastards, when they didn't even get near court? "Yes. Sergeant."

Vaughan nodded. "By the way, I hear you caused a fuss in town last night. Had a fight with those movie people?"

"Not quite how it went down."

"And you gave the director an earful."

He sounded almost hopeful. Had Alex pissed in the man's cornflakes or something? "Do you...know her?"

"She came through here first thing this morning looking for you."

She did? "Why?"

"Something about your injury? I told her that was a police matter and none of her concern. Who knows why people want to know when a police officer's incapacitated? It's not like she knows you; she's from out of town. And it's not like you make new friends." He smirked.

And screw you, too.

He leaned in and his voice became conspiratorial. "Told her if she was angling to get around you somehow, figure out when you were away so she could get up to something dodgy on that film set of hers, I'd be on her like a blowfly on shit."

Oh boy. "And what'd she say?"

"She called me an asshole." His nostrils flared. "When I objected, she said, 'Oh, sorry, I thought you knew.'"

It took every ounce of willpower not to react to that, but a laugh was dying to burst out. Sam's eyes watered with the restraint. "Oh. I see. Anything else?"

"Not much." Her boss started packing up his paperwork. "Nothing to trouble you. You just keep watch on all your little spot fires out here and leave me to sort out the big fish, okay?"

Lovely bit of condescension. It would have almost been worth the pain to plant her boot in his ass on his way out. But then she'd have to burn her favorite boots.

He put a folder under his arm and grabbed his car keys. "By the way, what's this I hear about you having a new nickname? *Hukapapa*?"

"The Wild Boars are being smart asses again. Dino thinks he's skilled in psychological warfare."

"*Hukapapa*...that means ice and hard frost, right? Why are they calling you that? Isn't it a good thing to be cool?" His brow puckered.

If he couldn't work out the nastier subtext to that slur, she wasn't about to enlighten him. "Not a clue." She opened the door for him. "Maybe Dino just admires me."

"*You*? Oh sure. That'd be it."

Sam narrowed her eyes. What an asshole. Alex really did have a point.

Chapter 8

Not Just a River in Egypt

ALEX STARED AFTER THE RETREATING form of one properly enraged Sam Keegan. Why did everything keep going pear-shaped between them? She'd made an effort to stop by the police station this morning to see if the other woman was any better after she'd staggered out of the pub the previous night. And maybe…she felt a little guilty.

Alex stood by her words. No one had the right to judge her or *Shezan* without having all the facts. But maybe she could have saved it for a less public place, given Sam was the local copper and all. When Alex had been starting out, how many times had people questioned her professional decisions, often in front of her crew? Even though she ran her own indie production company?

So, first thing, Alex had hoped to smooth things over. It was good business, she'd told herself on the drive over: Don't piss off the local law. Only problem was that instead of Sam, she'd found an officious sergeant at the station, acting as if Alex was after state secrets. So…she might have said a few things. And a few more. Christ, she needed to work on her censor button.

"Do you want it eight- or ten-feet high?"

"Hmm?" Alex's attention was drawn back to the set builder. His eyes kept darting to the exit as if half expecting Sam to come thundering back for round two. "Oh." She tried to gather her thoughts. "I'll let you know. I just have to check on something." Alex marched over to the production trailer.

"Quincy, what the bleeding hell did you do to Sam Keegan?" she said by way of hello.

"Ah, that." He shrugged. "Headed her off at the pass. Told her we wouldn't pay her a cent. Insurance won't touch it because you didn't even hit her."

Oh hell. "I pulled off the main road like a maniac. Reversed across her path, gave her nowhere to go…"

"And yet *didn't* hit her. It's done. You're absolved."

"But…"

"No. It's settled. This is my purview." His tone firmed. "I don't tell you how to direct, do I?"

Her lips compressed. "Could you not be so Hollywood for just one minute and do the decent thing?"

"Definitely not. Decent sends a signal that we're easy marks. You'll have a bunch of locals faking accidents and sticking their hands out for money."

"Oh, come on, the Kiwis aren't exactly known for being a litigious bunch."

"I'm not about to test the theory." Quincy shrugged. "Gotta say, we're damned lucky she didn't poke this through official channels. 'Cop-killer Director' wouldn't have looked pretty in the news."

"But I didn't kill her!"

"Like that would make a difference." He snorted.

"Why *didn't* she press charges?" Alex asked curiously.

"Because she reeks of honesty." Quincy's eyes lit up as if that was an unexpected, useful weakness.

"And we're screwing her over for it. That's wrong."

He shrugged. "Only morally wrong. I'm just doing my job. Banging down our costs is why I was hired. So not paying a dime to Roger's A1 Mechanics is an excellent place to start."

"God, I hate money sometimes. It causes weird shit."

"Well, I just made your weird shit go away. You're welcome."

Alex inhaled. Glancing at the timetable on the white board behind Quincy, she said, "I should go. I'm late for 'Shezan meets Poacher's Daughter' rehearsals."

"Wouldn't want to miss that," Quincy said dryly. "There'll be enough wooden acting to start a forest fire. And that's before you get to the crap dialog."

She couldn't argue. "I'm tempted to tell the actresses not to bother to learn their lines yet because that scene stays as-written over my dead body."

"Careful, Levitin. Directors with grand visions on B-grade flicks tend to get cut off at the knees in this business."

"What's so bad about having a vision for excellence?"

"Nothing. Usually. I'm just reminding you to lower your expectations. Yes, you can make it a *bit* better. I hope you do. But always remember we're not making *Schindler's List* here."

So much for him not telling her how to direct. To hell with that. She'd lower her expectations when she was dead. Alex stood to go. "Nice pep talk."

"You're welcome." Quincy snorted and turned back to his work.

Alex paced the paddock outside the poacher's tent set, waiting for Melody to deign to appear. Studio exec's kid or not, this was unacceptable. Alice had gone to drag the actress's pretty blonde ass back here more than five minutes ago. Melody was obviously putting up a fight.

Chloe was sprawled out on a canvas chair nearby, checking her texts. "Hey, did you know Summer's buying goats for villages in Africa?"

"Of *course* she is." Alex paused her pacing. "What does Bess say about it?"

"The usual. Not much beyond affectionate eye rolls. And something about how one goat should be named after their former showrunner." Chloe pocketed her phone. "Bess is so whipped."

"Oh to be that whipped," Alex murmured.

"Yeah." Chloe chuckled. "Hell, I'd endure being mocked 24/7 by my friends to be that happy."

"Wouldn't we all?" Her words came out far too wistful.

Their eyes met. This was weird. Their best friends were in an intense relationship and yet she and Chloe were barely acquaintances. It was an artificial intimacy—there, but not really. Throw in Alex being Chloe's boss, and it didn't get any less weird.

"Maybe one day I'll be in a love affair so sappy I won't care how 'out there' my lover's whims sound," Chloe drawled. "*If* I worship at the altar of the right deity, of course."

"Oh? Which deity did you have in mind?"

"Chocolate goddess," Chloe said. "I like the daily sacrifices required."

Alex laughed. "Sounds legit. But please convert to Her Cocoaness *after* my movie. I don't want Skye having to resew all the costumes again."

"Fair enough. Hey, when are we getting an eyeful of *Shezan*'s new threads?"

"Soon." Alex dropped into the canvas chair beside Chloe, drumming her fingers on the wooden arms. "This delay is ridiculous," she grumbled. "Melody's only got two dozen lines in the whole movie." She glanced over to the First Assistant Director. "Leslie? Can you try again on Melody?"

The woman reached for her walkie talkie. "Alice, can we get an ETA on getting Ms. Howard to set?"

"I can't find her!" Alice's voice squawked back.

Alex sighed and turned back to Chloe. "Are you excited about your first starring role?" she asked.

"I know it's getting flamed and shit, but I'm really stoked. I'll be the first ever Maori chick to play a fantasy lead for a major studio."

That made sense. This would be a big deal for Chloe and her community. All the more reason to fix the rot. And as much as the other woman tried to hide it, Alex could hear the worry underneath her laid-back answer. Alex gave her a measured look. "I promise I'll make it worthy, Chloe. You won't be embarrassed by it when I'm done."

Chloe looked intrigued. "Cool. But honestly, I figured even if the movie was complete crap, I'd still get an all-expenses trip home to see my family." Something caught her eye, and she pointed. Alex followed her finger.

Melody was prodding her way slowly across the paddock in heels, somehow looking regal despite all the ruts and manure. Leslie leaped onto the walkie talkie to notify Alice.

"Our megastar's arrived," Chloe said.

Mega-something. "You're being kind," Alex muttered.

"If you'd met her dad, you'd say it's a miracle she's so normal."

"Really?"

"Met him at one of Skye's big industry parties. He never let anyone forget he's a someone. Spent most of the time making these passive-aggressive jokes about how he'd get more work done if his family wasn't around bugging him. Skye never invited him again."

"Hmm." Alex tilted her head, considering the parallels. "How interesting she took this role. Angry daughter faces off with abusive father."

"Think maybe someone's sending Daddy a message?"

"No idea." Just as likely Melody didn't realize why she was drawn to it. After all, that required self-awareness.

Chloe tapped her script. "So this scene is the first meeting with the daughter and Shezan, right? How do you see it?"

"Shezan would look at her fancy hair and impractical outfit and think she's an oddity, something exotic that draws her in. She's never seen a white woman before, either." Alex inhaled. How trope-filled was this damned movie?

Chloe eyed her. "You don't like this, do you? The whole racial and social divide shit? Or, um, any of it?"

"Well, not as it is, I admit. I tend to prefer movies with messages. But don't worry, I'll make this much better." She gave Chloe her most reassuring smile.

"So what's *Shezan*'s message?" Chloe asked, sounding curious. "Has it got one?"

Make the studio VP's daughter famous? Alex hoped she sounded confident when she replied. "I'm still working on a different approach to what's written. Something fresh."

"Choice." Chloe yawned, then stood, stretching. She ran her fingers through her long black hair. "Course it might be a bit hard for some people if you come up with anything less than entirely wholesome." She snorted.

"What do you mean?"

Chloe's eyes settled on the slowly approaching Melody. "Haven't you noticed how full-on religious my co-star is? She wears this huge crucifix and quotes scripture all the time. This morning, the caterer copped an earful of Proverbs. Something about a calf fattened with hatred?"

Alex took in Melody's blonde cheerleader looks and don't-care-about-anything expression and tried to marry them with Chloe's words.

Chloe added more quietly, "Look, she hasn't strayed into Leviticus territory yet, so I don't think she knows about you and The Gay. I won't tell."

"I see." *Great. A powerful diva on a religious crusade? Lucky me.* She appreciated Chloe's loyalty, even though Alex's sexuality wasn't a secret. One internet search would be all it took. "Right. Shall we get to it?"

"Sure." Chloe grinned. "I'm all set to look shocked and awed by the sight of some white chick in safari pants."

God. This script.

The rehearsals did not improve Alex's opinion of Melody's abilities. In fact, she was getting worse. Her delivery was flat, she sometimes stepped on Chloe's lines, and her gaze never stayed on her co-star, instead meandering off to nowhere.

Maybe Quincy had been right: It was ridiculous thinking about a vision when all she had was mediocre to work with.

Except that wasn't quite true, was it? Alex had a top cinematographer, a leading costume designer, a stunning backdrop, and a decent lead actress. Chloe was gamely holding her own in spite of Melody's efforts. Also, their bad-boy poacher was off-the-charts creepy, and all his scenes were memorable at least. So, really, all she had to do was fix the rest. But right now, the absolute worst was right in front of her.

"Okay," she called to Melody, "can we try it again, but this time, really *up* the energy? Pretend this is real."

"What do you think I've been doing?" Melody pouted.

That was her trying? Out of the corner of her eye, Alex caught Chloe's smirk. "All right, you two, step closer. Let's try a deeper frisson. Maybe you're each the most intriguing person the other has ever clapped eyes on? Can we try that? Just turn up the intensity to a hundred, okay?"

With a shake of her blonde hair, Melody took two steps closer to Chloe and began her line. "Where on earth did you come from? What *are* you even?" she demanded.

Chloe, instead of answering immediately, gave her a long, considering gaze and then took one more step, right inside Melody's space. After an amused, appraising look, she teased, "What are *you*?"

Alex's mouth went dry. The line was supposed to be delivered like a challenge, an annoyed comeback for the arrogant newcomer, but that had come out almost...sultry.

Melody's face slackened as she stared back, not saying her line. "I-I'm Jennifer," she finally said. "I'm here with my father." Her voice was lower, huskier now.

What the hell is happening?

The actresses stared at each other. Then, slowly, Chloe dropped her eyes to Melody's lips.

Redness flooded Melody's cheeks. "And you can't be here! You're setting all those traps for my father and he's furious." Her words came out in a breathy rush.

Chloe offered a crooked smile. "Why do you care if he's mad?"

"I don't!" Melody gave her a frosty glare. "I'm my own woman."

Chloe laughed. It was gentle and faintly mocking and, God, it was *perfect*. "Sure you are."

The rest of the scene rehearsal played out. Alex remembered to call "cut," but long after the word tumbled from her lips, she sat unmoving, staring at the actresses in astonishment. The entire set had gone eerily still.

Melody swung back to face Alex with her usual resting bitch face. "Well?" she asked. "Was that more intense? Enough energy?" The derisive sneer would have been insulting if not for the redness that still lingered on her neck and cheeks betraying her. Her fingers were wrestling together in a nervous tangle.

"Much." Alex hid her jubilation. "Great job, you two," she said briskly. "Everyone, take five. Chloe, a word?"

She hurried Chloe away from the set as Melody plonked her perfect ass into a canvas chair and grabbed her phone, expression back to vacant.

"Oh my God," Alex said in a low voice.

"I know, right?" Chloe snickered. "I think I woke the dead. Shit!"

"She responds when you flirt. You hit a nerve of some sort."

"I was barely even flirting. Like, I was feeling pissed off after our Leviticus conversation and thought of doing something to stir up her shit. I had no idea she'd..." Chloe blinked at Alex, "...go all breathless and weird."

Alex's mind whirred. "You two have chemistry. Keep doing what you're doing and see what happens. Don't overplay it, though. And I think it'd be best if we don't explain any of this to Melody."

"Sure." Chloe paused. "So, do you think she's a closet job? Or maybe she doesn't even realize she's giving off lez vibes?"

"No idea. The reason isn't the point. Let's just harness it." She strode back to the main group, Chloe in tow. "All right, people, moving on..."

Chloe went all in on the next few run-throughs, stepping into Melody's space each time, touching her arm, smiling, holding her gaze...

If Melody had worked out what her co-star was up to, she gave no sign. Not...consciously. However, the longer scenes went on, the more she began to mirror Chloe's actions and expressions. At one point, Melody drew in a breath, held it, and looked into Chloe's eyes as though her co-star was utter perfection.

It was...oh Lord, it was everything. Lightning in a bottle. So real, so damned brilliant. So much so that Chloe drew in a deep, surprised breath.

In that moment, everything became clear to Alex. A vision was crystallizing, a plan for how her movie could be rewritten and shot. Shezan would fall for the daughter, not the father. It would be subtle, layered, subtextual. And above all, Alex would make it beautiful.

In that last scene, Melody had smiled at Chloe with a flawless mix of coyness and confidence. Where had *that* actress been hiding? What emotion did Melody think she was playing?

This would work. She rose from her chair. "Melody, when we shoot, do it *exactly* like that. You were perfect."

The woman glowed.

"And Chloe? Just what I needed."

Chloe's eyes were gleaming.

"Everyone take ten." Alex returned to her chair and began to make copious, frantic notes.

A few minutes later, Skye Storm slipped into the seat beside her. "Well, well," she said, "Someone's up to something."

"Hmm?" Alex said as she scribbled. "Regarding?"

"Chloe and Melody. Don't pretend you're not up to mischief with those two." Skye's eyebrows lifted. "You know exactly what I mean."

Alex looked up to meet her costume designer's amused expression. "Is it that obvious?"

"To me." Skye regarded Melody in the distance, talking on her cell phone. "But I suspect one particular participant is quite oblivious, isn't she? So I have to ask." Skye lowered her voice to an intrigued whisper. "Are you *Ben-Hur*ing the innocent Miss Howard?"

Alex gave her a sheepish look. "If by that do you mean am I letting one possibly homophobic actor think she's merely playing a close friendship, and I've told the other one to play it as gay subtext, then yes, I'm absolutely doing a *Ben-Hur.*"

Skye nodded. "As I suspected. What do you think Melody will do when she finds out?"

"By then I'm trusting the film will be done and it'll be too late for her to complain. Besides, I'm sure someone in Publicity will tell everyone it wasn't written that way but they love that people are free to interpret it any way they like."

"What of the studio? You can't pull the wool over their eyes the way you can one actor."

"I know. I'm hoping the movie's been so badly slammed that there's nothing to lose at this point. I won't know until I ask for my changes, but I get the impression they're so humiliated they'd try anything." *God, I hope so.* "Right, how are the new costumes coming along?"

Skye flipped through a large notepad. "That's what I was coming to see you about. The Amazons are warriors. They'd have access to leather, feathers, wood, and woven grasses. They wouldn't have access to metal, so forget heavy bodices or anything like that. So here's my concept." She passed Alex her notepad, turned to a sketch. "I know it's unusual, but before you say no..."

Alex held up her hand to stop Skye talking so she could absorb it fully.

The outfit was in two pieces, with tight leather pants in a rich, rust brown and a basic tan leather tunic top. An intricate, plaited pale-cream leather belt was woven around the waist several times. Unexpectedly, a reddish, spotted, thin fur pelt came over one shoulder, protecting the left breast and diaphragm. Leather straps bisected the breasts and held a quiver over the right shoulder.

The boots were dark brown, leather, mid-calf height. Bare forearms were adorned with thick, hard-leather, fur-lined bracers, and thinner, intricately carved decorative leather wrapped around the biceps. The effect was sleek yet functional, emphasizing both the lines of the bust and the warrior's muscles. "What sort of leather is it?"

"Mostly buckskin, a lightweight leather. It would be easy for any Amazon to make this outfit, dye it with berries, and manipulate the material through plaiting and so forth. The half-shoulder vest is for warmth and protection."

"Why only half shoulder?"

"She needs her bow side free to get a full draw."

That made sense. "What's that vest made out of? I've never seen spotted copper fur before."

Skye's eyes lit up. "Well, I've been doing research on the Valdivian Rainforest we're basing our world in. Did you know it's famous for all its miniature animals?"

"Annoyingly," Alex grumbled. "It's hard to manufacture a threat out of the world's tiniest carnivores and cutest marsupials."

"How terrible for you!" Skye broke into a light laugh. "It's glorious for me, though, because they have these beautiful miniature deer, called pudú. That's what the pelt's made of." She tapped the sketch. "We'd use fake fur and just make it look like pudú, of course."

"Well, I really love the belt," Alex said. "And is that a pouch at the side?" She peered closer. "Skye Storm, did you just give my Amazons pockets?"

"I did, sweetie. Every girl needs her pockets." She nodded earnestly.

Alex snorted. "It's bold, Skye. But I don't think sexy movie Amazons are supposed to wear pants."

"The ones living in a temperate rainforest would. It's chilly at night."

"You know what I mean. Showcasing some boobs and bare skin is the rule. And don't start me on showing off rippling abs. That's a prerequisite."

"You've been watching *Wonder Woman*." Skye sounded amused. "Have you been envisioning a training montage, darling? I'm afraid Themyscira's Amazons didn't have frosty mornings and drenching, icy rains to worry about."

"And Alex Levitin's Amazons don't have anywhere close to a $120 million budget. Your costumes are beautiful, but it's quite a departure from what the studio will be expecting and I'm a little concerned about the costs on such an extensive overhaul."

"Costs won't be a problem. I can salvage a lot of material from earlier costumes—the first ones, I mean, before the second director opted for near-nudity. I have certain suppliers who can do me excellent prices, too." Skye's expression turned pensive. "This all comes down to whether you want authenticity or not. Or will you tell me to drop the substance for style?"

Alex gazed at the concept. It really was stunning. Clever. Sharp. It made sense. "You've turned our Amazons into huntresses," she said appreciatively. "Warriors, not eye candy. Can you do me a prototype?" Alex asked. "I want to see it worn."

"Of course."

"How's our heroine's look coming? Has Shezan been overhauled, too?"

Skye smiled mysteriously. "That depends."

"On?"

"Her origins. I've thought hard about this." Skye hesitated. "If she were raised by wolves, as the script says, she'd have a certain look. Lots of fur. She'd use what's around her."

"Okay." Alex waited.

"But what if she's actually originally an Amazon herself?" Skye turned the page and tapped a new design. "Then *this* is what would make sense to her. A variation on what the Amazons wear, half remembered from her childhood if she was separated from her tribe young."

Alex's breath caught in her throat. "Oh." What a captivating idea. Her mind whirled. "So the distant Amazon allies are family she once lost?" She stopped. "And neither of them realize?"

Skye beamed and flicked to a new page. "I knew you'd understand. The story would be much richer if it had that thread to it."

Alex examined the sketch before her. The costume was more home-spun than the huntress outfits, clearly intended to look like it had been made by a woman with less skill than an Amazon—as if it was something she'd tried to re-create from memory. The stitching wasn't as good, the belt thicker, and the boots were different, as well—thinner and lighter, to enable speed. She also wore a woven grass headband to keep her hair back.

A story began to form as she traced the sketch with her eyes. A young Amazon girl, separated from her tribe. Maybe it was some ritual, where a girl spends a night in the forest as part of a custom, but for some reason, she doesn't find her way home. "She's lost," Alex said slowly. "A lost girl, searching for home. Her whole life is about finding that missing home."

"And don't forget the family who lost her," Skye said. "The Amazons never stopped feeling like a piece of them is lost. So evocative."

"This changes everything." Alex was working out how to spin it to the studio when Skye clasped her forearm. "Finding home is the theme, yes? So what if Shezan finds both her old home—the Amazon tribe—and a new home with her love?"

"Home as both a place and a person? That's good."

"Yes."

"Well, it's better than we had." Alex chuckled. "It has substance at least."

"I knew you were the right person for this job." Skye smiled.

There was just something about the way she said it that made Alex's head snap up. "What do you mean?"

"You understand how close I am to Chloe? When Summer first befriended her, I adored her immediately. I couldn't help but take her under my wing as another daughter."

Alex nodded.

"Well, I had to make sure Chloe's first leading film role turned out better than it was on paper, and to do that I needed allies. Talented allies who think outside the box."

Wait, what?

"So..." Skye slid her a knowing look. "I dropped your name into a few ears, raving about this marvelous indie director I worked with years ago who'd be perfect to make this film shine."

Alex's mouth dropped open. "*You* did this?"

"Yes, dear. I wanted Chloe's film career to take off. And I knew you needed work soon, for...erm, certain reasons."

Bettina. "Thank you," Alex said grimly to fill the silence. So...she couldn't even get offered the worst movie ever under her own steam? How depressing.

"You're welcome!" Skye beamed at her. "I like to look after my friends. Besides, I wanted to work with you again."

"So you got me this job," Alex repeated, feeling numb.

"No, you did that. See, the ears I dropped your name into already knew who you were. And I knew you'd be perfect to fix this. By the time you're done, this film will be fabulous."

"I admire your optimism."

"What optimism?" Skye's eyebrow lifted. "I'm a stone-cold hard realist."

Alex couldn't help but laugh. "Uh-huh."

Alex was slumped at a table in the pub after dinner, her back aching after a long day, and trying to think of how to compose the world's most compelling email.

Dear studio execs, please let me make your mainstream flick hella lesbian, but don't worry, it's on the downlow. Plus, I've put everyone's tits back in their costumes. Cheers, Alex.

Somehow she doubted that'd fly. She took a sip of her beer, opened her iPad's mail program, then CCed every studio executive she knew of associated with *Shezan*.

Dear gentlemen and Ms. Bassett,

I've been working on ideas for improving Shezan: Mistress of the Forest, *which I'm presently directing in New Zealand.*

Improving quality will require a costume overhaul (already completed), a different back story for Shezan, *a theme, and a new ending.*

The theme I propose is 'finding home.' It's a universal goal, and it's especially empowering for our younger female target audience. To achieve this theme, I propose making the following changes to the script:"

She paused to work out how to say it.

"Don't stop now." Skye had appeared, leaning over her shoulder. She was clutching a handful of knitting. "I'm all aquiver."

"Didn't anyone ever tell you it was rude to read someone's emails?"

"I didn't think you'd mind, dear. I'm waving the flag for Team Lesbian *Shezan*."

Alex snorted.

Skye dropped into a seat beside her and resumed knitting.

"What are you making?" Alex waved at the blur of plastic needles and wool.

"Socks." Skye held up the magenta woolen mass.

"Why?"

"It's relaxing. And they will match the suspenders."

That probably made sense somewhere.

Skye eyed the iPad. "So what's the thrust of your email?"

"That two women going off into the sunset together beats a cliché-ridden, straight romance."

"Sounds like quite the task. Well, go right ahead. I won't get in the way. I'm not one to interfere." Skye turned her attention back to her sock.

Alex resumed tapping out her email.

"1. Delete Shezan's romance with the morally dubious poacher and turn him into a straight-up villain. He's problematic given he shows no remorse and only stops killing to win over Shezan. Then he takes her back to his city home, isolating her from where her heart lies—and he knows it. This is controlling and robs her of her identity. She is a creature of the forest. This is not *a happy ending.*

2. Kill the villain. Give the audience what they'll be rooting for. A creepy villain killed by an animal he's stalking. Audiences love karma.

3. Give Shezan a history of being a lost member of the Amazon tribe. Connecting her back into her community is a powerful message of belonging. Reunions are hugely popular.

4. Have Shezan also find a personal sense of "home." To do this, beef up the role of the poacher's daughter, played by Melody Howard, and give her and Shezan a close friendship—so much so that Melody's character stays on in the forest at the end with Shezan. This ticks the happy-ending boxes. Our hero is not alone, and feels safe, and loved, and at home.

Close friendships and/or sisterly bonds between two women resonate powerfully with female audiences. That's the reason Frozen *is so popular. There's a huge clamoring for this overlooked dynamic. We can use that. Conveniently, Ms. Howard has superb chemistry with our star, Chloe Martin, so they could pull off this friendship convincingly."*

"Oh, very nice," Skye chuckled, peering at the screen, "given you've CCed her father. I know Richard. That man will puff up like a balloon at the mention his daughter's great at anything."

"You don't say." Alex was well aware that flattery got you far in Hollywood.

Skye suddenly waved at someone in the bar area. "Oh, he's so nice."

"Who is?" Alex asked, distracted.

"Sid. Our set guard." Skye's eyes sparkled. "Did you know who his foster sister is? That police woman. The one you were fighting with in here the other night."

Alex's jaw tightened. "Let's not discuss her. She's judgmental, arrogant, cold… Just no. Sam Keegan can drop off the face of the earth as far as I'm concerned." She ignored Skye's lifting eyebrows and continued typing.

The effect of these simple rewrites cannot be underestimated. For one, we shift from the unpalatable message of a woman of color giving up her sense of self to a white man who is cruel and manipulative. The message instead becomes about found family, being accepted for who you are, and embracing one's own power.

The poacher's daughter, in turn, finds the courage to be herself, to discover her own path. And that is a huge box office earner. Just look at Finding Nemo.

"*Frozen* and *Finding Nemo*? I see you appreciate the animated classics." Skye smiled.

"Yes, well." Alex eyed her pensively. "I looked up the studio execs. Except for Caroline, all of them have kids. They'd know first-hand the power of those titles. Too much?"

"Not at all. Continue."

> *Historically, box-office sales in sci-fi/fantasy movies where the romance is peripheral to the female star's hero journey have been impressive. In other words, fans in* Shezan*'s genre aren't there for the romance, they're there to see their heroine succeed. Examples proving this point include* Wonder Woman *and* The Hunger Games.

"Good choices." Skye nodded.

Alex snorted at the woman's apparent inability not to snoop.

"Sorry. I'll be quiet. I'm not interfering!" Skye declared. "Keep going."

Alex inhaled and tapped out her next paragraph.

> *I'm aware that deleting the romance may still concern you. Let me remind you that the highest grossing* Star Wars *movie of all time is* The Force Awakens. *This was a female protagonist's hero journey; it made a billion dollars and contained no romance. And* Captain Marvel, *also a romance-free female-empowerment story, made even more than Rey's adventures.*

"I loved Rey," Skye said cheerfully. "Costumes were divine, too. One day I'd love to…"

Alex glanced at her. Skye mimed zipping her lips.

> *This is where the world is now: Audiences demand films about women's hero journeys* first, *regardless of romance. And the top thing* Shezan *can do to overturn its negative publicity and claims of misogyny is to shout that we're making a film celebrating "girl power."* That's *what audiences are looking for now—not outdated tropes about women subsuming all their power, desires, and brilliance to make bad boys better humans.*

In the meantime, we've taken great strides to fix the biggest criticism about this film.

She turned to Skye. "Can you email me the sketches of the costumes? I assume you made photos? I'd like to share them."

Skye put down her knitting needles and dove into her bag, pulling out her phone.

Our costumes have been overhauled to reflect this 'girl power' concept, and address the movie being dismissed as exploitative and demeaning. See attached. Our women are now powerful, sleek huntresses. We'll have a prototype ready for photography soon. May I suggest getting the Publicity department to blitz the internet with them? It'll change Shezan*'s social-media buzz overnight.*

She glanced at Skye, who nodded in pleased agreement, then returned to knitting.

Alex looked around the pub. "I can't think of what else to say. Have I covered everything?"

"Mention the fallout surrounding Harvey," Skye said, unfurling more wool from her ball. "Subtly, though. That'll set the cat among the pigeons over there. Trust me."

"Weinstein? Isn't that radioactive territory?"

Skye smiled a secret smile.

"What aren't you telling me?"

"Now that would be telling."

In these heightened #metoo times, it's especially important to present our studio and our movies as celebrating women, not demeaning them. By providing powerful role models, strong heroines who can find 'home' without needing a man, we make Shezan *a story of our times.*

If you approve my suggestions, I'll get a new script written ASAP.

On a related note, I've cut costs in several areas to allow for any budget increases my above suggestions may incur. See attachment 2 for details.

I look forward to hearing from you soon.

Sincerely,
Alex Levitin
Director, Shezan

Alex added a list of the budget-trimming measures she'd cooked up earlier with Quincy and added that to the email. Then she collected Skye's costume photos and attached those, too.

After a moment, she typed one last line.

PS: Can we please do something about that title?

She sat back and reached for her beer.

"Very nice," Skye said mildly. "You're so good at this."

"Sometimes I wonder about all the secrets you know." Alex eyed her speculatively.

"I have no idea what you mean, dear." Skye gave her an innocent look. She finished her knitting and held it up. "What do you think?"

The maroon sock had the word "Hollywood" knitted in gold up the ankle.

"Very…um…cheery."

"Exactly!" Skye laughed.

"So how do you think they'll take my email?" Alex asked, giving it a final, worried look. "Did it sound too…feminist-y for the dinosaur execs?"

"Oh, the old boys will squirm a bit. But they're very interested in following the money. You made good arguments. For instance, Nolan's daughters are besotted *Frozen* fans; he complains about it constantly. Adam failed to get the rights to *Wonder Woman*, so he knows how successful a female-hero film can be. It's a sore point with him. Meanwhile, Richard has a vested interest in Melody's role being boosted. Caroline just wants something, anything, to get her noticed. All that together, and a few other factors, and you might be surprised."

"Hope so." Alex slid her finger to the Send button. "Now or never." She pressed it. *Done.* Looking up, she asked, "So where's Chloe tonight? Don't you two usually hang out over dinner?"

"I don't think she likes my mother-hen vibe when she's trying to chat up a certain local boy who's caught her eye." Skye smiled.

"Still crashing and burning on Sid, huh?"

"You noticed, too?"

"Well, Chloe gets a little distracted around him. I don't think he's aware, though."

"No. She says he just can't seem to take a hint."

"Tough crowd if you're a gorgeous movie star and can't get noticed." Alex laughed.

"It happens more often than you think. Beautiful women often intimidate men."

"They intimidate women, too. God, you should have seen me the first time I clapped eyes on..." She faded out, realizing Skye didn't know her secret. And it probably wasn't the best idea to share it with the mother of the woman Bess was now besotted with. "Oh...um."

"Elizabeth Thornton," Skye finished.

"How did you know?" Alex gave her a quizzical look.

"Back on the set of *Heaven's Blood* I put two and two together."

That far back? "You know that Bess and I were over years ago," Alex said hastily. "And my best friend's deliriously happy now, in her own terribly reserved, Bess kind of way. Summer, too, by the looks of things."

"Yes, that's true. They just seem to click together, don't they? But that doesn't make it less hard for those who haven't been quite so lucky, does it?" She shot Alex a knowing look.

Alex refused to let envy creep in, and she doubly, no, triply, refused to dwell on Skye's words. "Ancient history," she said forcefully.

"Oh, I know, dear. Anyway, all I'm saying is that I hope you'll find someone one day who thinks you're the most wonderful person they've ever met. The way I have with my Brock." Her eyes warmed. "And maybe next time she'll be someone who doesn't ruin your credit rating in the process."

"Ugh, Bettina! I still don't know how you found out."

"I know many people and many things." Skye's smile was mischievous.

"Yes," Alex agreed, glancing back at that sent email. "You really do. Thanks for your help on this, by the way."

"Nonsense." Skye resumed knitting, a serene look on her face. "I'm never one to interfere."

Chapter 9

Reflective

TWO BLOODY WEEKS OF DESK work, and Sam had been officially going crazy. She'd rather be falling off bikies' walls or chasing dope-head messengers around town than pushing paperwork from one pile to the next. She'd also been really missing Dino's dogs. At least Bruce had kept her company at work most mornings, curling up at her feet when she'd been most prone to climbing walls. Metaphorical ones, of course. She'd never felt so useless, but at least her ribs felt better.

Her incapacitated state must have become common knowledge, because this morning she'd found "*hukapapa*" spray-painted across her home's front door in red and black—the bikies' club colors. Brazen, brash, and newly emboldened. Just great. When she finally had enough dirt to bring down the Wild Boars, it'd be the sweetest damned day of her whole career.

"Wake up." Dr. Linn clicked her fingers. "I don't know where your mind just wandered to. I asked if you'd been taking your drugs daily these past two weeks." She pressed into the ribs at Sam's back.

"Shit," Sam protested at the pain. "And yes."

"I know it hurts, but it's much better. And the X-rays confirm it."

"It was even better before you started prodding me."

"I thought you were a big strong cop, all bravado last time. Or to be exact, *every* time I've seen you in the past ten years." Dr. Linn smiled. "What's changed?"

Sam's expression fell. "Nothing."

The doctor's smile disappeared. "Are you okay? Officers manning police stations alone have so much on their plate. I'm researching it. Did I mention that?"

"Yeah." She only brought it up every single visit.

"Aside from the physical toll, there's anxiety, stress..." Dr. Linn paused and weighted the next word meaningfully: "Depression."

"Are we done?" Sam wasn't about to be the doc's prime guinea pig in some new study, no matter how well-intentioned she was.

"Yes. Get dressed. I'll give you some privacy." Dr. Linn stepped away from the examination bed, closing the curtain behind her.

That seemed a little silly, since Sam had been sitting here in only her work pants and sports bra for ten minutes, but whatever. She drew her uniform shirt back on and was buttoning it up when Dr. Linn spoke through the curtain.

"I can recommend some people to talk to here at the hospital, if you need that. It's free and discreet. No one would know."

"I'm fine. I'm just..." She cast around for the right words. "Kind of wound up a little tight?"

"Well, I do have that love-struck intern if you need to...relax." Dr. Linn sounded amused now "She's most attractive, according to her peers. I couldn't possibly comment because I refuse to notice such things."

"I'm sure you're not supposed to be pimping out your underlings, Doc." Sam tucked her police shirt into her belt. "Probably some rule about it." She drew the curtain open with a flourish.

"Probably," Dr. Linn conceded. She studied Sam thoughtfully. "So, why are you so pent up?"

"My bike's still in the shop."

"Ah. It has been a while since you roared up our main street."

Sam inhaled. It felt too...juvenile to admit how much she missed it. A grown-ass woman wanting her shiny toy.

"I love to dance," Dr. Linn suddenly said, and her brown eyes became unfocused. "My husband and I take every opportunity to whisk ourselves around the local club and dance the night away."

"O-kay?"

"But three weeks ago, Eric broke his ankle. It's made us grumpier than caged cats." She paused. "We need dancing as an outlet. Everyone needs a way to blow off steam. You're not special in that regard, and it doesn't make you weak to need it." She leaned in. "While I'd prefer you chose a safer outlet..."

Sam rolled her eyes. She'd heard that speech a few times too, along with motorcycle accident statistics.

"...I know I can't change what you love. Would you like me to call up your mechanic and tell him it's a matter of some urgency he fixes your motorcycle? For the good of Ika Whenu, of course?" Dr. Linn's eyes sparkled at her joke. "I'd do it if it'd stop you brooding."

"Wouldn't matter anyway. Mechanic's left a message it's ready. But I just can't find the..." *Money.* Sam sighed. The timing of this was crap. Her savings were non-existent since she had been pitching in to help out Gina's ancient pub kitchen with a flashy new commercial oven. Gina had grand plans to turn Te Wharariki into a big-deal gastro pub to lure in tourists from all over with gourmet delights.

"No time?" Dr. Linn guessed. "Make it happen." She wagged her finger at her. "As your doctor, I'm telling you that's your top priority, okay? Don't need you getting into a funk. Well, a deeper one." She paused. "Were you always this moody when we were at school together, or did I suppress the memory?"

Sam snorted.

"Well, anyway, we're just going to assume that I've also lectured you once again on riding safely, and not doing any of those stunts you're infamous for."

Sam rolled her eyes. "I haven't jumped Dry Creek in years. Everyone else keeps bringing it up."

"Well, you know my thoughts on that by now. But, apparently, it's another reason my intern adores you. You have attained mythical status."

"Uh-huh." Sam's thoughts drifted. The doc was right: She needed Tiger. It was messing up her equilibrium not being able to escape. Maybe she could ask Roger for a payment plan? "Thanks. I'll make my bike a priority."

"Meanwhile, are you absolutely sure you don't want to meet my intern? Cathy's smart, funny, sweet, and, I'm sure you'll appreciate this bit, not prone to breaking the law." Dr. Linn winked.

"Not this time," Sam said diplomatically. Or ever. She sounded young and star-struck; tragic mix. "Maybe when I'm in a better mood."

"Yes. There is that. You'd only scare her off today. Your black storm cloud was evident from three blocks away when you came in."

It was?

"Go on then." Dr. Linn pushed a prescription for more painkillers Sam's way. "I expect to see you roaring past us in Te Aroha again soon."

Sam smiled at that image, just as her phone rang. Her enthusiasm faded, hearing the ringtone. A call had automatically switched through from the station. "Sorry, I need to get this. It's work."

Alex sipped her coffee in Craft Services, going through her notes after breakfast. They were in an unsettling pause, waiting for studio approval of her script overhaul ideas. They'd been filling in time doing only technical prepping and second-unit location filming that wouldn't be affected by any of the suggested changes. The actors not needed by the second unit were spending their time being drilled in stunts.

Meanwhile, Skye had finalized her prototypes and was starting costume fittings. The outfits looked incredible—even better than her sketches.

Finishing her coffee, Alex went over the day's rundown. They should be on schedule for a Wairere Falls shoot this afternoon thanks to the weather clearing. It was just a few sweeping establishing shots for use near the start of the movie, unaffected by any script rewrites. Shezan would be breast-stroking around the waterfall's pool, looking all 'forest mistress-y.' It'd be freezing. Alex shivered in sympathy with Chloe and her stunt double.

This morning involved a scene at the so-called Reflective Pool. Shezan was supposed to catch a glimpse of her reflection. A special effect sequence would be added later, where she'd glimpse the girl she once was. Originally, that had been listed as a flashback of growing up with wolves. If their script changes were approved, they'd instead drop in a montage of her life as an Amazon child.

She sighed in impatience. How long did these people need to decide whether to greenlight a new direction for a middling holiday flick on a shoestring budget?

Sid suddenly sprinted into view, his body rolling to a heaving stop. "Boss, you gotta come with me," he panted, pausing to suck in a breath. "Sorry, there's a problem."

Alex jumped up. "What sort?"

"Aren't you shooting at the pond today? On the call sheet, it says Reflective Pond?"

"Yes."

"Right," Sid nodded. "And, the thing of it is, it's been drained."

"Drained?" Alex's stomach clenched. "How?"

"You'll see." He led her to the tree-shrouded location, five minutes away.

When they reached the area, Alex could make out a lithe female figure leaning back against a tree, in running gear, looking unsettled. She recognized her. Kiri Cooper, Chloe's stunt double.

Alex eyed the now-empty mud hole and cursed. The artificial pond had been created near a beautiful stand of weeping willows. The set-design team had dug it a month ago, lined it with rubber, and filled it with mud and water. The idea was that by leaving it awhile, it would attract moss, bugs, and various other natural elements that would make it look real. Now muddied scuff marks replaced where the moss had been. Some rocks had been overturned and looked out of place. Even when they pumped water back in, it'd look less than ideal.

"What happened?"

"I was doing my morning run," Kiri said. "I saw this. Called Sid ASAP."

Alex glanced from face to face and back to the hole. "Why call Security? What am I missing here?"

Sid squatted and wiped away some mud against the rubber. "Puncture holes all over it. Someone did it on purpose." He squinted up at her.

Her lungs deflated. "Why would anyone do that?"

Sid shrugged. "Dunno. Maybe Fletch wanted payback? You did make him look like a bit of a goose at the pub."

Kiri cleared her throat. "Or it could be that someone wanted to stop filming. Some locals don't like the direction of the film—the revealing costumes and so on. They think it'll make Ika Whenu a laughingstock."

"But we're changing that! For God's sake, we're waiting on getting changes approved and the costumes are now incredible."

"Well, yeah, boss," Sid said, "but that's not common knowledge, is it?"

No, it wasn't. Alex regarded them. "You're both locals. Can you spread the word?"

"Sure." Kiri thrust her hands into her tracksuit pant pockets and hopped from foot to foot a little to warm up. "But people believe what they want to. Minds get made up and stay made up."

"Then *un*make them." Alex glanced at Sid. "Call the cops. Or…cop. We need to get to the bottom of this. Whether it's Fletcher or protesting locals, it's unacceptable, no matter the reasons."

He nodded. "Yeah, sure thing. I'll do it and come right back." He jogged away.

Staring at the empty mud hole, Alex sighed. *Great.* Just what she needed. She'd have schedule delays, repair bills for Quincy to grumble about, and more immediately, she'd have to deal with one of those people whose minds "get made up and stay made up."

Wiping her hands down her jeans, Alex hoped her meeting with Senior Constable Keegan would go better than the last one. Which wouldn't be hard, would it?

Sam arrived an hour later. Alex wasn't nearly suicidal enough to ask why the delay.

The woman's dark expression was more imposing than usual. Her crisp uniform encased Sam's strong, tall body with a sky-blue short-sleeved shirt, and a dark blue multi-pocketed vest. Around her waist was a bulging black utility belt, stuffed with what looked to be a yellow Taser, various pouches, and pepper spray. Sam's navy police cap kept her short blonde hair out of the way. Her uniform pants stretched across her ass in a pleasing way that Alex was absolutely not noticing.

She strode over, looking no-nonsense and commanding. "Sid, Kiri, 'morning." Sam's gaze slid to Alex. "And…Ms. Levitin. I understand you have an urgent matter of minor sabotage?"

"Actually, it's major sabotage to me because it'll put a big dent in our schedule and cost us time and money to fix. It took us a month to prep this to make it perfect." Alex waved at the empty pool. "Now we have a bunch of holes in a rubber-lined pond where there should be water and healthy plant life."

"I found it wrecked when I was jogging," Kiri said. "Little puncture marks all over it. The rocks were kicked to the side, too, and the moss all disturbed."

Sam crouched beside it and inspected the damage.

"I'm told it wasn't like this last night," Alex added. "Had to be done first thing today."

Sam pulled out a pocketknife and cut a small square out of the rubber lining.

"What are you doing?" Alex asked.

"Getting a sample." Sam held it up to the light. "I'm thinking pitchfork. Farm-sized? Where is Joe, anyway?" She glanced toward the farmer's house. "I'll see if he's lost any tools."

Oh. That sounded smart. Not to mention professional. Alex nodded.

"Um, do you mind if I finish my training run?" Kiri said. "My muscles are starting to seize, and I didn't really dress for standing around in the cold for an hour."

Alex's eyes fell to her outfit. Sleek navy tracksuit, white sneakers, and a thin beanie. She must be an icicle.

With a curt nod, Sam waved her off.

Kiri sprinted away over the paddock, sure as a jack rabbit.

Sam wiped down the rubber square on the dewy grass and put it in her vest's chest pocket, along with the pocketknife. "So, any suspects? Anyone on set being a troublemaker?"

"It wouldn't be someone on set. It's a local who hates what we're making here. Or a certain young asshole I embarrassed in the pub. Fletcher?"

"That's a big assumption." Sam's tone was icy. "Disgruntled employees would be most prone to committing sabotage. Far more likely than some local who thinks it's a genius idea to get out of bed in freezing temperatures to poke holes in your movie's little pond. And they had to know it even existed, right? It's not signposted or well known, is it? You think Fletcher or his ilk know about this place?"

Oh. True. "No."

Sam turned to Sid. "Any scuttlebutt about this pond around town? Has it ever come up?"

"Nah, Sis."

Sam looked pointedly at Alex with an expression that said *see?*

"Well, that doesn't prove anything," Alex said in exasperation. "And it absolutely doesn't mean one of my crew would do this. Why would they?"

"People have their reasons," Sam said. "Grievances fester. Is it possible someone thinks they're owed money, for instance?"

Oh for God's… "Hey, I didn't know Quincy would do that—"

"Sure you didn't," Sam cut her off. "Look, the question is, is the perp a local or someone on set? I don't know; I'll make inquiries. That's all I can do." She straightened.

"I really don't appreciate being called a liar." Alex took a step closer. "I tried with Quincy. He wouldn't roll over, so I fixed it myself. Should I get out my hair shirt as well or parade through the village naked?"

"Heh, naked." Sid snorted.

"What did you fix?" Sam snapped shut her notebook. "I've got a steep repair bill, and now you've got me dropping serious crimes to investigate some pinpricks in your kiddie pool."

What does she mean, what did I fix? Of all the insufferable, idiotic, self-righteous, annoying women… Alex dug through her wallet and found the mechanic's receipt shoved in the back of it. "I tracked down Roger's A1 Mechanics last week and paid for your damned repairs." She threw the paper at her. "Out of my own money. Exactly as I promised."

Sid gave a soft, amused snicker from somewhere behind them.

Sam's cheeks started to burn red as she stared in surprise at the receipt. "Right. Well. Why didn't you just say?"

"I thought you'd been told. Roger said he would tell you when you went in to pick up the bike." Alex glared at her, then at the empty mud hole costing them money by the minute. "Sabotage is no joke. Even a small thing like pinpricks in a *kiddie pool* can throw out our whole schedule. This is not trivial or a game. So, if you wouldn't mind doing your job, I'll do mine, and we can stay out of each other's way the rest of the time I'm here. Okay?" Alex shouldered her way past Senior Constable Keegan, furious beyond words.

Quincy was waiting for Alex when she stormed back to the Production trailer, her jaw grinding.

"Yes?" she asked as he met her at the door. "Another crisis?"

"More like a win. The powers that be have replied to your script overhaul ideas. Check your inbox."

"Oh?" She couldn't read his expression.

"Fess up," Quincy said curiously, "who told?"

"I don't follow."

"Don't play coy, Levitin. I know you're smart. How'd you know to put the #metoo hints in your email? The studio bosses told me on the quiet that's what pushed it over the line for you."

Jesus. What *had* the execs been up to? It did explain the exodus of suits at the studio around the time Caroline Bassett had been hired. Skye must have known something. All her innocent "I never interfere" lines. *Please.* Alex shot Quincy a bland, neutral smile.

"Anyway," Quincy continued, "I suppose you also know that's why you were hired, too? They wanted a diversity pick—a female, feminist, lesbian, whatever, someone they could hurl back at their critics."

So much for it being her impressive CV that had won her the job. "Right." Alex gritted her teeth. "So they've approved my changes then?"

"With one stipulation." He hesitated. "They want you to slot in a male character, someone easy on the eyes. A nice guy." He paused a beat. "White. American. Relatable. Not as a love interest," he added quickly, "more, um, as rugged wallpaper. All looks, no action. Well, no romantic action. Okay?"

Was that all? Alex could live with that. "I'm sure the existing anti-poacher ranger could be made to fit the bill."

"A white ranger out here? Wherever 'here' is?"

"Maybe he's here on exchange? Or married a local?" Alex stuck her tongue in her cheek.

Quincy snorted. "Yeah, okay, whatever. They want Mr. Good Guy to pop up at various intervals and provide a bit of square-jaw scenery to offset your..." He flapped his hand... "wall-to-wall girl power."

"God forbid anyone might feel irrelevant for three seconds," she murmured.

"I didn't hear that." Quincy smirked. "They said no to a title change. One of the VPs loves it. No accounting for taste. Anyway, the main thing is, your ideas have been approved. Kick your requests over to the writer."

"Great." *Finally!*

"And a heads up that I'm grabbing the First AD to organize Chloe and Melody for costume publicity pics this afternoon. The studio loved that idea. They want to start showering the internet in publicity stills of the new and improved looks." He exhaled. "Oh, and Levitin?" Quincy's voice lowered. "Good strategy keeping the gay out of your email. They'd have definitely shot it down if you'd asked for it outright."

How had he known? The email wasn't obvious. Was it?

Quincy rolled his eyes at her expression. "Come on, I saw those two in rehearsal. It's not exactly subtle, their eye-fucking. I put two and two together."

"People can choose to see their chemistry as either friends or lovers," she said evenly.

"Ri-ight. I don't think the studio's as stupid as you think. They'll spot it, too. Look, just don't name the horse and everyone'll live with it. They have way more to worry about right now than a bit of subtext in a B-list fantasy flick everyone's already written off. Right?"

"Okay."

"Hell, I can't believe I'm about to say this, but this thing's turning out so damned subversive that I'm almost *wanting* to watch *Shezan* now. Even if it's just to see if you can land this fuckin' nose-diving plane." He looked faintly stunned.

Alex knew the feeling.

Chapter 10

The Hardest Word

Sam glanced at her watch again, and then peered at her beer. The seven p.m. dinner stampede was about to come through Te Wharariki's doors.

Staring into her amber brew, she sighed. It was a bit hard not to feel like the worst piece of *pekapeka* shit since she'd found out two days ago that Tiger had been paid for and was just awaiting collection. She'd asked Roger why he hadn't thought that was worth mentioning, and the elderly mechanic had just waved her off, saying he had a lot of things to remember and an old brain. Either way, her day off couldn't come soon enough; she was anxious to pick it up and hit the trails.

In the meantime, there was the matter of a certain apology.

"You okay, bub?" Gina asked from behind the bar. "Need a top up?"

"I'm good."

"You haven't been in here much lately, not since your big dust-up with the movie folks. I was starting to wonder if you were going to avoid the pub for the rest of the shoot. Yet here you are, right on seven. That's interesting." Gina leaned forward as if waiting for some delicious confession.

"Can't a woman just enjoy a beer?"

Gina lifted her hands. "You really okay? Fletcher packed a wallop."

"I caught up with him and charged him. That put me in a good mood."

"Your face doesn't look like it heard you're in a good mood. Is something going on, love?"

"Don't you have someone else to shakedown for gossip?"

"Why would I do that when you're here?" Gina chuckled, glancing up when the door opened. "Ah, my best customers are here." She bustled away, calling to Dutch to get ready for incoming orders.

From behind her beer, Sam watched the motley group of Americans and Kiwis head for the ordering counter. A few made straight for their now-favorite tables. Alex brought up the rear, in discussion with some crew members.

"Hey." Sid appeared at her side. "Didn't expect to see you here."

Did everyone have to look so shocked whenever she socialized? "Just enjoying my downtime."

"If you say so." He grinned. "How many locals cornered you tonight?"

"Only three. There's the case of the lost farm duck, graffiti on a garage door written in an ex-boyfriend's handwriting, and a hubcap thief at Buy-Lo's Supermarket."

"We get the best criminals around here, eh?" Sid's easy-going smile relaxed her tension.

"Yep." She sipped her beer.

"So why are you in here when the crew of a certain oh-so-evil film are here now, too?"

She didn't bother arguing; he'd buy it was a coincidence about as much as Gina. "I'm investigating the sabotage." Sam hoped that sounded plausible. "Maybe you can help? With your insider intel?"

"Sure." He plonked himself onto the bar stool next to her. "Happy to help. 'Specially since I was the investigating officer at the time of the incident."

Investigating officer? Time of the incident? Sometimes Sam wondered if Sid still dreamed of becoming a cop. He'd applied a few years back but had just missed out due to his test scores. Books weren't his strong point. It was a shame. Sid was genial, honest as the day was long, and far too big to shove around. She gave him an indulgent look. "The pitchforks at Joe's farm didn't match the holes in the pond lining. Then I went through the movie set's tools with one of the assistants. No matches."

"Thorough," Sid said approvingly.

"Mmm. Maybe one of these days I'll get to solve a real case. You know the one."

"The meth? I hear George at the hardware store's now hooked. Why'd he go and do that? He's got a young family!"

Damn it. She'd wring Dino's ugly neck for turning Ika Whenu into a drug town. "Shit." Taking another stalling gulp of beer, Sam finally aired the question she most wanted to know the answer to. "So back to the set vandalism. What do you hear about your boss?"

"You think Alex did this? Torpedoed her own shoot? No way, Sis. No. Way. She's dedicated to this *Shezan* thing. And, like, wicked smart, right? First day on the job, I heard she just walked in, took one look at a set, and chewed through all the shit she saw. Had the builders and props guys redoing the whole thing."

"So she's a pedant? Picky?" She wrinkled her nose. "That's unpopular."

Sid snorted. "You can talk. You're the most details-crazy person going. You think I don't know you've been feeding Dino's dogs for months on the off-chance you have to raid him later?"

"That's just practical forward-planning. And they're nice dogs when you get to know them." She stopped. "How'd you know?"

"Dutch. Okay, remember that time when we were kids, and you caught a bully at school taking Kiri's lunch money off her? You demanded it all back, not just that day, all of it, and you calculated interest he had to pay."

It sounded so mercenary when he put it like that. "He needed to pay restitution."

"He shit his pants you scared him so much."

She shrugged. "I fail to see what any of this has to do with your director."

"Right, so, here's a list: Detail-oriented, dedicated, driven, goal-focused, smart, risk-taker, community minded."

"Wow," Sam drawled. "She's a damned saint."

"Actually, that's you." Sid met her eye. "*And* it's her. Ever think that's why you're butting heads?" He bumped his fists together. "Just two sides of the same coin."

Sam gaped at him. "I'm nothing like her!"

"No? Tell me how you're different."

"I respect the locals."

"So does she. The new costumes?" Sid shook his head. "Amazing. She's respectful as hell of our people."

"Well, I do good for the community through my job. Not shallow… tripe."

"Alex and her film employ stacks of people, though," he said cheerfully. "Many of us are locals."

"I don't have a felon for a father."

All humor drained out of Sid's face.

Oh. Why had she said that? Sam desperately tried to turn it into a joke. "Come on, I'm a cop, I'm not supposed to like criminals, right?"

"*Sam.*"

One word, but it was layered with so much disappointment that she felt the deep shame of it. Yeah. It had been a shitty, shitty thing to say.

Sid's voice cooled. "I don't think you get to judge someone based on their parents, do you? Your dad bolted before you could talk, and your mum…wasn't able to do the job."

Shame burned under her ribs. "I'm well aware."

"Bottom line: Alex is great, and I think you should get to know people properly before you write them off."

"People only disappoint when you give them a chance." She cocked an eyebrow.

Sid sighed. "Sad thing is, you act like you're joking, but I know you mean it." He gave her a long look. "Y'know, I'm going to go hang with people who don't hate their life so much." He left, joining his *Shezan* workmates gathered at the bar.

That was unfair. She didn't *hate* her life… It was just…hard to explain what her issue was. Sam's mood was shot to hell.

Maybe I should just cut my losses and leave.

Standing, she wiped her hands down her jeans and debated her options. Leave now with her dignity intact. Sam slid her eyes over to Alex, now seated at a table with two other women. The director's shirt—white and stiff at the collar, with three buttons undone—flattered the curve of her delicate neck. Alex ran a hand absently through her red hair and then dropped it back to the table with an amused slap to punctuate some point. Her gentle, low laugh infected her companions, who joined in. Then Alex smiled, small and teasing, flashing white teeth.

On the other hand, Gina had never raised a quitter.

No, she damned well hadn't.

As the weeks rolled on, Alex had begun looking forward to time out at the pub at the end of each day. She no longer noticed the worn floors, dated décor, or faded memorabilia tacked to the walls of Te Wharariki Hotel. Photos of winning sports teams long past their glory days dotted the walls, and now she was starting to recognize the people in those yellowed photos within the lived-in faces at the bar.

Tonight's drinks to celebrate the approval for script rewrites was something she'd been eagerly anticipating, even if it had trapped her in a typically random discussion with Skye and Chloe.

"Why," Skye asked with immense seriousness, "does everyone assume pumas are black? They're honey brown."

"Because of panthers," Chloe said after a beat. "Which *are* black."

"That makes no sense," Alex chimed in. "But yeah, that's why."

"So everyone just wrongly remembers them as black?" Skye pondered. "How interesting to be an animal so misunderstood."

"Or...it could be because the Puma sporting logo is black?"

At the new, familiar voice, Alex glanced up to find Sam standing over their table. Irritation flooded her.

"Can we talk?" Sam's expression was tight.

"No—" Alex started to say, but Skye clamped onto her wrist, halting her objection.

"Why, hello there, dear, you must be Sam?" Skye cut in. "I've heard all about you from our security guard. Darling man, Sid. And yes, I'm sure you're right about pumas. Maybe advertisers have far more to answer for than any quirky mass delusion?"

Sam slid her hands into her jeans pockets.

Skye barreled on. "I'm Skye Storm."

"Really?" Sam blinked.

"I know, dear, I've heard all the jokes. Anyway, I do *Shezan*'s costumes. The new ones." She laughed. "Let me stress that point! And this is Chloe Martin, our film's talented star."

Sam nodded a hello.

Chloe waved in greeting. "Can I just say, your bro is so nice. Is he single? He's...arghh...*divine*." She fanned herself.

"Um..." Sam squinted at her. "Who, Kev?"

"No, Sid. The security guy with a voice to die for."

Sam glanced back at the bar as if trying to mentally picture the odd pair together: a genial, rough-around-the-edges, heavily tattooed giant of a man and a beautiful, sleek, otherworldly international model. "Seriously?"

Chloe shrugged. "Sid's been totally useless at hints, so I wondered if he was taken."

"Nope. Single but clueless. Be less subtle."

"Hold up a sign," Alex suggested, amused.

"Or wave your panties," Skye said. "I hear that was popular in the seventies."

"So were perms," Alex countered.

"Good point," Skye said. "Do not start me on flammable leisure suits."

Sam shifted from foot to foot, as though wondering if she was still a part of this conversation.

"Right." Chloe beamed. "I'll up my A-game, cheers. Hey, Sam, I hear you went to school with my stunt double?"

"So you *do* all know each other in New Zealand," Skye teased.

"School was a long time ago," Sam said. "But yeah."

"Kiri said you jumped some huge dry creek back in the day, which makes you better than whitebait fritters, eh?"

"Oh, I've heard of whitebait fritters," Skye said enthusiastically. "Are they a thing in New Zealand? Where do we get them?"

"Um, here?" Sam pointed at the item in question on the large blackboard menu.

"Well, I'm feeling bold. Chloe," Skye said smartly, "be a dear and come help me figure out what else to get for dinner. Maybe you can accidentally trip over Sid while we're there."

The two women headed for the bar, discussing absurd romancing tactics, leaving Sam standing awkwardly in front of Alex.

"Right." Sam's eyes darted everywhere else.

"Well," Alex said, eying the aggravating woman...a woman who suddenly had turned endearingly awkward, and it just wasn't fair. She took pity on her. "Since Skye's obviously manufactured this time for us to speak, you may as well sit."

"She has?" Sam asked before dropping into a chair.

"Pretty sure," Alex said evenly. "So is this about work? You have a sabotage update?"

"No. My leads haven't come to anything yet."

"I see."

Sam inhaled deeply. "I came to thank you."

"Right."

"For my bike."

"I see." Alex kept her eye on Sam as she took a sip of wine. "It would be the polite and obvious thing to do."

"Right." Sam's gaze dropped to the floor. "I think I said some things that were out of line."

"You're not sure?" Alex asked.

"No, I'm sure. I was out of line."

"And?"

Sam gave her a blank look.

"This is usually where someone says sorry."

Sam pressed her lips together. "I thought that was obvious. I'm sorry."

"Mmm." Alex eyed her. "Okay, so that's that then."

Sam's shoulders sank as if she were being dismissed. She rose to leave but paused uncertainly.

Alex took her in properly. Slim-fitting pale jeans. A black T-shirt and leather jacket. A silver necklace at her throat. A thick, black leather belt that looked sexy as hell around the woman's trim waist.

Maybe it'd be better if she did go. With Alex's frantic job, she didn't have time for complications or complicated people. "Tell me more about the investigation." *Oh geez.*

Sam's fine ass dropped back into the seat. "Not much to tell. The weapon of choice doesn't match the tools available. The locals in town are unaware of your artificial pond. And the *Shezan* crew is outraged anyone would harm their production."

Alex's eyes sharpened. "See? I know my people. Besides, what possible motivation would they have for sabotaging their own paychecks? It wouldn't be one of us."

Sam shifted in her seat. "I'm not so sure."

Annoyance shot through Alex. "Don't you think I might know a little something about how sets work? I've spent a lot more time on them than you."

"It's not that." Sam hesitated. "I'm genuinely not sure what's going on here. I can't rule anything in or out. I don't like to make assumptions."

"That's new."

"What do you mean?"

"You made assumptions about my movie. Several times."

"Not without any evidence. Come on, those costumes…"

"Are history. The new ones are phenomenal." Alex pulled out her phone. She scrolled to her photos and lay the phone down. "Have a look."

They were the raw shots she'd sent to LA, which would be used for publicity once the studio tweaked them. First was the Duncan sisters in Amazon outfits, beaming, hands on bows, looking ready to hunt insanely cute marsupials.

"They look much happier," Sam said after a few moments. "Skye has talent."

"She's one of the best." Alex swiped to the next photo. "That's Chloe, who you just met, as Shezan. The girl in the safari pants is Melody. She plays Jennifer, the poacher's daughter."

The two stood back to back. Both women's arms were folded, and they were facing the viewer. Chloe's head arched slightly back into Melody's. Although the star was facing the camera, Chloe's playful gaze was sliding toward Melody, whose lips were curving a little.

On its own, Melody's expression was innocent. However, paired with Chloe's naughty, teasing look, it was as if they shared a secret.

"What sort of movie are you making?" Sam asked.

"An action/adventure fantasy hero thing."

"Do *they* know that?"

"What?"

"They look like lovers."

It isn't supposed to be so obvious, for God's sake. Alex regarded her thoughtfully. "Fine. You wouldn't be wrong. But it's being done as subtext. It won't be explicitly spelled out that they're a couple; the studio wouldn't go for that. So please don't share that. And if you ever find yourself talking to this woman"—she tapped Melody's face—"never breathe a word of what we've talked about."

"She doesn't know you're making a love story?"

"Actually, no."

"You're serious." Sam looked startled. "That's...unexpected."

"People aren't always self-aware. And some don't neatly fit boxes, either."

"Well, that's true."

"Although you seem pretty aware of a great many things not obvious to everyone." Alex leaned back against her chair and eyed her. She waved at the photo of the two women. "So...is that a cop thing? Reading between the lines?"

Sam chuckled. "Y'know, no one's ever asked me if I'm gay quite so subtly before."

"That didn't answer the question." Alex offered a smile of her own.

"I'm surprised the gossips haven't filled you in already.

"Nope. You remain as mysterious to me as the day I almost flattened you and you cursed my very existence."

"I'm shocked." Sam leaned in and asked quietly, "So, this lovers thing... is that your big plan to fix your film?"

Sam hadn't answered the gay question. She hadn't denied it though, either. Interesting. "Well...yes, it's a part of the fix." Alex regarded her curiously. "Why? Don't tell me you have a problem with a lesbian-themed movie?"

"Everyone needs their heroes, especially gay kids. *If* they're done well."

"Do you think I'll do it well?" Alex batted it back.

"That depends." Sam's eyes became half lidded. "I mean, maybe it'd help if *you* had an interest in the topic."

"Forest guardians?"

"The other topic."

"That has to be one of the most subtle ways anyone's ever asked me if I'm gay." Alex smirked.

Sam's lips twitched in amusement.

"But if you have to ask, I guess it means you never Googled me," Alex continued.

"Now why would I Google someone who almost ran me over?" Sam's eyes seemed brighter.

"Know thine enemy?" Alex suggested. "If you had, you'd have discovered not just that I'm gayer than a Melissa Etheridge concert, but that I'm a total nerd. *Serious* book nerd. I have Shakespeare-junkie friends. We party like it's 1590."

"That's quite a confession."

"Am I too tragic to know now? Especially for someone cool, of mythic creek-jumping skills?"

"Actually, the only person around here with mythic stature works on your set."

"Really? Who?"

"Breaker Bob."

Alex frowned. She didn't know everyone yet. "Sorry…I…"

"He's your motorcycle stuntman. He's been doing all the mounted camera stuff—like zipping through trees for a camera running effect? He taught me a few stunts over the years. He's great to have a beer with." She petered out, looking as if she'd overshared and regretted it.

Everyone needs their heroes, huh? Looked like she'd found Sam's. Alex smiled. "So are bike stunts how *you* party?"

Sam shook her head. "A few years ago, maybe. Not now."

"I can't even ride a pushbike without ending up in a tree, so that's impressive. Aren't you full of surprises?"

"Me? I'm not the one sneaking a lesbian romance into a mainstream jungle flick." Sam gave her a measured look. "That's *so* not where I thought *Shezan* would go."

"I know the feeling." Alex paused. "So you never said whether you thought I'd do it well. I mean now that you know I have a vested interest in the topic."

Sam's gaze fell to the photos on Alex's phone, a line knitting between her brows.

"You're taking a long time to answer." Alex sighed, and sadness filled her at what it meant. "Never mind. It looks like your mind really is made up about my film. I didn't mean to put you on the spot."

"No." Sam seemed startled. "I was just weighing up things. I'm…well, I'm evidence based. That's how I work things out. Yes, you could do it justice. I was just thinking it'd have to be better than some of the lesbian films out there. I've only ever liked a handful."

She'd watched lesbian films? Plural? *Well, well. So gay.* "Which did you like most?"

"*If These Walls Could Talk 2.* The middle story set in the seventies. I've seen it maybe thirty times."

"Wow. A favorite. Okay." Alex wondered at its appeal for her. "That had some great layers to it. The butch girl with a sensitive heart falling for the popular femme, and all the pressure is on her to be less masculine." Alex wondered if Sam had faced any bullying as a kid. "All that stuff about being different—is that why you love it? The message of being true to oneself?"

Sam's eyes danced. "Nah. The motorcycle. It's beautiful." Her voice warmed. "A Harley Sportster, K model. I keep trying to figure out when it was made. I've narrowed it down to 1952 to 1956."

Alex laughed. "And you mock my nerdy adoration of Shakespeare."

"I didn't mock it. I just couldn't relate to it."

"Is this where you tell me you hate Shakespeare? That he's a boring, old, dead white guy?" Alex drew in a breath.

Sam regarded her curiously and the air seemed to shift between them. "Would that bug you?"

Truthfully? Yes. So much yes. A thousand times yes.

"Now you're taking too long to answer," Sam said, eyes intent.

"I know. I'm sorry. Let's forget it." Alex stared morosely into her wine glass.

"Hey, I admit I've never read Shakespeare beyond *Macbeth* at school, but I have an open mind. Anyone still loved after four hundred years has gotta have something going for them."

Oh thank God. Alex gripped her glass, shocked by the depth of her relief. It wasn't hard to figure out why: Shakespeare mattered too much to her to have someone in her life hate or laugh at it. Someone like that would be incompatible with Alex.

And I really want Sam to be compatible with me.

Her heart clenched at that admission. *Oh Christ.* "By the way, I owe you a thanks," Alex said. "I should have said something earlier."

"For?" Sam's eyebrow cocked.

"Not arresting me for dangerous driving. It had to be tempting when Quincy said no to paying your repairs."

"You're not worth the paperwork." Sam smiled. A pair of dimples appeared. *Damn them.* Sam's phone rang, and she dug through her jacket pocket for it. "Sorry, it's work."

"They sure call you late. Aren't you off duty at this time of night?"

"I'm always on call. Unpaid overtime is one fun perk of my job. And for some reason, Tuesday nights are usually my worst." Sam answered her phone with a sharp, "Senior Constable Keegan," then put a finger against her other ear to drown out the background noise. "How many cars did they set on fire?" She frowned. "Yes, I understand. Okay, I'm on my way."

Sam rose from the table.

"Duty calls," Sam said. "It's been…well, fun." She grinned as if she hadn't expected that. Her broad shoulders squared, and her long-legged stride was efficient and fierce as she left the pub, leaving Alex feeling suddenly bereft.

She couldn't tear her eyes off the retreating form.

Chapter 11

Let There be Light

Sam yawned again. A glance at the clock—4:03 p.m.—showed she wasn't much closer to home and an early night than the last time she'd checked. Last night had involved running around in the aftermath of a mob of violent males setting fire to cars. Today she'd spent hours on the paperwork and trying to match each perpetrator's description to a known person of interest, without much success. She ran her hand through her hair and tried to focus.

Her tiredness wasn't entirely due to work. She'd woken this morning exhausted and frustrated, thanks to a dream involving Alex telling Sam she was gay, over and over. Why had her subconscious chosen to dwell on irrelevant matters? Really, who was Alex to Sam, anyway? A Hollywood blow-in who'd blow out again soon enough. Even if she was sort of interesting. Sort of amusing. Cute. Sort of.

Sam swallowed the dregs of her coffee, her sixth tasteless cup for the day. Supermarket brand was the best you could get around here. Alex, living in LA and being English, probably drank ethically sourced organic tea from sun-drenched fields in the ruins of an ancient civilization. She probably drove a Prius, too.

Her desk phone rang.

"Oh, thank God you're in!" a female voice squeaked. "It's stolen! Just now! The M90 lamp! Um, sorry, I mean, hi, it's Alice Benson."

The name tapped at Sam's brain. Oh, that's right—the assistant on Alex's movie. The young woman had helped Sam on her fruitless pitchfork hunt. American. Softly spoken. Smart. Somehow managed to make Alex Levitin look tall.

Sam glanced at the clock as she digested the woman's panicked ramble. 4:07 p.m. Okay, how could some crucial piece of lighting go missing in broad daylight? Especially with Sid on duty? "Alice?" she interrupted. "How come you're calling me, not Sid?"

She stopped. "Oh, he went to talk to his brother."

"He..." Wasn't Kev working in lighting now? Oh hell. *He wouldn't... would he?* "I'm on my way." She hung up. *Damn it.* If Kev couldn't straighten himself out at his age, when would he?

Sam slammed the patrol car door and stalked onto set. Sabotage and now a theft? Two crimes were definitely a trend. Alex was not going to be okay with this.

Why do I care again?

Sid met her at the gate, his black, bushy eyebrows wrestling in a civil war.

"So," Sam said, "what's going on? Got yourself a crime spree now?"

Sid looked baffled. "Beats me. Anyway, everyone's waiting for you to grill the crew. And it's *not* Kev."

"Better bloody not be."

"Yeah, nah, I know how it sounds." Sid pointed out their destination, and Sam adjusted her trajectory as he continued, walking beside her. "The gear that got nicked weighs a ton. It's not merch you can shift on the quiet. Besides, Kev loves this job. It's not him."

"We'll see." Sam headed toward an olive-green tent with a crush of several dozen people standing around. Sam's pace slowed. Among them was Alex.

The director was dressed the same as the day they'd met: tailored, slim-fit black pants, black boots, white button-down cotton shirt, and a fitted black linen jacket that had a masculine cut. The look really worked for her. Cute nerd chic. Sam's brain gave an approving *mmm.*

Alex's red hair had been cropped quite short the first time they'd met, but it now flopped forward to touch the top of her black-framed glasses.

"Search everywhere," Alex was saying. "Dave and John, grab some crew, anyone spare, and go over every inch of this place. We need that lamp or we'll be unable to do tonight's shoot. Or any night shoot, for that matter."

"Um, small question," a crusty man with wild gray hair spoke up. He wore weathered motorcycle boots and a crimson shirt that read "I do all my own stunts."

Sam couldn't prevent her smile. Breaker Bob. How often had they compared notes on the gruntiest motorcycles and craziest jumps at the pub? The legendary stuntman had texted her a congrats when she'd jumped Dry Creek. It was her most valued text.

"Wouldn't the missing gear be long gone?" Bob continued. "It's been over an hour. Whoever did this obviously knew what they were doing."

"Check everywhere anyway," Alex said. "We need to be sure."

Quincy cleared his throat. "And people, if one of you stole this equipment, it's not only a firing offense; you'll be sued for the damages and time lost on the shoot. Got it?"

Sam tried to find her younger brother's face in the crowd. *Kevin Mahuta, you had better be innocent this time.*

"Where's Steven?" Alex asked, head snapping around. "Can you bring me that photo?"

"Sure, boss," came an American twang amid the throng. A tall, mustached man with worried eyes passed over an iPad.

Alex held the tablet up to show everyone, turning it slowly. A photo of a blue-and-chrome cylinder was on the screen, with black flaps at the front. "This is what we've lost. The ARRI M90 EB MAX. Commit it to memory. It costs a fortune and weighs a ton, and we only have three on set. But we need all three to work together or we may as well have none." She handed the iPad back.

"Emphasis on costs a fortune," Quincy chimed in, folding his arms.

"Alice?" Alex called.

The production assistant stepped forward, anxiety radiating from her. "Yes?"

"You have one job now." Alex grasped both her shoulders and crouched a little to meet her eyes. "Do *nothing else* but find us a replacement. Steven will get you the full specs. I want you to scour everywhere for another one. If you have to hire it, borrow it, buy it, or drive all the way to Auckland to horse trade for it, I don't care. We need it, preferably within the next few hours. Okay?"

The young woman's head bobbed up and down.

"Cool in a crisis, eh?" Sid murmured, nudging Sam.

She folded her arms and refused to reply. *Sort of.*

After Alice scampered away, Alex looked around. "Where's the First AD?" she muttered. "Leslie!"

A plump, intense-looking woman wearing red glasses stepped up, and Alex addressed her in a no-nonsense tone. "If we can't shoot this evening, I need options. Work out a way to redo tomorrow's schedule so we can squeeze in tonight's poacher shoot, too."

Alex's gaze shifted to Sam, and she waved her over impatiently. "Senior Constable Keegan. Thank God. This is a bloody nightmare."

"I'm here." Sam projected confidence, suddenly wanting to reassure her.

"The lighting team's been gathered." Alex pointed at the tent. "These are the last people to have seen the M90. All we know is it went missing between three and three-thirty today. Please get to the bottom of this."

"I'll do my best."

"I can't overstate enough how much of a disaster this is." Alex gave her a beseeching look.

Sam inhaled. *No pressure.*

Kev poked his head out from behind a towering stack of boxes. "We're not pulling the plug on tonight's schedule yet, are we? We should keep prepping, yeah?"

Sam glanced at her brother in surprise. He actually sounded invested.

"Correct." Alex darted a look at him. "Let's not give up yet." She glanced back at Sam. "Our missing lamp is exceptionally powerful. When used with the other two M90s, it literally turns night into day. Without it we're screwed, but I don't want to scrap this evening's schedule until the last gasp." She pointed Sam to a tent. "This way. I've cleared a space which should be good for you to interview the crew. Oh, and thanks for coming so quickly, Senior Constable. It's appreciated."

Her expression was laced with so much genuine gratitude that Sam was suddenly glad she'd hauled ass out here instead of first finishing her vehicular-arson report.

Someone tugged at Sam's arm just as Alex was also pulled aside by Quincy.

Kevin's hand was on her forearm, his face beseeching. "I didn't do it," he said quietly. "I promise, Sam. I love this job. I'm learning so much. I didn't even know until a week ago you could make night look like day. And shit, I wanna see it in action! Why would I nick something like that?"

"Then why do you look like you did?" Sam asked, to test him.

"This is my resting face, eh?"

Alex turned back suddenly. "Wait, you think the lighting PA did this? *Kev*?"

Sam never shifted her gaze from the wide-eyed man in front of her, who began shaking his head vigorously. She answered with her gut instinct. "No, actually, I don't think my brother did do this."

He sagged in relief.

"Kev is your brother?" Alex asked in surprise.

"I have a matched pair," Sam said dryly, inclining her head at Sid. "All right, I'll interview everyone now, one at a time, if you don't mind."

Alex nodded. "Right in there." She pointed. "Good luck."

Alex listened in briefly at the tent as Sam asked the gaffer, Steven, some questions.

"How much does it weigh?" was the first.

"About hundred and seventy pounds with change."

A silence.

"Like, um, almost eighty kilos," Steven added. "Of course, last I saw it, it was pelleted. Boxed up, it's a crap-load heavier."

"Thanks for the conversion," Sam said. "My imperial is useless. Okay, so this is not something you could haul out of here on your own, is it?"

By the time the interview was done, Alex was still fixated on that first point. Only someone incredibly strong could have taken their lamp. It's not like you could just back up a truck and drive off with it, either. If someone had tried, Sid would have noticed it leave.

Alex returned to work and tried hard not to focus on the fact that her movie's schedule was hanging by a thread.

An hour later, Sam found her in the Production trailer.

"Want a drink?" Alex asked, taking in the tired eyes.

"I'm good." Sam flipped through her notepad, brow creased, and sat on the hard plastic chair opposite the desk.

"I can offer hot chocolate and marshmallows today." Alex grinned. "It's the weather for it."

"Figured you more for some organic, ethical, fancy tea for lefties, to be honest."

Alex tutted. "Dreadful cliché. I'll have you know I usually prefer organic, ethical, fancy *coffee* for lefties. But at least I have the originality not to enjoy it."

Sam smiled.

"So that's a no to the hot chocolate?" Alex checked.

"Can't. That stuff'll make you sleepy."

"Right. How'd you go?"

"I've finished my interviews with anyone who was on set when the M90 went missing. Two things are clear: This lamp can't be easily carried, and it can't be easily sold."

"No."

"Your head lighting guy, Steven, tells me it's worth thirty-thousand US. For one lamp." Sam shook her head.

"Sounds about right." Alex shifted in her seat. "Any suspects?"

"Going through the work schedule and everyone's alibis, I can rule out all the lighting crew. That includes Kevin. The only time he was away from the crew, Sid was with him. Besides, he might be tall, but he's a lightweight. Doubt he could even drag it, let alone lift it."

"But why did you think it was him in the first place?"

"I didn't really. It's just, he's had a few issues in the past so I keep a close eye on him. Stealing tech's not really his MO, though."

"Okay, so if not the lighting crew, then who?" Alex asked.

"Well, of the people with the physical ability, that just leaves the weight-lifting cook in Craft Services, but he only seems interested in food, and three stuntmen who didn't even know the set had any lamps that do what this one does. On that note..." Sam's lips twitched ever so slightly, "They've asked if they could watch when you find a new M90 and turn it on. They sounded pretty impressed by it."

"For God's sake, I'm not running a carnival," Alex growled. "Tell them to amuse themselves on their own time."

"I may have taken the liberty to already suggest something like that—only meaner." The gleam in Sam's eye was pure mischief.

Alex chuckled. "Good."

There was a bang at the door, and it opened.

"Alex?" Alice's head poked in. "Um, hey. I have news."

Alice Benson was a damned genius. And she was getting a raise, Alex decided, as she watched their replacement lamp being driven off to their forest set. The brilliant production assistant had phoned Matamata, the same town that had made a few Hobbits world famous. And someone there knew some people who knew a Peter Jackson second-unit crew sitting around who weren't using their M90s this month.

Her assistant had saved the whole day. Well, night. A bit behind schedule they might be, but they'd be able to shoot very soon.

A group of crew members had gathered to cheer the borrowed light's arrival. Among them was Sam, who was scribbling a few lines in a notepad.

"Hey," Alex said, drawing Sam away from the group, out of their earshot. "Didn't think you'd still be here."

"I wasn't. I came back when I heard a lamp had turned up. It wasn't clear if it was the missing one or a replacement and I needed to know for my report, so..." She glanced back at the M90. "You weren't kidding about the size of it."

"Yeah." Alex shook her head. "So can you figure any of this out? If you can't easily sell a thing, why steal it?"

"Why did someone poke your little pool lining full of holes?" Sam replied quietly. "Seems to me that just because it's less obvious this time, sabotage is still sabotage."

Alex felt something inside her crumple. "But that means...it's definitely an inside job." *Does someone hate us—me—that much?*

"I'm sorry. It does look that way."

"But...I run a good set," Alex whispered. "I'm a fair boss. Fuck."

"I'm sure that's true," Sam said kindly. "And maybe it's not you that someone has an issue with. You're not the only boss, are you?"

"Quincy?"

"Not just him, although maybe he's rubbed someone else up the wrong way, for a variety of reasons." Her eyes crinkled. "You think like a director. This is *your* production, *you're* at the top, and everyone works for you or Quincy. But every department has its own supervisors, doesn't it? There are multiple bosses, any of whom could be in conflict with someone else."

Wait, there were dozens of suspects? That felt...horrible.

Sam drew in a deep breath. "Look, sorry I have to ask this, but have you received any threats?"

"Of course not."

"Any enemies?"

Alex regarded her. "I suppose fewer now? Since we fixed some things, I mean. I've given the Duncan sisters permission to post the new costume pics, for instance. People in town are warmer now."

Sam nodded. "They are. But I wasn't just asking about Ika Whenu people. Does anyone want you to fail?"

Fail? What a disturbing thought. "Not that I'm aware of."

"Well, okay, just thought I'd ask. I'll work my way through my list of people disgruntled with *Shezan* and see what comes up."

"You have a whole list?" Alex's mouth went dry.

"I do."

"Who's on it?"

"Frank Buddins, the man Quincy fired who does waste pumping. Fletcher and a couple of his aggro mates who like to cause trouble around town from time to time out of boredom. It's a long shot. I'll let you know if anything pans out. Leave it with me."

"Sure, I trust you." Alex paused. Funny how true that felt given she barely knew Sam.

"Thanks." Sam's eyes brightened. "I appreciate that."

"Right, I have to go," Alex said, with a smile. "My evil poacher isn't going to catch himself in Shezan's traps. Well, actually, he kind of is." She laughed.

A sudden gust of wind whipped through, rattling equipment, and Alex shivered. New Zealand just didn't get any warmer. She reached for the zip on her jacket but, in her haste to do it up, managed to catch her shirt in it.

Bits of white cotton stuck through the teeth. *Oh, smooth.* A few tugs failed to fix it.

Finally, Sam stepped forward, shoving her notepad under her arm. "I can't take it anymore," she murmured. With a sharp jerk, she brought the zip down, liberating the shirt.

Alex's cheeks were considerably ruddier than the wind had made them.

Sam did it up again, neatly. "There," she said. "Happens to the best of us."

Alex wasn't sure what to feel about the invasion into her space. And Sam hadn't moved back yet, either. "Thanks again, um, Senior Constable."

"No problem, *Ms. Levitin.*" Sam's eyes were teasing.

Alex sucked in a breath. *Mercy.*

Chapter 12

The Body

RESPLENDENT IN HER TARTAN FLANNEL pajama bottoms and blue tank top, Sam tossed some bread into the toaster in her kitchen. The pitiful room had seen better days...most likely in the 1950s. She stared at the chipped Formica bench top, the brown lino tiles on the floor, the threadbare chocolate-brown carpet in the lounge. Her battered, hulking TV sat on six Yellow Pages because she'd never gotten around to buying a stand. Why hadn't she?

Sam's worn-out, one-bedroom rental next to the police station had been home for so long that she'd stopped seeing it for what it was. For the first time in ages, she could see its morbid decay through the eyes of a visitor. A visitor who might pop around on a rainy day for a hot chocolate with marshmallows, for example. A visitor she hadn't seen in six days.

Everything was clean, of course; Sam ran a spotless, neat-as-a-pin house. She'd brightened her bedroom with nice curtains from this millennium and maintained fresh flowers in the kitchen. Okay, so, the orchids, a gift from Gina, hadn't died yet despite Sam's occasional neglect. That counted as "maintained," right?

Still, what her modest home lacked in charm, it lacked double in everything else. There was no disguising how dated it all was.

Her gaze wandered over to the living room wall and the giant corkboard decorated with dozens of vibrant postcards from around the world. Originally, she'd set up the board to puzzle out ongoing police cases in her downtime, but it hadn't worked out that way. Most cases in her first five years had been minor and easily solved, not requiring earnest, TV-crime-show level corkboarding.

Sam inspected the postcards' glossy surfaces. Paris, London, Rome, Spain, Singapore, and Sydney competed for attention in the middle. She picked out the one from Pfeiffer Beach, California. In the twelve years since her ex's card had gone up on the board, very little had changed. And yet Sam still held the view that living minimally meant she was free to drop everything at any moment to scratch her travel itch.

Except "any moment" had never come.

And in all the years she'd lived here, she hadn't bought a stick of serious furniture because that meant she was staying for good. Denial was preferable to admitting that.

And now, here she was. Thirty-six, living in a (neat-as-a-pin) dump, doing a frustrating job, being largely avoided by the people she'd grown up with, and not once having left New Zealand's shores.

The toast popped. After heading back into the kitchen, Sam spread it with butter and Marmite, then made a coffee. "Travel's overrated anyway," she told the kettle. "Too many pushy and annoying tourists."

Which reminded her of Alex, who, okay, had stopped being annoying long enough to accept her apology. If she squinted, maybe Alex's pushiness was more assertiveness really. She had to respect a woman ready to stand her ground. Couldn't be easy in her line of work. Sam appreciated assertive women—especially those who punched well above their weight.

Her mind slunk back to the *Shezan* case. Well, cases. None of Sam's leads had turned up anything. Frank, the fired waste-management guy, was now happily working in Matamata on a road crew, resurfacing roads. It was Sid's old road crew, as luck would have it, so it was easy to check the man's alibi. That was how life was around here. Everyone knew everyone, and sooner or later, everyone worked everywhere at least once.

Fletcher and his chaos-demon mates had had rock-solid alibis, too. So now she was stumped. Damn it. She'd really wanted to haul some bastard in and get this annoying business off her desk.

That was the only reason, of course. Sam was all about justice.

Her phone pinged.

Hey, officer K. Been stuck on night shoots all week. Any luck with my lamp theft? - Alex

Sam replied: *No leads. On the bright side, I haven't given up yet.*

Bright side? Senior Constable Keegan, are you punning with me?

Smiling, Sam texted back: *That would be out of character.*

Would it though? Do you have a secret life as a stand-up comic? Hey, need me to coerce my cast and crew into dropping hundreds of glowing five-star reviews on your act? ☺

Her phone pinged again a minute later. *I was kidding btw. Not only would the optics look wayyy 2 suspicious, but I do have a few ethics, despite living in LA. Besides, didn't u say u hated cons?*

Sam snorted. *To confirm: No cons, no puns, no comedy routines. I bleed pure blue.*

There's a depressing thought. I don't like the idea of you bleeding one bit.

Sam stopped chewing. Was Alex flirting with her? Wait, why was she assuming Alex was even single? God, and here was Sam trying to see her home through an arty Hollywood director's eyes. For all she knew, Alex was married to some hot movie star and had ten adopted kids.

Funny how I've decided she's married to Angelina Jolie.

Sam grabbed her phone and Googled the woman. Hundreds of stories appeared about Alex's movies. Some titles sounded a little…eccentric. *Heaven's Blood?* What on earth? An angel in demon form? Whatever. She clicked through to check out the box office. *Ouch.* That one had sunk.

Working her way down the list, she saw that Alex's work had grown in both budget and positive reviews every film. That climate change one, *A Quiver in Time*, sounded good. Maybe she'd see if she could get it on Netflix.

She found a video of Alex at a GLAAD event where she'd won an award. Her speech had prompted laughs when she talked about being the "scariest creature in Hollywood—feminist, lesbian, and fiercely independent."

Fiercely independent? Obviously pre-*Shezan*.

Google had a few photos of her out at various Hollywood events. Alex's friends were beautiful. Sam blinked. No, not just that. Gorgeous. Stunning. Summer Hayes? Elizabeth Thornton? Grace Christie-Oberon? Amrit Patel? Every one of them could grace a magazine cover. These people didn't even look real. They were about as far from Sam's world as you could get.

That simplified things, didn't it? Even if Alex was single, she wouldn't want to hang out with Sam in her daggy dive of a rental. Besides, it was pointless. What would happen when the movie was finished? Did she think Alex would just park her boots under Sam's bed and stay on in Ika Whenu, population 2,735? That'd worked out so well with Nicole, hadn't it? And it's not like Sam could just toss in her job here. People relied on her. Probably a good thing Sam had worked out their complete unsuitability for one another before she'd made a fool of herself by asking Alex out or something.

Which she definitely hadn't considering doing.

I really like her.

Sam rammed the last of her toast in her mouth. Not helpful. A decision had been made. That was that. It was simpler to keep things as they were. Friendly but arm's length.

A streak of orange bisected her kitchen curtains, the rising sun creeping over the distant Kaimai Ranges. Time to collect Bruce and hit the road.

Today was the first day in a month she felt okay enough to climb the Boars' wall again. What if the dogs weren't friendly to her anymore? Maybe she'd have to start from scratch again, tossing meat from the top of the wall as she had in the early days.

Sam was still debating that choice when her phone rang.

Work? At this unholy hour?

"ALEX!"

Alex lurched out of a deep sleep.

"Wake up!" a familiar voice boomed.

"Sid?" Alex opened one eye. "What the hell are you doing in my trailer?"

"What?"

Oh. Right. He was outside. "S'wrong?" She called back and reached for her glasses.

"A body! There's a body in the dam!"

"What?" No way had he just said... She staggered out of bed and wrenched open her door to find Sid and a bedraggled group of cast and crew crawling out of their own trailers in various states of dress.

"I was doing a perimeter check." Sid waved his enormous arm. "And I saw it." He held up his phone. "Took a pic."

Alex reluctantly peered at it. A large male body in dark clothing was floating face down in the water.

"It's Joe's dam. The farmer whose property we're on? He waters his sheep there. And we have to get the body out before the water's tainted."

Was her set cursed? A horrible thought suddenly slammed into her. "Sid, have you done a head count? Is anyone missing? Alice, can you...?"

"On it." Alice nodded, sounding the model of efficiency although her hair was sticking up and she looked barely ten percent awake.

"Where's Quincy?" Alex's head whipped around as she scanned the crowd. Goddamn it, if it was Quincy who'd drowned his annoying-but-useful butt, she'd wring his neck again. "Wake him first." Her gaze darted back to the breathless Sid. "Have you called the police?"

"Yeah, Sam's on her way. And, um, she's not sounding too happy."

Can't blame her. Hell, her job sometimes meant pulling bodies out of dams.

Sid's stressed voice looped in Sam's head as she drove. *There's a body.*

A sickening jolt of fear had lurched through her the moment he'd first said the words, and she wondered if the set saboteur had finally gone too far and revealed more sinister intentions.

Her first thought had been chilling. "Is Alex okay?" she'd croaked out. The wave of relief at hearing the body was male had been unsettling.

Sam had called the coroner's office in Hamilton to send someone up to deal with the remains, but they'd emphasized the need for her to be sure before they dispatched anyone. It was a long drive and only barely sunrise. They'd informed her they'd be on standby, awaiting her confirmation.

Half an hour later, Sam pulled her checkered blue-and-yellow Holden Commodore patrol car into Joe's drive. She got out and glanced at Sid's solemn form, waiting for her by the gate.

Sam's mood became grimmer with each step. It wasn't just that she'd have to haul a deceased person out of a dam, or the condition it might be in due to water being involved, although the near-freezing temperature would help. It was that it might be someone she knew.

She'd attended road accidents and seen mangled, bloodied, and broken bodies of kids she'd gone to school with, and people she'd bought groceries from, and it made her sick to the gut every damned time.

Sid waved her in. "This way." He looked pensive. "Over here."

She trekked over the undulating grasses of the field, dodging sheep manure and divots, until she came to the wide dam. Joe crouched at the water's edge, peering at the body floating in the middle. Along with someone else.

The sight of Alex, strong and well and shooting Sam a warm but worried look, shook her equilibrium a little. Relief washed through her.

Damn it. She was supposed to be all professional and stoic. She slapped on her most aloof mask. "Good morning. I see we have a situation."

Alex nodded, expression apprehensive. "Thanks for coming."

"You okay?" Sam wondered if Alex had seen a body before. Maybe she had, being from LA? Didn't people shoot at people all the time in California or something? Hadn't she read that somewhere?

"Not really." Alex fiddled with her jacket sleeve. "Everyone from *Shezan* is accounted for. No one's touched the body, We don't know who it is. I can't believe this is happening.'

"Okay. I'll get this sorted. This is a police crime scene now." Sam peered at the dam. *Shit.* The body was right in the middle. "How deep is the water?" She turned to Joe, whose craggy brow furrowed. "Can I get my waders on and...?" Her waders went up to her mid chest, and she tapped the height of them to explain.

"No." Joe shook his wrinkled head. "The water'd be about chin-high on you out in the middle."

Just great. She could call in police divers, but it'd take ages for them to arrive. With a sigh, she began to undress.

"What the hell are you doing?" Alex's eyes flashed wide open. "It's freezing out here!" Her breath came out in misty huffs. "Sun's barely up."

"What would you have me do instead?" She toed off her boots, then peeled off her socks.

"Wait for the coroner? Let them do it! Or wait till it's warmer? I could get my crew to rig us a really long pole with a hook and—"

"Can't," Joe cut in. "I need the remains out of my water supply ASAP or my sheep'll get sick. She's right doin' it now. Longer it's there, warmer the temperature gets, worse it'll be."

"And the coroner's office isn't coming." Sam undid her belt. "Well, not yet. They're on standby until I call back to report what I drag out of here."

"Maybe Sid could do it then?" Alex darted a hopeful look at him.

"I'm the police officer on duty," Sam cut in. "Besides, your guard can't swim."

Alex blinked in surprise.

"Never learned." Sid shrugged. "Sorry."

Sam slid her pants down, leaving only her black boy-shorts. Her skin pimpled in the freezing wind. It was only going to get worse in a minute. She steeled herself, then began unbuttoning her shirt.

"You are bonkers," Alex muttered, pulling out her phone. "Alice? I need you at the dam. Bring a thick towel and one of those ankle-length coats with the extra padding."

"Thanks." Sam drew off her shirt.

"While you're on our set, you're my responsibility."

The old farmer wore a distant look as Sam straightened, now clad only in her sports bra and shorts. *Probably thinking of his sheep.* Alex was staring at her like she'd never seen her before.

"What?" Sam asked churlishly, not quite sure what to make of the scrutiny. She was now freezing, displayed like a lamb chop, and about to wade into a gross, muddy pool to bring a corpse to shore.

"Nothing. Just…" Alex's hand flashed out to squeeze her arm. "You're so brave." Her gaze lingered for a moment before she glanced away.

Brave? "Just doing what they pay me the big bucks for." But the compliment warmed her far more than the tendrils of sunlight starting to peek through the trees edging the border of the property.

Slowly, Sam waded in until she could no longer touch the bottom and then breast-stroked her way to the middle, careful to keep the water out of her face and ears. Shivers overtook her, but she pressed on. Teeth chattering, she neared the body and slowed to tread the water.

Wait a minute. It wasn't floating right. Too high and...

She scowled as she realized what she was looking at. Fury flashed through her, followed by relief. She grabbed the body by its rigid arm, towing it. Her annoyance gave her numbed limbs a burst of energy. Reaching the banks, Sam hauled it out.

"Who is it?" Alex asked, avoiding looking directly at the body.

"Maybe we should call it a 'what,' not a 'who.'" Sam hauled her find over onto its back. Waterlogging had easily doubled its weight and it landed with a wet, heavy thunk, sending a spray of mud over Sam and Alex.

"Shit," Alex muttered, glowering at her spattered clothes. Her expression narrowed as she digested what Sam had dumped at their feet.

"Fuck me dead, eh!" Sid gaped. "It's just a mannequin!"

The "body" was dressed in a nicely tailored suit. Its sculpted face was rather realistic. Sam had never seen anything like it, not even in Auckland's fancy, top-end clothing stores.

Alex stared at it. "Why's that thing in the dam?"

Joe's shoulders sagged in relief and he offered a toothless grin. "Who cares? Least it means I can water my sheep, no worries." He stood and dusted down his worn jeans. "I'll leave you all to it. I've got to feed my animals." He trudged off back toward his farmhouse.

"So?" Sam turned on Sid and Alex. "Looks like I was hauled out of bed on a wild goose chase."

Alex frowned. "Yes. But my people didn't do this."

"You sure?" Sam poked at the dummy's smart-looking outfit. "Can you get your costume woman to come up here?" She shivered and rubbed her arms. "Skye, wasn't it?"

The assistant—Alice—materialized, holding a towel and a puffy jacket bigger than she was. "Oh my goodness," she said, eyes as big as headlights.

"You must be freezing!" She thrust the towel at Sam the second she reached her.

Sam dried off gratefully, then handed it back. As she jerked her pants back on, Alice pointedly looked the other way. Alex was on the phone, asking Skye to join them. Whether she knew it or not, Alex's gaze was drifting appreciatively all over Sam's body.

After getting back into her uniform, which felt far too thin after her swim, Sam slid on the padded blue jacket Alice offered. Stamping her now booted feet for warmth, she waited for the costume designer to appear.

When she arrived, Skye took one look at the dummy, crouched before it, and said, "Oh, I see. How interesting. Did you know you can't even buy these mannequins here? And the suit? Very familiar."

"Familiar?" Sam and Alex asked at the same time.

"Oh yes. It's one of *Shezan*'s previous costumer's early concepts for the poacher. I decided to go in a different direction. These colors, red and black, are a little too strong. Besides, he can't wear that now his tent interior contains red tones."

"Where's the red?" Sam asked in confusion, gaze raking the dark, sodden material.

Skye flipped the jacket open to show a red lining. She studied it closely for a moment, her brow creased as though about to say something profound.

Sam waited in anticipation.

Alex held her breath.

"Ah yes," Skye finally exhaled. "*Definitely* the right decision. Not the best look at all. Our poacher needs something coarse and rustic, not some suit." Her gaze drifted.

Oh for God's... "Can we focus on the main point?" Sam cut in. "This suit was stolen from your set?"

"Yes, dear." Skye nodded. "Not just the suit. The mannequin, too."

"Why?" Alex stared in dismay. "What does that achieve?"

"That's the question." Skye sounded philosophical. "Motives are everything. From poachers to saboteurs." She glanced at Sam. "What do you think?"

"I think I'm too frozen to be standing around debating anything." Her teeth chattered again. "Sid, could you haul that thing back to the set? I'm going to cancel the coroner's office."

Sid lifted the dummy, grunting at its weight. "Bugger. Water's got in it."

Skye jumped in to help, grabbing its feet.

"Hey, thanks." He grinned. "Weird start to the day, hey? How you doin', anyway?"

Sam leaned away from her brother. Some days he was too damned cheerful before breakfast.

As the pair awkwardly marched the dummy back to the set, they chatted amiably. Skye was now talking up the virtues of Chloe. "Goodness me, that girl! First time I met her, I knew I'd take her under my wing. She was so sweet and too far from home! Oh, she's an amusing soul to have around, I'll tell you. It's a complete mystery to me why she's single."

Subtle.

Sid nodded and agreed it was indeed a mystery.

My clueless brother. She wanted to slap him. *Seriously.*

A shiver rocketed through her.

"You need a hot shower," Alex noted. "You can use mine."

"Thanks. Sounds good."

"And then I think it's time we talked about what's really happening." Alex inhaled. "Because have you considered we're not the target here?"

"What?" Sam stopped. "Then who is?"

"You."

"Three more," Alex was saying down the phone as she paced her trailer; she'd taken an urgent business call from LA a minute ago. "And not a single one more." She thrust a fluffy towel at Sam and waved her into a cubicle at the end of the trailer as her voice became sharper. "That's what I'm saying."

Sam could still just hear her muffled voice before she stepped under the shower. She mulled over Alex's theory while soaking up the blasting heat. How could she be the target? All the disruptions had messed with *Alex*'s set. And...okay, sure, they'd inconvenienced Sam. But *Shezan* was the target. When people were unhappy with their local cop, they usually left their complaints on her doormat, in her letterbox, or spray-painted across her home's walls.

Except today's false alarm had nothing to do with the set at all. It screwed with Sam, no one else. Was someone getting their jollies having her running out of town every five minutes? Which begged the obvious questions: Who wanted the police out of their hair, or who wanted to punish her?

Most of her enemies were too lazy to bother getting up before dawn for any reason, including her boss. Though she doubted even Sergeant Peterson was that petty. Besides, he was stuck in a Crime and Justice Organisation conference in Tauranga all week. So that ruled him out.

Which brought her to the most glaringly obvious perp. Who would dress a dummy in a red-and-black suit, which also happened to be the Wild Boars' colors? The more she thought about it, the more it fit with their obnoxious asshole leader, Dino, and his twisted sense of humor.

Sam turned the water off. Beyond the door, she could hear Alex still on the phone, issuing orders. She dried off and leaned in a little to hear Alex in full-on boss mode as her footsteps neared and retreated, up and down the trailer.

You go, girl.

She tucked in her shirt, then combed her hair with her fingers, peering in the small mirror. *It'll have to do.* The talking had stopped, so she opened the door. And froze.

Alex's bare, pale back was to Sam as she bent over, pulling tight jeans over blue bikini briefs. A flash of the side of her boob appeared then disappeared.

God, she was beautiful. Fine-boned, delicate, lean, gorgeous. Heat flared across Sam's face, and she backed into the bathroom and shut the door as quietly as she could.

A minute later, a knock sounded. "It's safe to come out now." Amusement laced Alex's tone.

Sam sheepishly opened the door and exited, praying the redness in her cheeks wasn't obvious. "Thanks for the, um, shower." She edged past Alex, inching to the trailer's door.

"Where are you going?" Alex asked. "We haven't discussed this."

"This?" Panic flooded Sam.

"The perpetrator. The motives. Why, what did you think I meant?" Alex's eyebrow lifted.

"This. Yes." Sam turned to sit just as Alex took a step forward.

They found themselves pressed together, breast to breast, in the narrow passage between the kitchen table and seating. Immediately they shot apart like opposing magnets.

"That wasn't awkward in the least," Alex muttered, dropping onto the nearest bench seat. Her cheeks were pinker than a minute ago.

"No." Sam sighed. Sitting on the opposite bench, she wished she could burn from her mind the distracting memory of Alex's soft body. "So, I think you might be right about the motive."

"Oh?" Alex was suddenly sharp and interested.

"Mmm. It's almost certainly Dino Taumata. He's always taunting me. Wouldn't put it past him to bribe someone on set to commit sabotage to distract me, fuck with me, or both. And the dummy was wearing red and black. Those are his colors. He may as well have stuck up a sign with his name on it."

"I see." Alex pursed her lips. "How can I help?"

"You can't. I think the fastest way to solve this would be for me to have a nice chat to Dino."

"Is that safe?" Alex put a staying hand on Sam's arm as though she was about to run off that second. "On your own?"

"Sure. It's just a chat. And I know this guy. I'll be fine."

Sam had gone to school with Dino, where he'd distinguished himself by being a bully. Anyone who looked at him sideways copped his wrath. But she had his measure. He was harmless if you approached him the right way. So, she'd just talk to him. Maybe he'd kick her out of his compound; maybe he'd invite her in and boast about his deeds. Either way, no harm, no foul.

"Sam?" Alex squeezed her arm, her touch burning through Sam's uniform. "Please be safe, okay?" She leaned over to kiss her cheek, just as Sam slightly turned away.

Alex's lips met Sam's ear instead, which felt even more intimate.

Arousal flared, sharp and strong, catching Sam by surprise. *Oh hell.* "I should go." Her eyes darted to the door, and she stood.

"Sam? Aren't you forgetting something?"

"Hmm?" Sam glanced back.

Alex pointed to her police belt, still slung over the back of the chair where Sam had dumped it on her way in. Only slightly essential! Geez, where was her head?

"Oh right." Sam grabbed it, yanking it on as fast as she could manage; quite the feat given all its bulging pouches. "Thanks."

"You're most welcome." Alex stood, leaned in, eyes darkening, and this time her farewell kiss connected on Sam's cheek.

Her lips were as soft as the rest of her.

Chapter 13

The Boy I Knew

Sam pulled up to the Wild Boars clubhouse in her patrol car. This time she was on official business. Uniform, badge, police cap, the whole nine yards, so there could be no misunderstandings. Her hand fell to her belt, loaded with her Taser, baton, and OC spray, reassuring herself that she was prepared for anything. No need to break out her police-issue Glock 17 or the Bushmaster XM15 Patrolman rifle that sat in the lock box in her car's boot. That'd send the wrong message. She was just here to talk.

She'd left a message for Sergeant Peterson that she was going in for a "quick interview" with the Wild Boars' boss. Of course, Vaughan should have been with her for back up, but he was at his conference, so there wasn't much use asking. He could chew her out later, by which point she could explain why it had been worth it.

Leaning on the buzzer at the sliding metal door to the compound, Sam waited.

"What?"

"Senior Constable Keegan. I'd like a quick word with Dino. It's business."

"Fuck off, eh. He's busy."

"Really think Dino should be the one to tell me that." Sam wondered if Dino had a clue how much that movie lamp he'd nicked was worth. He could do up to seven years for it. That'd be sweet. "I think he'll want to hear what I have to say. Be in his best interests, trust me."

A colorful curse on the other side of the metal was followed by the grating noise of the gate opening. "Get in, talk fast, then fuck off," the voice said through the door. Then followed a warning shout to the compound: "Pig on deck!"

Sam stepped inside to see the usual mass of dead cars and rusted metal. She eyed the man who'd let her in. Fleabite. Well, Aaron Wells, age twenty-two. His slippery parents ran house-repair scams around Matamata.

The sound of gang members entering the compound brought her up sharply. They didn't thunder in to try and cow her as some thugs would. No, they creaked up to her gradually in their thick, worn motorcycle boots. The Wild Boars always got off their ample asses slowly and walked languidly so you had plenty of time to take in their massive bulk, intimidating facial tattoos, and pissed-off expressions.

She headed toward the clubhouse building; a familiar sign on the front read: *Trespassers will be shot. Survivors will be shot again.* As she walked, she did a quick head count. There were more than the ten men she'd expected.

Has Dino been recruiting?

A sliver of doubt nudged her confidence. She should know the numbers, damn it. Uncertainty prickled through her. Since when did she throw careful planning out the window? She calmed herself with the reminder that this was *Dino*, for God's sake. Not exactly an evil mastermind.

Sam came to a stop between several wrecked cars as the rush of black-and-red bodies pushed in all around her, taking up position. Within moments, she was surrounded by Dino's army. She squared her shoulders and eyed his second-in-command, Dogsbreath. "Your boss in?" she drawled. "Need a few words."

Dogsbreath disappeared with a grunt.

As she waited for Dino's arrival, she assessed her exit options. She'd hemmed herself in. At least two men now stood behind her, forming huge human bollards. Still, if push came to shove, literally, she could probably jump on the roof of the nearest rusty car. Up, over, and out. She'd be fine. Her fitness had to be superior to these grunts, who looked as if the most exercise they got was bending their elbows at the pub.

Dino emerged, all swagger and corpulence. He wore a black gang T-shirt with a red logo, black jeans, and a studded, fat belt. His unwashed, collar-length hair hung around his face, partially hiding an ugly scar bisecting his eyebrow. Dino's beer gut perched above spindly legs encased in leather pants. Man was one big topple risk.

He scratched his fingers through a bushy brown sideburn. "You're trespassin'. Unless you got some paperwork, *hukapapa*."

"Actually, Fleabite let me in when I buzzed at the gate."

Dino glared at Fleabite, then back at her. "Well, now you can buzz right out again."

"No, Dino, we need to talk…"

"No?" His eyes narrowed into slits. He nodded at someone behind her.

Sam's legs were kicked out, her knees landing hard on the ground. A foot jabbed into her kidney, and a flurry of clawing hands jerked her OC spray and Taser from her body. A rushing boot came into focus, then agony exploded in her skull.

Dino stood over her. "Think you're so fuckin' cocky, storming in here, demanding my attention like you got a right to it."

"For God's sake, Dino, I just came to talk. But fine." She gritted her teeth. "I tried to do this nicely. I'll have your place raided unless you let me up *right this bloody minute*!"

Dino's expression stiffened. He took a fistful of Sam's vest, lifting her to her feet with one jerk. He switched to hold her from behind, then nodded to Dogsbreath, whose hands wrenched apart the vest, sliding in and out of pockets, before yanking the shirt out of her pants.

"What the hell!" she hissed, fear lancing through her. "Get your damned hands off me!"

With roaming fingers hot against her skin, Dogsbreath skimmed her stomach and small of her back. "No wire. Not even a phone," he told his boss, then then shoved Sam back at Dino.

"I thought we had a deal," Dino continued speaking to Sam as though nothing had just happened. He walked back to the front, grabbed a tight fistful of her vest, and jerked her closer. "Sure, we can fuck up each other's shit around town, but you stay off my turf. This little visit breaks our rules."

"What deal?"

"It was *understood*. Callin' me a liar? In front of all me boys? You suicidal?"

This was not the Dino she knew. Then again, she usually didn't deal with him in front of his crew. That had clearly been her mistake this time. *Is it too late to get the hell out of here?* Her legs twitched, ready to bolt or fight, but her training leapt into her head. *De-escalate first.* "Not calling you a liar, Dino. But I think we have a misunderstanding."

"I could do anything to you," Dino muttered, his bloodshot eyes penetrating deep into her. "Anything at all."

Her fear spiked. "I'm a *police officer*," Sam snapped. She held his stare evenly. "My boss knows where I am. *Anything* happens to me, you're done. All of you are." Her eyes darted around to the gloating men.

"Your…*boss*. Fuck that's funny, eh?" He let go of her vest with a dramatic flourish and smirked. "Your sergeant tell you he's at a conference right now? In Tauranga?"

How could he possibly know that?

"Hey, Axel?" Dino called out. "How much does Vaughnie owe to that little operation your brother-in-law runs?"

"Twelve grand."

"Dogsbreath? How much does he owe our club?"

"Nineteen Gs."

Dino sucked in an exaggerated breath. "See, your boss has a tiny gambling problem at some of the private, off-the-books clubs up and down the Waikato region, including one we own. That's where he is right now, tryin' desperately to gamble his sorry ass out of debt. He's been borrowing money all over to pay for his habit, too. Every time you harass one of my couriers, I call up your boss to get him released, all polite like. He doesn't even argue anymore."

"I don't believe you." Except it felt a lot like truth. The warning signs jumped into her head. Her growing doubts. Nothing quite lining up. How Sergeant Peterson's "special interest" cases never resulted in convictions. Not that she could prove any of it. He'd always kept his explanations vague enough to drive a bus through.

"You know it's true. He'll never approve a raid on my compound, so you're screwed."

Well, she'd just go over his head then.

"Besides, you got no grounds to ask for a raid. Not one shred of evidence against me. And even if you did, Vaughnie'd make it all go away. So, now what I'm going to do with the world's most annoying fuckin' cop?" Dino prodded her nose.

"Do that again and I'll bite it off."

"Hmm. I could let you walk." He smiled. "For a price."

"I don't take bribes."

"No, you idiot. You pay *us.* A groveling apology to me and the boys for trespassing. That's just for our amusement. Plus, some confessions you've been on the take. On camera. A little insurance, in case you ever got the urge to share what we've discussed with any higher authorities."

"No. Not for sale."

"No? You came in here, disrespecting me in front of my crew. If you don't take the deal, the boys are gonna want some payback. To kick your ass a little."

The hell? There was no way this was going to be a *little* ass-kicking, with all Dino's boys, built like brick shithouses, having their blood up. This was insane, even for him. Illegal gaming houses, pushing drugs, even blackmailing a cop was one thing. As serious as all that was, it was nothing compared to beating a cop into a coma or a grave. It was the kind of attention she thought even he was smart enough to avoid.

"Dino, you don't have to do this. You made your point. These things get out of hand. You do this, you and your boys will do serious time. The cops will never leave you alone. Don't do it. You're not some brainless thug and you're sure as hell not a murderer."

Dino grabbed her collar again. "You always acted like you knew me. You don't."

Alex stepped out of her trailer, thoughts drifting back to Sam. She hoped the woman knew what she was doing, because confronting a man with a grudge, on her own, sounded an awful lot like insanity. Or maybe this was just a regular day for a small-town copper. She was a professional. And maybe Sam did know the locals well enough to know how far she could push them. And this was some old acquaintance, so…

I should have kissed her properly when I had the chance.

At the production trailer, she picked up her messages and had a quick chat with the First AD about the updated schedule. "Good," she said, pleased at Leslie's efforts. "Looks like we're back on schedule, finally."

"Mmm," Leslie agreed. "Thank Alice for that. Imagine trying to get anything finished without our M90s. It gets dark early out here."

"I know. Right, I'm going to talk to the set designer. I swear the man adds a dozen more ferns to the Amazon camp every time I turn around. We'll be losing our extras in the foliage at this rate. While I'm gone, can you talk to Max K about scene thirty-two? It's still not right. You know what I mean."

"Sure." Leslie nodded. "I'll see you out there."

Alex headed over to the poacher's set, trying to steady her nerves after the chaotic start to the day. The "body" that wasn't. Seeing Sam's gorgeous body in very little. All that glorious muscle and flesh. Jesus, she was only human. Then Sam blushing after catching Alex getting changed? That charged air afterward? She'd been so tempted to just...

Totally should have kissed her.

Chloe's head was bent in conversation with her stunt double as Alex neared.

"He's sweet. Truly," she was saying. "But all Sid ever talks about is his sister."

Apparently Chloe was still trying to get Sid's attention. He hadn't even caught a clue when she'd managed to find a signed 5XL All Blacks rugby shirt and dropped it in his lap at the pub one night with a smooth, "Hey, Sid, saw this and thought you might like it." He proudly wore it everywhere and told everyone how "cool those *Shezan* people are, eh?" Yet he remained sweetly oblivious.

"That's weird. Why's Sid so focused on Sam?" Kiri asked.

"He's worried she's obsessed with bringing down some bikie boss. But the whole time he's talking about her obsession with Dino, he's kinda missing the point that *he's* obsessed with her being okay. He can't see what's right in front of him."

Alex's blood ran cold. "Dino runs a biker gang?"

Chloe's head whipped around. "Alex? What's up?"

"Tell me everything you know about this Dino," Alex demanded.

"I only know what Sid tells me," Chloe said, frowning. "That he's a bully and a mean bastard who runs the meth trade around the district. Why?"

"Is he...dangerous?" *Stupid question.*

"Alex?" Chloe frowned. "You okay? You've gone pale."

Fear invaded every pore in her body. "Sam," Alex whispered. "Sam's going after Dino. Now. Alone. She thinks he's behind our set sabotage."

Kiri gasped. "Oh hell." She grimaced. "Dino's a real knuckle-dragger. He's scary."

Alex grabbed her phone and called Sam. It rang and rang, then clicked over to an answering message with Sam's voice.

You've reached Ika Whenu Police Station. Senior Constable Keegan is currently not available to take your call. If you have an urgent local matter, the nearest station is Te Aroha on 884 8999. Or call triple one for the national emergency switchboard. You can leave a message after the tone, if the matter is not urgent.

"She's not there." Alex hung up and began to pace.

Chloe scrambled to her feet. "Sid. He'll know what to do. I'll get him." She bolted.

Alex called the Te Aroha police number. A man's recorded voice kicked in.

You've reached Te Aroha Police Station. Sergeant Peterson is presently at a conference and not available to take your call. If you have an urgent local matter, the nearest station is Ika Whenu on 884…"

"Shit! Sergeant Asshole's unavailable, too." Alex scowled, waited for the voicemail tone, then left a message.

"You mean Sergeant Peterson?" Kiri asked. "Mightn't have mattered if he was there. He's useless. All hot air and full of himself."

Alex's jaw worked. "Who else do we call? Main police switchboard?"

"Not much point. Police from the outer districts would take too long to get here."

"Fuck," Alex muttered. *Damn it, Sam. What part of "stay safe" didn't you understand?*

Blood dribbled out of Sam's nose. The blow had come from nowhere, snapping her head sidewise. Wiping the blood away slowly with her fingers, she tried to get a look at Dino's eyes in the darkness. He'd hauled her into his shed for a "private chat," amid disgusting hoots and calls from his men.

Christ, how has it come to this? When she closed her eyes, a face swam into view. Cute. Nerdish glasses. Curling smile. *Oh. Right.* Sam's motives were obvious. She'd wanted this asshole to leave Alex's movie alone. She had wanted Alex to succeed. Wanted her to feel safe.

Wanted *her.*

And right there was the number one reason not to let emotions get in the way of policing. Mistakes could get your head ripped off. She sighed.

Was Dino going to kill her now? Here? How could anyone change this much?

Dino snapped on the light.

Her eyes adjusted, blinking. Wait, where was the meth lab? The stockpile of drugs?

The dusty room appeared to be a shabby man cave, a receptacle of empty beer bottles and topless girlie posters. She took in the ripped armchairs that looked like they'd lost an argument with Killer and her brothers, a bird-shit covered pool table, a framed poster of a gorgeous red Ducati 1299 Superleggera, and a stainless-steel home brewing kit. Plus a ten-kilogram sack of… She squinted… Baking soda? *Um, what…?*

Suddenly Dino shoved his face right up next to hers, eyes bright and furious. "You stupid fucking bitch!" he snarled. "God damn it! Fuck you!" He slammed his fist into the shed wall. "Fuck, fuck, fuck!" Then both his hands slapped the wall and stayed there, his shoulders shaking as he pushed against it. The whole structure gave a little wobble.

"Where's the meth?" she asked, desperate to distract him from whatever had just set him off.

"You're looking at it!" He shot her a withering stare. "I don't fucking have any, do I?"

"The hell you don't. Ika Whenu's swimming in it."

"I know. But it ain't comin' from us."

Sam glared at the denial.

"Jesus! Use your bloody eyes, woman. Do you *see* any drugs?"

"Is it… I mean, you keep it in the house?" That made no sense. The drug-making process was highly flammable, not to mention the toxic smell would make the place reek.

"Fuck you! My cousin died from that crap. Why would I push it? That'd be like pissing on his grave."

She blinked. Oh. She did vaguely remember something about that a few years back. But… "Your couriers are convinced you deal meth." Hell, she'd interrogated enough of them to work out what the idiots were trying so hard not to confess.

"Those dopeheads believe what I tell them. They get weed for ferrying my parcels around as long as they ain't opened. But if they *did* sneak a look or get collared…know what's really in them? Baking soda. Since they think it's the real deal, they act shifty as fuck." He laughed. "Best acting is believing it. Then Dogsbreath goes around and picks up their packages after the drops and we recycle them for the next one."

"You're full of shit."

"Am I?" He waved at the sack of baking soda. "You think I bake cakes?"

He had a point. "Why the charade?"

"It's all about respect. Some rival gangs were fucking with us, trying to steal our territory, muscle in on our gaming establishment. Soon as word went round we'd stepped up with the big boys into hard-core drugs, they all backed off real fast. Jesus, it was almost funny."

God, that did sound just like the Dino she'd known at school. All talk.

"Don't the Hornets care you're stealing their credit?" It was an educated guess. She'd sighted a Hornets bike parked at Dino's one morning, two months ago. There was no reason at all for a Tauranga-based rival gang member to be anywhere near Dino's compound, let alone be allowed to stay the night.

"We did a deal," Dino said, not noticing her little trap. "All we have to do is keep the local cop out of their hair on the nights they drop their stuff."

Wait, *that* was why every second Tuesday was always so busy? "Those car fires? That was you?"

He shrugged. "No comment. But I hear you were miles from the drop."

Miles from the drop. She did her calculations. Wherever the drop was, was probably in the opposite direction to where she'd been sent. She drew a mental line from the burning cars through Ika Whenu, out the other side, and… There wasn't a damned thing out there except…

"Train yard," she muttered. "The disused one." That'd definitely be deserted any night of the week.

Dino's eyes grew wide. "How the fuck did you know that?"

"Good deal for the Hornets. All reward, no risk. Target's on your back, not theirs."

"Like I give a shit. People don't mess with us now. All a man has is his rep. You know where I came from, what I had at home. Christ, everyone at school knew. Same reason I knew all about your shitty life."

Anxiety shot through her. "Don't you dare go there." She scowled. "I mean it, Dino."

"Or what?" Tone mocking, he added, "Hmm, yeah. Remember it well. Your dad shootin' through. Your mum, cracking up, and walking around town in the nude, talking to people who weren't real. You rushing around at all hours to try and find her and haul her ass home again. What were you? Eleven?"

Nine. And *ten.* And *eleven. And fuck you, Dino, for that reminder.*

"Know what I remember most? How much you hated everyone who saw you like that. Sometimes I think you still resent us for knowing, for seeing you at your weakest. You pretend to be strong, but we all know what you looked like, all helpless and useless." He heaved out a sigh. "Fucked as it sounds, I relate." He walked over to the pool table and picked up a cue. His knuckles turned white around it. "My old man was a fuckin' animal. Used to hit me with one of these."

That was common knowledge. Dino's brutish father had spent more time in jail than out of it for what he'd done to his family.

He tapped the scar above his eye. "When I went to school with bruises, everyone knew my ole man was at it again. I *hated* them for knowing. Soon as I was big enough, I waited till he was asleep and beat the snot out of him. With one of these." He rapped the cue against the side of the table. The wooden thud sounded loud in the stillness.

His laugh was mirthless. "Told everyone it was a fair fight, but that was a lie. Whatever. He left me alone after that and I made my own family. You gotta do that." He gave her an intense look. "You *gotta.* No use waiting for our own fucked-up parents to give a shit about us."

That was more than Dino had ever said to her in his life. "Why are you telling me any of this?"

"Who else am I gonna tell this to? Dogsbreath?" Pain edged his eyes. "I got a reputation, not just in town but *here*. Besides, your ass is gonna be fucked up in three minutes. Not like you'll be spilling anything but your guts." His voice cracked, his face twisted, and finally she saw it.

Fear.

It dawned on her. "Oh Jesus, Dino…you don't even want to hurt me, do you? You're just doing it to not lose face. You're in here, building up the courage. Or stalling."

His anger returned. "Goddammit, Sam! Why'd you have to force my hand? I gave you a way out! You were supposed to take the bloody deal!" His eyes were pleading now, even as his words dripped with fury. And he'd said her name the way he used to at school. Half exasperated, half mocking.

This was the boy she remembered. Huh. Maybe people didn't change so much after all.

"Dino," she said quietly, "you didn't give me a way out. You gave me an impossible choice. I can't accept it. Like you say, reputation's everything."

"You'd walk out of here!"

"At what cost? Every day knowing you could demand something from me the way you do my boss?"

"Don't make me do it," he begged her. "Take the fucking deal."

"Give me a better one—better for both of us. One that won't see the Boars all tossed in jail for years."

"That's the one on the table. My boys won't accept any less."

"Twenty against one? And some of them are big enough to count as two. What could go wrong? You're not a murderer!"

"Take my deal and you won't have to find out if that's true."

"I won't be compromised, so no. But I know who you are. Bad as your old man was, even though you were a bully at school, I also never saw you lay a finger on anyone."

"Because I got the others to do it," he said morosely.

"Even so. *You* didn't do it." Was she clutching at straws? It was a weak argument, and at any other time she'd mock it. "It's not you. *You* don't kill people, and you sure as hell don't put them into comas, either."

He threw the pool cue back on the table and turned on her. "For the last time, you don't know me. I was someone else at school." He stared at her for a measuring moment. "So were you."

She gave him a wary look and firmed her jaw.

"You had fight in you then," Dino said. "Now look at you. You're just a hundred percent stinking cop. No life. Nothing. *Hukapapa* suits you, eh? All ice, no heart. Know what? When you bailed on this town after school, I thought, hell, good on her. Anyone who gets out of this dump is smart in my book." He looked envious for a moment, then shook his head. "And then you came crawling back, lookin' like cat-sick warmed up."

The reminder felt as brutal as a slap. Sam glared at him.

"It's such a hole here," Dino continued. "And everywhere you turn, people remember: Who you were, all your secrets, and they *know* how you look broken in half." He drew in a deep breath and said with sincerity, "The fuck's wrong with you, Sam? Why'd you come back? You shoulda stayed gone. If you had..." Regret filled his eyes. He turned away.

"So why didn't *you* leave?"

"Got family now," Dino's thumb jerked over his shoulder to the door, indicating the meatheads behind it. "Can't leave them. We got each other's backs, loyal to the end."

And there it was: the truth as Dino saw it. The unspoken knowledge sat between them, heavy and dark: He was never going to choose her over them. Didn't matter how bad he felt about it, this was always going to end the same way.

"Look, you gotta understand, I got no choice here," he said tightly. "None."

A silence fell, then Sam said, "I see that you believe it."

He looked down, hands forming balls. "Look, I'll call off my boys after a little bit. Let them get their pound of flesh and all, but I wouldn't just leave them to it, to y'know..." He trailed off, looking faintly sick.

How fucked up. He really didn't want to do this. Sam sighed. So that was it. Fear surged, warring with adrenaline. She inhaled, mentally planning her escape route, wondering how far she could sprint before they caught up with her. Well, nothing left to lose now. "Look, since our cards are on the table, can you tell me one thing? What was the deal with the movie-set shit? The sabotage? Who were you paying there to do it?"

Dino squinted at her. "The fuck? I wouldn't go near them Hollywood mincing poodles if my life depended on it."

"You didn't do that?"

"Why would I waste time on that crap? Does that frou-frou shit sound like me?"

It really didn't, now she thought about it.

He ran his hand through his hair. "It's been five minutes." Dino now looked nauseous. "Can't put this off any longer."

"So." Sam straightened and gave him a cool stare. "You're going to beat the living hell out of a girl you went to school with? This'll haunt you forever. Stick between your ribs every day. I've seen it."

"You think I don't know that?" He glared. "You already know the answer. I have to."

"Then you're weak—letting others dictate the man you are, even when you know it's wrong."

His eyes narrowed. "You want a black eye to go with the mauling?"

"Fine. Let's just get this over with." Sam turned to the door. "Cos I'm done talking to a coward."

For a moment, Dino looked about to strike her and she braced herself.

Instead, he swore. "Samantha Keegan. Fuck it, woman, I *really* don't understand you."

"I know," she said and then added the truest thing she knew as she pulled the door open. "I don't think anyone really does."

Chapter 14

Rescues and Rumbles

ALEX BOUNCED ALONG IN THE front seat of Sid's open-backed pick-up truck that he called a "ute." It turned out he was exactly the right man to call in a crisis. He not only knew where the Wild Boars lived but exactly what to bring. Which is why he diverted to pick up half a dozen bulky members of a Matamata road crew he'd once worked with.

Now hanging on for dear life in the ute's rear, the men had apparently been dead keen to get out of tarring a road outside a pig farm.

So somehow they were all going to a rescue. Or was it a rumble?

Guilt was threatening to swallow Alex whole. She'd seen the look in Sam's eyes when she'd left the set. So determined to find their saboteur—*for me*. And she could be getting her beautiful ass killed over something that didn't matter much in the scheme of things.

She was well-trained, though, right? Strong. Smart. Cunning. Sam probably could handle a bunch of rough old bikers who probably just sat around all day drinking. Right?

They bounced over a pothole, which prompted a few good-natured shouts from the back, and a rattle from the chains, shovels, pipes, and a Stop-Go sign that one roadworker hadn't let go of. Weirdly, he looked familiar, but she couldn't place him.

"I should've left you behind," Sid told Alex, as he hammered it. "How'd you talk me into this again? Sam'll kill me for getting you mixed up in this."

She doubted that, but the thought made her heart quicken. "Because I gave you no choice? Oh, and I'm your boss."

"Oh, right. Well, when we get there, you stay out of sight, in the ute. If it looks like we're losing, you floor it outta there as fast as you can, then call triple-one." He sighed. "Though this'll be over long before any cops turn up. Main thing is, you haul your ass to safety."

"Okay, small problem…" Alex waved at the gear stick. "I only drive automatic."

"Oh hell." Sid began slowing. "Right, I'm gonna drop you off here then."

"No way!" Alex gritted her teeth. "I'll stay out of your way."

Sid grunted.

Eventually the ute lurched to a halt. For a second, they both stared at the sight of Sam's parked patrol car. *Still here.*

The heavy crunch of men's boots hit the dirt road.

"Right," Sid said to the men jumping off his vehicle, "we'll just go in, all polite, and ask for Sam. If there's nothing wrong, they'll hand her over. If they say nah, here's what we do…"

Alex let his words fade out as she stared at the imposing, brick-walled compound opposite, its enormous wrought-iron gate shut.

A ferocious cacophony of barking sounded from inside. Then came shouts, howls, and a voice—definitely female, sharp and angry—in the middle of it.

"Or we just barge in right now," Sid snapped. "Okay, move your bloody asses." He spun around to Alex. "And you—don't leave here or Sam'll have my gizzards for breakfast. Um, boss." He disappeared to the back of the truck and reappeared holding a concrete-splattered garden fork in one hand and a heavy shovel in the other.

Sid and his burly friends rushed to the gate. When they prized the huge door open with their garden tools, Alex had a good view inside. About two dozen men in black-and-red jackets were crowded around something on the ground…no, *someone*…as terrifying snarling sounds rose above their shouts.

Sid and his crew thundered in. The bikers turned…and it was on. Fists pounded; legs swept out in brutal kicks.

Where was Sam? Alex had never felt so helpless in her life. All she knew how to do was make movies. How useless was that?

The tangle of scuffling legs and boots parted, and for a brief moment, she saw a flash of navy on the ground.

Sam!

Growling dogs were leaping all over her. How many were there? They were snapping and snarling, flecks of spittle flying from their yapping mouths. Sam, pinned beneath the vicious animals, was struggling to crawl to her feet.

With shaky hands, Alex rang 1-1-1, reached the emergency switchboard, and tried to explain the mess before her.

"Where are you, ma'am? Exactly?"

"I-I have no idea. Wild Boars? The clubhouse? It's a biker gang."

"A biker gang?" She sounded puzzled.

"Um, motorcycles, what you call bikies? They're in the Waikato region somewhere."

"Ma'am, that's a very big area and I'm afraid that club's not listed in our directory." The voice was sympathetic but impatient.

"Near Ika Whenu?"

A rattle of keys, then... "I've sent a request for the nearest police to that town to attend and they will most likely be aware of the location of the gang compound you mention."

"Great, except the nearest police station is in Ika Whenu, and its only cop is right now being attacked by dogs and bikers! Can't you tell where I am from my phone's GPS or something?"

"If you're using an Android phone, ma'am. Which you're not—"

"Cell tower then?" Alex demanded. She'd seen that in movies. Surely...

"If you're on the Spark network." The voice was faintly apologetic. "You're not."

For God's sake...

There was a clatter of keys. "Attendance from a larger station will take about forty-five minutes to reach..."

"Forty-five minutes!" This was pointless. "That's too long. I have to go..."

"Ma'am, no, you need to stay on the line so we can determine—"

"It won't matter. You'll be too late." *Damn it.* "For what it's worth, send an ambulance. That'll probably be more useful in the end."

"Ma'am—"

"Tell them to hurry." If they could even work out where she was.

"Of course, but you need to stay at a safe distance—"

Safe? When Sam was getting her ass flattened? Screw that for a joke. No, there needed to be a record of what was happening. Proof. She ended the call just as a huge biker tossed a haymaker that smacked Sid's head sideways, dropping him to the ground with a pained "ooof". She frantically flicked through her phone's apps, glancing up periodically.

Sid was already on his knees, swaying out of the way of a low-sweeping boot.

Alex jumped out of the vehicle. She might *only* know how to make movies, but to hell anyone was getting away with anything on her watch. She'd use her one skill and work it.

Hitting the record button on her social media live feed, Alex began to speak as she darted across the road toward the compound.

"The bravest person I know is a cop in Ika Whenu, New Zealand—Senior Constable Sam Keegan. Right now, she's trapped inside a motorcycle gang compound, the Wild Boars, where she went to confront the gang over criminal activity. They've set their dogs on her."

The sounds of howling, snarling, and biting carried on the wind. Alex tapped the button to swap to the rear camera and focused on the swirl of bodies, swinging fists, twisting limbs, and enraged dogs.

"Senior Constable Keegan's brother and his friends have just gone in to try and rescue her, but they need help. I'm putting out this feed in the hopes anyone in the area can get the word out. If there are any police nearby, come urgently! You can see Senior Constable Keegan on the ground, fighting to get up, despite the dogs pinning her down."

Alex was too far away.

"I'm going to get closer," she told her audience of…sixty-three. *Damn.* Still, any one of those people could help. "Spread this video," she urged them. "Please. If you know anyone in New Zealand, alert them, tag them, get the word out. We need help *now*. As for the local police?" She focused the phone's camera on Sam's twisting legs as a Rottweiler snarled and stood on her. "There's only one. You're looking at her."

The dog had blood on its muzzle. *Shit! Come on, Sam! Get up!* Her stomach twisted at the sight.

Sid was bellowing for the gang to "give me my sister or this'll get *real* ugly."

A biker tumbled, crashed over the shell of a rusted car, and skidded in front of the gate, at Alex's feet. He stared up at her with a dazed look before his eyes fogged over and shut.

Alex jogged around the outside of the compound, staying close to the wall, searching for a better vantage point. There. A big leafy tree overhung the wall.

"I'm going up," she said. "Stand by." Clambering up its limbs, Alex reached wall height, then slid across a branch and looked down, centering the phone's camera.

She gasped. The four rampaging Rottweilers were spattered in blood. One was on top of Sam, and, wait, was it...*licking* her? The other three were snarling and snapping at anyone getting too close.

Are the dogs protecting or attacking the cop? Someone posted a comment on her live feed. *Or licking her to death?*

Good Q, said another.

Some gang members were waving chains at their dogs, faces twisted with fear and rage. Periodically a Rottweiler would lunge at one and take a chunk out of him.

A fat man with shaggy hair was calling out attack commands to the dogs, to little avail. Sid thundered up and crashed him to the ground in a tackle.

Messages kept pinging down her page.

Oww! Nice 1

Got him!

Boom! Fucking legend!

Sam pushed away one Rottweiler that kept bounding over her and managed to crawl to her knees. A biker towering over her kicked at her head. She ducked to one side, caught his ankle, twisted sharply, and crashed him to the ground. Her fist connected with his stomach in follow-up. He grunted loudly enough for Alex to hear.

Her phone started blooping reactions. Multiple thumbs up wafted across the page.

This isn't supposed to be damned entertaining, Alex thought in annoyance. "We need urgent assistance here," she growled. "We're outnumbered.

There's an officer down; she could be hurt. This isn't a joke." She crawled farther along the branch and held out her phone.

Sid and the Matamata crew had now surrounded the biggest biker, the enormous bruiser who'd taken Sid down earlier. The man glared at the dogs, then Sam. "What the fuck did you do to them?"

Alex glanced down at the latest alert.

1 NEWS here, where exactly are you? Wild Boars aren't listed. We want to send a TV crew

Hell if I know, Alex thought, then inched farther along the branch.

Sam's boot lashed out at the giant, supplying a crunching stomp on the top of his knee. She jerked her head away just as a meaty fist came down at her.

Alex gasped, marveling as the brute of a man grabbed his knee with a howl and sank to the ground. *She's holding her own. Actually, she's magnificent.*

The human mountain flung his hand up, grabbed Sam's foot, and jerked her to the ground. Jumping on her back, he flattened her.

Bollocks! He had to weigh more than three men. The pain on Sam's face was terrifying.

The nearest dog flew at the brute with a snarl, attaching teeth to the giant's arm. The biker roared in pain and tried to fling the dog away, but it clung to him, biting harder. While he was distracted, Sid waded in and attempted to drag the man off Sam's back.

As he did, Sam clawed her way out from under him. Her face was red, and she was gasping for breath. She seemed stunned and shaky.

"Sam, get out of there fast!" Alex whispered.

Messages were flashing up constantly by this point. Now a thousand people were watching.

Hold on Officer Keegan!

Hey, I think the dogs r winning!

Am posting google map co-ords for 1news.

A map appeared.

Then a reply from the station. *Thx. On way.*

Then another message. *Ive called Hamilton cops. Theyre closest big station and got xtra muscle! Could take a wile tho*

She suspected it'd be long over by then.

A few new faces had joined the fray—familiar ones.

"Oh crap," she muttered. "Those are three of my film's stuntmen," she told her audience.

Had Chloe and Kiri told them about the desperate situation, or had they seen her feed? Either way, she was going to have a hard time explaining this to Quincy. It was bad enough she'd just bolted. At least she had Leslie to take over for her. Stuntmen had no replacements.

The three men, all muscled, Maori, elite fighters, were wading into the fray with glee on their faces. The first stuntman grabbed at bikers one by one, giving each one a shake, and then tossing them behind as he went, where the next stuntman followed up with dizzyingly fast punch combos, before shunting them to the final man. The last stuntman latched onto each Boar by the collar and belt and hurled him out the gates.

It was as coordinated as one might expect for pros who performed well-constructed fights for a living. Alex shook her head at how casual they made it look. The compound was rapidly starting to empty out as a result of their actions.

Holy crap! When's this movie coming out? Looks awesome!!!

Wait, Alex, is this ur new movie?

Oh! I thougt this was reel. Is this a promo?

"No, it is not a bleeding promotion!" she replied hotly. "This is *real.* Lives are at stake." *One in particular.* She tried to pick Sam out of the crowd but had lost sight of her when she'd spotted her stuntmen.

A siren wailed in the distance.

Three bikers were now on Sid, who was buried in a sea of red-and-black jackets. Suddenly Sam flew into the frame, hauling them off her brother by their long hair and seats of their pants. All the while, snapping dogs were everywhere, darting between people's legs, taking opportunistic chunks out of Wild Boars.

A loud crack sounded, and before Alex could react, her branch snapped. Suddenly she was in the air, tumbling over. The next second, the air slapped out of her lungs. The pain was searing. For a few moments, she could only register her senses. The smell of dirt and dust, the sound of grunts, shouts, and barking, and the taste of blood from inside her lip.

Everything hurt.

A muscled body went tumbling past her, landing easily on his feet. "Oh, hey, boss," one of her stuntmen said in surprise. "Cool fight, eh?"

He jogged back toward the fray. "Maybe get out of the kill zone, but?" he tossed over his shoulder.

The kill zone?

I'm in a damned kill zone.

A roadworker's Stop-Go sign flashed by, smashing into someone's face, and a grizzled man appeared above it. He leaned casually on it and looked down at her. "Fancy seeing you here. Still working for that film company?"

What? Wait, Frank? The You Dump, We Pump guy? *What?* No. *I'm in hell.* Alex closed her eyes.

"Alex?" Sam's concerned voice sounded in the distance. "What the hell are you doing here? I'm coming! Don't move!"

Move? Not likely. Alex opened her eyes and drew in a tentative breath.

A frothing dog sprinted past, its eyes wild. It screeched to a halt, turned, and eyed her.

Oh shit!

It slunk over to her, tail down, mouth open, teeth bared.

She covered her face with her arms.

It jumped on her abused chest, its full weight pressing on her. Alex tensed, waiting for the worst.

"Killer! Down, girl!" Sam's authoritative voice sounded close now.

Hot canine breath fanned her cheek. Suddenly the enormous animal bounded off Alex, and she lowered her shaking arms.

Sam's hand shot into view, wrenching the dog farther away by the collar. Then her face was right up in Alex's. "You're insane! Why would you come here? What the hell do you think you're doing?"

"Dying," she whispered. "Slowly."

"Nope, no you don't." Sam's blood- and grime-streaked face hovered over her. "Not on my watch. Come on." She hauled Alex to her feet in one yank.

For half a second, Sam just held her upright while a swaying Alex found her balance. Had Sam always been this strong? Not to mention brave...

"You idiot!" Alex said, suddenly remembering why they were all here. "You didn't tell me Dino was some biker boss. If you had, I'd never have let you come here alone!"

"Let me?" Sam's expression grew quizzical, head turning in the direction of the fast-approaching sirens. "And who the hell called the troops? I had it handled."

Alex folded her arms. "You mean your brother and his friends did."

"They weren't necessary. I'd been planning this for months. I had the dogs' loyalty." Her eye twitched. "I'm assuming you were the one who called the police?"

"Well, yes and no. I didn't know the address here, so I called in reinforcements." At the reminder, Alex looked around for her phone. Where it had gone when she fell? "I've been live streaming to get you help."

Sam's eyes went wide. "You let *live footage* go out of a police officer in a bikie brawl?"

"Um, yes?" What was her issue? "You needed help; I got it."

"You…" Sam looked appalled. "I can't even… I *was* handling it. This is my job. Do you have any idea what you've done?" As she spoke, a trickle of red ran down her neck. Sam wiped at it, peering at the blood.

"You're hurt!" Alex reached for her head. "And you're welcome, by the way."

"It's nothing." Sam gritted her teeth. "Sid had no right letting you anywhere near this disaster. I'll brain him."

"I didn't give him any choice. And what's so bad about gathering evidence of what happened?"

"You really can't see it?" Sam glared at her.

Alex stared at her in confusion. "See what? I only shared the truth."

"Don't be so naïve. Jesus, Alex, I trusted you."

Alex's heart dropped into her shoes at the accusation, as if she'd betrayed Sam somehow. "I don't understand. What are you—"

Blue uniforms suddenly swarmed the compound, accompanied by officious shouts. The remaining fights broke up. Wild Boars were dragged outside, bleeding and cursing.

"Are you all right, Senior Constable?" A salt-and-pepper-haired police officer appeared at Sam's side. His assessing gaze flicked from the blood on Sam's neck to Alex, and back again.

"Yes. Thanks. Sergeant…?"

"Hawkins." He nodded at the blood. "There's an ambulance outside. Get that looked at," he ordered. "I'll clean up this lot." He suddenly froze and his face paled.

Alex followed his gaze to see the prowling Rottweilers eying the new intruders. Their hackles were up, and their teeth bared.

"I'll take care of them," Sam told the sergeant. "Stay back. Don't go near them." She whistled. The dogs bounded over to her. "Come on, kids, let's get you locked away." She led them behind a shed.

Hawkins watched her go, shaking his head in disbelief.

Suddenly the pinched features of Sam's boss came into sight. Sergeant Peterson's expression was harried. He waded through the chaos, gaze sweeping around, searching.

Wasn't he at a conference? How'd he get here so fast?

The man spoke briefly to Hawkins, who pointed him behind the shed.

Alex crept closer, wondering exactly how much trouble Sam's boss was going to rain on her for taking on a biker gang solo. Maybe none? Didn't they forgive their own, or something?

She caught snatches of conversation from behind the shed. "Stupidest actions ever… reckless… insane… have your badge."

Alex moved closer, hearing Sam's retort. "I guess when you owe twenty grand to bikies, it's a bit hard to turn on them, isn't it? Someone had to look into this, especially since you kept blocking me on the Boars."

Wait, was Sam's boss on the take?

"You have no idea what you're talking about," came Peterson's voice. "I'll have you investigated!"

"You can't stick a damned thing on me. No proof. Your word against mine. And I have seniority and a spotless record."

"No proof? Okay, how'd you get back from Tauranga so fast? Maybe you were at some local gambling den instead? Got any proof you were ever at that conference?"

"I'll have your badge in two seconds if you push on this. *And* I'll deny this conversation even took place."

"Try me. You'll find, like Dino did, that I can't be blackmailed."

Peterson stalked into view and caught sight of Alex. "What are you looking at?" he snapped. "This is a police matter. Get back behind the cordon."

Before Alex could answer, more police surged past them to clear the area.

"Hey, whose is this?" one officer shouted, lifting a dirty phone out of the small bush it had rolled into.

"You found it?" Alex rushed over and grabbed it gratefully. "That's mine." She studied it anxiously. Oh. *Still live streaming?*

Wait, eleven thousand viewers?

She glanced at the screen. The comments made little sense.

OH SHIT! That dudes ass got owned.

Ill deny it, Ill take ur badge – haha – um, hey cop dude, the whole world just heard u!

His ass is 2 seconds from being investigated. Burn!

Alex's eyes widened.

"Ma'am, please step this way," a police officer said to her, pointing to the gate. "We'll need to take your details and question you on what has occurred. Thank you for your assistance."

She obeyed his instructions.

Outside, bikers were sitting cross-legged up and down the road, handcuffed behind their backs. Some were bleeding. Shirts were torn. Faces bruised. A couple were unconscious, with paramedics looking them over. Police milled around.

"You want your lawyer, eh?" one female cop was saying to the biker Alex had seen earlier shouting commands to the dogs. "Hope it's a good one. We don't take kindly to one of our own being assaulted. You and your men are in deep trouble."

Your men? That little pissant was Dino?

"Hey, we were just here, minding our own business, and these thugs came and attacked us!" Dino protested. "Nothing illegal about defending our place."

The cop snorted. "Tell that to everyone who saw you on a live feed trying to order your dogs to attack a cop. Good thing for you they ignored you."

"I didn't do that." Dino squinted at her. "The hell you on about, woman?"

Suddenly Alex's phone came alive and she looked down to see laughing emojis all over the screen and comments about Dino being "in for a surprise."

Ah, right, still live.

"Um, thanks, everyone, for getting the word out," she told the viewers. She blinked at the numbers. "All fourteen thousand of you. You saved a good woman today. Thanks again."

A slew of thumbs up and heart signs greeted her just before she ended the feed.

Dino was now staring at her and her phone, realization dawning.

She turned it around to face him—not that he'd be able to see the screen. She smiled slowly.

Alex half expected him to look murderous, but instead he deflated. Defeat settled around him. *Pathetic man.* God, even she could just reach over and—

"Nah, boss, you can't do that," Sid said as he passed. "Not once they've been arrested, at least."

"How'd you know what I was thinking?"

"You looked evil." He chuckled. "So, you okay?"

"Yeah."

"Pretty sure I told you to stay in my ute."

"Yes."

"Figures you'd ignore me." Sid nodded at Sam, now being examined by a paramedic. "What'd ya do to Sam? Me, she wants to drown in free beers while calling me an idiot. You, she's just full-on mad at."

"I told her I live-streamed the brawl. Fourteen thousand people were watching by the end."

"Oh." Sid's grin disappeared. "Yeah, bugger. That's not good."

"She was kicking butt!"

"She won't see it that way."

"But everyone watching helped save her ass! We did good."

"Cops and cameras, eh? Not a great mix, seein' as she wasn't supposed to be here alone. She'll be investigated and you just gave them all the evidence they need to tear her a new one."

"But—"

"I know you meant well. It was a good idea. But Sam being a cop, it's a whole lot of complicated for her now, right? She's used to saving her own ass, so she'd be embarrassed it even needed saving. All those witnesses? She does not like being talked about or looking stupid."

"So she hates me." Alex glanced at the sullen woman in question. Sam was standing with her hands on her hips, getting bandaged up by the paramedic.

"Yeah, maybe, for now. She'll come around. You just gotta give her time to think it through and realize she maybe owes you one." He grinned.

"Really?" Alex asked hopefully. "What if she doesn't come around?"

"Well, that'd suck. Having Sam mad at you is the worst thing. Trust me."

Great. "Well, I should go thank everyone," Alex said. "Your road crew. *Shezan*'s stuntmen."

"Y'know, everyone'll be at Te Wharariki pub tonight. Might be better to have a word to them then." Sid glanced over at the ambulance. "And, you know, give Sam some space."

No kidding.

A TV van screeched up, and soon a cameraman was out and panning the scene, while a crew began to interview the enthusiastic Matamata road crew.

"Ah crap, I better sort this," Sid muttered. "Those boys aren't supposed to be off work. I gotta spin it right. Don't want anyone getting fired."

"Sure. By the way, Sid"—Alex grabbed his arm as he was leaving—"Thanks. You were amazing."

He grinned and left with a wave.

Sergeant Hawkins walked over and handed Sam a pepper spray canister, baton, and Taser. The wind picked up, carrying their words clearly.

"Think you may have lost these in the confusion."

Sam offered a tight look and nodded. "Thanks. How'd you get here so fast?"

"It's Matamata Cup Day. the Waikato Police District had a couple of extra units over here to help keep an eye on the racing crowds. We got the call of an officer down near us. Then we all start getting texts from friends and family, with links to some live feed." He winced. "Higher ups are going nuts. Reckon you'll be all over the news tonight. There'll be fallout."

Alex winced.

Sam's expression became grimmer. "Figured. Thanks for the assist. I did have things under control, though." She slid the items back on her belt.

"Sure," he said neutrally. "I look forward to your report." He left her to it.

After a moment, Sam glanced up, her gaze intersecting Alex's.

Alex's small smile was met by a wall of ice. Nonetheless, she couldn't tear her eyes away. She stared at Sam, trying to convey that she'd only done any of this for her. Everyone needs help sometimes. Alex kept on staring, her heart clenched in dismay at Sam's closed-off expression.

Oh hell.

Chapter 15

Viral Sensation

ALEX'S HEAD WAS THUMPING LISTENING to so many excited, enthusiastic Te Wharariki Hotel patrons buying each other drinks and recounting tales of bravery that rivaled *Beowulf*. The two dozen bikers were now numbering forty. It'd probably be a hundred by evening's end.

However, the woman whose name was on everyone's lips was missing. Sam was resting at home, according to Sid. He'd also said that Sam had learned the Wild Boars were not behind the sabotage.

That seemed like the sort of important piece of information a police officer might have wanted to discuss with *Shezan*'s director. Unfortunately, Sam hadn't responded to Alex's text or call. Maybe she was asleep? Or still angry?

So, Alex sat in the boisterous pub, staring into her beer, analyzing just how pissed off Sam was.

Skye's was the only other somber face in here tonight. Any attempts to talk to the costume designer had been foiled by another cheerful local buying Alex a drink. Turned out the Matamata road crew appreciated her for making them social media legends.

Not the point, she'd tried to explain. They didn't care.

On the largest New Zealand news site, "Locals wade into brawl to save their cop from rampaging bikies!" had been trending worldwide for hours.

The national media had descended on the pub, much to Gina's delight, and she'd managed to squeeze into every interview that she'd be relaunching Te Wharariki as a gastro pub soon. Media were interviewing the locals, working their way through them as adeptly as vultures on a carcass. Alex had become an expert at ducking out of sight to avoid telling them to sod off.

In the space of three hours, Sid had become a media darling. His beaming face was all over the news talking about how "smacking a few bikie heads in to save my sis" was not something he'd thought about, and he'd "just acted on instinct, hey." He'd thanked his road-crew mates and also paid tribute to Sam for saving her own ass by befriending the dogs.

Alex watched the interview on a TV above the bar—the sixth time she'd seen it so far—and marveled at what a natural he was. Sound-bite perfection. Photogenic, too, with those flashing white teeth and warm eyes. No wonder Chloe had been flinging herself at him in her own laid-back, "sooo, buy you another garlic bread, Sid?" way. Not that he'd noticed. Still.

"That's Sam. Always doing the smart thing," Sid concluded in his interview, and for a moment his expression faltered.

Alex interpreted that as: "Except for today—I have no idea why she was even there."

Neither did Alex. It was insanity. What had possessed her?

The guilt crept back, knowing exactly what had possessed her. Sam had put herself on the line for *her*, to find the saboteur. A saboteur who was still a mystery—so all of this had been for nothing.

A new beer appeared on the bar next to her elbow and she sighed. "I don't think I can."

"It's not for you. It's mine. God knows I earned it today." Quincy eyed her.

Oh hell. She'd been avoiding him, too.

The executive producer perched on the bar stool beside her. "I wish you'd said, 'I don't think I can' four hours ago when you decided to attend a gang brawl." His expression hardened.

"About that..."

"No, I don't care why." He scowled. "We're half a day behind production now. You left the set, not telling anyone anything, and didn't return. And I had to find out from our lead actress what was going on—a woman who was so upset about what could be happening to you and our equally missing security guard that she was unable to actually *act*. Which was fine, since it turns out we were lacking a director at the time."

"I'm so sorry." Alex rubbed her brow. "I acted on instinct."

"I'm aware; I saw the footage. So did half the planet, including the studio bosses, who want to know why their *Shezan* director's hanging out of a tree, filming biker brawls, instead of making the movie they're laying down tens of millions for. It's a good question."

Shit. Alex dredged up her most contrite expression. "I'm sor—"

"Don't bother. Look, this town already has a cop and it isn't you. These locals are more than capable of sorting out their own squabbles without an assist." He shook his head. "Know what? I have no clue what to tell the studio. What do I say? She dropped everything and ran after the cop she's got the hots for?"

"What?" Alex almost choked. "I don't—"

"It doesn't matter. That's what the locals are saying around here. Well, they have a whole bunch of theories, but that's the leading one. It's how it *looks*."

Jesus. Was she so transparent that even some random barflies could see her feelings?

"I don't care either way," Quincy continued, "but I need this to *never* happen again."

Like two biker brawls being live-streamed was on the cards.

"Just focus on nothing else but the film, is all I'm saying," he continued. "We both know how bad the stink surrounding *Shezan* is. We can't afford one more bit of crap about it. This film's more diseased than my ex-wife's boiled cabbage. My second ex-wife," he clarified.

"It has been a bit cursed."

"And that ends here." Quincy tapped the bar hard. He met her eye. "So…here it is: If your commitment to the project is not a hundred percent, I need to know, because I've had it up to my eyeballs with fuckin' *Shezan*. I'll tell the studio that's it. We can't start again with a fresh slate and a new director. The media would flay us alive if we had to get a *fourth* one. It'd be better if they just tossed a match on the gasoline and walked away."

Alex stared at him. She'd only disappeared for *half a day*. A disturbing thought slammed into her. "Wait, is that what you want? Is that what this has all been about?" Alex lowered her voice. "Have you been sabotaging things so I'd look like shit? Your beef is with me and you wanted me gone?

Or did you just want to go home because you're so sick of this movie, and ruining it'd speed things up?"

He hissed in a breath. "Of course not! I'd never screw over my own production. To me wasting money's like taking an acid bath. Can you just commit to the fucking film, so we can all move on?"

Alex eyed him closely. He seemed genuinely aggrieved. With a tired nod, she said, "Of course. So, do we have a revised schedule? Did Leslie work up something while I was gone?"

"Yes. Tomorrow and the next day, it's a sparrow-fart-early start to pick up lost time. Five a.m. That way everyone's ready to shoot the moment the sun hits their pretty faces. Leslie's already put it on the board in Production."

It was freezing, dark, and miserable at five out here. She pitied the actors, who'd need to be up even earlier. "I'll be there. Obviously."

"Good." Quincy picked up his beer and made to move away. "Alice has told the rest of the cast about the pre-dawn starts. They're leaving now if you want to catch a ride back."

"Yeah."

"Hey?" Quincy tilted his head.

"What?" She eyed him morosely.

"Work aside, you okay? You look like shit."

"Thanks," she drawled. "And I'm not the one who decided to single-handedly go and beat up the biker gang believed to be sabotaging our film."

Quincy considered that. "She did do that, didn't she?"

"Mmm. As to what to tell your bosses? I was protecting our assets. I believed our film had been harmed by that gang. Incorrectly, as it turns out. But I wanted to ensure they were held accountable for sabotaging *Shezan*."

"Christ that's bad," he grumbled. "But I'll try and spin that. And I'll leave out the bit about you chasing after the hot cop."

Alex narrowed her eyes. "I don't know what you're talking about. This was *business*."

"That's what I said, too," Quincy said ruefully, "right before I fell for wife number three."

Chapter 16

Fifteen Minutes of Fame

THE DAY AFTER THE BRAWL Sam would rather forget, her phone rang all morning. She let the calls slide through to voicemail as she gingerly worked her way around her kitchen, making toast for an early lunch—or late breakfast. Her phone was full of messages from Sid, Alex, Kev, and Gina, not to mention a bunch of other locals checking she was alive. Probably just didn't want to break in a new cop.

There were also work calls—Police Media regarding dozens of media requests for interviews worldwide, the drug squad responding to Sam's call about what she'd wrung out of Dino, and the Police Commissioner's office. That last call she was putting off returning, well aware that her lowly ass being in her big boss's sights could not end well.

Her phone pinged with a new text message. Great. Te Aroha's bossiest doctor.

That's it, I'm using you as my primary case study in my next paper on unsafe practices in solo-officer stations. What were you thinking?! Never mind, just see me soon. I mean it!! If you don't show I'll have my intern haul you in by the boots. This is not optional.

With a sigh, Sam took another painkiller and reviewed yesterday's events. The moment Dino had ordered his men to attack, everything had flipped upside down. Sam's grand plan to sprint out of there had been stopped cold when her arms were grabbed by Dino's largest bikie. Then Dino had kicked her knee out, dropping her to the ground.

Suddenly, four Rottweilers had rushed at them out of nowhere, a blur of muscle and bared teeth. Finally the hounds of hell lived up to their reputations, turning into snapping, ferocious beasts and lunging at anyone getting too near to Sam.

The Boars hadn't been sure what to do at first, alternating between hitting Sam and fending off the dogs. For every hit they got in on her, sharp teeth were sunk into them in return.

Truthfully, Sam wasn't sure how long she could have held them off, even with her snarling allies. By the time the compound's gate had burst open and Sid and his crew had poured in, Dogsbreath's boots had been driving into Sam's ribs while she tried desperately to protect her head from the others.

The sight of her brother storming to the rescue had been both sweet and terrible. *She* was the police officer. And she'd needed rescuing. By a civilian. Everyone in Ika Whenu knew that now. Hell, tens of thousands of strangers did, too, thanks to Alex Levitin.

She'd seen Alex's missed call and text but didn't trust herself to talk to her right now. That woman was the reason she couldn't leave her home without facing half a dozen staked-out reporters. This morning's earlier walk to get the newspaper in had been especially fun.

"Are you a hero, Senior Constable?" one had shouted as she plucked the paper off her path.

"Tell us how you got the dogs on your side!" called another. "What'd you do?"

"Is it true you took on eighty gang members solo?"

Eighty, was it?

"Why did *Shezan*'s director rush to your aid? Are rumors true that you and Alex Levitin—"

"No comment," Sam had cut in. "And there will *be* no comment, so there's no use you all trampling my garden." She'd glanced at her half-dead plant bed. "Such as it is." That had earned snickers. "Take it up with Police Media." She'd gone back inside, slamming her door.

A trip next door an hour later to fill out paperwork and various reports had involved more media excitement. Her "no comment" had been more snarl than polite that time.

Bloody Alex Levitin.

She pushed aside her half-eaten toast—cold, anyway—and finally faced the call she'd most been dreading. The Police Commissioner.

For ten excruciating minutes, she had her ears pinned back while he explained all the reasons why her being the most visible cop in New Zealand right now was not a good look for the department. Putting civilians in harm's way had been reckless. Unprofessional.

He was somewhat mollified that she'd found the source and drop location of the meth so the drug squad could intercept the next delivery. Sam would not be allowed to attend the stake-out, given her work situation was currently "under review."

A nice way to say she was suspended. An acting replacement to run Ika Whenu station was being sent over from Hamilton.

Yes, she was well aware she'd screwed up big time, and the whole world had witnessed the results. *The whole bloody world.*

After a few more litanies of Sam's failings, the Police Commissioner ended the call.

She flopped back on her bed. *Great.* So, here she was: Ika Whenu's suspended, disgraced, reckless cop. Probably about to be fired after that "work review." No other job prospects. No life outside of Ika Whenu.

What, exactly, was she going to do now?

She closed her eyes, too tired for any of this. She'd deal with it all later.

Chapter 17

Blue Skye

Five in the morning was just as cold and miserable as Alex had expected. It was considerably worse with a hangover and drizzling New Zealand rain. As the minutes slowly ticked by, Alex stared miserably at the ferns, sets, and waterlogged, shivering extras, wishing she could slip away for half an hour to check in on Sam. The longer the silence dragged on, the more Alex's equilibrium suffered. However, Quincy's stern directive to focus, and her own desire to prove she was committed, kept her feet cemented to the set.

Alex pulled up her thick shirt collar to get the icy chill off the back of her neck and adjusted her "lucky" director's hat, a stylish, sharp, straw fedora she'd found at a hip artists' market a decade ago. She could use a bit of luck right now.

"All right, Chloe? Melody?" Alex called, then paused, gazing out at the weather again. So bleak. How apt.

Chloe cleared her throat. "Alex?"

Alex blinked. "Sorry. Yes. On 'Am I strange to you,' I need you to step up close to Melody." She waved them closer to each other. "Get right up inside her space, okay?"

"Aren't they good friends at this point?" Melody asked with a small frown. "Why is she being all challenging?"

Because it's sexual now, too? God, Alex so wasn't in the mood to tap dance around Melody's obliviousness today. Chloe's amused expression wasn't helping.

"They like to tease each other. A little playful one-upmanship, trying to throw the other off a little," Alex said. "Know what I mean?"

Melody's frown deepened. "Who does that? If I tried that shit on my friends, they'd tweet that I'd lost my mind."

"Think of it as trolling for fun. In person," Alex said, fighting to keep the sarcasm at bay.

"Oh." Melody gave a smile. "Right."

"Okay," Alex said in relief. "Chloe will go almost nose to nose with you and you'll be startled and stare at her for a bit, wondering what she's doing. Yes?"

"Sure." Melody sounded bored now.

"Great. Marks, people," Alex called. She retreated to her director's chair, called out a few final instructions, heard the clapper board come down, tried not to wince at how loud it was, and called, "Action."

"You're strange." Chloe said, her voice the low, smoky timbre she used for Shezan. "I don't know any others like you. Do you swim in streams where you come from? Hunt for food? Am I strange to you?" She stepped inside Melody's space and slid her gaze to the other woman's lips. "What do you see when you look at me?"

"I see a woman unlike anyone I've ever met before." Melody's voice hitched. "I can never go back to the life I had, knowing you're out here somewhere. Alone."

Chloe smiled softly. Her hand floated to Melody's arm and squeezed.

An ad-libbed gesture. *Sisterly solidarity*, Alex would tell the suits if they ever asked.

"I'm not alone," Chloe said. "My family is all around me in the forest. Who do you have?"

"I-I have you."

Oh yes. Melody had nailed exactly the right amount of vulnerable and hopeful. The girl was disturbingly good at faking sincerity. *Just hold the intense eye-fucking a little longer…* "And…cut. Excellent job. Get ready for close-ups."

"Um, Alex?" Melody stepped well away from Chloe, then darted a look back at her co-star. "About this…"

"Yes?"

"Why would Jennifer want to stay with her friend in the middle of the forest? No creature comforts? I can't go five minutes without my curling iron. Why would Shezan be worth giving up all that? Especially since she's only known the woman for, like, a few months."

"Because they're *really* good friends." Alex's head pounded. She needed another aspirin. "BFFs. Okay?"

Melody squinted. "But I wouldn't give up all that for my best friend I've known for five years." She paused. "Then again, the bitch did take my boyfriend to a concert last week." Melody shook out her beautiful blonde ringlets. "Hell, never mind. I guess it's why they call it acting."

Alex gave her a tight smile. "Exactly. And you're acting so well. I'll be right back."

She slunk off to find an aspirin. After a long swallow and a tired sigh, Alex grabbed her phone and anxiously looked at the texts. Three from Bess. One from Rowan. Nothing new from Sam. Well. Maybe the hero of the hour was still asleep. It was ridiculously early.

It took most of the day and a shift of location, but eventually Alex finally started to shake off her miserable start.

She glanced up to find Melody watching her.

"So what's the big deal?" Melody asked, wandering over to Alex. "Why's everyone acting so excited about our next scene?"

"Because we have your character's poacher dad to kill off," Alex said. *Which you'd know if you'd bothered to look at the script sides.* "Jennifer has to decide who to save: Shezan or her father."

Melody smiled. "Ooh. I won't even hesitate."

Seriously, this girl has issues.

"On that note, sit, please." Alex indicated the canvas chair beside her.

Melody promptly dropped into the chair and reached for her phone. Apparently conversing without simultaneous texting was a failure of multi-tasking.

"Okay, listen, we're shooting *the* pivotal moment of the movie," Alex told her. "We need Jennifer looking like she'd rather die than lose Shezan in this scene. But you can't make the choice look easy. Show us her conflict of deciding who to save. And then, when it looks like Shezan might be in real trouble when she's fighting the poacher, I want you to show us devastation, then resolve."

"Devastation? Over a friend she's kinda just met?" Melody gave her an odd look.

Alex forced a smile. "But it's intense. They've almost died twice now, and saved each other's lives. It's been a whirlwind journey of emotions and jeopardy and now here they are. Maybe imagine someone in your life you couldn't bear to lose."

Melody's gaze faltered.

"Your...boyfriend, maybe?" Alex tried.

Melody's expression soured. "He really is on my shit list right now."

Alex exhaled. "What about your family?"

She shrugged. "They're so annoying."

"Close friends?"

Nothing.

"Pets?"

Melody's face lit up. She pulled up a photo of an adorable white lapdog with an oversized pink bow in its fur. *Yikes.* "This is my good boy, Valentino."

"Right," Alex said. "Imagine you have to choose between saving Valentino or yourself. That's the conflict we're going for in this scene."

Melody's eyes widened. "That's an evil choice. Okay, I get it."

Alex rose and addressed her team. "Right, everyone, you know the drill. A puma, to be added in later by special effects, will bound toward Shezan and the poacher." She waved at the actors. "Jennifer has an old rifle and only one bullet. If she shoots from the left, the impact will throw the enraged puma away from her father and into Shezan's lap. If she shoots from the right, the opposite occurs. Spoiler alert, the villain gets a lapful of puma."

A murmur spread as everyone prepared for the shot. If this went well, it could make the movie. The drama, the power of the story, everything hung on whether Alex could pull this off. She'd worked on the angles with her crew for days, figuring out how to up the tension

"Hell of a way to die," Jeremy, the poacher, joked, with his trademark creepy grin. "But I've got a face people want to kill, so I get it."

"Nah, mate, you're not so bad," Chloe said.

"You do," Melody said bluntly. "Sucks to be you."

Oh Jesus.

Jeremy merely laughed.

Alex called action and leaned forward as the scene unfolded. At various moments, she shouted where the puma would be. "He's almost right on you now. Jennifer, choose! You can't decide!"

Melody's face transformed into horror and fear, her finger tightening on the gun. At the last second, she leaned to the right and squeezed the trigger.

"Bang!" Alex shouted. "Puma's rolling your way, Poacher. It's hit, it's crazy with pain and it'll maul you with its dying breath."

Jeremy acted terror, screamed, then clapped a hand over his jugular. The bloodied throat effect would be added later.

Melody cried out, half sobbed, then turned away. "I'm sorry."

"And...you're dead!" Alex called to Jeremy.

He stopped moving, his jaw falling slack. *Brilliant.*

Melody was crying. Actual tears. Dear God, she really could act!

Or she really loves her dog.

Chloe crawled to her side. "Don't cry," she whispered.

"I'm not crying for him." Melody's face crumpled. "I'm glad he's gone."

"You are?"

"He was not a good man," Melody said sharply. "Being honest about him hurts. And until I met you..." Her voice became softer. "I didn't understand." Her eyes dropped to Chloe's lips. Chloe swayed closer.

For a half a second, Alex wondered if Chloe would kiss her despite Alex's clear keep-it-subtext instructions. She seemed sorely tempted, her gaze slipping all over Melody's plump lips.

Alex held her breath at the delicious anticipation.

Instead, she kissed Melody's cheek, then stroked it with her thumb. "I'm glad I could be here for you. You'll always be safe with me."

They slid into a soft hug that was sensual and stylized rather than comforting. It was an allegory for sex, something she'd worked out in advance with Chloe. Melody simply mirrored Chloe, as she often did.

Alex called cut and felt strangely unsettled. *Why?* The scene looked gorgeous. Of course it did: Alex had spent hours designing it that way. She'd made her plans with exhaustive detail and figured out with her experts how to use their cinematic tools to maximize tenderness, softness, and beauty, extracting every beat of pathos. But still, she was unsettled.

The words of the scene slithered around her head.

You'll always be safe with me.

The first time she'd read that in the script, it sounded like typical fantasy-hero nonsense. No one was really like that. Everyone looked out for themselves. Alex knew that for a fact. Even with people who cared for her a great deal—family, friends, lovers—there always were limits. She'd never been anyone's top priority, and they always held something back. Human nature, she supposed. Such was life. And then…

Alex drummed her fingers on the wooden armrest as her thoughts galloped. Then Sam had rushed into danger, had risked her life, without a moment's thought. For Alex. It was terrifying. Startling. Humbling. Astonishing. And so unsettling. People just didn't do that. Not people in real life.

Alex glanced over at the sound of clapping. Crew members were helping Jeremy stagger to his feet, and the villain was hamming up his death by jungle cat.

Chloe was trying to readjust her costume, which had torn slightly at one shoulder amid the chaos; Skye assisted, her fingers tugging and pinning like a pro.

Alex studied her costume designer more closely. Her face was pinched, and her lips drawn tightly down. Skye had been in the oddest of moods all day.

After Skye finished, Kiri pulled her aside for a hushed, furtive conversation involving a lot of vigorous head shaking.

Alex cocked her head in surprise. What would a stunt double and a costumer have to argue about? Skye had made the woman's costume weeks ago. It fit. End of story.

Suddenly, Skye jerked her hand away and strode over to Alex. Every muscle in her tiny body turned rigid.

"Skye, no!" Kiri called out.

The cast and crew stopped dead and turned to watch, expressions uneasy.

Dread seeped into Alex's veins. She inhaled slowly and lifted her head. "Yes?"

"I'm so sorry," Skye said. "I'm really very, very sorry. I caused this." Her fingers tangled in front of herself. "And that lovely police officer was almost killed because of me."

Alex stared, speechless.

"Officer Keegan should never have been at the biker's compound," she continued. "And that was my fault."

Alex's blood ran cold. "Skye? What are you talking about?"

"The dummy in the dam. It was an accident. I put it there. I'd been experimenting, testing how certain clothes react to the elements, to see what would be better for costumes. And, well, I got distracted. I can be a little scatterbrained."

Alex stared in dismay.

"I got called away that evening by some minor drama and forgot I'd left it there until the morning, by which time the alarm was raised. Next thing I know, Officer Keegan is bravely rushing off to see the bikers and I feel terrible! I'm so sorry, dear."

"Why didn't you say anything at the time?"

Skye blew out her cheeks. "Well, I felt foolish. And I assumed it wouldn't matter because the investigation would be over in two minutes. No leads, no clues, and so on. I thought, 'I'll just say nothing, go back to work, and that'll be that. Where's the harm?' You know the rest." Skye looked distraught. "Well, except for the fact there is no saboteur."

The lack of reaction from cast and crew was even more disturbing than Skye's bombshell.

Alex noted several guilty faces looking away, including Kevin and Kiri. "And why do you claim we have no saboteur?" she asked, voice chilly. "Because that doesn't explain the other events. The destroyed pond? The stolen lamp?"

"We don't have one," Skye said with certainty.

Kiri shot her a dismayed, warning look.

"We *don't* have a saboteur," Alex repeated slowly. "And what does our stunt double have to say? Kiri, didn't you discover the pond had holes in its lining?"

"Um…" Kiri's hands turned into knots. "Well, I'd been running, like I said. I had my spikes on, because the ground gets so muddy in the morning. A bird swooped me, and I was so startled I ran through the pond. My spikes made a mess of the lining. I apologize for not telling you. The thing is, this is my first major stunt-double job, and I really didn't want to lose this opportunity. Sorry, Alex."

"I...see." Alex gazed at her for a long beat, noting how Kiri's eyes slid to Skye and back.

"Let me guess," Alex turned to a frozen-in-place lighting team, "there'll be some innocent explanation for why one of our most critical lamps went missing?"

Kevin began inching away.

"Kevin? Anything to share?" Alex asked, tone warning.

A clipboard clattered to the ground, and Alex turned to see Alice's white face, her eyes wide.

"Or Alice? Perhaps you have some insights?" Alex eyed her production assistant with annoyance. Surely not Alice, too?

Alice's mouth opened, then shut tight.

"Don't blame Alice," Kevin said, running a hand across the back of his neck. "There was a mix-up. I made a stuff-up with the M90. I read the call sheet wrong, and thought I was supposed to move it to the poacher's tent set so I took it up there."

"Took it? How?"

"I used the forklift." He shrugged. "I just drove it there, same way I always shift our lights. No one saw me. But when I got back, all set to move the next M90 up there, I found out some urgent meeting had been called. Then I find everyone's going nuts and you're in the middle of a big speech about saboteurs and tracking down a new M90, so I figured I'd keep my trap shut and go along with it. I was already on notice over breaking a light. I was pretty sure losing your most expensive flamin' light would get my ass bounced."

Alex regarded him with rising anger. "You thought I'd fire you for a misplaced lamp? Things go missing on sets all the time! Are you seriously telling me you couldn't even admit to a simple mistake? You think I'm some sort of ogre?"

"Um...no... That's not...not all of it." He scratched his ear. "Look, I knew I was on thin ice, and maybe you'd fire me, maybe not, but either way, well, word spreads around here, real fast. And I really didn't want to be known as the dickhead who couldn't even read a call sheet right, on top of the guy who broke a light in week one."

He chewed on his lip and flicked a glance at her. Finally, he dropped his gaze to his boots. "I've made a lot of mistakes in my life, really stupid shit, and I've got a bit of a rep now. I didn't wanna see the look on my family's faces if I screwed up yet again and everyone knew it. I love this job and I wanted to be a success. I just don't want to be *that* guy again. I wanted it to be different this time."

Alex stared at him in disbelief. She turned to Alice. "So why does my loyal assistant look so guilty?"

Kevin darted a look at the quailing woman. "I called her when she was five minutes up the road to find a new light and told her what happened. I suggested I get the original light back and say it was a replacement she'd found. She could then save the day and no one'd get fired or humiliated. Or, specifically, um, me."

"So we don't have Peter Jackson to thank? No wonder he didn't answer my thank-you email," Alex muttered. She glared at her PA. "Alice? Why did you go along with this nonsense?"

"I didn't want Kevin to lose his job or anyone's respect. He's been doing so well." She gave Kevin a sympathetic look. "It didn't cost us anything to pretend I'd found a new light. I really didn't want to throw him under the bus. He's really nice."

Kev reddened, and Alice looked utterly stricken.

"So basically, *everyone* here knew there was no sabotage." Alex scowled.

"I didn't," Melody said, barely looking up from her phone. "And I'd fire all your damn asses."

Murderous looks greeted her proclamation, but Melody shrugged and went right on texting.

Alex took in the shamed faces gathered around her. That not one of them felt she could be trusted with the truth filled her with a profound sense of failure. "You people lied to me, day in, day out. Quincy and I believed we were being targeted. What were you thinking? You're all adults. Someone could have died!"

Abashed looks greeted her. Alex wondered if they truly understood how close their stupid stunts had come to getting Sam killed. Then there was Skye. Of all people, she'd trusted Skye to be the grown-up in the room and to have her back. And all this time, she knew and had said nothing.

"I can't even look at you right now," she continued. "I just don't know what to say. Actually, yes I do. Alice? You're now working with the second-unit director. Kevin? Not only were you dishonest and irresponsible, you manipulated someone else into covering for you. You're fired. Kiri, I'm taking the cost of the destroyed rubber matting out of your paycheck because you lied to me. Be glad I don't deduct the amount it cost us in time lost, too. And Skye?" She shook her head, dismay filling her. "I don't know where to start."

"Alex—" Skye stepped forward.

"Don't...don't even talk to me."

Skye's protests faded out after a glance at her dark face.

Alex stared grimly at her team. "It's not the damage done to the property. It's the damage you've done to my trust. I have no words for that. Now, I need to explain all this to Quincy and get a new assistant."

With that, Alex walked off the set toward the executive producer's trailer, beyond devastated.

How had it come to this?

Chapter 18

Clearing the Air

THE BANGING ON SAM'S DOOR was loud enough to wake the dead. If this was another damned media hound looking for a scoop, she'd toss them in Wairere Falls. She glanced at her watch. Four-thirty in the afternoon? Her eyebrows lifted. *Someone's persistent.* The journalists usually bugged out long before this time of day. Deadlines and all that. Swinging her front door open, ready to offer an icy serve, Sam almost slammed it shut again.

Alex.

No. Too soon.

Sam wasn't ready to explain how being displayed for a baying crowd to judge was the worst thing Alex could have done to her—not just professionally but personally. Explaining any of her reasons would involve emotional expenditure Sam didn't have in her right now.

Still…did the woman have to look that hangdog?

Sam sighed and widened the door. "Come in."

Silence fell after she'd entered.

Alex paced the lounge, looking more unsettled than Sam had ever seen her. She didn't even seem to notice the threadbare minimalism and fifties "dump chic" Sam had once been so certain would send her running for the hills.

"Drink?" Sam asked. "I have…" She screwed up her face, trying to remember. It'd been a few weeks since she'd found time to properly shop. "Beer, coffee, and water."

"Beer." Alex stopped. "No, wait, not beer. That'll bypass my censor button, and I might say something I can't take back and I know he's family, so I don't want that, but damn it, Sam!"

Family? She frowned. "What's Kev done now?"

"How'd you know I meant him?"

"It's always him. He attracts trouble like a magnet. So, what's he done?"

Alex started pacing. "Lied. They all did."

"All? All who?"

"Skye, Kev, and Kiri."

"I don't follow." Sam drew Alex over to her worn green couch.

"The sabotage," Alex said, sitting. "They all knew who did it because *they* did it. You were right. It was an inside job."

"What?" Sam dropped heavily beside her. "I'm sorry, *what*?"

Alex filled her in on the events, including Skye's out-of-character confession, and how crushed Alex felt by it. "And then I fired Kev," she finished. Her gaze flicked up to Sam. "I had no choice."

Disappointment kicked Sam in the stomach. She'd really hoped this job had changed him.

"But for me, he's not the worst of it," Alex continued. "It's Skye I'm most hurt by. I was so fond of her. We'd become so close, and I can't even look at her now."

Sam's mind tried to make sense of this. "So there's no saboteur?"

"No. Just people being self-centered and inconsiderate."

"I'm so sorry."

"Me, too." Alex slumped. "Let's not talk about them anymore. It's breaking my heart." She jumped back to her feet and began to pace again. Finally, she stopped in front of Sam's colorful display of postcards and leaned in. Intrigue crossed her face. "Who sent you these?"

"The escapees."

Alex turned. "What?"

"It's an in-joke. When people leave Ika Whenu, they send me a postcard of where they are. It started with a few friends I had in school doing it because they knew I dreamed of travelling. Then it sort of caught on and became a tradition. I don't ask them to, but anyone who leaves town does it." Sam joined her. She tapped a postcard from Singapore showing a city lit up by fireworks. "Peta works at a media company over there now." Sam unpinned it and turned it over.

Kia ora to my fave cop! Check out the view from my office window. Wish you could see it too. Cheers! Peta. xx

Alex's eyes fell to the card from Pfeiffer Beach. "This one's well worn. Do you like it best?" She studied it more closely. "Gorgeous beach."

Sam shrugged. "It is. That card's from the ex I was with when I was stationed in Auckland. We broke up when I moved back home." Sam's gaze trailed the beautiful sands of the beach, heart lifting, as it always did, at the sight of it.

"May I?" Alex asked, fingers trailing the card.

Sam waved for her to go right ahead.

Alex picked it up and read.

See where I am? Shame you're not here because that odd little town and family of yours come first. If you ever change your mind, look me up. N.

"Geez. What a bitch."

Sam laughed at how aggrieved she sounded. "Yeah, well, she was hurt I had to choose Ika Whenu over her. That was years ago. I keep her postcard now because I love the photo, not the sender. And Nicole was right about one thing: I am tied here in a way I can never be free of."

Silence fell between them. "Never?" Alex finally asked. "You're never leaving here, *ever*?"

"It's fine. I can live vicariously through other people's adventures. Use my imagination for what's out there. Maybe it's easier this way. Besides, I don't need to go anywhere or do anything to feel complete."

"I get it," Alex said quietly. "It hurts to watch people leave and never come back. It's easier to just not put yourself in that position. To not get too invested in them or your old dreams."

So starkly put. Sam blinked, unsure of how to deny it. "No, I just mean it's not for everyone. The great big dreams: Exotic places. Fancy jobs. Long-haul relationships. Whatever. I'm fine."

"You do know that a *little* investment in dreams is okay, too, right?" Alex said. "Not everything is about huge life goals. You're allowed to be happy for as long or as short as you want to be. Where's the harm in the short-term dream, if everyone goes into things eyes wide open?" Her gaze was soft, intense, and…lingering.

Oh.

"What are you…?" Sam stopped uncertainly. Was she reading the undercurrent right? "Are you asking for a fling or something?"

Alex's expression became rueful. "Is 'or something' an okay answer? Because Sam, there's something here between us. Something powerful. I think you feel it, too. Because when I'm with you, I feel a pull I never expected to. Is it just me? That connection? I'd like to explore that…if you do, too? Even knowing how it will end?" Alex's hopeful look burned into her.

How it will end. Sam inhaled and fixed her gaze on the Pfeiffer Beach postcard, drawing her finger across the glossy surface. "It's a bit pointless, though, isn't it?"

"The point is what we make of it."

There is that. Sam glanced up to find Alex standing much closer, her eyes longing. It'd be so easy… *Oh, hell.* Sam kissed her.

Alex's lips were hot, exploring, and teasing under hers. Her fingers curled into Sam's hair, tugging her down, closer.

Sam's stomach fluttered. Then came the burn of arousal. *How long has it been?*

When they finally pulled apart, Alex's eyes were bright, and her lips swollen and tempting.

"I feel it, too," Sam admitted. "But this is still pointless." She stared at those lips, craving more of that rush. "You'll leave soon."

"So tell me to stop and I will." Reaching for Sam's hand, Alex pulled her fingers toward her chest. "See how fast my heart's racing? That's for you. You're an incredible woman. I want more of you; so much more. Or…do you want to tell me to stop?"

The rapid patter beneath her fingertips was as arousing as the touch of Alex's lips had been. Sam imagined sliding her hand under Alex's shirt, just inside the cup of her bra, to feel the softness of her breast. She shivered at the thought of other places that would be just as soft. What did Alex's inner thigh feel like? How might it taste under her tongue?

"Sam?"

"I don't want to tell you to stop."

"Then don't." Alex kissed her this time.

It was like fire coursing through Sam's nerve endings. All consuming.

Too soon.

Sam had to slow things down while she still could. She pulled away, with regret. "I don't want you to stop but I think we need to."

"Oh." Embarrassment edged Alex's face. "Have I read this wrong?" she asked. "Are you seeing someone?"

"No. I think you're special, Alex. It's only right I take you on a date first. Get to know you a little better than the crazy movie woman who almost ran me over. You deserve more than just us falling into bed in the heat of the moment. Both of us are worth more than that."

"Old-fashioned, huh?" Alex smiled. "All right. I'd like that."

"How are you with dawn starts?"

"I've had quite a few lately for work. Although thankfully they're over for now."

"Think you can face one more? How about coming by here at dawn tomorrow? I want to show you who I am and what I do. All part of the Sam Keegan experience. There'll be coffee. And snacks. Plus cuddles and wet noses."

Alex snorted. "Why do I think this isn't what it sounds?"

"You'd be right." Sam grinned.

"All right. I'm intrigued. Just as long as I'm on set by eight. Meantime..." Alex's mouth twitched up. "Do you mind if I borrow your lips for a little while until then?"

"Does that line ever work?" Sam's eyebrows lifted.

"I wouldn't know. First time I've tried it. You tell me." Alex's eyes sparkled with mischief.

"Come here." Sam leaned in. "Just this once I'll reward a tragic line. Only because you're cute and a little bossy." She gathered Alex in her arms and kissed her the way she'd wanted to for far too long.

The sigh that followed was soft and approving, and Sam had absolutely no idea whose it was.

When they pulled apart this time, Alex's eyes were sad.

"Hey," Sam whispered. "What is it?"

"I'm wondering if you and Quincy are now my only friends left in New Zealand. And given I know Quincy can be a bit of a prick, that's kind of tragic, isn't it?"

"I'm sure that's not true. Well, it is about Quincy," Sam teased. "But the part about having no friends. I thought you and Skye were close? Even after today, surely you still…"

"I'm not so sure. She's acting so out of character. I'm starting to wonder if I ever really knew her if she could do that."

"I feel the same way about Kiri." Sam frowned. Kiri had been a loyal ally since Sam had stopped a bully giving her trouble back in school. She'd always thought of Kiri as one of the good ones. "I don't understand any of this. Kiri's solid. Decent. Reliable. And one thing she's never done is lie. Not on something big. It's just not her."

"It is now."

This didn't feel right. A grown woman not owning up to something as silly as a minor set accident? So she'd run through a pond, not attacked it with… Sam stopped and mentally rewound. "Hey, do you remember Kiri's shoes the day the pond was destroyed?"

"No."

"They were clean and white. They'd be muddy if she'd run through the pond." Sam pondered the woman's story for a moment. "How big do you think running spikes are?"

"No idea."

"They're like needles compared to the chunky holes I saw in the lining."

"Kiri was lying?" Alex started. "Well, I mean, again?"

"Yes. Or covering up for someone else."

"Is everyone lying? Skye, too?"

"Maybe."

"Skye claimed the dummy slipped her mind," Alex said slowly. "But what's weird about that is she's actually so sharp. She's eccentric, yes, but not scatterbrained. Yet she would simply forget some big experiment on the effects of water on costumes?"

Sam looked at her thoughtfully. "When I pulled the dummy ashore, it weighed a ton; far more than those cheap mannequins in stores."

"Costume designers do like the best."

"I didn't think of it till now, because at the time it was waterlogged. But even dry, how could a featherweight like Skye have dragged that dummy anywhere? Let alone all the way to the dam? It weighs more than she does."

"Then who did?" Alex blew out a frustrated breath. "Are they all protecting the same person? Is Kev covering up for them, too?"

Sam mulled that over. "Kev doesn't do that, though. I love him, but that's his flaw. He's selfish. He always points the finger at someone else to save his own hide."

"Then what's going on?"

Sam glanced at her watch. "When everyone hits the pub for dinner, we'll confront them. We'll do it all together, so no one can weasel their way around anything."

"It's like a Miss Marple mystery." Alex half smiled. "Just my luck: I come to New Zealand to make the world's worst movie and get caught up in a weird, real-life sabotage plot. At least I get a cute cop love interest." She winked and nudged her. "Blonde, too. You'd be studio approved."

Sam snorted. "I'm just going to assume that was a compliment."

"Good move," Alex said, now smiling fully. "So tonight… Just like Miss Marple we do the big denouement. Everyone sitting in the parlor while we point fingers."

"I'm not really into Agatha Christie."

"How can a cop not dig a good whodunit?" Alex looked askance.

"I don't really have a huge amount of spare time, especially since the meth hit. Aside from riding Tiger, I'm all about work. This town owns my ass."

At Alex's puzzled gaze, she explained: "It's a one-cop-town thing. Even your days off and after-hours are seen as fair game."

"You mean when there're emergencies?"

"No, not just emergencies. It does make for long days. Of course, the big downside is sometimes I *can't* unwind; I'm always primed for the phone to ring. I can't really get caught up in a movie or a book anymore, because I'm always low-level tense."

"Seriously? That's awful."

"You get used to it. That's life."

"Have you always worked here? I mean straight out of the police academy?"

"No. I spent a few years posted in Auckland before I came home."

"What was working in Auckland like?"

"Good." Sam smiled. "Busy, lots of variety, and I got left to my own devices on my weekends."

"So why come home?"

The million-dollar question. She debated how much to answer. "For family. Sid heard Kev was sniffing around the bikie gangs, doing odd jobs for them. That's how they lure in new members. Give young men a bit of splash cash for minor work, make them feel special, part of a new family, give them respect, and from then on it's a slippery slope, sucking them in deep."

"Oh hell."

"No one could convince Kev to leave his shitty new friends. He was on his way to being a career crim, just like them. Getting caught would mean serious jail time…unless someone was around full-time to prevent that happening."

"Let me guess who."

"Yeah. Gina begged me to apply for the local station. Ika Whenu's officer had just retired and we knew the bikies wouldn't want a member who had a police relative breathing down their necks."

"So it was the perfect solution," Alex murmured. "On paper, at least."

"Right. How could I say no to the woman who took me into her home, treated me like her own child after my mother was…" She ground out the next word: "Committed." Sam stared at her hands. "She'd hear voices, sometimes, that told her she was being followed and she'd hide. One night I found Mum behind Gina's pub, looking like she'd crawled there. Knees and hands were all dirty and bloodied. It was winter, she was naked and shivering, but nothing I could do would convince her to move. Gina found us. She fed us, clothed Mum, then took me to one side and told me I'd done really well but that this was too much for a kid to have to handle. They took Mum away the next day. Gina started the process to become my foster mother."

Sam braced herself for the reaction. There was a reason she avoided discussing this. She hated pity. Sometimes she was met with anger, as though her mother had deliberately done this to her. No, she'd tried so hard to get better, but drugs hadn't helped; nothing had. It wasn't her fault.

"Takes real guts to keep getting back up after life knocks you down."

Sam darted a look at Alex. The knot in Sam's stomach eased a little. No judgment there. "Maybe. Or maybe I'm just stubborn. Or too stupid to quit."

"Just take the compliment." Alex's eyes crinkled.

"No." Sam was unable to stop her own smile.

"Do you still see your mother?"

"She's passed away now."

"What about your dad?"

"Don't remember him. Don't know if he's dead or alive and I never cared enough to find out."

"I'm sorry." Alex regarded her. "And this is why you've given everything to your foster family."

"It's the least I could do. They've never given me a cause to question my loyalty. At least, not until today." Her expression fell again. "Damn it, Kev."

Chapter 19

Curiouser and Curiouser

THE *SHEZAN* CROWD WERE WELL into their meals by the time Alex entered Te Wharariki Hotel, with Sam hard on her heels.

Alex approached the crew table, noting the furtive looks as her sharp gaze went from eye to eye. Skye looked downright despondent.

"People." Alex cleared her throat. The chatter at the tables died down. Eyes swung her way. "We need to resolve some things."

Quincy peered at her questioningly, silently asking what was happening and whether she needed his support. She gave him a minute head shake.

"It's come to my attention you all told me a pack of lies today." Alex folded her arms. "Now I'd like to know what the truth is. And so help me if you lie to my face again, I'm tempted to fire the lot of you. Most of all, I'd like to know why you'd do this to me and our movie. I thought you believed in *Shezan* the way I do. Why would you conspire to hurt it? Hurt us?" She paused and glanced at Skye. "Hurt me?"

Skye's gaze dropped to the table. Her fingers skidded restlessly up and down the stem of her glass.

"Let's start with the punctured pool. Kiri? What really happened? Your sneakers weren't muddied, and the puncture holes were too large to be caused by shoe spikes."

"I'm so sorry. I'm so, so… I never wanted to hurt you, and especially not Sam."

Sam moved closer to her. "What does this have to do with me?"

Kiri darted a look at the others then shook her head. "I can't say."

"Can't or won't?"

"Both."

Alex's lips thinned. She turned to Skye. "You aren't forgetful. And there's no way you could carry that dummy to the dam in the first place."

Skye dipped her head. "You're right, I didn't."

"Then how did it get there?"

"I'm devastated you're hurt by this," Skye said. "Please believe that. It was never my intention. But this story is not for me to tell."

"You're covering up for someone?" Alex pressed her. "Who?" She glanced around. "You barely know these people!"

"That's not correct." Skye folded her hands on the table.

Maddening answer. Alex stared back at her in confusion.

"Kev," Sam cut in, stepping forward, "did you accidentally move the lamp to the wrong place or did something else happen? Was someone else involved?"

"Um, Sam…" Kev began.

"Right now it's Senior Constable Keegan. I'm asking as a police officer. Who is lying?"

Eyes shifted from person to person. Silence.

Alex's tensed shoulders began to ache from bunching up.

"Jesus Christ," Melody piped up, "this is one bat-shit-crazy set. To think I thought it'd be boring out here in Outer Buttfuck."

"Melody," Alex snapped, "if you're not involved in this conspiracy, I strongly urge you to keep your mouth shut. And while you're at it, please resist denigrating the home of many of your colleagues."

Melody rolled her eyes and mimed zipping her lips.

"Are you really going to fire everyone? Even those not involved?" Chloe asked quietly. "Because if you do, *Shezan* will be seen as an even bigger joke than it was."

Alex folded her arms. Of course the star, in her first leading role, would have the most to lose. But right at this moment, Alex was starting to see the appeal of Quincy's threat to throw gasoline on the whole thing and walk away as it burned.

"It's more than a little tempting right now."

"Is what happened really that big a deal?" Sid piped up. "I mean, if you break it down, a couple of delays aren't huge, are they? How much time did you even lose?"

Heads nodded nervously.

"You're really not going to tell me what's going on?" Sam's gaze darted around the group before landing on her youngest brother. "Do you really respect me so little?"

"It's not that," Kev said, eyes solemn. "I promise it ain't. But you'd seriously fucking hate us for telling you the truth right now. Maybe later? Somewhere less public, when you're less...um...scary?"

When the others backed him up with adamant nods, Sam gave them all a look of disgust.

Alex took in Skye's face. It was paler, and the woman was peering at her half-eaten plate of fish. "You, too, Skye?" Hurt filled her as she asked, "You really won't tell me?"

"It's not my place to." Skye met her eye. "Not without the consent of all concerned." Her determined expression didn't alter one bit. "And Kevin is quite right, dear. Definitely not now, not here."

Alex gaze shifted from face to face. "This is disrespectful on a level I've never seen on any set. I'm appalled at everyone involved." She stared at Skye. "All of you."

"Alexandra, dear, please remember what I said the day at the dam. Motives are everything."

"And what does that mean?" Alex asked.

Skye merely offered a tiny, rueful smile. "A question for another day."

Chapter 20

My Kind of Crazy

ALEX COULD COUNT ON ONE hand the number of times she'd been willingly up before dawn. Work didn't count, of course. But this was anything but work. It was a chance to see Sam in her natural environment, so yes, she was game, even if she was still waking up.

Yawning, she climbed out of her car in front of Sam's worn timber house next door to the police station. She smoothed the wrinkles out of her jeans and flannel shirt, suddenly self-conscious that she was kitted out like a lesbian cliché. Alex glanced up at a small whuffing sound and broke into a smile.

Senior Constable Sam Keegan, resplendent in black motorcycle leathers, was sitting on the top step of her home's two concrete steps, playing with a small dog. The animal was in her lap, leaning up to lick her face while Sam scratched it behind the ears, eyes filled with affection. The yellow and white dog seemed very old, with graying ends to its coarse fur.

Sleek, powerful Sam Keegan turned to mush by a tiny dog? Alex bit back a laugh.

"Hey." Alex ambled over. "I see where the cuddling and wet noses component of our date comes in."

"Yep." Sam grinned. "Meet Bruce. He'd normally be riding shotgun with us today, but while I'm suspended, my replacement got my patrol car." She did not look pleased at this development.

"We could take my hire car." Alex jerked a thumb over her shoulder at the vehicle. "Although, given my track record, you should probably drive."

"I had a better idea. Something a bit more fun." With a final scratch of Bruce's head, she rose and picked up the pair of motorcycle helmets beside her. "Wanna come for a ride?" she asked. Her smile turned roguish. "I promise I'll be safe. No wheelies or anything."

Alex smiled. "Sure." She glanced at the dog who had bounded over to sniff her ankles. "Sorry, Bruce, I'm gonna steal your ride."

Sam handed her a helmet, then slung a small backpack over her shoulder. She led Alex around the side of her home, to a small garage.

"So you have a dog?" Alex asked. "I hadn't realized."

"Nah, he's my neighbor's. Actually, Bruce sort of comes with the station. The previous officer owned him and took Bruce out every day. When he retired, he and his wife moved next door on the other side of the station to me, which gives Bruce easy access to plague the resident officer in charge." Her smile was warm. "Even though the retired officer's passed away now, Bruce still expects his morning rounds regardless."

"Wait, how old is he?"

"Twenty-two now. Quite a legend around here. Jack Russell terriers usually live to about sixteen."

"Must be all this clean New Zealand air and good living," Alex teased. "Not to mention getting to go for drives in the countryside every day with the cute local cop."

"Cute, huh?" Sam lifted the door to her garage and wheeled out her motorcycle. "Well, between me and Mrs. Fenley, he's probably the most pampered pooch going, so that's definitely a factor. He's just always happy. Who wouldn't want to live forever if they're that happy?"

"Can't argue with that."

Sam poked her backpack into a small storage box at the rear of the motorcycle and settled on her seat.

Alex put the open-faced helmet on as Sam did the same.

"Done this before?" Sam asked.

"Once or twice. I have a motorbike at home."

Sam regarded her, then her lips curled in amusement. "I just can't picture you streaking along on the back of a beast." She slid onto her bike.

"Well, not exactly streaking—more like I cruise along at a sensible pace on this sweet little Honda Unicorn 160CC. But it's not exactly bat-out-of-hell transportation like yours."

"A...Unicorn?" Sam squinted at her in disbelief. "Never heard of it. And trust me, that's weird—about as weird as its name."

"I bought it from an ex-Bollywood producer who'd had it shipped over from India. Top speed isn't too hot. But it's a gorgeous pearl color and it does the job—helping me avoid insane traffic jams on the I-405, and letting me tell people I ride a Unicorn." Alex laughed.

Sam chuckled. "Oh well, I suppose sometimes good things come in tiny, underpowered packages." She grinned and patted the seat behind her. "Okay, climb on."

Alex did so, curling her arms around Sam's waist.

Sam's hand drifted to where Alex's clasped her stomach, and she rested it there for a few moments before pulling black gloves from her pocket and sliding them on. That simple gesture, checking Alex was okay, warmed her.

"Where are we going?" Alex finally thought to ask.

"Rounds. All up it'll take about forty minutes. Then we get breakfast with a view. Something you won't have seen before."

Alex smiled into Sam's back. She couldn't wait.

The Wild Boars' compound was a mess. Sam stared at the front gate, which had been completely flattened. That had happened after she'd left. Had it been police or a rival gang picking through the entrails?

Alex's hands tightened at her waist.

Sam looked down in apprehension. "You okay?"

"I just never thought I'd have to clap eyes on this place again." Alex slowly retracted her arms and gazed around. "I'm fine, though."

Sam slid off her bike and met Alex's concerned look with her own. "Sorry we're here. This won't take a minute. I just want to do a health check on the dogs. I'm not sure if they got impounded after I left, or if they escaped in the chaos later, and I'm worried they've been forgotten. Stay here if you want. There won't be any trouble, though—all the Boars are now in the remand center, awaiting trial." She took out her backpack. She'd packed meat for the hounds just in case.

Alex slid off and shot her a determined look. "I'm coming, too."

The clubhouse seemed weathered, shabby, and angry, like an old man left forgotten in the dust. Sam headed past it to the large, rusting cage behind the work shed. Fur and dog droppings caked it, but it sat empty now. Sam wrinkled her nose. The smell was as potent as ever. Would it have killed the Boars to wash the cage once in a while?

"I'll just try the clubhouse. See if anyone's around." Sam headed back to the front, Alex on her heels.

A grizzled, stooped man flung the front door open before she'd even reached it.

Sam stared up at the enraged face of Dino's abusive old man. He was gray now, and not just his hair; all of him seemed more worn out and leathery. Even his traditional Maori facial tattoos seemed withered. His eyes filled with resentment at the sight of her.

"You? Back to piss on my boy's shit?"

Strange how loyal he was to a son he so often tortured. "Where are they?" Sam asked.

"All arrested. Course, that's bullshit. Boars didn't start a damned thing! They were just defending themselves from trespassin' pigs."

"Defending themselves by attacking a lone police officer," Sam argued. "It's all caught on video. No wonder the judge refused them all bail."

He glared. "All your asshole cop mates tore the place apart later. Didn't find nothin'. Fuckin' sorry to disappoint." Hatred dripped from his voice. The man squinted, and the tattoos around his chin, cheeks, and eyes transformed into a patchwork of disconnected scribbles.

Sam folded her arms. "I came about the dogs. Where are they?"

"Pound has 'em. They're gonna be put down for being people eaters." He spat on the ground. "Be nice if they actually *were* people eaters, hey? What they are is fuckin' useless, seein' you're still alive." He paused. "But since you're here, Dogsbreath's woman told me to pass on a message if you came by."

"What message?"

"Dino wants to see you. I got no fuckin' clue why. Now clear off. You've done enough damage." He went back inside the clubhouse and slammed the door.

Sam headed back to her bike. What the hell did Dino want with her? Not that it mattered; she couldn't be talking to him. She'd be a witness in the case against him and the rest of the Boars. She should just steer clear. No point getting her ass in any deeper trouble.

On the other hand, if it wasn't about the trial, if it was about something else... She frowned. Not the drug drop, surely? He knew she'd figured out the who and where of Ika Whenu's meth supplies now. If Dino had warned the Hornets that the cops knew...if the next drop on Tuesday night was a set-up... Shit, it could put an entire police team in danger.

Well, if that was what this was about, it made Dino a confidential informant, or near enough. Hell, she could always argue that line if meeting him blew up in her face later.

She couldn't see Dino today; she had a lengthy meeting scheduled with two officers from the NZ Police Professional Conduct Group who were investigating her boss and his gambling habits, and a backgrounding with the drug squad on the meth problem. But tomorrow morning, sure...

"What's up?" Alex asked as she slipped onto the bike behind Sam. Her hands settled against Sam's stomach once more.

"Just figuring out some logistics."

"About Dino? You're going to see him?"

Sam wondered if Alex would try to talk her out of it. "Why?" She twisted around to meet her eye.

"I'm sure you'll be fine." Alex gave her an even look. "I saw him. He's pathetic. You can take him."

Sam relaxed immediately. "Yes, I think I can handle one whipped bikie boss in a locked remand center." She leaned forward, about to start her bike. "Okay, the annoying component of our morning's over. Let's go see a man about a cow, a woman about a bread delivery, and Mother Nature about a view."

"Um, what...?"

"You'll see." Sam grinned. "Hang on."

Alex gazed in wonder around the clearing Sam had brought them to. Surrounding them were giant tree ferns, enormous trees caked in vivid green moss that seemed hundreds of years old. Old logs were peppered with tiny bright-orange mushrooms springing from their decaying forms. The smell was delicious—sweet, peaty, rich. This was ancient earth, like the beginning of time.

"Wow," Alex whispered. "What *is* this?"

"It's a croissant, baked fresh by Dutch. Don't you get these in LA?"

"Not that." Alex laughed at the flaky pastry on the crumpled paper bag in front of her. "Although it is good. I mean *this*. I half expect a dinosaur to peek out of the foliage."

Sam's eyes smiled, even though her lips didn't move. "It's New Zealand. It rains a lot. Stuff grows wild. And it's protected by the government. So there are hidden places all over where nature wins. This particular spot? I'm the only one who knows about it."

"I love it." Alex lay back on their picnic rug. "There's nothing like this anywhere where I live."

"Then how do you relax?"

"Parties with friends mostly."

"The Shakespeare crowd." Sam sounded amused. "But nothing back to nature?"

"Actually, I did use to connect with the great outdoors regularly. I used to love stargazing. I called it inspecting the universe one star at a time. Haven't done it in a while, though."

"No?

"I used to do it at my best friend, Bess's, place," Alex said. "She has this amazing house high on a hill overlooking LA. Sometimes we got lucky and there'd be a break in the clouds and smog. We used to lie on deckchairs and stare up at the skies."

"Sounds beautiful."

"It really was." Alex took a bite of cheese and moaned in appreciation. "So good."

"Of course it is. It's from Matamata Dairy. They make the world's best cheese," Sam said with absolute certainty.

"Sometimes you're so fiercely parochial. Such a good Kiwi," Alex teased, finishing off the slice.

"Can't help it. Lots to be proud of." Sam grinned. "Wet Wipe?" She offered Alex a moist tissue.

Alex took it and wiped her hands. "You're like a perfect Girl Scout. So organized."

"It's my training. New Zealand's finest are prepared for everything."

"You'd make a good director with that attitude."

"Somehow, I don't think so. Too many divas and douches involved. Much easier when you can just arrest the people annoying you." She grinned, then wiped her hands meticulously before expertly packing away the rubbish. Her little pile was so neat, it was mesmerizing. Sam looked up when she was done. "So...stargazing? Why'd you stop?"

"Well, at the time, Bess and I were dating, so it was wonderful sharing it with my girlfriend. But when we broke up, I stopped."

"You miss it?"

"I hadn't realized I had, but yeah." Alex plucked at a few grapes. "I've been remiss. I've looked up after a long day's shooting out here and my God, it's so special. Amazing. So little light pollution. The stars are like glitter."

"I meant dating Bess," Sam said quietly.

"She's just a good friend now."

"Why did you break up?"

"Scheduling conflicts. Distance. Location shoots. I was never around."

"And the real reason? Because scheduling conflicts don't make someone sound as sad as you just did. It's okay," she added gently. "We all have that one ex who sticks with us longer than others."

"The real reason then." Alex huffed, hating admitting it. "She was in love with someone else."

"She cheated on you?" Sam's face tightened. "I hate that."

"No! God no, she'd never. It was unrequited. She was stuck on a straight woman for years and desperately trying not to be."

Sam winced. "That'd be the worst."

"Yeah." Alex squared her jaw. "I was completely into her, but Bess was always holding back. I doubt she even realized she was doing it. *I* felt it, though. I ended things because it was just too hard on me." Alex blew out a breath. "Cue the tissues, chocolate, and white lies so she never knew how much she broke my heart. But that was fifteen years ago; we're great friends now. And here I am: better, stronger, wiser."

"Simple as that." Sam gave her a knowing look.

"Is anything? But I did power through three movies back to back to keep my mind off it. My career boomed. Choice, hey?" Alex laid on her worst Kiwi accent.

Sam laughed, and her gaze became soft. "Just so you know, when I'm with someone, she's all I think about. In case you're worried I play the field or anything else. I don't do that. My focus is absolute."

Alex paused. Uncanny how Sam had tapped into her biggest fear: not being enough. She thought about the beautiful woman beside her. Sam's loyalty. *You'll always be safe with me.* "I can see that about you," she said quietly. "I appreciate that."

"I appreciate you." Sam's eyes were warm. "And I confess I'm glad you landed in my corner of New Zealand."

"Even though I almost ran you over?"

"Okay, maybe after that bit."

"What about when I thrashed you at darts, tore strips off you in the pub in front of everyone, had you up at dawn *twice* to investigate set sabotage, including that time you were forced to strip..."

Sam lifted her hands in defeat. "Okay, that does sound kind of crazy. Maybe *you're* crazy."

"Who, me?"

"Yes. But I think you're my kind of crazy."

They gazed at each other.

For the longest moment, Alex was unable to stop staring. Those eyes were so kind, so interested. Sam's lips, just slightly parted, ticked into a soft smile at the corners. Just a little. Her hair, blonde, shoulder-length, and sculpted, suiting those perfect cheek bones. *Gorgeous.* Alex's cheeks filled with heat. "I'm enjoying our date."

"I'm pretty glad, since this is who I am," Sam murmured. She whisked a stray hair out of Alex's eyes. "So who are you?"

"That's a complicated question. It's something I can't easily share—how I see the world. There's a movie in my eye and it plays all around me, all the time, and I'm constantly working out the shots, the angles."

"I can see why you became a director. But why move to LA?"

"London's not the epicenter of filmmaking. Besides, all my closest drama school friends left for Hollywood, so it was a pretty easy decision to go with them."

"And you've always wanted to be a director?"

"Yes. No question. What about you? Was law enforcement always for you?"

"Seemed the best fit. Does that sound strange, always wanting to be a cop?"

"It sounds like you. Protective."

Sam snorted. "Or maybe I couldn't think of anything better. Something that let me work outdoors a lot, do what's right, and I'm largely left alone by people." At Alex's flicker of concern, she added, "I get it. No one likes to hang out with the cop."

"You like that?" Alex asked, picking up something in her voice. "Being the outsider?"

"It suits me. Most of the time."

Alex leaned on her elbow and studied Sam. "I think I know your type. You like to be invited to the party even if you say no often."

"Doesn't everyone?"

"Maybe." Alex smiled. "What music do you like?"

"Sid's." She grinned. "My brother whips his guitar out at the pub every Sunday afternoon and has the smoothest voice. He does traditional Maori songs. And the Eagles."

"Really? I'd love to hear him some time."

"I'm surprised Chloe didn't tell you all about it. She's in there, every Sunday, front row, looking like she wants to fling him down and have her way with him on the spot."

"He *still* hasn't noticed?"

"He thinks she's just really friendly."

"God. Someone should just tell him. But where would be the fun in that?" Alex laughed. "So do you like anything other than Sid's greatest hits?"

"I appreciate world music, all kinds. New Zealand does have the most beautiful songs of anywhere, of course." Sam's eyes twinkled at her shameless parochialism. "Ever hear *Hine e Hine*?"

"No."

"Most spine-tingling lullaby ever—a Maori princess wrote it a hundred years ago. But I love traditional stuff from all over the place. Some of my music is more out there than others."

"How 'out there' are we talking?" Alex asked curiously.

"I'll play you some." She pulled out her phone, flicked through the menu, and hit *play*.

A rich, gentle, almost wailing female voice started, with other women's voices layering it, like leaves on the wind. It was so wistful and aching that Alex shivered and closed her eyes. "Play it again?" she asked when it ended.

Sam did.

"God. Beautiful," Alex exhaled when it finished. "You know, I could see this in my movie, at the start when we do all the wide, sweeping scenery shots. What is it?"

"It's a modern take on a traditional style of music from Bulgaria. The song's *Malka Moma—Little Girl*."

"Bulgaria? That's...unusual."

"Yeah, well. I can do unexpected sometimes. Sid teases the hell out of me for my 'cat-killing music.' Don't tell anyone I love this stuff, okay? Years ago I spread the word I like pub rock."

"You and your tough cred," Alex teased. "You know, you don't have to be anything but you with me."

Sam didn't really smile, but she relaxed. That was way better than any smile.

Alex drew in a breath and appreciated all over again the peaty smell. She'd miss this. "Do you come out here often?"

"Not so much these days. Work's been busy since all the meth hit town. But before that, whenever I was climbing the walls to get out of town, I'd often ride out here." She regarded Alex. "You're the first person I've ever brought here. But I thought maybe you'd see it the same way I do."

"What do you see?"

Sam hesitated. "This might sound as crazy as my music."

"Tell me."

"The essence of life." Sam's fingertips touched the soft, springy moss on a log. "Like a living, breathing thing—Earth...exhaling."

"I love that. You know, I could see my Amazons running through here. It's got that forgotten-by-time, ancient warrior feel. So, I was right all along then. You *are* an Amazon."

Sam rolled her eyes, which sparkled. "No need for insults."

"I meant it in the best sense. My Amazons are powerful huntresses now."

"I know." Sam reached for her orange juice bottle. Condensation ran down the glass, and she flicked a finger through it idly. "I've been hearing about all the changes. Your film sounds nothing like it was. I might have to watch the bloody thing now."

"How times change," Alex teased. "I'll make sure to invite you to the world premiere. It'll be in Te Aroha—closest cinema to Ika Whenu we could find."

"Count me in." Sam smiled but it faded. "That'll be long after you've finished filming and gone home."

"Yes."

"I wonder what will have happened between now and then." For the briefest second, disappointment flitted across her face.

"Ah." Alex inched closer. "Sam, you're thinking about things that haven't even happened yet." She took Sam's hand, trailing a thumb over the back of it gently. "You're stressing about us parting ways and feeling let down before we've even gotten together."

Sam took a deep breath. "It's not unreasonable."

"So…what about Bruce?" Alex asked. "He seems happy, doesn't he? Take a leaf out of his book. Do you think that old dog worries about what's happening eight months from now?"

"It's not a bad philosophy, living in the now. It's just hard for me. I'm used to protecting myself; and taking unnecessary risks is not something I often do."

Alex stared at her. "Sam, you took on a biker gang. Alone."

"I did." Sam gave a wry smile. "But normally I plan such things to the tiniest detail. Research. Figure out all the contingencies and so on. Then along you come and all that's out the window."

"Oh dear. I'm a bad influence. I've stoked your reckless side."

Sam laughed. "Well, I've always had a reckless side, it's just I usually minimize risk a lot better than I did that day."

"You? Reckless? I'm not seeing it." Alex really couldn't. Sam always seemed so contained.

Sam rose. "Okay, come on then."

"Where?" Alex stood.

Sam pointed through the foliage. "This way to meet Reckless Keegan."

Alex followed her through a few twists and turns, then a steep climb down. The sounds of rushing water began to fill her ears.

Pushing aside one large fern frond, Sam held it for Alex to step past. A thrashing, churning stream rushed in front of them.

"Where are we?"

"Dry Creek."

"Doesn't look very dry."

"Kiwis have a sense of humor about these things. And some years back, in a fit of madness, I did what everyone said was impossible, and jumped it on my bike."

Alex's eyes widened. Her gaze darted up and down the embankment on either side, seeing nothing but rocks and thick foliage. "How? Where did you take off? How did you even find anywhere to land?"

"Landing was fun. I ended up, after a few bounces, halfway up that thing." She pointed directly across from them at a bushy native tree. It looked thick enough to break a fall…and take some chunks out of someone in the process.

"But that would mean you crossed the river here." Alex turned. A jagged rock was on the right of her, dense foliage on the left. The embankment under her feet was much higher than the other side of the river, and slightly rising. But it didn't seem enough. Worse… "There's no room for a ramp."

"No. That's why it was seen as impossible. In fact, the moment Breaker Bob told me it couldn't be done, I decided to prove him wrong."

"How?"

"Hours of practice—I re-created the jump in a safe area over a different river. I also had rising ground on this side, speed, a big tail wind, knowledge of how to angle my body to the aerodynamic position needed, bravado, and sheer dumb luck. It all came together."

Alex stared at the churning water and the distance again. "You're crazy."

"I planned it well. It was a managed risk."

"Even so!" A chill shot through Alex at the danger. "Crazy!"

"Crazy would be doing it without any planning. This was just me being bold. Sucking it up and doing it even though people said I couldn't. Sometimes a calculated risk's worth the reward. Are you saying you haven't ever risked everything, bruises and all?"

"Well…I did take on *Shezan*. Do you make a habit of this?"

Sam smiled and suddenly looked nervous. "I once kissed a beautiful woman I liked even though she was way out of my league."

"Who hasn't?" Alex muttered. "When was yours?"

"Oh, about two seconds from now." Sam leaned in, capturing Alex's lips with hers. It was nothing like their kisses the day before. There was no tentativeness this time; it had passion behind it, and a powerful promise of much more.

Alex melted a little. "Sam? I'm not out of your league."

"You are to me. So…too crazy?" The way her eyes burned with desire, Sam wasn't asking about the kiss.

Alex clasped the back of her head, pulling Sam down for another dizzying kiss. And then she hung on tight, kissing her over and again. "Turns out I'm fond of crazy."

"Me, too." Sam drew in a deep breath. "It's still early. Will you…come home with me?"

"No," Alex said with certainty.

"No?"

"I can't wait." Alex pulled Sam away from the surging river, leading her deeper into the greenery behind them. Her eyes darted around. The smell was sweet and woody. Dense ferns and thick, tall timber pressed in on them, closing out the world. Alex's eyes lit on one solid, smooth-barked tree. "Here."

Glancing up at the towering specimen, Sam's lips curled. "Against a *tōtara*?"

"Why's that funny?"

"Of all the trees you could have picked, you chose an iconic one. It's used by the Maori for…"

Alex pressed Sam hard into the trunk, then dragged her whole body slowly up against her.

"Oh." Sam's breath caught. "Doesn't matter."

"No." Alex grinned and kissed her hard. "It doesn't."

Taking Alex's head in her hands, Sam claimed her mouth fiercely.

The kisses were perfect. Hot, delicious, sexy, demanding. Arousing. So arousing. Alex's legs lost a little cohesion.

Sam spun them around until Alex's back was against the trunk. Her hand flicked down the buttons on Alex's jeans. They popped, one after the other, like soft gasps. She pulled open Alex's shirt and pushed up her

T-shirt, eyes sharp on the light-blue bra she'd revealed. Sam tugged it up, baring Alex's small breasts and hardening nipples.

Sam's eyes darkened. "Oh yes," she muttered, then her mouth descended on the closest tight knot.

"God," Alex whispered.

As Sam's tongue kept playing with Alex's nipple, her fingers slid down, inside jeans and underwear. She played with Alex for long, slippery moments.

It was delicious, naughty, and Alex couldn't get enough, rolling her hips forward to meet her.

"You like that," Sam murmured. She stroked Alex's crease harder, and the wetness was audible.

Alex groaned and closed her eyes, warmth gathering in her cheeks. "I'm only human."

Sam's lips shifted and her breath feathered Alex's ear. "So am I. I'm so wet right now. I might come just from how you feel under my hand." Her fingertips shifted lower, curling, drawing wet trails up to tease her clit.

Flares of arousal radiated from Alex when those roaming fingers settled in to rub in rhythmic patterns. "Oh…" She curled her arms around Sam's smooth, leather-jacketed back, pulling her in. "Don't stop." Her stomach clenched.

After a few more determined strokes from Sam, Alex's knees and thighs began trembling. The orgasm flooded her as she bucked against Sam's firm fingers.

She opened her eyes to discover her own white-knuckled fingers clenching tight fistfuls of Sam's jacket. Alex lifted her gaze to meet her half-lidded eyes.

"Did you enjoy that?" Sam purred.

Alex swallowed. Her mouth was so dry. "I'm sure you could tell I did."

"I had an inkling." Sam withdrew her glistening hand and reviewed the evidence.

"So cocky." Alex gave her an amused, challenging look. "And what would we find if I put my fingers inside your pants right now?" She splayed her hand against the leather in question and cupped Sam, then rubbed with the heel of her hand.

Sam pressed her center into Alex's hand, inhaling sharply. Her eyes became glassy and unfocused.

Alex dragged her fingers slowly up and down Sam's fly, enjoying the shudders each time she pressed against it. She pulled down the zipper. *Oh yes*. Alex could smell her desire.

Sam gave a soft, strangled moan. "Any time now would be good," she growled.

Alex smiled at her impatience and peeled the leather down, over Sam's perfect ass. She admired its pleasing contours, covered in black boy-shorts. "I remember these." She gave the waistband of the underwear a playful twang. "From the dam. My brain flailed around from the sight of you. Didn't know where to look."

"I'm glad I made someone happy with my sacrifice that day." Sam's teeth were gritted, and her chest rose and fell more quickly. "Could you…?" She waved at herself impatiently.

"So eager." Alex drifted her hand to the front of Sam's boy-shorts, curling under them at the vee. Cupped in her hand was shadows and heat: the darkness of the material, forbidding and sleek, under which she could feel a repressed fire. She gave a testing rub.

Sam's thighs locked at attention.

"Are you close?" Alex asked. "Just from me doing this?" She rubbed again, harder, pressing where she imagined Sam's clit to be.

This time Sam's breath hitched, her back snapped into a sharp line, and the smallest hiss escaped from her lips.

"Are you…fighting it?" Alex asked, amused. She rubbed again.

Sam trembled.

Alex peeled the boy-shorts down Sam's muscled thighs. "Beautiful." Her gaze lingered on the exposed skin. "So much power in your whole body, but I love your thighs especially." Her fingers trailed the body parts in question. "Strong, lean…" Her fingertips drifted higher until the back of her hand faintly brushed Sam's sex.

"God." The word was a whimper.

With one finger, Alex ran a languid, light line between Sam's lower lips, pausing to trail over every tuck and fold. "You really want this? Want me?"

"Have I been so cryptic?" A tremor stole through her. "Please?"

Sam's swollen folds swallowed Alex's roaming fingers as she pressed deeper. It was like drowning in silken softness. "Ohh," Alex said softly. "You're so aroused. And yet you're trying so hard not to come, too." She smiled. "How stubborn."

"*Alex.*" Sam's breath caught, then came faster in ragged gasps. Her mouth dropped against Alex's neck, and her heated lips slid across Alex's collar bone. "The things you do to me."

"Tell me," Alex urged her. "What do I do?"

"So hot. I want to touch you. I always want to touch you." Her hips bucked, then her body went taut. "Oh…I'm…"

"Don't hold back." Alex skidded her fingers over the slippery folds. Her thumb found Sam's clit, and she pressed in. "Let go. Now."

Sam's thigh muscles locked together, her neck went rigid, and her mouth fell open in a cry. "Oh. *Oh!*" Sam's fists formed tight bundles. Her sharp, incoherent cries carried on the crisp air, then faded out as she gasped. "I'm there." Her expression transformed to pure wonder.

Alex gazed in amazement, never having seen so much joy on her face. She slipped her hand from Sam's heat, pulling up her clothing after one last, appreciative look at the delights she'd been playing with.

Next time I'll taste her. Her sex gave a sharp, approving clench at that thought.

After doing up Sam's pants, Alex's fingers lingered on the leather and came to rest on the backs of those powerful, tantalizing thighs.

I'm there.

What did she mean by that? The words could mean she'd reached her peak, but Alex didn't think it was just that. The distant look in Sam's half-closed eyes said she was far from here. Far from her life spent existing in a rundown rental next to a police station that asked too much of her. Far from all of it.

"You're free," Alex said in sudden understanding.

Sam didn't answer. Her eyes fluttered shut and she offered a small, contented sigh. Her whole body seemed to relax.

Chapter 21

Secrets

SPRING HILL CORRECTIONS FACILITY, AN hour away in the Waikato, comprised a gray-walled series of hexagon-shaped buildings with a grassy courtyard in the center of each one. The idea was every room had a view of greenery. Sam trusted Dino appreciated it.

She parked, packed her motorcycle jacket in her bike's lock box, then straightened her uniform. Sam tried to focus on the business at hand, but her mind drifted. Maori ancestors might have made their canoes and carvings out of *tōtara* trees, but Sam would have an entirely different appreciation of them forever more.

Sam still tingled at the way Alex's divinely talented fingers had made her body sing. Last night, she'd been all Sam dreamed about. She'd woken today exhausted, aroused, and grumpy as hell that Dino was forcing her out of bed.

She glanced around. Sam had phoned ahead, explaining the delicacy of the situation, and the need for confidentiality. Dino had been moved into the innocuous-sounding Health Team Leader's room. A guard posted outside the door eyed Sam warily as she entered.

"He's got a mouth on him, that one," he warned.

"Sounds like Dino." She went to close the door behind her.

"Senior Constable, are you sure you should be alone with him?" The guard's eyes widened.

"This is a confidential police matter." She darted a look at Dino. He seemed smaller out of his gang leathers. A prison-issue white T-shirt stretched tight against his gut, and gray tracksuit bottoms hung loosely around his skinny legs.

"Yeah, *confidential.*" Dino ogled Sam and sneered at the guard. "Bug off now. We need to be alone."

Sam rolled her eyes. "I'll bang on the door if I need you," she said firmly, and then shut it in the guard's face to end the discussion. She turned to Dino. "Was that really necessary?"

"Man has a reputation," Dino grumbled. "Or I had one."

"Why do you think I didn't meet you in the visitor's lounge? Bikies don't talk to cops. Which makes me ask, why am I here?"

"How's my clubhouse?" He soured. "What's left of it?"

"Gate's flattened but the rest looks about the same old shithole. Your old man's taken it over, and seems busy shouting at the universe."

Dino looked disgusted. "Laughing at the mess I've made of things, probably." He glanced out the slatted window. "I almost didn't ask for you, but this is important."

"Is it about..." She lowered her voice. "The Hornets' drug drop? It's tonight, isn't it? At the old railyard?"

His teeth bared. "Fuck you for figuring that out."

"Dino, I have to know: Did you warn anyone that the police know?"

"Are you fuckin' nuts? My rep would be worth shit if people knew I'd narked."

"You didn't nark. I figured it out."

An odd gleam entered his eye. "Gotta admit, it's not a bad result."

The hell? "You don't care what happens to the Hornets?"

"Those little shits? Hooking people on their deadly crap? Nah. Fuck 'em."

Well. Sam stared at him, digesting that twist. An unexpected opportunity slid into mind. "Shame I don't know what time it'll go down," she said casually, flicking lint off her uniform pants. "Maybe someone could give a few Hornets gravel rash for you—for what happened to your cousin."

"That'd be narking," he said, but his eyes became speculative. She could almost see his cogs whirring.

He didn't speak for a moment. She waited.

"Don't blame me if you're stupid enough to freeze your tits off at eleven."

Eleven. Thank you, Dino, you useful bloody bastard. She'd slide that tip over to the drug squad. Sam leaned back. "This isn't why you asked me to come, is it? So why am I here?"

"Look," he said, meeting her eye properly for the first time. "I need you to save my dogs. They got seized. And they seem to like you." He scowled. "*Obviously*, or you wouldn't be still standing. I love those stupid, disloyal bastards, even though I put out the word I abused them to sound meaner. I couldn't hack it if anything happened to them." A redness crept up his cheeks.

"So basically you want me to save the dogs that will likely be put down for attacking a bunch of people."

"Hey, they didn't attack *you*, so what's your problem?" He glared at her.

"Excuse me?" she said, outraged. She distinctly remembered Dino at one point throwing out panicked attack commands in the middle of the melee. "You tried to get them to!"

"Not seriously! Well, okay. *Once*." He somehow managed to look both indignant and sheepish. "Only after they'd taken chunks out of all me boys. Besides, they ignored me, so I don't know why you're all bent outta shape. So, can you save them? I mean if anyone can, it's a cop."

"Why should I help you?"

"I'll do a deal."

Sam snorted. "What do you have that I'd ever need?"

"Man like me hears a lot of things. So I know what happened on that movie set you were asking about. So, you spring my dogs, find them a new home, and I'll spill."

"A new home? Can't your friends take them?"

"For fuck's sake, they're all in here except Dogsbreath's woman, and she won't help. She's got little brats at home. I don't trust Dad not to hurt them. And it'll be years before I get out of here again." His face hardened.

Sam quickly weighed up the pros and cons. She'd replayed the video a few times and had noticed that Killer had snapped, snarled, and lunged like her brothers, but hadn't bitten anyone. She'd be a good candidate to be saved. *I must be a sucker to be considering this.* "There's no guarantee I'd pull this off," Sam warned him. "In fact, odds are low."

His eyes brightened. "So argue the case, hey? Try."

"I'm probably mad to agree," she sighed, "but okay. I promise to do my best to rescue your dogs and find them good homes."

Dino's eyes filled with relief. "Okay."

"So? Let's hear it."

Dino shot her a suspicious look. "How do I know you'll stand by your word?"

"Dino, for God's sake, you already know the answer. I've always been an honest cop. That's why you're in this mess—I wouldn't cave to blackmail. And it should have been obvious to you by the way your dogs protected me that I love 'em, too. Okay?" She threw her hands up. "Stop trying my damned patience."

"Yeah. Yeah, okay." He actually looked a little shamefaced. "Right, so... the person behind the sabotage, the person who made you run around in stupid fuckin' circles is Sid."

"Bullshit!"

"On Killer's life, that's the truth."

"My brother would never—"

"He would and did. Don't know why. But it was him. Your bro ain't as perfect as you think."

Sam's anger kicked in. "No. Kev, maybe..."

"Kev? You're kidding, right? That boy couldn't stitch a fuckin' plan together if his life depended on it. It was a goddamned relief when you dragged his sorry ass out of the Boars. I was so glad to be shot of that dumb shit that I didn't even charge him the usual exit fees."

Exit fees. When everyone beat the crap out of an exiting member. It was true that Kev, then only seventeen, had never seemed worse for wear despite leaving the gang at Sam's furious insistence.

Realization dawned. "That wouldn't have stopped you any other time."

Dino shrugged and looked away.

"Why'd you spare him—really?" Sam asked.

"Let's just say, I think you had one too many shit sandwiches at school. I know I served half of them, spreading the stuff about your mum, making sure everyone knew. I...probably shouldn't of done it, 'specially since my home life was as crap as yours."

Since when did Dino develop a conscience? Her eyebrows lifted as he continued.

"Look, the thing of it was, with Kev, I wasn't going to add to your crap pile, eh? Least, not more than I already had." He really did look guilty now. "So we got a deal, right?"

Damn it. She really was nuts. "Okay, fine. I'll do everything I can to help your dogs."

Relief shone in his eyes. "Fuck off then," he barked, out of habit most likely, since his words contained absolutely no venom.

She made to leave, but before she opened the door, he added, "And hey, Sam, you stupid bloody bitch? Get the fuck out of Ika Whenu. Okay? You're too smart to let that boring hole suck any more life outta you than it already has. Shit, why are you even still here? Don't be a dickhead." He dropped his voice to a mumble. "Don't be like me. Just don't."

Sam stopped by at the pound on the way home, and after an official monotonously cited Section 33A of the Dog Control Act 1996 at her ad nauseam, she was redirected to Matamata-Piako District Council.

On the way over there, she couldn't get Dino's words out of her head. Maybe he was lying? Leverage to get her to help? Although, Dino was many things, but she'd never caught the ugly bastard lying to her.

Sam pulled her gloves off and leaned on the desk at Matamata-Piako District Council, waiting her turn for the on-duty Animal Control officer to meet her.

"Hey," the woman behind the counter said, "aren't you that cop from the internet video thingy?"

Sam gritted her teeth, then remembered she needed a favor. "I suppose." She attempted a charming smile. Well, a smile at least.

"Thought so. My boss loves you. Watches the video on repeat."

"How nice for him."

"Your Animal Control officer's just come in." The woman nodded behind Sam as an office door opened. "He's new."

Sam turned to find Sid staring back at her in surprise, wearing a thick, padded black vest with "Animal Control" emblazoned on it.

"Sam! How'd you find out I was here?" He beamed at her.

Jesus. Yet another job? She tugged him away from Nosy Nora at the counter. "A bad penny's got nothing on you, Sid. Lemme guess, you were fired from *Shezan*?"

"Oh yep. Real hard. Apparently leaving my post to save your scrawny bum didn't fly with Quincy." He shrugged. "He's a bit of a shithead, eh? You were right about him."

No arguments from her. "Okay, I need…" *To know if you're the brother I thought you were. I need you to tell me you weren't behind the conspiracy…* "you to action some paperwork on Dino's dogs to declare them non-menacing."

Sid's eyebrows shot up. "Um, Sis, those Rotties were chewing on everything that moved."

"Only chewing Boars attacking me. They didn't go for anyone but people hurting me or them. They're heroes in my book. I want to get them new homes. But I can't if they've been declared dangerous under Section 33."

"That's asking a lot."

"They deserve a second chance. It's not fair they'll be put down for who their owners were."

Sid dragged out a sigh. "Look, sorry to say this but two had to be put down already. Badly injured."

Sam's stomach clenched as if she'd been sucker punched. "W-was one of them Killer?"

He consulted his notes. "Killer and Demon are fine."

Thank God. "Okay, good. Look you should rewatch the video. Killer didn't actually bite anyone. Maybe Demon didn't either? Surely that'd save them? And, hey, I'll find a dog expert who'll say in writing that they'll retrain them to be good, safe dogs."

Sid studied her. "That's a long shot, Sam. You have to know that."

"So argue my case. Ask your boss—doesn't he like me in that video? Can't you work that angle?"

"I don't think I can. I've only been here a few days."

"Sid, come on! You owe me."

"For what?" He squinted at her.

"Gee, I don't know, time-wasting a cop with bullshit sabotage on a movie set?" She watched his expression closely, almost afraid of what she'd see.

"What? No. Who told you that?" His left eye twitched.

She'd know that 'tell' anywhere. Betrayal welled up inside. "How many times are you going to lie to me? You had me running all over the Waikato region at all hours. Going in that dam. That's disrespectful as hell. I could charge you." Sam looked him square in the eye, her anger mounting.

"Look, it was never supposed to get out of hand. It wasn't supposed to be serious. And the dummy was s'posed to stay a lot nearer the shore. It drifted." This time his tone was pleading.

"So this was all a game? You were amusing yourself?"

He looked pained. "It's complicated."

"I'll make it really simple: Did you ask Skye, Kiri, and Kev to tell me a pack of lies and get me chasing my own tail or not?"

"I...yes. I talked them into it."

All the faith and trust she'd had in her brother crumbled. She folded her arms. "I could have died because of your stupid stunts."

"I never thought you'd go rushing off to accuse the Boars! And I'd never have let you get hurt!"

"Hurt? I was almost *killed*, Sid."

Horror crossed his face. "I'm sorry. You *know* I'd never put you in danger on purpose."

"So tell me why you did this, and make it damned good."

"I can't. Not yet," he pleaded, expression helpless.

"Damn it!" Frustration surged, choking her. "Don't you get it? Your stupid stunts got me suspended!"

"I'm really sorry." Sid sounded contrite. "And I know it looks bad, but your job isn't everything, Sis."

How cavalier could he get? "Just because you go through jobs like most people change socks doesn't mean I do. It took me years of doing the hard yards to become a senior constable and earn my own station. And you've stuffed it up for me in five seconds. You lie to my face and then have the gall to call me 'sis?' I don't even know who you are anymore." She walked away in disgust. "I don't know you at all."

"Sam!" he called after her, sounding crushed.

Screw him. He'd brought this on himself.

Chapter 22

Beginning of the End

Sam sat on her battered green couch, staring at her wall of postcards. Bruce had decided to grace her with his presence tonight, which meant Mrs. Fenley had already turned in and he was bored. She ran her fingers through his coarse fur. Each postcard represented people she knew. Some she'd liked a little. A couple she'd liked a lot. One she'd even loved—and then not so much. All were gone, far from Ika Whenu.

Except her. Despite the grandest of girlhood dreams, she hadn't stepped even a toe outside of New Zealand's shores.

How much she'd wanted to, especially in her twenties. Always, though, duty called her back, duty to family. And look at what family had done to her.

Her brain ached from trying to make sense of what had possessed Sid to jerk her around for some elaborate joke.

Family meant everything to Gina, and Sam had soaked up those lessons at her knee. She'd absorbed her words, believed them, and she'd loved Sid more than any man alive. Loved Kev, too, despite their sometimes-contentious relationship. She'd have done almost anything for them.

But now this.

The Police Commissioner had summoned her for a meeting tomorrow in Wellington to review her suspension. She could be losing her job. And if that happened, and if she meant so little to her own family, what was even holding her in Ika Whenu?

That was too big a question for one exhausted brain. Maybe it wasn't even the right question. Too much thinking anyway. She glanced at her wall clock and stood. Time for action.

She pulled on her black boots, to match the black T-shirt and pants she'd donned earlier. A black beanie followed, and she carefully tucked her hair out of sight.

Glancing at Bruce, still curled up on the couch, she asked: "Want to come watch some bikies get their sorry asses arrested?" She tickled behind his ear. "Don't worry, the bad guys'll be outnumbered ten to one. We'll be away from the action. And the railway yard's not too far to walk, which is good since your furry butt's not designed for motorbikes, hey?"

Bruce climbed to his feet, tail wagging.

"That's the spirit." She lowered her voice to a conspiratorial whisper. "Just don't tell anyone we're doing this."

Her orders had been clear. Sam was suspended and her acting replacement, Senior Constable Murray Snell, would be the local officer advising the drug squad tonight, even though his "local knowledge" could fit on the back of a postage stamp.

Sam had to be especially careful not to get caught, given her meeting tomorrow. As if she could stay away, though. Trying to stamp out the meth trade in Ika Whenu had swallowed her life for so long. She'd agonized over it, held the hands of people she'd known her whole life who'd lost a family member to the addiction, and arrested locals for crimes they'd never have committed without being under its influence.

But if the drug squad did things right, which included simultaneously raiding the Hornets' headquarters, there'd be no more drugs washing through the Waikato region. Finally, Ika Whenu's streets would be clean for the first time in almost two years.

"Come on, Bruce." She scooped him up. "Let's go watch it end."

Sam lay on a small rocky cliff that overlooked the disused railyard. Enormous, stacked shipping crates sat around it, rusting and forgotten. The company that used to run this place had gone broke years ago and just walked away.

In her left ear, she could hear Bruce's soft panting. In her right was the distant, haunting cry of a *ruru*—the native owl some Maoris believed foretold the coming of an ominous event. Well, it'd be ominous as hell for *those* two.

A pair of Hornets were sneaking into the yard. One hung back, playing lookout, while the other ducked behind a small, brown service building, sticking to the shadows. Somewhere down there, a team of police would be waiting to pounce. She hadn't seen them yet, but she'd recognized their unmarked cars on her walk here, hidden out of sight, four streets away.

The *ruru* called again, and the lookout Hornet turned nervously, peering into the darkness. Maybe he was a superstitious type. He pulled out a torch and aimed it at the low, sloping corrugated iron roof, lighting a path.

The first man climbed up an old crate and rammed a small, sausage-shaped black bag into the shed's wide guttering. Sam pulled out her phone and started video recording as he repeated this twice with other bags. It was grainy as hell, but the Hornet shining torchlight on the guttering for his friend had illuminated their faces for a few seconds.

A scuffle in the distance drew her eye. She turned to see a swarm of officers surrounding a stooped man next to the main railyard building, holding a paper bag. He twisted away and a streetlight caught him. Why the hell were they bothering Larry the crazy hermit?

They were shouting now: "Police! Drop the package and step back!"

For God's sake! Wrong man!

The Hornets she'd been watching froze, then pinned themselves against the wall, well out of sight from the police, looking agitated and fearful.

Sam cursed, ended the recording, and texted Murray.

Behind brown shed. North end. 2 Hornets. Packages in roof gutter.

One of the figures surrounding the cursing hermit stepped away from the crowd, pulled out his phone, then turned slowly, surveying the area. *Murray, obviously.* He pointed at the brown shed, said something, then bent over his phone.

Sam's phone pinged seconds later.

U shouldnt be here.

Jesus, Murray, just take the damn tip. Sam scowled, wondering how much shit he'd put her in. She texted a reply.

Just passing thru while out for a jog

She looked up. *Oh crap!* She fired off a new text.

Theyr on move!

Police broke cover, emerging from every dark corner, and bolted toward the brown shed. The pounding of booted feet alerted the two bikies, who took off in opposite directions. One turned directly into the face of a cop who had him faceplanted and cuffed in seconds, only feet from the Hornet's motorbike. *Efficient.*

"One down," she told Bruce in approval.

The other sprinted for the cliffs. Toward her.

Bruce sat up, ears pricking.

"Yeah, I know, boy. Not too lucky, is he? He's gonna be toast, one way or another."

She pulled out her phone again.

Cliffs. Northeast

This guy was much faster than the first and had a pretty good head start on police below.

The bikie's head eventually bobbed up above the cliff edge, his wheezing announcing him long before she saw his round, brown face.

"Hi." Crouching at the top, Sam met his startled eyes. "Going somewhere?"

He eyed her outfit. "Who the fuck are you?" He hauled himself over the ledge, rising to an enormous height, and sized her up properly.

"I supposed you'd know me as *hukapapa*." She stood.

He scowled. "The fuckin' cop. Shit." He looked around as if he was deciding whether to run or attack her. He probably could flatten her quite easily with one swat of his meaty fist.

"I wouldn't. Best you just sit down right now." Sam injected cool menace into her voice.

"Or what?" He snorted.

"Or you'll piss off my dog." She pointed at Bruce, who was now happily sniffing out the exciting new smells of the intruder's boots, tail quivering with delight.

"That thing? Doesn't come up past me ankle."

"True, he's small," Sam agreed, "but Balltearer can jump to crotch height, which is all he needs."

"Ball...tearer?" He eyed Bruce. "You're bluffing!"

"Am I? Well, let's see. How brave do you feel?" Sam asked curiously. "How much *do* you like your bits where they are?"

Five minutes later, the drug squad arrested a surly Hornet frozen on his knees at the top of a cliff, his wary eyes fixed on a small, ancient Jack Russell terrier.

Murray came to stand beside Sam. "Out for a jog, eh? At eleven-thirty at night?" He took in her black beanie, matching dark top and pants, and heavy boots. "Very, ah, sporty. Cool monochrome, too."

"Black's slimming," Sam drawled. "I've emailed you a video of the drop since you were all busy roughing up the wrong suspect. Don't want those two wriggling off the hook. Just don't make me regret it."

Murray checked his phone, eyes widening at what he found. "Thanks. No probs. After all, you were just out for a jog." He nodded, then smiled. "Did ya hear the Hornet HQ raid got the entire bloody meth factory? They're toast. Whole lot of them. The Tauranga drug squad are losing their shit they're so happy, cos that one factory was drowning their whole city in drugs."

"Good." Sam relaxed. So it really was over. No more climbing bikie walls or trailing dopehead couriers around town. "Couldn't have happened to better assholes."

"No arguments from me. Closer to home, they just caught a local man trying to collect the drugs at the drop site." He waved vaguely at the railyard below. "Not too bright. An aggressive little shit called..." He rummaged through his pocket and pulled out his police notebook. "Fletcher Norton. They're rounding up his mates now for questioning."

Sam's eyes widened. *That* asshole was who'd hooked half the town on this crap? "Just when I thought I couldn't hate someone more, they prove me wrong."

"Well, he's in deep shit now. You won't have to see him for a long while." Murray turned at the shout of his name. "Gotta go. But this feels great, doesn't it? It's why I became a cop!"

Sam watched him jog away, envy surging through her. Yeah. It *was* great. They'd done it. Cut off the snake's head. And now it was over. And maybe that was the last arrest she'd ever attend. She might never get to feel this way again; the sense she'd helped serve justice. She rammed her hands in her pockets at that bittersweet thought.

"Come on, Bruce," she said gently. "You did great, boy. Really intimidating. I totally felt it." She snorted. "Let's get you home."

As she headed off, her mind filled itself again to the brim with the blur of questions, riddles, and stress she'd been pushing from it for the past hour. Sid's betrayal flooded her mind once more and she scowled, picking up her pace. *What. The. Hell.*

Chapter 23

Being There

Alex woke to a thumping on her trailer door. Blearily she rose, glancing at the red numbers of the clock on the microwave. 1:02 a.m. She opened the door a crack.

Sam was outside, agitation all over her face, hair mussed. She looked more disturbed than Alex had ever seen her. "Sorry to wake you."

"Don't be." Alex widened the door and shivered against the cold air Sam was letting in.

Sam's gaze trailed over Alex's sleepwear—striped blue pajama bottoms and a faded Clannad T-shirt. Alex suddenly wished she'd worn something less tragic than her favorite Irish band shirt.

"I shouldn't have come," Sam said, regret troubling her eyes. "It's so late. I was having the worst night trying to get my head straight, and I found myself here. I don't know what I was thinking, bothering you."

"I'd say you were thinking pretty clearly if you chose me." Alex smiled. "Get your ass in here before we both freeze."

After a second's hesitation, Sam clambered inside and closed the trailer's door.

"Want a drink?" Alex asked.

"No."

"To talk?" Alex asked, curious about Sam's strange mood. She'd never seen her so unsettled.

Sam glanced around. Her gaze shifted restlessly from the kitchenette to the couch, the ajar door to the bathroom, and finally the rumpled bed.

Alex lifted her eyebrows. "Oh." She smirked.

Sam's cheeks reddened.

"Is that why you came?"

"I…" Sam looked uncertain.

Alex's low tone contained heat. "You know, I've been thinking about you all day. My wandering thoughts haven't exactly been G-rated." Alex tilted her head and a smile ghosted around her lips. "So if you felt the same, if that's why you came, I have no objections. So…is it?"

For a moment, Sam didn't speak, and then she looked down, a blush feathering around her cheeks. "You mean more to me than that. You're not just someone I want to…you know…whenever I'm out of sorts."

"I know. But is that why you came? For…*you know*?"

"Not…consciously."

"Subconsciously then?"

Sam's gaze darkened and her chin lifted. "Yes."

Alex couldn't believe how arousing that admission was, torn from Sam's throat like a naughty secret. Her nipples tightened and want coursed through her, leaping from nerve ending to nerve ending. "Then I think you'd better kiss me."

Waking in Alex Levitin's arms was glorious. Sam breathed in the scent of her skin, the aroma that was all Alex. Intoxicating. Sweet. Subtle.

She only barely remembered how she'd wound up here. Her talk with Sid yesterday had started an emotional tsunami that kept rising the longer she thought about it. It turned up all sorts of issues, including the choices that led her to stay in Ika Whenu. It was all so confusing.

But one thing that wasn't confusing was Alex. Her warmth and easy acceptance, her comfort, had been a steady presence in the darkness. It went deeper than their attraction. Of course their chemistry burned and arced between them. But this was something else. It felt like where she was meant to be.

She studied the sleeping woman, curled up tight against her, just like the sparrow she'd likened her to the day they met. The memory of Alex surrounded by Wild Boars made her want to tug her closer. Sam's relief at finding her unharmed that day had been overwhelming.

What was it about Alex Levitin that got under her skin? Why did Alex feel so different to any other woman she'd dated? Why did she crave her so much?

Sam trailed her fingers down Alex's arm. Clever, funny, focused, dedicated, and adventurous. She was someone who picked up and saw the world on a whim. How amazing that must be.

Playing with a tuft of red hair at Alex's temple, Sam tried to imagine existing in Alex's life. It was so foreign. Everything Sam did was so cut and dried. Seek out crime, stop crime. That was it.

Alex is so beautiful. She smiled at herself. Funny, given Alex looked so rumpled.

The woman she was admiring stirred, confusion filling her eyes for a moment as she focused. Alex's expression cleared and she smiled. "Morning, beautiful. I love that look you have for me."

"I don't have a look," Sam replied, confounded.

"Sure you do. You look at me with wonder and…hmm…a hint of envy."

"Envy?" Sam's eyebrows rose. "I don't."

"I don't mean it in a bad way. It's like a wistfulness. I must seem to float around the world on a whim. You find that very attractive."

"I…" Sam deflated. Was Alex a mind reader? Was it written on her forehead?

"Sorry." Alex hesitated. "Sore point?"

Sam sighed. "I didn't know it was obvious."

"Well if you put the clues together, maybe. You stare at postcards from distant places, listen to world music, race out of town every spare minute on Tiger. I see someone craving escape."

"Maybe," Sam conceded. "Is that so bad?"

"Of course not. It's only natural. Why do you ask? Do *you* feel like it's bad?"

Sam couldn't answer that now any more than she could last night when her feet had taken her straight to Alex's door. It was too confusing.

"A rare sight." Alex's eyes crinkled. "Senior Constable Keegan looking stumped."

Sam regarded her thoughtfully. "You never did take my police officer side too seriously, did you?"

"How do you mean?"

"You always say my rank like it's something admirable or even amusing. But it's never a negative."

"Why would it be negative?"

"Try being a police officer for a day. All anyone sees is the uniform. When I enter the pub, conversations often switch topics, in case I hear something that'll get them in trouble. It's human nature. Not with you, though."

"Well, it's not that I don't take it seriously. It's just that's not even close to everything you are, is it? I like *all* of you. In and out of your uniform." She smiled at the double entendre.

"You see me."

"Yes. And I like what I see a great deal." Her fingertips trailed Sam's arm. "Besides, I know what it's like, being only seen as your title."

"Oh? Are directors treated in some weird way I don't know about?"

"It's more how the film industry is. People are so desperate for their big break that anyone with a whiff of power is fawned over. It's disconcerting. I get actresses flinging themselves at me—as if I can't tell what they're really after. Worse, most are straight. God, it's exhausting. So, I get where you're coming from. People often don't see *you*." Alex's eyes suddenly lit with amusement. "Although I notice you never cared that I was some Hollywood director either, did you? In fact, you hated me for it."

"Hate's a strong word," Sam suggested, tone teasing. "I'm protective of Ika Whenu. If there was any hate, it was about your appalling driving skills."

Alex laughed. "Damn—sexy, *and* a sense of humor."

"Who's joking?" Sam deadpanned.

"Uh-huh. So tell me: What had Ika Whenu's sexy cop out of bed and on my doorstep at one a.m. in the first place?"

"Couldn't sleep."

"I think that's self-evident."

"I have a lot on my mind."

Alex paused. "Us?"

"No. Well, yes. But that's not what had me up." Sam inhaled. "All my life, I've done everything I could for my family. I love them and I'm grateful for them, so I never minded. They made me feel like I belonged."

"You do belong," Alex said. "Gina adores you. Sid, too."

Sam's whole body felt tight. "He adores me so much that he admitted yesterday he was behind the set sabotage."

"What?" Alex's eyes snapped open. "No!"

"I had to find that out from Dino. That was lovely."

"Why did Sid do that?" Alex demanded. "Was he being paid by someone?"

"He wouldn't say. Whatever the reason, it hurts. Years ago, Gina begged me to move back home and help Kev. I made a promise to her that day to always be there for them, because that's what family does. But now...I've been wondering if the respect goes only one way."

"Oh, Sam. They respect you."

"Do they? Or maybe it's a sign."

"A sign of what?"

"Nothing. Never mind." Sam shook her head. "Anyway, in the middle of it all, I realized I have no idea where I'm heading. For years I've assumed I'd die here with my boots on like the last cop."

"You have so many choices for the first time," Alex said. "It must be overwhelming."

"And this afternoon the Police Commissioner wants to see me. If I'm sacked or lose my station, then what?"

"Okay." Alex studied her. "Close your eyes. What's the first thing that comes to mind when I say, Sam Keegan, what would you most like to be doing right now?"

"I'm on a beach."

"Ooh, nice. Where?"

"There's a beach I always wanted to go to. Pfeiffer Beach in California. I saw a documentary on it once and I'd never seen anything like it before. The sand is a purple color because it contains crushed garnet. There's a keyhole arch the waves burst through, too. And the ocean is clearest blue. The temperature's perfect, not freezing like here. I always fantasized about camping near my beach and gazing out over the sea." She hesitated. "My first girlfriend, Nicole, knew that was my dream place—"

"Wait, her postcard? That's Pfeiffer Beach?"

"Yes. It's why she sent it. She was mocking me, saying, 'Look, I went to your precious beach because you never will.'"

"She really is a bitch." Alex scowled.

"She was hurt. We'd always planned to go there together but I had priorities here I couldn't ignore. Maybe she was right, though. Maybe I never will see my beach."

"Why do you believe that? Even if you stay in Ika Whenu, you could still have a holiday anywhere you like."

"This probably sounds silly for someone like me who enjoys her own company, but I never wanted to be at my beach alone. I don't want to travel alone at all. My dream is to enjoy the adventure *with* someone. The world's meant to be shared."

"I understand," Alex said. "And now you're at a crossroads, wondering what you are going to do now."

Sam regarded her pensively.

"You're allowed not to know," Alex continued. "You don't even know right now if you have a job. So why don't you table all this till after your meeting with the Police Commissioner?"

Silence fell. Finally, Sam said, "That's a good point. Okay."

"And after you see him, come and find me."

"I may not be in the mood to talk."

"Then we won't talk. Will you come anyway?"

"Okay." Sam heaved out a breath. "I don't want to think about this anymore now. Take my mind off it? Tell me: How many places have you been to? Where have you visited?"

"Hmm… Well, let's see. I've been all over Europe. I've also visited Singapore, Japan, Vietnam, the US, of course, and would you believe, the Sahara?"

"The Sahara? Seriously?"

"I made this film about climate change not too long ago, *A Quiver in Time*. I needed some footage involving a local tribe and quiver trees." She waited. Everyone always laughed at the quiver trees. But seriously, when your water-storing succulents die off, the whole ecosystem gets in strife. That was important.

No laughs from Sam. She just nodded. "Where else?"

"Lord Howe Island. I think that's probably most similar to New Zealand, at least climate-wise. Not to mention the richness of greenery, the close-knit people, and the gorgeous waterfalls."

"Nowhere's as beautiful as Wairere Falls, though," Sam said with certainty.

"Is that so, proud local?" Alex poked her ribs. "And how would you know?" she teased.

"I'm a Kiwi. We just know these things," Sam declared.

"Really," Alex drawled.

"Yup."

"It'd be very weird for you, wouldn't it, if you were no longer able to be a cop in Ika Whenu?"

"I suppose," Sam conceded. "But at least the main thing I wanted to fix is now sorted. The meth."

"It is?"

"That's the reason I was up so late to start with last night—there was a raid. I wanted to know how it went. The Hornets were all arrested. The meth supply in Ika Whenu and the whole the Waikato region just got cut off."

"Well that'll win you big brownie points with your boss, won't it? That's all because of you, isn't it?"

"In part."

"We could protest, you know, if you got fired. All those people who saw the live feed, who fell in love with your bravery, we could whip up a PR campaign to save your job. I'm sure the locals would rally around, too. I know you do a lot for this town and these people who expect so much from you. But they know it, too. They'd stand with you."

"Maybe. But getting more attention will get the brass even more pissed off." Sam closed her eyes. "I'll just see where my cards fall. All I can do now."

Chapter 24

Judgment Day

Outside the New Zealand Police Commissioner's office, Sam checked her uniform's sharp lines down the pale blue short sleeves and needle-fine creases in her navy pants.

"You can sit if you'd like, Senior Constable." The commissioner's personal assistant indicated the guest chairs. "He's running fifteen minutes late."

"I'm fine. Been sitting too long as it is."

Sam wondered how long this meeting would take. Would her boss just fire her on the spot? If so, he could have gotten someone else to do that. Maybe he wanted to read her the riot act first? Was there a lot of precedent for this? Cops caught on live video in a bikie brawl they'd brought on themselves?

Gazing at the giant windows, broken up by strips of beige wall, Sam wished for a distraction. What was Alex doing right now?

In the early hours of this morning, she'd been like a beacon, drawing Sam in. On the hour-long flight from Hamilton to Wellington, remembering how wicked Alex's mouth and hands had been, how teasing and skilled, had been a pleasant distraction from fixating on all the creative ways her boss might fire her.

"Commissioner Fraser will see you now."

Sam nodded and marched through the doors into the office on less than steady legs.

As she took in her boss's minimalist office with its view over the nation's capital, she wondered again why a nobody cop from a provincial backwater was even in the man's presence.

Commissioner Fraser greeted her then nudged a plate of ham sandwiches her way. "Hungry?"

She stared at them and then back at him. "No. Thanks." Her mouth was dry. "I'm fine."

"Probably a wise choice." He smiled. "They're from the staff cafe."

She nodded politely.

"So, Senior Constable Keegan." He flipped through her file. "You've put us in a bit of a tough situation, eh? I know we talked briefly on the phone, but it bears repeating. Trying to single-handedly raid a compound full of bikies and attack dogs—"

"Sir, I—"

"No." He lifted a stilling finger at her. "I've read your report, so I know what you're going to say, but no. First, all motorcycle gangs see official police visits as raids, whether *we* do or not. And those dogs were trained to attack regardless of whether they mauled your person or not."

She bit her lip.

He continued. "Brought a civilian along to document proceedings. I cannot tell you how inconvenient that was." He gave her a narrow look. "We've had media interest on this incident from all around the world."

"Um, she brought herself along," Sam said. "I wasn't initially even aware Alex was there."

"Alex. That would be...Alexandra Levitin. A movie director," he noted, shuffling through his papers. He shifted his gaze back to her. "So you know her?"

Her cheeks warmed. *Biblically? Sure.* "I've met her a few times, yes. She's filming a movie in our neck of the woods."

"Well, it was so *nice* of her to be so comprehensive in sharing her video. Half a million views now." He thrummed his fingers against the table.

Half a million? Holy... "Yes, sir."

"Your brother then turned up and started throwing his fists around. One..." He consulted his notes. "Sidney Mahuta."

"Yes, sir." Sam shifted impatiently.

"So, while it's all very amusing to the public, your actions have made New Zealand Police look like amateur hour. The Opposition Leader asked in Parliament whether funding's so short in regional stations that officers have to feed the criminals' dogs and drag their brothers along on raids. The Police Minister loved having to answer that question."

I'll bet, she thought, wondering what his reply had been.

"Your report states you had cause to believe the Wild Boars had a drug-manufacturing operation underway, and were also sabotaging those movie people."

"Yes, sir."

"Both allegations proved unfounded, correct?"

Sam inhaled. "They did, yes. But my intervention did lead to intel that dismantled the Hornets' methamphetamine operations throughout the Waikato region last night. I was able to ascertain who the manufacturers were and when the next drop would be and the drug squad intercepted it and performed various raids."

"I'm aware." He tilted his head. "I'd say well done but, overall, it wasn't really, was it? Everything you did was ham-fisted, risky, short-sighted, and failed to follow procedure."

Technically correct.

"You endangered the lives of multiple civilians," the commissioner went on. "And you could have gotten yourself and them badly injured or killed."

Also technically correct.

"It was reckless and frankly, I have no recourse but to officially censure you for it. There is no way we can say what you did was acceptable behavior, or we'd have every officer thinking they can play Rambo. Of course it'd have been much easier to deal with this discreetly if there hadn't been that video." His lips pursed. "But it's everywhere. So..."

Sam wiped her hands down her pants surreptitiously. *Here it comes.*

"You'll no longer be allowed to run a regional police station. Keep your nose clean, and in a few years you might be eligible again."

She wasn't being fired? "Yes, sir."

"Officers with your experience, and the skill to hold their own against a violent motorcycle gang, do not grow on trees and I'm not about to throw that away, especially when we have a recruitment shortfall. How you went about this was not ideal, but you're not a bad officer. Your record is otherwise exemplary."

O-kay?

He shot her a wry look. "Besides, how would that play to the masses? We can't demote you. You've become a hero out in the burbs. Your bravery's inspirational. Recruitment's up. People want to *be* you. I know, I know, they're delusional if they think braining bikies is what policing is. But still, you're somewhat valuable to us."

"How? I mean, I can't run my station now." Would she be some grunt posted somewhere else?

He turned and waved at the poster behind his head that read, *NZ Police Recruiting Now!* "You like to make a difference, right? Well, I think you'd make a great new poster girl for New Zealand Police. We're looking at doing an international ad campaign. Get some of the Aussies, Canadians, and Brits to give it a go over here. What do you think? Job's based here in Wellington. You'd have to move."

Sam looked at him, then the poster—with some grinning young recruit on it—then back to him. "You want me to give up my station, move to the city, and sell the wonders of policing? And I'd what? Just do media interviews, pose for photos, and talk up policing all day long?"

"Essentially."

"How would that look to other officers? Me becoming a poster girl for 'playing Rambo?'"

"The consequences will be made well known internally—that for all your high profile, you're now no longer an active-duty police officer." His gaze was sharp.

My career is *over then.*

"If you say no, we can find you something else, but it'd be around the bottom of the pecking order. At least this way the pay and office are better."

"As a *poster girl.*"

"As the face of New Zealand Police." His gaze sharpened. "That's nothing to sneer at. Besides, I know what those small regional stations are like. They're stressful as hell. Especially the one-officer ones." He gave her an aggrieved look. "And if I didn't know, there's this persistent doctor in Te Aroha who keeps sending me her long damned reports."

Go Dr. Linn. "Right."

"But the bottom line is we don't have enough police to go around. And as for non-sworn Authorized Officers, well, hell, I wish we had more civilian AO recruits to plug the gaps, too, but we don't. We're doing the best we can with limited resources. Which brings us back to my offer. You could do more good for New Zealand Police as our recruiter than you could doing on-the-ground policing. Imagine how much pressure you could take off those smaller stations if we had a lot more police to spread around? And you're just the woman to make it happen."

"I'd be little more than a face stuck on a poster, though."

"You'd work with our media and publicity department, do whatever they need best. That's why I asked you here, so you could meet them, do the full tour and so on. Why? Do you have any better offers?" His smile was faint but all-too-knowing.

Sam didn't appreciate that one bit. How condescending. Did he really think he had her over a barrel? Sounded like it. "I might explore my other options," she said tersely, and made to rise.

He looked genuinely surprised. "Senior Constable? If you walk out now, the offer's off the table for good."

"I can't be what you want me to be here. That's not me. Besides, I need to be based in Ika Whenu. I have responsibilities."

"Are you...resigning?" His shock was almost worth it. Funny how powerful, career-climbing people always assumed what motivated them, motivated everyone.

"You leave me little option, sir, given Ika Whenu only has one police posting and I won't be in it." Hell, even if she wasn't needed at home, re-starting her career at the bottom again as a disgraced junior shit-kicker based who knows where didn't hold any appeal. Sam paused as an idea struck her. "But were you serious before? About helping regional stations?"

"Of course."

"Okay, I have a proposal. A win-win solution. And you'll get your recruitment pin-up after all."

Chapter 25

Confessions

ALEX TRUDGED BACK TO HER trailer after work to find a slightly crumpled Sam in her police uniform, sitting on the steps.

"Sam?"

She looked up, her expression distant.

"How'd it go with the Police Commissioner?"

Sam didn't reply.

"Oh, love, okay. Let's talk inside," Alex murmured. She punched in her code, opened the door, and waited.

Sam headed in.

Alex followed and closed the door behind them. "Sam?"

Sam's lips were on hers almost immediately, frantic and heated.

"Oh?" Alex's eyebrows rose. "Well, hello there, Senior Constable."

That earned her a warning nip at her earlobe.

Alex smiled into her neck. "Want to talk about it?"

Shrugging, Sam mumbled, "I lost my job today."

"Sam!" Alex pulled away.

"No, it's not like that." Sam eyed her for a moment, then glanced away. "I quit."

"Quit?"

"They took my station off me. I'm no longer Ika Whenu's…anything." She ran a hand through her hair.

"That isn't fired, though. Where are they sending you?"

"They offered me a desk job that'd mean I was little more than the face of New Zealand Police on posters." Sam scowled. "Police Barbie."

"You know, you'd be an effective recruitment tool," Alex suggested lightly. "I'd sign up immediately."

"You're biased." Sam rolled her eyes.

"That's true. Besides, I doubt New Zealand Police would let my sparrow ass anywhere near a police uniform. One stiff breeze and all that."

Sam almost smiled that time.

"You're allowed to laugh at my hilarious jokes, you know."

"I'll bear that in mind when you make one."

"Ha-ha." Alex leaned forward for a kiss. "Well, what would you like? To talk some more? To be flung down for unforgettable sex? A soothing massage? Go out to dinner?"

Sam chuckled. "Just picturing you trying to fling me anywhere. I've got a good deal more muscle mass on you. And I won't mention the height difference."

"Better not if you know what's good for you." Alex grinned. "Would you like to see if I could?"

"I've seen you try to lift Tiger. That ended well." This time Sam laughed.

"A bike doesn't do what you ask it to," Alex countered saucily. "I bet *you* would."

"Can't deny it." Sam's eyes flicked toward the bedroom.

"That's what I thought." Alex smiled and led Sam to her bed. She turned and sized up her lover. "As hot as you look in that uniform, right now, it's in the way." Even so, Alex spent an admiring few minutes mapping out its sharp creases and lines with her fingertips. Finally she popped the clear, small buttons of Sam's crisp sky-blue shirt, before tugging the material from navy pants. She parted the shirt, just a little. Sam's sports bra and a long strip of skin came into view.

Sam lowered a hand to her large black utility belt and, with slow, trembling fingers, undid it.

"Are you okay?" Alex asked, as she drew the shirt reverently off Sam's shoulders,

"I just realized. Today's the last time I'll ever wear this. End of an era."

"Start of a new one?" Alex suggested. "We don't have to do this. If you're not in the moo—"

"You're all I could think about on the ride back from the airport," Sam interrupted. "All I wanted." Her eyes were dark. "I need—" She stopped.

"This?"

"You." Sam kicked off her boots in two thuds, skidding them down the trailer's length. Then she wrenched down her uniform pants and tossed them in the same direction. She straightened, now only in her underwear. Then, with a casual yank, she tore off her bra, and dropped her boy-shorts to the ground, kicking them aside.

What a canvas she was, muscles and planes. Leanness and beauty. Alex drank in her body. "I'll never get used to seeing you like this. Beautiful."

"Nah, I'm all muscles and sinew, like someone made a scarecrow out of crowbars." Her hands reached for Alex and deftly peeled her out of her clothing. "You're the beauty. How did you get to be so flawless?" She trailed fingertips over Alex's bare body.

Alex looked down. She was paler than paper. Her stomach was soft and flat, lacking the muscled leanness of Sam's. Her breasts were small—tiny handfuls topped by the palest pink points. Goosebumps broke out across her arms under those watchful eyes. "I'm not—"

"You are to me. I love how delicate you are. All the things I'm not. Gentle, warm, soft…fine, like porcelain."

"I'm not fragile, though." Alex shot her a warning look. "Don't you dare go gentle on me."

"Wouldn't dream of it." Sam chuckled. She dropped onto the bed and lay back, legs naturally falling apart in a casual, sexy invitation. "Anyway, didn't you say *you* were going to ravish *me*?"

"True." Alex admired Sam's impressive body, then knelt before her on the bed. Her voice became mischievous. "That's definitely the plan."

For a moment, neither spoke. Sam's breath caught and held, and her smile fell away.

Alex's eyes locked onto Sam's burning ones as their excitement rose. She slid forward, fitting herself between Sam's legs, pushing them wider. She played with the softness of Sam's pale inner thighs, using backs of knuckles and nails, barely touching, until wetness gleamed, and slippery flesh swelled and reddened. Alex's hot breath shifted Sam's short blonde hairs, matted with slickness, as Sam's body jerked and arched, desperately seeking more contact.

Low moans rose in the back of Sam's throat.

Alex leaned in closer and closer, until her whole vision was framed in erotic sights and scents. Inhaling was a spice trail that tantalized and hardened Alex's nipples.

"Touch me." Sam's words were part command, part plea.

Alex met Sam's eyes. She recognized hunger in that gaze. Arousal curled through her belly. No matter how many times Alex saw proof of Sam's need, she still couldn't quite believe it.

Bending her head, Alex's mouth at last touched Sam's heat. She took her time, explaining with her tongue and fingers in meticulous detail all the ways she knew that desire could be teased, flamed, left trembling on the edge, and then…when Sam's defenses finally tumbled…sated.

Sam looked so vulnerable as she came. She seemed harder in places, too, as well as softer. Younger, freer, lost, taut. Naked and needy. All Sam. *All* of her.

Alex studied her in wonder, seeing the vision both before her and also in her mind, playing like a sumptuously shot, arthouse movie. Neck straining, back, stomach, and thigh muscles all clenched, twisting, pulling, releasing. So much beauty.

It was so honest. At that moment, Alex had never wanted someone more. Desire rose painfully inside. Wetness coated between her thighs, and her stomach clenched and swallowed. She desperately wanted to see that vulnerable, blissful look on Sam's face all over again. Alex bent forward once more.

God, how she loved women's bodies. And this body—this powerful, strong, honorable woman, who trembled as Alex stroked and licked every crevice, crinkle, and fold—suddenly became the most beautiful she'd ever had the joy of pleasuring.

Sam's toes curled. Her core clenched and drew Alex's exploring fingers deeper, pulsing against them. "I'm there."

There. Wetness coated Alex's mouth and fingers and she tasted Sam's escape. Piquant, salty. Sweet.

Sam's eyes that had clenched hard and tight as she'd sought her release, fluttered open. "Oh God. That was…" She inhaled.

"Hey," Alex said gently, withdrawing her slick fingers from Sam's heat. "Welcome back."

Sam smiled, her gaze still unfocused. The walls rebuilt; her defenses with them. But this time there was something lighter about her. "I needed that."

Alex smiled back at her. "Apparently telling your boss where to shove his job gets you a little worked up."

"I didn't do it like that," Sam protested with a lazy wave. "I was entirely professional. Said 'sir' and everything when I nuked his Police Barbie proposal." She laughed suddenly and pulled Alex into her arms. "By the way, you have a lot of talent."

"Mmm," Alex said, warmth spreading through her. "Flatterer. So now you're a little more relaxed, want to tell me if you're really okay? It's a huge deal losing your station."

"You sure you want to talk when I could be returning the favor?" Sam's fingers walked across to Alex's nipple and flicked it playfully.

"I'm a patient woman. You can owe me." Alex curled into Sam's side and slipped a leg over her hips. "So?"

Sam exhaled. "I know I should be shattered. My career went up in smoke and being a police officer is all I know. But…" She paused. "In some ways it felt like a weight lifted."

Alex nodded. The lightness she'd noticed. She'd long suspected Sam had been more miserable than she'd realized. In a rut, maybe? "Good for you."

"I don't know what to do now." A lost look entered her eyes.

"Knowing you, you have some options. So what's on your to-do list now? You feel like maybe revisiting some of your old dreams? Traveling?"

Sam became wistful. "Maybe. All I know is the world feels different right now."

Alex drew in a deep breath, wondering how this would go. "So, I've been thinking about something. How you want to go to your dream beach? It's just…you already know someone who lives in California, who'd be more than happy to take you there if you wanted." Alex snuggled closer. "I want you to know, that offer stands, in any capacity at all. I'd be honored."

Sam stared. "But Pfeiffer Beach is hours from LA."

"I don't care. It's not every day I help someone achieve a dream. But I'd love to show you more of my world, too, if you wanted. I move around a lot for work. It'd be fun. A couple of months' break and you could go home if you want. Or…stay longer, if things work out."

Disbelieving eyes met Alex's. "You don't mean that."

"I never say things I don't mean. Sam, I think this could be great for you. A reset; a change of scene. And for me? Well, I can't seem to get enough of you. It'd be nice if we didn't have to say good-bye quite so soon."

Sam bit her lip. "It's an incredible fantasy, but I doubt I can afford such an amazing adventure. Thank you for the offer."

"You know, as shallow and annoying as Hollywood is, it does have some perks," Alex said with an eye roll. "I'm getting paid extremely well for this movie, far more than I need. So...if that's all that's stopping you, we could work something out."

It took a beat for Alex's words to register but then brilliant, blinding hope flared across Sam's face. Just as quickly, it bled away, disappointment left in its wake. She'd really considered it...for a second. "I can't. My family needs me."

"But if all that stuff with Kev getting in trouble with the law is behind him, how do they need you?"

"Gina's not as young as she used to be. I help her out a lot," Sam said stiffly.

"Well, can't Sid and Kev help out if it's just chores?"

"It's not just that." Sam's pensive expression seemed to radiate a fear that Alex might argue. "When I came back home? I promised Gina I'd stay. A person's only as good as their word." She chewed her bottom lip.

For such a powerful statement, Sam didn't sound entirely certain.

Alex understood. She'd dropped a grenade in Sam's lap. For Alex, there was no debate about whisking a beautiful lover off to a few sights the woman had always dreamed of seeing. And if that led to something more, something deeper, well, Alex would be delighted.

But from Sam's point of view, Alex had just suggested she ignore her whole family-focused, ordered existence and go swanning off with her on a whim for months. Alex gave her a reassuring smile. "Well, I understand it's a lot. Think about it. You don't have to decide now."

"It's an amazing offer." Sam pulled Alex closer into her arms. "Thank you." She kissed her passionately, pressing her into the bed.

"God, Sam—"

A knock sounded on the trailer door. "Alex?" a female voice called.

Alex's eyes sprang open. *Damn it.* She sighed and reached for her robe. "A director's job is never done."

Sam hauled a sheet to cover herself, although the bed wasn't visible from the door.

The movement distracted Alex. Even shrouded by the sheet, her body was like a smooth, powerful sculpture. She'd never tire of that sight. *So beautiful.* She headed to the door, pulling it open.

Skye was on the top step, holding a bunch of color swatches. *Oh right.* Alex had asked her to bring them by as soon as she was done for the day.

"Alex," she began. "I..." Skye's gaze shifted to Alex's hair...then to the floor. Sam's heavy boots lay in a heap. A little farther along were her police pants. "Oh! Sorry to interrupt your...police business," she said with a gleam of amusement. "I have the swatches you were asking for. I'm leaning to viridian green."

"Right, excellent." Alex nodded briskly. "I'll think about it later. If that's all?"

"Not quite." Skye handed over the swatches. "Are you and Sam doing anything in twenty minutes?"

"Why?"

"There's a meeting."

"With whom?"

"I'll explain at the meeting. I'll knock on the trailer door when it's starting. Okay?" Skye didn't wait for an answer before disappearing.

"What was that about?" Sam asked.

"Beats me." Alex closed the door and dropped the samples on the kitchen table as she headed back to bed. "But we now have a mystery meeting to attend."

"That's weird." Sam shifted as though about to get up.

"Not so fast." Alex eyed her. "We have twenty minutes to fill and I believe you owe me. Besides, I hear New Zealand's finest have a reputation for efficiency."

Sam nodded earnestly. "There is that. Far be it for me to let down the side. C'mere."

Alex's eyes gleamed.

The next time Skye knocked, Sam was dressed and still tingling. The heat and want in Alex's eyes not ten minutes ago had been so addictive. The other woman hadn't needed long to finish, coming hard under Sam's hand, quivering with tension. Then there'd been that burning, naked appreciation that followed when Sam had slowly slid her uniform back on. She smirked at the reminder. It was clear that at least some part of Alex would miss Sam being a police officer a great deal.

As she was closest, Sam opened the door. She discovered an unlikely trio. Sid, Skye, and Kev. *The schemers.*

"What?" she asked acidly.

Breaker Bob suddenly jogged into view, muttering something about "just getting the message." He grinned.

Et tu, Bob?

Alex appeared behind Sam.

"Right, so. Okay, better jump right in." Sid shifted from foot to foot. "It's time for you both to know what happened."

"Oh?" Sam headed down the trailer steps, followed by Alex. "I'm all ears."

"You're right that we told you both a pack of porkies, but we did it for a good cause."

Alex shook her head in disbelief. "I'd love to know how you think you can spin this positively."

"Or at all," Sam grumbled.

"The first night you were both in the pub, having that big fight about how crap *Shezan* was...um, no offense..." Sid glanced at Alex.

Alex gave him a wave to get on with it.

"You were tearin' strips off each other. Well, I saw it. The spark, Sis. There's *fire*. And the *Shezan* people I was sitting with, they saw it, too—how Alex was reacting."

Alex peered at Sid. "What?"

"*Totally* into each other," Sid explained. "So, sure, we'd had a beer or four by then, but the more we talked about it, compared notes and the like, the more we realized those sparks were way out of the ordinary. And that maybe it'd be good if you saw more of each other. Like, a lot more."

"What does that mean?" Sam asked.

"Well." Sid coughed. "Um, romantically."

The breath seemed to leave Sam's lungs. *No.*

"Oh God," Alex murmured. "You've been *matchmaking* us? That's it?"

"Pretty much. You were like a couple of circling sharks, so we figured if we could just get you together, you'd see what we saw. So I punctured the pond, put the dummy in the dam, and asked Kev to hide an important light. It made sense at the time."

"This is crazy as hell." Sam scowled at him.

"Definitely," Alex agreed.

"No, crazy is what you two look like together. Fireworks, eh." He gave them a cheesy grin.

The others nodded adamantly.

Sam glanced at Bob, who was scratching the gray stubble on his chin. "You, too, Bob? I expected a bit better from you."

He shrugged. "What can I say? Everyone deserves to be happy. Specially you. To quote Mother Theresa—"

"Oh God," Sam muttered.

"—The most terrible poverty is loneliness."

"Kill me now," Sam groaned.

"Don't you think your plan had a few glaring flaws?" Alex broke in.

"Well, yeah," Sid conceded. "We made a mess of it cos we threw our stories together over a long, boozy night, so we didn't exactly notice any plot holes."

"Okay," Sam allowed, "but what about when you'd all sobered up?"

"Yeah." He looked rueful. "We should have sat down the next day and talked out the details and then we'd have noticed what a pile of shit it all was. But we didn't, cos we weren't focused on that side of it. It's like when someone points out the obvious, you go, 'Huh, why didn't I think of that?' But we were so fixated on our huge endgame, bein' big-picture thinkers and all, that we didn't see the little stuff that gave it away, right?"

"Christ," Sam muttered in disbelief. "None of you should ever become criminal masterminds."

"No argument from me." Sid cleared his throat. "So when you saw through our explanations, we had to get together and figure out some really good plan-B stories that sounded more plausible. Only problem was, they sounded plausible all right. They made you hate us. Kiri's totally crushed."

He peered at Sam. "She's looked up to you since school and here you were thinking she's a selfish brat. All she wanted was for you to be happy."

"That's all any of us wanted," Skye jumped in. "Alex, darling, this is the happiest I've seen you looking in years. Goodness, it's been a revelation seeing you light up like a Christmas tree around Sam."

"I see." Alex's cheeks flamed. "How flattering that you think my dating history is so awful it needed an intervention."

"It's not just you, dear. I'm a serial offender at matchmaking. Don't hate me because I'm a romantic." Her eyes sparkled with amusement.

"Anyway," Sid cut in, "we hadn't even finished with half the stuff we were planning before Sam got it into her hot head that Dino was behind it and rushed off to confront him."

"Well, next time don't dress your dummies in the same colors as the Boars!" Sam said in exasperation.

"Yep, Sis, point taken. Small tactical error there." Sid nodded sagely. "And obviously it wasn't meant to go that way. Anyway, what I'm getting at is what happened was pretty simple: You're always there for everyone else, Sam. And you had no one for you. Then along came Alex—cool, smart, easy on the eyes, likes chicks, has a job." Sid gave the thumbs up.

Alex snorted.

"It *was* a little more sophisticated than that," Skye tried.

"Did you ever think to ask?" Sam cut in.

"Whaddya mean?" Sid said.

"How do you know I didn't prefer things the way they were? Maybe I like my own company?"

"Sam," Sid said quietly. "Come on, that's such bull. You never wanted to sit on your ass alone in Ika Whenu for the rest of your life. That isn't you at all. Least, it didn't use to be."

Sam held up her hands, "Look, even if your intentions were good, why didn't you tell me any of this when I asked?"

"With the entire pub earholing in?" Sid gaped at her. "You'd have died of humiliation. Most of Ika Whenu was there that night."

She shuddered at that image. "So what about when I confronted you alone?"

"You weren't ready. You weren't invested enough in Alex yet."

Alex coughed. "Oh boy."

"Risk was that you'd toss away any chance with her just to spite us," Sid said. "I told everyone the puppy story so they understood."

"The puppy story?" Alex asked curiously.

"That's ridiculous!" Sam groaned. "I was a bloody kid."

Sid turned to Alex. "She was fourteen, right? I was seven. Kev hadn't been born yet. Old man McGregor's dog had had a litter of six beautiful puppies. Gorgeous little things. Mum had promised Sam she could pick one out for us. When we get there, it's obvious which pup is for Sam."

Sam made a soft pained noise.

"There he was, blonde and white, so bouncy and beautiful, with these bright eyes, and it was like meeting Samantha Keegan in puppy form," Sid said. "Amazin'. None of us could believe it. The McGregors were asking her what she was gonna call him. Mum and Dad were suggesting silly names. I was trying to shove the pup in her arms and do whatever a seven-year-old thinks will help his sister choose a thing. And the more all that happened, the more Sam got as stubborn as a chest cold."

"I did not!"

Sid eyed her. "You so bloody well did. You made a face, stamped your foot, and said you didn't like that puppy at all and you went and picked the runt. Even though Mr. McGregor warned you it was pretty sick and mightn't live long. So you dug your heels in, we took home the sick pup, and later that day the McGregors gave away all the other puppies. So how long did our puppy live Sam?"

Ten days. "No idea."

"You sulked for six months when it died. And we never did get a dog after that. You said you didn't want one again."

"I can't see the point of rehashing all this."

"So why didn't you pick the perfect puppy?" Sid eyed her for a long moment. "Because you hate being pushed into things, made to feel like you've got no choice in it. Even if it costs you happiness, you make damn sure it's *your* decision."

"Wait, did you just call me a puppy?" Alex asked.

Sam folded her arms. "A puppy is hardly the same thing as who I date as an adult, Sid."

"Not so sure about that. If you'd known we were fixing you up with Alex early on, you'd have shoved her away and given us all a what-for."

"I…" It was true. Absolutely true. But still! Galling much?

"So," Sid said, "your friends did what they had to so you didn't feel backed into any corner, even if they looked like assholes in the process. Cos you can't be trusted to grab onto a good thing if you think someone else chose it for you."

"I'm not that bad," she protested weakly.

Sid shook his head. "No? How does it feel every morning when you take Bruce for a ride? Every day, you know Mrs. Fenley has that perfect dog you never claimed because you're so pig-headed."

How do I feel? Idiotic, but glad Mrs. Fenley loves him, too. "I'm not pig-headed."

"Then why are you so mad your friends wanted you to have a shot with someone awesome?"

"It's not that. It's just you could have butted out and left us to it."

"And that'd have left you two staring daggers at each other till the clock ran down on *Shezan* and Alex went home. So sue us for caring enough to throw you together to make you face all that chemistry."

"And why are you spilling this all now?"

Sid beamed. "Um, we heard your relationship had *developments*." He put air quotes around the word.

"For God's sake, this is not how sane people do things," Sam protested. "You're all certifiable."

"Sam's right," Alex agreed, sounding amused. "Certifiably crazy."

"*Good*-crazy, though," Sid suggested cheerfully. "Y'know, Skye said ours was an A-grade plan and that she was an expert at dark arts-level matchmaking."

Skye offered a sheepish look. "I was sure this was *the* most genius idea in human history, but in my defense, I may have been on my fourth mojito at the time."

Sid snorted. "Except you were the most sober one of us."

"Which wasn't saying much." Skye's expression became somber as she regarded Alex and Sam. "I truly wish the next day we'd all sat down and thought about how it might backfire or hurt you. Instead, I got all caught up in my costume redesigns, and I know Kiri and Bob were flat-out, too, and so we didn't give it much thought beyond 'Oh, how lovely if it all comes together.' Not our most brilliant moment. But we really did mean well. It was for the greater good."

"Did no one stop to think about how much this cost the movie or the police in lost time?" Alex said.

"Exactly!" Sam glared at Sid.

"It wasn't supposed to delay production," Skye said. "I was clear on that from the start. And every incident was chosen for most minimal impact. Well, until things got out of hand."

Kev snorted. "One word for it."

Sam gave them both a look more stony than an Easter Island statue. "I'm sorry I can't see the funny side right now." She retreated back into the trailer, shutting the door with a bang.

"Give her time," Alex said, voice muffled through the trailer door. "I know you meant well. But she's had a tough day and she's got a lot on her mind. Your big confession just adds to it."

Sam sighed inwardly. That wasn't even the half of it.

Ten minutes later, Alex discovered Sam staring into space on the couch of her trailer. Her posture was unnaturally stiff.

"Well, that was fun," Alex said lightly. "I've never been match-made by my own crew before."

"I'm a laughingstock."

"More like you're an unmade bed. An unstraightened painting." Alex gave her a wry look. "Weird thing about humans is they love to fix things. You know what people are like. *I wish my friend wasn't so alone. Oh look, two single lesbians, let's…*" She interlocked her fingers. "This isn't even about us. It's about them thinking they're helping and meddling because they can. At least it's from a place of love."

"It's from a place of annoying," Sam grumbled.

Alex snickered. "That, too."

"You seem weirdly happy."

"More like relieved. All this time I thought someone hated me enough to bring down my movie, and it's…"

"My idiot brother and his accomplices."

"Exactly. They'd be insufferable if they knew I'm not mad, but between me and you? Come on, it is a *bit* funny." Alex elbowed her. "And when Bob earnestly quoted Mother Theresa, I thought I was going to lose it on the spot."

"Bob's a man of many depths."

"Right." Alex laughed. "So why's this making you so grumpy? Your friends and mine just want us happy. That's not so awful is it?"

Sam closed her eyes. "I told you about my childhood. Everyone in Ika Whenu knows my business and my secrets. Every time I turn around I see that knowledge in their eyes. Today's just a tiresome reminder of how small a small town really is. Meddlers and gossips. It makes it tempting as hell to just..."

Alex blinked. "What?"

"Go." Sam sighed and then sagged again.

"Are you serious?"

The silence stretched on as Sam seemed to pick apart her response. "Sorry. No. It's a really nice fantasy but... Hell, I wish it were that easy."

"It could be. You have no job, no plans, and you have me...someone who'd love to spend a few months traveling with you. Then, who knows?"

Sam's mask was sliding into place, her features becoming more closed off. "Sometimes I let myself dream for a minute. Sometimes I even try to trick myself, too."

"How?"

"When I found out Sid was behind it all, it felt like, well, if he could just throw away family, then maybe I didn't have to stick to my promises to family, either. I wanted it to be a sign I could leave. But it was just an excuse, and I always come back to one thing: I'm the woman I am today because of Gina, and I made her a promise. Anyway, it's not just that. People need me here, too. I wouldn't want to let anyone down." She hesitated. "Maybe exploring the world's just not on the cards for me and it's time I finally accepted that."

"Sam?" Alex said gently. "Stay tonight? We could talk some more about this."

"What's there to talk about?"

"You don't need to make up your mind now."

"We both knew this was a short-term thing from the start. Aren't we kidding ourselves?"

"Maybe, maybe not. At least give us a chance?" Alex urged her. "Maybe do what I'd do: a pros and cons list. I'm good at those."

"I'll bet you are." Sam smiled softly. "I'll bet you're good at all sorts of things." Her face fell. "Feels like I've been saying good-bye from the moment we first kissed. I don't want to keep doing that for the rest of the time you're here. It hurts too much. It'll only get worse."

"It doesn't have to be good-bye yet," Alex protested. "Come on, it doesn't."

"But it will be good-bye eventually, so what's the point dragging it out? You belong out there, in a bright, shiny, distant world I don't fit into." Sam bent down, cupping Alex's face, and kissed her more tenderly than Alex ever had been kissed in her life. "And the truth is I'm needed here."

"Come to dinner tonight?" Alex said quietly. "Please?"

"I don't think it's a great idea. I need space to figure things out. I wouldn't be much company." Sam studied her and her gaze became soft. "I am really glad about one thing today. Finding out no one's been trying to sabotage you. No matter what else, that's a huge weight off my mind." Sam's fingers trailed down her cheek. "So beautiful." She inhaled. "G'bye, Alex."

Chapter 26

Space

Shezan: Mistress of the Forest was finally coming together, Alex thought with grim satisfaction. She'd thrown herself into work with ferocity after Sam's good-bye two days ago and told herself it was probably for the best. After all, Alex could focus properly now, not wonder what her life would bring, whether she'd have someone else to consider, or what plans to make.

Well, at least her love life was consistent. Why did she still even bother dreaming that someone might think she was worth taking a chance on, and going in boots and all?

Not that she blamed Sam. She'd known all along that what she'd asked was a lot for Sam to overcome, given her life and experiences.

Too much, it seemed.

It was almost seven, her eyes were gritty, and her head hurt, but the dailies waited for no one.

"There," Quincy said, pointing at the scene they were reviewing together. "Pause there. The sun hitting behind the mountain. That's spectacular." He exhaled in amazement. "Gold."

It was. One thing Alex hadn't counted on was just how stunning *Shezan*'s backdrop would be.

"Cinematography steals the movie," Quincy continued. "I can't believe I'm about to say this, but I actually believe you could win an Oscar for *Shezan*."

Alex burst into laughter.

"I'm serious!"

"I know. That's why it's funny." She shook her head. "Well, I can see why the first director insisted on filming virtually right under the falls. He had a good eye, even if the sound looping will kill us slowly."

They watched Chloe and Melody circling each other, the flirting and dynamic tension arcing up.

"Hmm," Quincy said. "I'm also starting to think you really know what you're doing."

"I'm sure there was a compliment buried in there somewhere."

Quincy snorted.

Alex trudged back to her trailer a short time later, considering her options. She wasn't in the mood for pub frivolity tonight. So...drink, sleep, or...

After a warm shower involving troubling thoughts about a certain cop she was already missing far too much for a short-term fling, Alex wrapped herself into her white "Shezan Rulez" robe and slipped on fuzzy socks. With a soothing cup of not-too-terrible coffee in hand, she reached for her phone and tapped Bess's number, already practicing her excuses given how late it would be in LA.

"Well, well, she lives," came the amused drawl after the second ring. Her best friend sounded wide awake.

"Hey. Sorry to call so late."

"It's fine. We're still up. Summer's learning a script. I'm reading a new biography—about that American media mogul Elena Bartell. Spoiler alert: She's a lesbian. Did you know they're making a movie about her? I should audition. I'm only one flattened vowel away from perfecting my New York accent."

Alex snorted and took another sip of drink.

"Do you never check your messages?" Bess continued. "I left several calls after your viral video. My God, I thought New Zealand was such a nice, quiet place. And when you landed smack bang in the gang compound, I about had a heart attack."

"Oh, that." Alex laughed. "Yeah, it looked worse than it was."

"It had better. So...who's the cute cop?"

"The what?"

"I'll jog your memory. The one who you had the camera focused on for fifteen minutes? Your *dear, brave* friend."

"Uh…"

"The one you dedicated the video to. The one who rushed to your aid. Don't forget that close-up, from grass level, of her gazing down at you looking scared out of her skull that you'd hurt yourself."

"Oh. Yeah." *Shit.* "We've gotten to know each other a bit."

"Quite a bit, I should imagine." Amusement laced Bess's voice. "By the way, Summer's requesting you do a New Zealand wedding. She's always wanted to go."

"Wedding!"

"Personally, I think destination weddings are elitist consumerism. Although she has a point about how lovely New Zealand is."

"Bess, stop joking about this. I don't even know how I feel about her." Actually, Alex had a disturbingly good idea how she felt. Their last conversation washed endlessly around in her head. Not seeing Sam for even a few days was disconcerting; nothing felt right knowing she wasn't just a call away.

"I'd say you feel a considerable amount given the panic in your voice on that video. And I'm really happy for you. *Really.*" Her voice was warm. "She's far better than Bettina. The worry in that woman's eyes for you was crystal clear."

"Oh."

"Why do you sound so stricken? Or…is it over already?" Bess sounded worried.

"I… Yeah. It went pear-shaped after I sort of invited her home with me."

"Ah."

Silence fell between them.

Alex winced at how lame that must sound. It was every lesbian U-Haul stereotype, wasn't it? Even if her offer was only about sight-seeing. Well, *mainly* sight-seeing—with hope for more. Much more.

Instead, Bess murmured, "So she must care a great deal if you asked her to do that? I mean, you're one of the most perceptive people I've ever met. You must know she has feelings for you."

Alex considered that. The gentle way Sam touched her. The loaded looks. The way she'd opened up to Alex with secrets not lightly shared. And she did also fling herself at a violent gang of bikers for Alex. Who does that if they're not…?

"The emotional side, that's not the issue, I don't think," Alex decided. "It's just I asked too much, too soon. Sam has responsibilities here. And she chose those over me."

Bess gave a knowing *mmmm.* "So you want me to tell you it's okay and not to worry; that it'll all work out? I can do that. So: What responsibilities does she have? Her police job?"

"No." Alex frowned. "Mainly some old promise made to her family, I think."

"And what's your plan to win her over?"

"My… Wait, I'm not trying to win her over."

"Whyever not?"

"Um." Alex stopped and considered that. "I'm being respectful?"

"Is that what you want? To respectfully wave to her from the airport and never see her again?"

Never see her again? Oh God. The clench in Alex's gut was almost painful. "I need her."

"As I thought. So fight for her. Anyone who gets you this worked up has to be worth it."

"Look, she's big on doing right by her community and her family. How can I fight that?"

"Are you sure that's her issue?"

"You think she's lying?" Alex's eyes widened.

"I think it never hurts to check on why people really do things. It's human nature, shying away from what scares us most."

Alex rubbed her temples. "Or Sam really *is* honorable and wants to keep her promises. She's like that." She sagged at the truth of her words. "Damn. I really have no hope, do I?"

"Don't count yourself out yet."

"It's fine. I'm used to being second choice." *Oh hell.* She bit her lip at the clumsy words.

Silence fell. Then Bess drew in a sip of air, barely audible. "Alex? I'm sorry about…when we dated. Truly. I was lacking a great deal of self-awareness, not to mention being deep in denial about my…situation back then. But we're better as friends, aren't we?"

"Definitely. It's not you, it's just…why does this keep happening to me?" Frustration filled her.

"I know it's a dreadful cliché, but when it's meant to be, it will be. And you can't abandon hope yet. You're good at research, so research. Talk to whoever knows her best. Come on, you're great at getting to the truth and heart of people. It's why you're an exceptional filmmaker."

"Why are you so sure it's worth it?"

Bess snorted. "Darling, I saw the video. You two… My God, if someone bottled whatever emotion was arcing between you, they'd be rich. I mightn't know Sam, but I know this: The way she ran over to you in that compound, the fear in her eyes over you, no one's that good an actor. I find it hard to believe you're her second choice on anything."

Hope soared fierce and strong.

Bess's voice faded out as she spoke to someone away from the phone, and then: "Summer's just come to bed."

"Right. I won't keep you."

"Before you go, may I offer some final advice?"

Alex went to her mini-bar and grabbed a bottle of water. "God help us all," she said dryly. "Come on, wasn't your grand idea of wooing Summer to ignore her for months?"

"That's out of context," Bess claimed in amused indignation. "I wasn't wooing her, I was protecting… Look, forget it, just listen."

"Okay." Alex took a gulp of the drink.

"Just don't underestimate yourself. You are witty, empathetic, clever, and cute, and unlike me, you have plenty of charm."

Alex knew that tone. "Uh-oh, what's happened now?"

"The gossip rags are claiming I've been indulging in eating baby placentas as a health kick. I think the subtext was I'm trying to live forever, wicked witch that I am."

"Life goals!" Alex burst out laughing. "At least they never suggest you aim low."

"There is that." Bess sounded pleased at the idea.

"Me, I'm apparently working on a film setting back feminism fifty years." Alex sighed.

"Fifty? That does sound impressive. Right, I'm turning in. Good luck on getting the girl." A low murmuring sounded, then she added, "Summer says to stay away from bikers and, also, that there should be an ancient Chinese proverb about marrying the woman who throws off two assailants to reach your side."

"I'll bear that in mind. If it's not too late. She may not still be interested."

"How could she not be?" Bess asked, a smile evident in her voice. "You're you. Special. Night, Alex."

"Night." Alex hung up, warmed to the tips of her toes.

Chapter 27

Permission

It's for the best, Sam reminded herself for the umpteenth time in three days, as she climbed off Tiger outside Mason's milking sheds.

She would have been kidding herself—well, both of them, really—dragging things out. Sam had so many responsibilities here. People needed her. She flipped the rusty latch over and tugged the door open.

Mason gave her a grateful wave, assorted cows mooed, and she trudged back to her bike.

Alex didn't understand. How could she? It was hard for Sam to explain all the little things that made up the press of responsibilities in Ika Whenu that she could never abandon. That was that.

Then why do I feel so miserable?

Her phone beeped with an incoming text. Alex.

Did I ever tell you how good I am with lists? I think I should help you with yours.

Baffled, Sam threw her phone back into her pocket unanswered, started Tiger, and roared back into town.

Gina greeted her at the pub door like usual, pointing the bread tray to the kitchen. Sam's phone beeped twice more but her hands were occupied with two dozen sandwich loaves.

"You gonna get that, love?" Gina asked after Sam set down the bread. "Your phone's going off like Dutch's microwave."

"It's nothing." She turned to go.

"You okay?" Gina cocked her head. "You don't seem yourself. Even more broody, if that's possible."

"All good."

"I'm sure there's something you want to tell me. Something about work?" Her gaze sharpened.

"Oh." Right. "I lost my job. Not much else to say."

"Quit's how I heard it."

"Well-informed as ever." Sam rolled her eyes.

"Saw the story in the paper. A certain new senior constable got phone video of the Hornets dropping drugs in Ika Whenu."

Sam folded her arms. "Great. Murray'll go far."

"Anonymous witness gave it to him, the paper said. Some *jogger*." Her eyes were knowing.

"Lucky."

"You miss it, don't you?"

Sam shrugged. "I don't miss being on call all hours."

"So what are you doing with all your spare time? Spending it with that director of yours?"

Of course GNN knew about her and Alex.

"If that's whose boots are under your bed these days, I'm happy for you," Gina continued. "She seems lovely, especially for a Hollywood type."

Sam sighed inwardly and kept her face neutral. "We're...on a break."

"Oh, bub, what's happened?"

"Nothing. Life goes on. Same old, same old. I'm needed here. Look, I better go."

"Wait." Gina drew her aside, away from the open kitchen door and Dutch's earshot. "What do you mean by 'I'm needed here?' Did she ask you to go off with her?"

Caught, Sam sighed and didn't answer.

Gina didn't need one. "She must care for you to make such an offer."

Sam scowled at being put on the spot. "It's only travel. A few months checking out the sights together. Thousands of miles away from everyone. From you. And Kev."

"Where you're needed," Gina repeated.

"Right."

"What has you so busy here? Most people don't quit a job without something lined up. But all I see is a lot of empty space in your day."

Sam drew her finger along the polished, worn wood bar. "I've been considering all my options."

"And what are these options?"

Sam shrugged. "I thought you could use some help maybe. You're not getting any younger. And you know I've helped out at the pub over the years; I know how it's done. I could be there for you all the time, especially when you do your big gastro-pub overhaul."

"Got it all figured out, hmm?" Gina's expression lacked any trace of the delight Sam had assumed would follow her offer.

"No one would give you any trouble with me around," Sam added. "If anyone got ugly, I could step in immediately."

"As could Senior Constable Snell—whose job it would actually be."

Sam stared at her.

Gina tutted. "It's not that I don't appreciate the offer, it's just—a better question is why you're not considering Alex's offer, too? Why'd you break things off?"

"How'd you know *I* did?"

With a snort, Gina eyed her. "Miss Responsible here wonders how I know."

"Fine." Sam folded her arms. "Cleaner to do it now. Just be harder later." Sam leveled Gina with a cool gaze.

"But why'd you turn her down at all? Don't say it's because you suddenly have a passion for running a pub. You'd be bored in two minutes. And don't say it's because you don't care about her, either. Bub, you're way more gone on her than you ever were that Auckland girl. The moping's ten times worse this time. And I *have* seen you two together. A mother knows these things."

"I have responsibilities here," Sam protested.

"Let's hear them."

"Lots of little things that add up every day, from picking up your supplies to doing Mason's gate. Kev needs me to keep an eye on him, most of all. People need me."

"When I stopped driving, the baker offered to drop off the bread for me, but I told him no because I liked seeing you every day. Can just as easily say yes. And I'm sure you don't need to stay in town just to lift or close a latch on a cowshed."

"But Mason…"

"Has friends, family, neighbors. Not everything's down to you."

"Well, there's Kev."

"Who's now a man."

"Who needs me."

"Does he, though? He's grown up a whole lot lately."

"He's turning out as crazy as Sid," Sam grumbled.

"I reckon so." Fondness filled Gina's eyes. She reached into her pocket and drew out her wallet, from which she plucked a photo, worn and faded.

Sam. Aged about twelve.

"I fell so in love with this little girl." Gina traced the lines of her young face in the photo. "It broke my heart the day I found you. I said to myself, 'Gina Mahuta, you will not let this child down. You will make sure she feels safe and loved and is protected no matter what.'"

"And I'm grateful. You kept that promise."

"Not always. I'm not perfect. I also let you feel obligated to fix your brother's situation. I sometimes wonder if that was the worst thing to do."

"I didn't mind. Gangs are a risky thing to get caught up in."

"True. But that happened years ago. Kev's safe. So I'm wondering, why are you still here?"

"Trying to get rid of me?" Her words, intended to be teasing, sat between them like an unexploded warhead.

"Never," Gina said forcefully. "You'll always be mine, whether you're in LA or Outer Mongolia. You'll always have a home here, too. But you don't need to stay here to make sure of that. You won't lose me if you go."

"Why are you so sure I should? I've been doing okay here, haven't I? Well, until the mess at the Boars compound."

"You have. And people here respect you a great deal."

Sam gave a cynical huff. "Sure. Respect me so much they pulled those sabotage stunts on me."

"Is that really how you see it? That they played some stupid pranks on you? No. That's their way of showing they care."

"More like they got plastered and thought it was hilarious. You know how bored people get around here. The scrutiny and gossip are constant.

Between what happened to Mum, you fostering me, and my coming out, I was a hot topic for years. This is just same old shit, different day."

"I know they hurt you badly back then," Gina said quietly. "And I also recall a lot of those doing the hurting weren't much older than you at the time. Now that everyone's all grown, they feel bad about the things that were done to you; I know it as a fact."

Sam paused. Hadn't Dino admitted much the same thing?

"And those shenanigans on that movie set?" Gina continued. "Well, I see people trying to show you how much they care about you. Wanting you happy. And all you're seeing is they're laughing at you. They aren't, sweetheart." She cupped Sam's cheek and met her eye. "The laughter's stopped. It stopped years ago. Sure, there'll always be gossips but it's not about hurting you. I promise, you don't need those ten-foot-high walls anymore."

Oh sure. Easy for her to say.

"Anyway, that's a thing for you to figure out on your own," Gina said. "In the meantime, what I can say is, if you want to leave us, that's okay. We'll all be just fine."

I'm that disposable?

"Hey," Gina asked in concern. "What is it? Where'd that squirrelly brain of yours just take you?"

"Nowhere," Sam said gruffly.

"Sam, just because you're free to go doesn't mean we won't miss you. I'll ache not seeing you every day. But I'll be happy, too, knowing you're off following your heart. And if your heart lay in pouring beers in my pub, I'd be thrilled to have you beside me. But that's not you. Your dreams have always been about seeing the world. And before you say you don't care about that anymore, I've seen your postcards. It's okay to go after your dreams. It is, bub. I promise, it is."

Hope warred with doubt inside Sam. Her dreams had seemed impossible for so long. Sam's thoughts lurched into a chaotic jumble.

"By the way, those movie people just paid the first half of my catering bill," Gina said. "Turns out they pay in American dollars—now that was a lovely surprise! Probably should have read my contract closer. But it means I'm getting almost half as much again as I budgeted for, so I'll have plenty for my new oven, and then some. I won't need your loan money. I'm giving it back."

"It was a gift." Sam eyed her uncertainly.

"I love you for that, I do, but you'll be needing some splash cash around all those fancy tourist places. And maybe you'll want to take Alex somewhere nice and romantic, too?"

"I haven't decided to go yet."

Gina shot her a knowing look. "Don't be stubborn now. If this is the puppy all over again—"

"I swear if anyone mentions Bruce one more time—"

"So prove us wrong."

"I've got to think about it. It's complicated."

"Or it's real simple."

Sam exhaled. "Nothing's ever simple with me. You know that."

"I'm well aware. You do love to overthink everything." Gina looked sad. "Just consider it. Okay?"

With a nod, Sam left before the annoying woman thought up any more probing questions. Outside, she plucked her phone out of her pocket and called up her new text messages.

*Sam's list – Pros and Cons of Having an Adventure with Alex Levitin**
**Because nothing is decided until there has been a list*

Nothing? Sam snorted. *Sure.*

Pro: I'll let you ride my Unicorn all over LA. Who needs some high-powered beast called Tiger when you can purr along on my 'sweet cream machine'. I'll even give you naming rights.*
**possibly a euphemism.*

Sam typed back:

Con – I don't have a US driver's licence for streets of LA. Nice try.

Alex replied immediately.

Pfft. We'll go off-road then. I've heard you know a bit about that. Rumor has it you even know stunts, like flinging yourself under cute directors' cars to show off.

Flinging herself under…

*Pretty sure that's *not* how it happened.*

Sam settled back on Tiger and drew out her helmet as her phone beeped again.

Semantics. Pro: In LA, I can take you to a set to see actual movie motorcycle stunts that'd set your hair on fire! Thrills, spills, and superstars. Ooh!

Sam did up her helmet strap. Then tapped a reply:

Con: It'd be easier to stay home and watch Breaker Bob. I'd get to save a bundle, share a beer with him, and my hair would stay un-napalmed.

OK, then. Pro: We can take photos of you swanning around Pfeiffer Beach to send to that bitchy ex who said you'd never get there. To go with it, I can enlist my comedian mate Rowan to come up with a clever, cutting message of restrained British shade. Bonus points: It'll be so subtle it'll take her a week to realize she's been insulted.

Sam smiled. Nicole wasn't worth it. Rowan sounded fun, though. She tried to picture him and came up with a young Hugh Lawrie. Random.

Pro: Sam, even you are allowed a break and to get out of dodge sometime

No attempt at humor this time. Sam could picture her pleading eyes. She pushed down her anxiety, that feeling of being boxed in. First Gina beating this drum, now Alex.

Con: I can't just abandon people who rely on me. It doesn't work that way.

Her phone beeped almost immediately.

A break isn't abandoning anyone. Final pro: There's me. You really matter to me Sam. I don't want to lose 'us'.

Sam stared at the message. Their...whatever it was...wasn't supposed to be about more. The pressure in her head started building. Why did everyone want her to take up Alex's offer? Why was everyone pushing her to go?

She already felt dispensable thanks to the letter sitting on her kitchen table. Official confirmation of her resignation from New Zealand Police. It included an order to turn in her equipment and uniform. And...the big one: a requirement she vacate her subsidized rental within six weeks to allow one Senior Constable Murray Snell to move in, now his appointment had been made permanent.

This was too much. She revved Tiger and debated whether to go home. She needed a clear head. Air. Sam pointed her bike out of Ika Whenu and floored it.

Roaring along Kopuku Road, the dark green forest pressed in on her, calling her into its depths to hit the hard trails.

Soon.

Tumbling, brittle, brutal thoughts spun through her head. Gina didn't need her. Kev didn't need her. Sid had never needed her. New Zealand Police sure as hell didn't need her. Even a certain neighbor's dog was perfectly fine without her. She'd caught Bruce happily curled up at the feet of her replacement at the station yesterday.

No one in her community really needed her. Funny how she'd always thought they had. The ego of her. How humiliating to discover she was about as essential as tits on a bull to the population of Ika Whenu.

So that was good, wasn't it? She was free to go. That's what everyone seemed to want, anyway. It's what Alex wanted. Everyone was pushing her that way. Sam gritted her teeth.

Why shouldn't she just leave? After all, Sam was now pretty sure her feelings for Alex weren't the passing-fling kind. The woman was intoxicating. She couldn't get enough of her.

So what was the damned problem? Stubbornness for the sake of it?

I'm afraid.

Oh.

Sam blinked. Oh hell. Had she left it too long? Lost her spontaneous streak?

She tried to pick apart the sensation, the threads and layers gluing doubt to fear.

What am I afraid of?

For a brief, absurd moment, Alex's love of lists leapt to mind.

The wind picked up, icy and frigid against her cheeks.

What do I fear? What if something happened to Gina when she was gone? Or Sid or Kev? Sam would never forgive herself.

What if… The next doubt curled inside her like a ball of prickles… What if she didn't even like traveling, after all these years banging on about it and moping over her damned postcards? Geez, that'd take the cake, wouldn't it?

That's not it.

What was it?

What if Alex gets bored with me? Then what?

The pain of that thought was so suffocating she knew she'd hit the mark. Sam was a *managed* risk taker. She didn't like being tossed into the darkest unknown. Hell, she'd quit her job rather than face being sent God knows where, to start at the bottom again, away from everything she knew.

Taking a chance that someone *might* want Sam in their life for as long as Sam wanted them, too… She couldn't control that risk at all. If she gambled and lost, the hurt would choke her. She'd be off, far from home, with a woman who no longer thought she mattered.

That was the crux of it. Sam had long wondered if she was easy to throw away. Her deadbeat father certainly thought so. Her mother hadn't managed to find a way back to her, either.

It wasn't her fault. It wasn't.

Doubts filled her. How would Sam deal with it if things with Alex crashed and burned? How would it feel if a woman who had come to mean so much to her looked her in the eye and said, "It was fun but I'm done."

Isn't Alex worth the risk, though? She clung to that thought. Of course she was.

It's not managed risk, the anxious part of her brain hissed back. *I can't manage that. I can't predict that. It would crush me if she wanted me then discarded me, too.*

That felt like the truest thing she knew. So, there it was. Maybe she should protect herself while she still could. Protect her brittle heart. Stay.

No! She didn't want to watch Alex walk out of her life.

What if, though, I let Alex leave now and decided later...maybe I could follow her if I realized I made the wrong choice?

Rounding a corner, she leaned into the tight bend, enjoying the speed, just as a flash of white came into view.

An enormous sheep truck was bearing down on her, taking up most of the road.

The driver honked, long and loud. The road was too narrow. Sam was going too fast.

Mouth dry and eyes widening, her hands crushed the brakes. She yanked the handlebars to the side, praying it'd be enough.

Alex headed over to the pub before work, determination building. Time to get to the bottom of a certain confusing, honorable ex-cop. She found Gina in a supply room, shifting boxes to and fro.

"You here for Sam? Just missed her," Gina said.

"No. I was hoping we could sit and have a chat?"

"Sorry, love, just had a new delivery. Gotta find space for it all. I can sort and listen, though. What's on your mind?" She cracked the lid on a carton.

"Sam."

"There's a surprise." She snorted. "Matters of the heart, hmm? Pass me the box of Jim Beam?"

"You know about us?" Alex tried to shove the carton Gina's way but almost threw out her back.

The publican laughed. "You'll never cut it in pubs, that's for sure."

"Highly doubt it, yeah."

"And of course I knew. You two haven't exactly been hiding those long looks. But before that, all your friends and Sam's were in here, hatching up schemes late into the evening the night you two had your big dust-up." She looked up. "Be glad they never got to releasing a wild pig on set. Breaker was sauced as hell and all ripe and ready to go trap one then and there!"

"Christ."

"So what do you need, love? Everything okay?"

"I was wondering if Sam's ever thought about leaving Ika Whenu?"

Gina paused. "She did leave. When she went off to do her police training and got posted in Auckland for a few years. But she came back when Kev got in strife."

"Since then?"

"I suppose I don't have to guess why you're asking?"

"I've asked Sam to come back to LA with me. See some sights. She said she can't leave." Alex frowned. "She didn't say she doesn't want to, only that she has responsibilities here. Reading between the lines, I gather she made a promise to you once and she doesn't break her word."

"Are you implying I'm keeping her here? Because promises about Kev were years ago. That's all in the past."

"*I* know that. *You* know that. But I'm wondering if she does?"

"What are you getting at?" Gina's eyes narrowed. "I'd never force her to stay."

"That's just it. You don't have to force Sam. She does everything out of love and obligation. Because she made a commitment and she's honorable. And sometimes, people want to do right by those they love or respect, and that matters more to them. You know her better than anyone. Tell me, does Sam strike you as that sort of person? Who'd put herself second over her own happiness if she thought it was the right thing to do?"

Gina's jaw worked. "She's always been the responsible one, even young. Always looking out for others. Me. Everyone. The whole town."

"So when does she get to look out for herself? Has anyone ever told her she could?"

"Think you have it all figured out, don't you?" Gina regarded her closely. "Sometimes people are a lot more complicated than you think. This isn't about me."

"I'm not saying—"

"Yes, you are. And it's not about some old promise I asked for when I was at my wit's end with Kevin. Sometimes things matter more to people than what's best for them."

"What matters most to Sam then?"

Gina sighed and leaned against the shelves. "As a girl, Sam was afraid of one thing: We'd stop wanting her. Didn't matter how many times I told her she was stuck with us, that's what terror was for her, that'd we'd toss her aside some day. So she made herself essential. I think in her head somewhere, she believed if she wasn't desperately needed, she's not wanted, either."

Alex sucked in a breath. *How sad.*

"She's always been this way," Gina said. "So you asking her to leave out of the blue, to do something where she's not essential to some vital thing will have her in quite a tailspin. She'll be agonizing over it for sure."

"Could you talk to her? Make her see this is a good thing?"

"I already did. And it's no use."

"I'm sorry?"

"It's not enough for me to give her permission to go, though I can see you came here convinced it was. She has to give herself permission. Afraid I can't help with that."

Disappointment filled Alex.

"But if it makes you feel better, she's still in two minds. Will certainly be brooding up a storm right now." Gina studied her. "In the meantime, what of you?"

"Pardon?"

"Why are you inviting a woman you barely know overseas with you? That seems awful fast."

"I know how it looks. But it doesn't have to mean anything big. Sam'd come for a few months, see a bit of the world, and go home. What's the worst that could happen? She's gotten to tick off a few things on her bucket list? She's always dreamed of traveling."

"Oh, love." Gina clucked her tongue. "I can see the lie all over your face. You want a lot more than a few months with her."

"I..." Alex didn't bother denying it. *Yes.*

The old woman didn't speak for a few moments. "Y'know, I fell in love with my Albert in just two days. Silly old duffer had been hitchhiking through town barefoot in the middle of winter and I just had to know who he was. Loved every one of our twenty-three years together before he passed. Sometimes it happens that way."

"That's so sweet."

"Mmm. So I can't really judge what feels right to another person, even if it is fast. All I can say is, I need you to promise to look after my girl. She's not nearly as tough as she acts."

"I will," Alex vowed.

Eying her thoughtfully, Gina said, "You know, when that daughter of mine commits to anything, she jumps in boots and all. If she agrees to go with you, remember that. This won't be a casual thing for her. It'll mean something. Something big." Her expression sharpened. "And I think you're the same, maybe."

Alex shot her a surprised look.

"It's in your eyes."

Alex dipped her head. "I'd really love it to work out. I tell myself, maybe it will, maybe it won't. But I can't *not* try. Sam's too...special...not to give it a go. I had to ask."

"Yes, love, I guess you did. And she'll decide before long. Be patient." Gina pulled a box over and tore it open. "Now get on with you. I'm sure you've got better things to do than trip over my merchandise." She waved her away.

Sam stared up at the enormous shape filling her vision with wide eyes as her hands crushed the brakes in a death grip. Anguished squeals of air brakes filled the air as the truck driver slammed on his, too.

It would be too late; they would never stop in time. Hemmed in on either side by trees and dense vegetation, there was nowhere to go.

This was it? She could smell the sheep manure, hear the panicked baas from the back of the truck, and taste a sharpness in her mouth.

In an instant, her life condensed into just the heartbeats thundering in her ears. Almost dispassionately, she saw the truck, the narrow black road, her reactions.

Time condensed again and warped, and suddenly she saw Gina's eyes the night she'd found Sam behind the pub with her mother. A dog dying against her chest, and Sam crying for days. Realizing she was gay. Kissing Nicole. Gina's plea for Sam to come home. Being named Ika Whenu's police officer. Nicole dumping her. Hauling Kev out of Dino's gang by the scruff of his scrawny neck.

Then nothing. Until Alex. A montage of Alex's amused looks and bright eyes and soft, soft lips flashed into her mind.

The other driver suddenly hauled his rig off the road and into the brush, flattening shrubs and saplings, and bouncing over rocks, roots, and ferns. It was enough...barely. A hand's breadth was all that separated them when she flew past the thundering metal giant.

The truck roared back onto the road with a sickening screech from clawing undergrowth scratching its sides and accelerated away again. A loud, obnoxious honk rang in Sam's ears.

She swallowed back her bile and looked around for somewhere to pull over. After another few hundred feet, she turned off into a clearing, rattled to her core.

Trembling, she sat there and simply stared back at the road. Christ.

"Death by sheep truck, news at six." That'd be some headline. She pulled off her gloves and wiped down her shaky, sweat-slicked hands. If she'd died like that, she'd probably be a standing joke in the pub for months. Well, until Gina gave them all clips around the ear.

God. Her heart thundered. The most exciting thing in her life for the past decade had happened in only the past three months. And she'd been prepared to walk away from it, for what? Managed fucking risk? Screw that.

I almost died.

She glanced around and choked out an almost hysterical laugh when she realized where she'd pulled over. At the end of the Forestry Road dirt trail. Just three feet from where Alex Levitin had almost cleaned her up the day they'd met.

That day came rushing back. The fright she'd had when Alex's car suddenly appeared. The pain on impact. Huge, wide, apologetic eyes peering down at her as though nothing could ever make up for what she'd done. Then the horror and fear on Alex's face when her tiny ass had failed in the mismatch of the century wrestling Tiger off Sam. If it hadn't been for the agony in her hip, Sam might have laughed.

She hadn't been able to bring herself to be too annoyed with her in that moment…at least, not until she'd realized where Alex worked.

But that was then. Now that impossible, beautiful, amusing woman who'd almost run Sam over had offered to show her the world. And what had she done? Almost caved in to fear, before coming a hand's breadth away from having her life reduced to a pub punchline.

Way to go, Sam.

She yanked her gloves back on. *Fuck that.*

Chapter 28

Much Ado About Something

"Cut!" Alex said briskly, pleased with the scene. Chloe and Melody were really nailing their interactions now, and it was seamless, needing little intervention from her. "That was excellent, ladies." She glanced at her watch. "All right, let's set up for the last scene before lunch."

Alice waved to get her attention. Alex's newly reinstated production assistant pointed toward the gate. "Alex? Someone's here to see you."

Alex looked over to see the dashing figure of Sam Keegan in motorcycle leathers striding toward her. Her heart did a merry little flip. How did Sam always manage to look so good? Alex straightened, and anxiety rocketed along her nerve endings, remembering how they'd left things.

Sam's mouth opened when she got within three feet of Alex. Then shut. A blush feathered her cheeks. "Yes," was all she said.

"Yes?" Alex asked, confused.

"Yes."

Oh! "Yes!"

Sam nodded. "I'm kinda scared, I'm not gonna lie. But it's a big yes."

Alex pulled Sam into her arms and kissed her soundly. An assortment of whistles and cheers went up behind them. Alex was more focused on Sam's soft lips parting in surprise, then moving under hers.

Coming up for air, Alex waved away her boisterous crew with a dry "yeah, yeah," and added "Let's break early for lunch, people."

Predictably, that earned more catcalls.

Sam darted a narrow look at their audience. "Loud, aren't they?"

"Enthusiastic, I believe. Let's find some privacy." Alex led Sam back to her trailer. Once inside, she gathered Sam's hand in hers and asked the only thing that mattered. "You do want to travel with me?"

Sam drew in a breath. "Yeah." She met Alex's eyes.

"Why?"

Sam's lips curled. "I may have a pesky case of feelings for you."

"Pesky, hmm?" Alex smiled as her heart lifted. "What kind of feelings would those be?"

"Oh, the big ones. They're the 'let's try out the beds in hotels all over the world' feelings. Let's watch sunrises in hotel robes on balconies like a romantic movie cliché, and talk about stuff that matters to us. And I want to try the most interesting local foods with you."

"And your responsibilities?" Alex asked with a hesitation. "What happened to them?"

"I think I'll always feel responsible for the people in this town, and my family. But a certain bossy publican recently pointed out that I don't lose my place in her family by doing what I've always wanted to."

Alex's grin spread wide. "That's huge."

"Yeah."

"And you're feeling okay?"

"Aside from a few fears, I know what I want now."

"What are your fears?"

"What if I don't even like traveling? And what if I love it, but maybe you've gotten bored with me? Then what?"

"That's the risk of any relationship." Alex squeezed her hand. "But I admit I'm having a really hard time picturing it."

"Good." Sam took in a deep breath.

"And you're really, really sure this time? You've decided?"

"Yes." Sam met her gaze evenly. "Look, I know me, and I don't exactly love uncertainty." She gave a self-deprecating smile. "But you're worth it. So why don't we stick with the original game plan? For as long or as short as this lasts, let's give it a chance. Assuming you still want to, too." Uncertainty filled her expression. "Do you?"

"Sam," Alex said with a wide smile, "in case it hasn't been blindingly obvious, you're for me."

"Oh." Sam's answering smile started tiny and spread until it wreathed her face and reached her eyes. "Okay. That's, um, good. Works out better that way."

Alex laughed. "Yes, it does."

Sam leaned over and gave her a kiss so sweet that Alex discovered, to her embarrassment, that swooning was in her wheelhouse.

"I can't wait to show you my world," Alex murmured. "But it's more than that. I want you to meet my friends. See my home. My life."

"Seems fair since you've already seen mine. Surprised you didn't die of boredom."

"Don't speak too soon. I warn you my world involves a lot of nerdy party nights and Shakespeare."

"I anticipated that. Come over tonight? I'll order in Monza's Pizza and I've bookmarked *Much Ado About Nothing* on Netflix to see what the fuss is all about. How about we watch it together? Also, you'll get to have me naked at some point."

"What an offer." Alex smirked. "I'd never say no to Emma Thompson."

That night in Sam's bedroom, Alex lay in her arms as *Much Ado About Nothing*'s end credits rolled up the small TV screen Sam had hauled in from the lounge. The film had a lot of charm.

Contentment filled Sam. Tonight, everything seemed right. She felt lighter, and now, with Alex snuggling against her, she had no regrets about what lay ahead, even though her fears remained. Maybe they'd always exist. It was in her nature, after all.

"What a great closing shot." Alex sighed happily. "All one take at the end. Did you see that? That's Kenneth Branagh for you."

"Did you just watch that whole movie with your director's hat on?" Sam asked.

"It's impossible not to. Doesn't mean I can't love it, too. Did you like it?"

"I did. Funny and clever. And I related to the brothers…one's black, one's white. No one even questioned that."

Alex regarded her. "Do you get questioned much about your family?"

"As a child, a lot. People are nosy. When I became a police officer, the uniform came with a lot less of an invitation to discuss non-police matters."

Alex considered that. "How does it feel now? Not wearing your uniform anymore?"

"Weird. It's all I know."

"Well, that's not entirely true, is it?"

"I don't follow."

"Breaker Bob came to see me this afternoon," Alex said. "Apparently there's some crazy rumor you might be going to LA with me."

Sam rolled her eyes at how fast gossip spread. "What did Bob want?"

"He's of the view you'd be an excellent film stunt rider. He offered to fix you up with some of his contacts."

Sam frowned. "I can't do that."

"Who jumped Dry Creek? Imagine doing kick-ass stuff on a motorbike every day. Oh, and they take stunts very seriously on sets, so your safety would be paramount. Anyway, once he said it, I couldn't believe I hadn't thought of it first. He also pointed out they're looking for more highly skilled female riders these days, as more female-focused action movies get made."

Sam's eyes were wide as saucers.

"I turned him down," Alex continued. "For now."

"What? Why? You just said I could do it."

"And that's true. But while Breaker's references are good, I can go one better. Skye's partner is Brock Hayes."

"Who's he?"

"A legend. And if Brock likes you, he can give you the world when it comes to stunts. Like Skye, the man knows everyone. I'll introduce you. We can keep Breaker Bob's contacts in reserve."

"I haven't said yes yet. How do you know I don't want to become a librarian or something?"

Alex laughed. "Call it a hunch. I see Sid wasn't kidding about that puppy story. You really do have a contrary streak."

Sam opened her mouth to protest, but Alex jumped in first. "Sam, you can do anything you want, from tap dancer to street cleaner, and I'll back you. It's just something to think about. Okay? But maybe you are destined for movie-making greatness, as Breaker Bob thinks."

"It's unnerving thinking he's sitting there, mapping out my future." She folded her arms.

"Bob means well. He thinks very highly of you, and it was obvious he cares about you."

Sam absorbed the words, reminded of what Gina had told her. No one's laughing now. They wanted the best for her. "Maybe," she admitted.

Alex laughed. "So many wins tonight: Shakespeare and a concession people care about you." She snuggled tighter against Sam. "On that note, all those locals can appreciate you as much as they like, but right now, you're mine."

"That so?" Sam drawled. "Then, Ms. Levitin, I suggest you prove it."

The kiss she received made Sam's toes curl.

Chapter 29

Clearing the Air

THE NEXT EVENING, SKYE AND Alex spent a few hours at Te Wharariki pub, breaking bread, imbibing the house red, and picking apart a fraught and muddied thing. Friendship was sometimes like that.

"Did you really think," Skye was saying, as her knitting needles clacked enthusiastically, "that I would ever mean you harm? You inspire me. That's one of the important things in life, really. Love, laughter, and inspiration. And, hopefully, grandbabies, if I can somehow put that thought into Summer's head without her noticing. But my daughter's far too smart. I'm worried she'll tumble to my scheme. I might have to work on my eldest girl instead."

"So many schemes, Skye. And I know you had a hand getting Summer together with Bess."

"I'm a serial meddler, it's true. But the thing is, I've found two stubborn people sometimes need to be pushed a little onto a path that makes most sense for them."

"The path *you've* figured out, though."

"Of course!" She smiled. "What other path is there?"

Alex chuckled. "You're impossible."

"So everyone keeps telling me."

"Well, it has worked out. I forgive you."

"Thank you, Alexandra. I do feel badly over how I upset you both. I promise when we were planning all this, we envisioned it playing out quite differently. I can offer some reparations to you though."

"Oh?"

"Bess once told me once how much you loved my dear friend Jean-Claude Badour's butterfly movie."

"She did?"

"The graceful, morphing watercolor effects especially."

"Oh, right." Alex nodded. "Yes, genius."

"He's offered to have his art effects person, his cousin, Amelie, do them for the start of *Shezan*, too, if you want. I sent him the opening page of the script and photos of the scenery a few months back. And Amelie sent her concepts back to show how it might look. I've only just received them." She put down her needles and reached for her phone.

Alex sat up straight. This was phenomenal. Presumptuous as hell, of course, and there might be some pushback from the studio, but she didn't care. She wasn't budging on this. Amelie Badour's art had been the best thing about Jean-Claude's eccentric little movie which had won multiple international honors.

"Oh, he was happy to offer. See, it tickled his fancy, sprinkling some French fairy dust over Hollywood's 'worst' movie. He's contrary like that. And he's absolutely fine if you say no to his offer, but he thought the otherworldliness of the setting might suit it at the start. Here, see?" Skye passed over her phone, cued up to the artwork.

Alex held her breath as she stared at the gorgeous watercolors. They were arresting, startling, sumptuous. Her eyes soaked in the images, picturing how it would look on the big screen. She felt a rush of excitement and relief. "That's...fantastic."

"Yes. It is."

With this, *Shezan* would be stunning. Alex would give their editing team in Auckland a head's up on this immediately. "I'll have to spin this to Quincy. It's...unorthodox. Well, for a fantasy flick."

"So tell him Amelia's doing it for next to nothing. She'll be displaying the artworks in her gallery whether you use them in your film or not." Skye's gaze drifted over Alex's shoulder. "Now then, I believe someone's here for you."

Alex turned and her pulse jumped. She hadn't seen Sam in here for dinner since the saboteurs had been unmasked.

Sam squared her shoulders as though preparing for battle, and headed toward them. As she waded through the patrons, several smart-ass comments and guffaws were tossed her way about Sid having to matchmake his standoffish sister. Alex winced at Sam's cold, unimpressed expression.

"Time for my exit." Skye patted her hand. "Oh, and before I go, a little advice, from one who's spent years loving her own proud, strong, silent type? The stoic ones need more love than they pretend. That 'tough's' only skin-deep."

"I know." Alex grinned. "Thanks, though."

"Good luck." She rose and left the table, taking her knitting with her.

"Hey, stranger." Alex smiled warmly as Sam arrived. "Fancy seeing you in here."

Sam sat and looked about, wariness in her eyes. "So we're still the topic of conversation in here," she grumbled. "I thought if I avoided the place for a while, they'd move on."

"You really do hate being the center of attention, don't you?" Alex asked with amusement.

Sam's eyes narrowed. "Only when I'm the focus of their annoying stunts. And, knowing this bunch of troublemakers, another could be around the corner any minute."

"Well, right now, they're busy working out whether or not you'll murder Sid as the sabotage scheme's mastermind. And if so, method of dispatch."

"Jury's still out. That man gave me so many damned headaches."

"Not just headaches, though." Alex pointedly traced the cuff on Sam's shirt with a trailing index finger.

"No," Sam conceded, humor lacing her tone as she looked down to study that roaming finger. "Which is why he still lives."

Gina bustled over and placed a beer on the table. "On the house. Sid's delighted to see you back in here and says he's paying for all your drinks tonight."

"Generous of him," Sam said dryly.

Gina smiled. "He also says to remember he's the boy who found your lost stuffed bunny toy. Rescued it from Mr. Harper's half-feral cat."

She bustled away.

"You had a stuffed bunny?"

"I can neither confirm nor deny." Sam took a sip of beer.

"By the way, I had a great time last night. And breakfast was...delicious."

"That was my pleasure. Literally." Sam's cheeks reddened. "I think we should watch more Shakespeare. I liked how it ends."

"With panoramic, rising master shots?"

"That, too."

Alex snickered.

Sam's gaze returned to wandering the room, her jaw tightening.

Alex followed her eyes, seeing locals quickly look away, talking in hushed tones.

With a sigh, Sam said, "It's still hard. I'm trying to focus on why people did this, not how."

"Skye wasn't wrong when she said motives are everything."

Gina reappeared and placed a plate of garlic bread in front of her. "This one's from Kev. Wants you to remember the time he washed your socks nine times to get the red out from being left in the machine with those sports shorts."

"He made my socks red to start with! Those were his shorts!"

"I'm well aware. But unlike Sid, he doesn't have a deep stockpile of favors you owe him."

"True." Sam grinned.

Gina laughed and left.

"By the way, Kev told me the other day he loved working on your film," Sam said.

"Even though I fired him?" Alex's eyebrows lifted.

"Well, you re-hired him when his motives turned out to be pure."

"Mmm. Well, that and he has a forklift license." Alex smiled.

"So he's decided his career's in lighting now. Some job he heard about from the crew beckons in Wellington. He even tried to convince me to ask you to write him a reference." She shook her head. "I know, I know—the cheek of him!"

Alex almost choked on her beer. "He broke a light in his first week and hid another one that delayed production for hours. But *this* is his calling?"

"Apparently." Sam grinned. "Trust me, it's still a better effort than he's contributed at some of his other jobs."

"Well, to be honest, he was a pretty decent lighting PA. And he may have had a hand in helping us get together. I might just give him that reference after all."

"Go, Kev."

"God, that smells divine," Alex peered at the basket of bread.

"Dutch is an amazing cook. You should see the gastro-pub menu he's been working on." Sam tore off a chunk and the rich, buttery garlic bread sent up a plume of steam. "Try some."

Alex took a bite and her taste buds did a happy jig. "I'm in heaven."

"Not yet, but soon." Sam drained her drink and set the empty beer glass slowly down on the table. "Maybe, you'd enjoy a walk? To…my place?"

"Why, officer, what *are* your intentions?"

"Strip search, ma'am. I'm quite sure I need to be thorough with your kind. Who knows where you're hiding contraband."

Alex laughed. "I appreciate the thoroughness. Of course, if we leave together, all these rubberneckers will have their theories about us confirmed. Well, the ten who didn't already know, I mean."

"That horse bolted days ago. Curse of a small town. I'm glad I'm leaving it."

Before Alex could answer, Gina arrived with another beer. "From Sid. He wants you to remember that time he turned up at the Wild Boars compound and wailed on a bunch of bikies for you."

Sam snorted and twisted her head around. Her eyes lit on her brother, who gave her a hopeful look and cheesy grin.

Grabbing the beer, Sam turned to Alex. "Give me five?"

"Sure."

Sam headed for Sid's table, which was close enough for Alex to eavesdrop.

"Fine." Sam slid the beer over. "You win."

"Forgiven for meddling?" He looked so pleading that Alex almost snickered.

"Yeah, yeah. Drink up. This one's on me."

He chuckled. "Um, pretty sure I paid for it, but."

"I know. Okay, shove over." She slapped the booth seat. "I've been meaning to talk to you about something. And I think you'll thank me."

Five minutes later, she headed back to the table and stopped in front of Alex. "Come home with me?" She held out her hand. The gesture was simple, bold, and could not be mistaken for anything else.

Sam Keegan willingly indulging in a PDA in front of all these people? Alex hid her surprise and took her hand. "Any time. So are you still going to do *the thing* before we go? If you're leaving Ika Whenu for good, it's time."

Sam hesitated. "I suppose I should. I'm just psyching myself into it. Facing the rabble head on is a solid plan. But *wanting* to? Not so much."

"You'll be great." Alex squeezed her hand.

Inhaling deeply, Sam nodded. "Time to clear the air."

Sam's heart was in her throat as she reviewed the pub. What had possessed her to do this? Now was a fine time to suddenly decide she should stare down the demons and ghosts that still stalked her in this town.

Who faced off an entire bikie gang?

Right.

Sam climbed onto a table...one of the sturdier wooden ones that had been known to serve as an impromptu karaoke stage from time to time. She held up her hands. "Everyone? I need a minute."

Sam's authoritative tone caused the hubbub to die down immediately. Although she was well aware it might not have been the tone so much as the rare sight of her actually inviting attention.

Sid pushed past bodies to get closer, frowning. Gina stopped wiping the bar, her eyes widening in astonishment.

Suddenly all Sam could hear was the pounding of her heart. She licked her lips. *Right, then.* "I have an announcement, and I thought it'd be better you heard it from the source for the first time in Ika Whenu history."

That earned a round of laughter.

"You're on with the director!" a wag called from the back. "Yeah, we know already! We got eyes!"

"No, that's not it. Although"—Sam's gaze darted to Alex, and her lips curved up the faintest amount—"I'm not denying it."

That earned a few whistles and cheers.

"Knew it!" Quincy intoned dryly.

With a deep breath, Sam continued: "First, I'm no longer going to be your police officer. I'm leaving."

This time there was no laughter. She'd expected at least a couple of cheers for that. Instead, crickets. Then the chorus of complaints began.

"Why?"

"No!"

"But you stopped the drugs!"

"Is this because of the video?"

"We could protest! They can't fire you!"

"Hey!" Sam lifted her hands to quiet them. "Yes, the video started it, obviously. They took Ika Whenu station off me, so I resigned because I didn't like what I was offered instead. All the protests in the world won't change that. Senior Constable Murray Snell's your man now."

"Murray's a dick!" someone called out.

"Murray is *not* a dick." Sam sighed. "And he's sitting right over there." She pointed at her replacement, now trying to melt into the wall. "Pro tip: Don't call your new cop names, hey?"

That caused a few snickers.

"We want you back, though!" someone else called.

"Well, you don't get me back because…here's the news. I'm going overseas. Time to see the world and maybe explore my work options, too."

"LAPD!" someone suggested.

"Marines!"

That caused a roar of laughter.

"Motorcycle stunts!" came a familiar gravelly voice. "In Hollywood!"

A series of awed *ooohs* sounded.

"Yes, fine… I *may* try some motorcycle stunt work, too, thanks to someone who shall remain nameless for suggesting it."

Breaker Bob mock saluted his worn blue beanie, looking pleased as punch.

"Assuming I don't break anything major, I'll be back here on the regular to make sure you're not all getting up to mischief." Sam's gaze slid over to her family.

Gina looked so proud; her hand floated to her heart, and her eyes glistened. Sid grinned from ear to ear and gave her dual thumbs up. Kev merely nodded, as if to say, *duh, of course my sister will now be a Hollywood stunt rider.*

Her announcement brought the house down.

"I see you approve," she drawled when they finally stopped cheering. "How nice that me putting myself in mortal danger amuses you."

"If you're in mortal danger, you ain't doing the stunt right," Breaker Bob shouted.

She laughed. "You'd know. How *are* you still walking?"

The room burst into laughter once more.

This time she joined in. A sense of camaraderie washed over her as she truly felt these people were laughing with her, not at her. "Now, while I won't miss you people *at all*," she teased, aiming for arch but ending up just sounding fond, "especially the way you corner your police officer at all hours for your missing horses, angora goat, and duck concerns—"

"Hey, that was an emergency!" came a cry from the back of the room. "Quack Sparrow's a working duck."

"Sure he is," Sam continued dryly.

The room roared with laughter again. She lifted her hands once more for quiet. "But don't think I've left you without backup. Policing's a big job, a draining one, even in a small town like this. So, I'm proud to announce that my brother, Sid, will have yet another new job—"

Laughter sounded at that in-joke.

"—as Ika Whenu's first non-sworn, Authorized Officer. As an AO, he'll fill in on minor stuff at the station, and take charge of anyone who's gotten their sorry asses arrested. Sid'll also be trained to become a proper police officer down the line, with some high-level supervision, to make sure he doesn't circle all the wrong answers on his exams again!"

The room broke into laughs, the loudest coming from Sid. He was the first to admit that his lack of academic focus had sunk him when he'd tried to become a cop even though he'd aced all the practical stuff.

"It's in New Zealand Police's interests to help him pass this time because...are you ready?" She lifted her eyebrows. "Next year, the new face of the police force will be Sid Mahuta."

The roar was deafening.

Sid raised his arms like Rocky.

"I know, I know," Sam said. "The mad bastards in charge think he'd be a great man to front their campaign to get more people signing up, since he's already internet famous. Personally, I don't know how they'll cope having to see his ugly mug on recruitment posters at HQ, day in, day out, but far be it for me to tell the Police Commissioner how to do his job."

Sid preened. "He should be so lucky to be as pretty as me!"

More laughter filled the room.

"And if you don't behave with Sid or Senior Constable Snell, I should warn you. Sid's going to be getting a dog, recently acquired from a bunch of arrested bikies who shall remain nameless."

Sam grinned with satisfaction. Sid and Gina had agreed to each adopt one of Dino's remaining two Rottweilers after the animals passed a Council-mandated, vet-run behavior-modification course. Gina had been delighted with the extra security for her pub, especially given her expansion plans and extra tourists who'd be on their way, and it gave Sam peace of mind for her safety.

Suddenly Sam felt nostalgic. "It's been an honor to be your police officer. I've known most of you all my life. I admit we didn't always see eye to eye." There was a sobering silence. "I'm sorry if I've been hard to know because of that. It's been pointed out to me recently…" her gaze drifted to Gina, "that maybe you're not all sitting around waiting for me to screw up so you can laugh at me, and maybe you do want the best for me."

Claps and whistles of agreement hit her powerfully.

"Well, I didn't understand before. It's…it's a big deal for me you feel that way. And I have no words." She stopped again, feeling the love in the room wash through her. Her throat tightened. Sam's gaze slid to Alex, who was beaming from ear to ear, with so much affection in her eyes. It was overpowering. "Thanks," she said gruffly to the room. "That's all I have to say. G'bye, stay safe, be good to each other, and don't nick shit." She jumped off the table.

The room erupted into hearty cheers and applause.

In seconds, Sam couldn't move for all the people slapping her on the back and shaking her hand. Claustrophobia welled up, but then, suddenly, Alex was on one side and Gina on the other, flapping her hands at them all.

"Back off, you lot. Let the poor woman breathe." Gina then ignored her own advice and pulled Sam into a mighty hug. She whispered hotly against

Sam's ear, "I'm so proud of you, bub," before stepping back and wiping a tear from her eye. "Now then, you two best make your escape while you can or you'll be here all night."

Sam nodded, and Gina bustled away. Turning to her other side, she found Alex's soft eyes on her. "Um," Sam lowered her voice. "So I didn't embarrass myself too much then?"

"You were perfect. You had them all in the palm of your hand. You'll be sorely missed."

"I don't know about that—"

"No, Sam. You will. Take it from me. You're a blockbuster hit. Rave reviews and all that." She elbowed Sam and tilted her head toward the door. "Now, I believe you promised a girl a walk to your place? Although a lot of people around here seem to want to tell you how sorry they are you're leaving. You could always stay a bit and talk to them?"

Sam's gaze took in the room. *Stay and have beers shoved in my face by boisterous, well-meaning, half-smashed locals. Or…* She glanced back at Alex. Sliding her arm around her shoulders, she said, "Nah. Let's go."

They made their way through the crowd to the exit, and the genuinely warm well wishes thrown her way burrowed into Sam's chest. She'd had no idea.

So maybe she would miss Ika Whenu a little bit.

Chapter 30

It's a Wrap

ALEX GAVE *SHEZAN*'S FINAL EVER scene a long, hard stare and then exhaled. "Cut. And…that's a wrap on *Shezan: Mistress of the Forest*. Fantastic job, people. Really awesome work." She turned and clapped at her crew and cast, hands above her head.

A cheer went up across the set, and she returned it with a tired smile. It was only five-thirty in the evening, but her day had started at dawn. Alex was mentally and physically exhausted. Not just because of the sizzling former cop she'd woken up to today, nibbling on her earlobe. That had become a frequent start to her day lately, and she wouldn't swap her lover's pre-dawn attentions for anything, even adequate rest. It did mean, though, that she was virtually dead by the time her sodding film had fallen over the finish line.

"There's a wrap party tonight," she reminded everyone. "There'll be a screening of a few scenes of *Shezan* along with a few surprises. Oh…and free booze."

The cheers got considerably louder.

Alex called her production assistant over. "I need you to invite a few extra people to the party."

Alice whipped out her notepad. "Sure."

"Invite Joe—it's his land, after all—along with Sid, Kevin, and Gina Mahuta. And Sam…who I'll invite myself. Just make sure all five are granted access at the gate, okay?"

Alice nodded, smiled, and disappeared.

She left final instructions for the First AD, Leslie, who was handling any technical work as they began shutting down the production. Then Alex headed for her trailer.

Flopping on her small couch, she punched out a text to Sam.

Hot date tonight @ 8. Just you, me, and entire Shezan cast + crew. We'll c a little bit of the film too. Want to come? Can promise fun, laughs + later, kisses from the director. :) btw your fam's been invited. Couldn't have made Shezan without them.

Her phone pinged a minute later.

Seriously? Didn't Sid sabotage your film, Kev lose a light, and what did Gina do for Shezan?! Of course I'll be there. Congrats on finishing!

Alex replied: *Your brothers were great when they weren't sabotaging. Gina fed us. PS wear something warm. It's an outdoor screening.*

RU just being nice? Inviting Shezan's black sheep + Gina? For me? Thnx on clothing tip. Will pack my flannel undies.

Alex texted back: *Flannel undies are NOT a thing. And I'm not nice. I'll have u know I'm as fierce as those dogs ur trying to rehab*

Since Killer's a complete softy, I agree. See you in a few hrs. xx

Alex stared at the two Xs, her heart warming along with her cheeks.

She wondered what Sam would make of the highlights reel of *Shezan* she'd see tonight. Their Auckland editing team had been working flat out all throughout filming. Most special effects were still missing, but Alex had ordered them to at least do a cut of the opening scene, with Amelie's watercolor art underlaid with the evocative Bulgarian song she'd chosen.

Alex couldn't wait to see all those elements together on the big projector screen the crew would be setting up next to Craft Services. Soon Alex was about to discover how much of a hit—or otherwise—her career would take from her insane decision to agree to this movie.

No pressure.

By eight that night, Craft Services had been transformed. Rows of plastic chairs, filled with cast and crew, lined the grassy, flat area. A giant white sheet had been strung up. All lights had been turned off, plunging the screening area into inky darkness—nature's own cinema.

The still, moonless night carried laughter and chatter from everyone crammed into the chairs, waiting for the entertainment to begin. For many, this was the first movie they'd worked on, and nervous tension rippled through the crowd.

Alex sat in the back row next to Sam, her jaw clenching and unclenching.

The show reel began amid rowdy cheers.

What if it's no good? Alex wiped her perspiring palms down her jeans. *What if Quincy and I just imagined it having redeeming features? Critics could shred it even worse than before. I won't be able to show my face in LA for years.*

Sam gathered her hand and whispered, "Relax."

The Bulgarian music began, with an aching, low, earthy rumble of traditional bagpipes, joined by layers of gently wailing female voices. It was ancient, longing, like calling for a home of millennia ago. The rich watercolors of fern-thick forest surrounding Wairere Falls appeared, earning soft, awed gasps, before they dissolved into the real scenery.

A Maori elder's narration began. The woman's deep, earthy voice had been recorded in the studio in Auckland only a week ago. Her gravitas brought goosebumps to Alex's skin.

> *In an ancient, distant land, there was born a girl child. Small of size, but strong and fearless, she grew to be ten seasons old. She had a gentle spirit, a curious nature, and a smile of such brightness as to make the stars envious.*
>
> *Shezan was beloved by the Amazons as their most precious sister.*
>
> *And the day she became lost, the whole world wept.*

The haunting lament of the Bulgarian singers rose with the music. The artwork itself wept, too, draining down the screen, bleaching it of color.

"Oh wow," Sam murmured. "That's beautiful."

Alex nodded, throat too tight to swallow.

The editing was sublime, even just in these rough cuts.

Several action scenes followed, before it jumped ahead again to just before Jennifer and Shezan's big puma showdown. The intimate close-ups and guarded looks giving way to longing were perfection. This was the powerhouse moment of the whole movie, and she'd been dying to see it in panorama size.

They were now at the moment where Jennifer had to choose between saving her father or Shezan.

A close-up of her shaking rifle filled the screen. Then Jennifer squared her stance, took aim with a determined clamp of her jaw. The tension rose, the music little more than a single taut violin string. Quivering, holding, waiting.

Alex's hand was suddenly crushed by Sam's. The crowd drew in a collective breath. A slide appeared.

Insert: Gunshot sound FX

Insert: Puma close-up FX

Jennifer flung aside her gun and ran, a fearful expression on her face.

Insert: Poacher mauled FX

Insert: Puma dead

Then...the poacher's crumpled form came into focus.

The audience cheered heartily.

Alex snorted at the response. Typical. *Everyone loves a good villain.*

Jennifer was now comforting Shezan. "Don't cry. Not for him. He's not worth it."

Oh yes. It was even better than Alex had dared hope. No one made the slightest sound.

Shezan slipped her arm around Jennifer and they walked slowly away.

"It's so cold." Jennifer gazed around them. "I come from warm lands. Here, the ground is frosted in the mornings. The trees shiver with winds. The leaves stay wet long after sun-up."

"Is it...too cold?"

"That's just it. It should be," Jennifer said softly. "But all I feel here is warmth. Shezan, *you* warm me."

"Then stay. Be warm here—with me."

Jennifer's smile could have lit the whole screen. "Always."

The crowd went nuts. Roars and cheers resounded.

The film's stars remained gazing at each other as the camera pulled back, rising toward ancient, green Mount Te Aroha.

Breathtaking. Quincy was right about the cinematography. It deserved an Oscar.

Next up came a few scenes showcasing Breaker Bob's riding skills, weaving through the trees, leaping a tiny creek, earning hoots and smart-ass comments.

But Alex's mind was still on that pivotal scene. Her movie probably shouldn't work at all. Some of their dialogue still was a bit too...over the top. She preferred understated. But somehow it seemed to work when paired against the magnificent backdrop. Something to do with larger-than-life characters in a larger-than-life setting.

A rhythmic Amazon dance was now playing under some hastily cobbled together credits, and this time the cheer was female—all the Amazon extras. It finished with more dazzling watercolor brilliance for the movie's end, weeping down the screen along with the music. The crowd erupted into hoots as they recognized their names.

Then the screen shifted into a series of bloopers.

"Fuck!" on-screen Chloe said.

"Line?" Melody replied, sounding bored.

"*Fuck,*" Chloe repeated. "*That's* your line."

"Wait, I get to fucking swear?" Melody deadpanned.

Chloe's face shifted right in the lens, larger than a house. "Fuck yeah."

Alex's barked "Cut!" sounded in the background.

Alex rolled her eyes at her exasperated voice. That had been a trying day. Everyone had been so tired they were punch-drunk. Making movies was always funnier in hindsight.

Local stuntees started flying across the screen in a short tribute to their skills, incurring more excited hollers and whoops from the audience.

"I think they like that." Alex laughed. "Or those three, anyway."

"They're really popular around here," Sam said. "Even more so thanks to you. Those stuntmen have their own fan page now, since your viral video."

"Ah."

The bloopers continued with a rubber arrow bouncing off a tree, Melody asking for her line three more times, and Chloe accidentally tumbling out of the high tree set, disappearing into a dense bush, followed by a muffled "I'm fine!" Next, Sid tripped face-first over a lighting cable, bouncing in and then out of frame, followed by Alex, hands on her hips, captured peering down at him, saying, "Seriously, Sid?"

Sam's laugh was as hearty as everyone else's in the cheers of delight at that.

Candid footage of Alex giving her cinematographer the thumbs up and a wide, genuine smile ended the reel in a freeze frame. As the projector was switched off, and the lights came up, the applause rose to thunderous.

Alex walked to the front and quieted them down. She made a short speech thanking everyone for their work, praising the efforts of novices and veterans alike. Then she paused.

"In years to come, I want you to remember *this* moment: Once upon a time you worked on the so-called world's worst movie and *you* made it beautiful. Be proud of what you've accomplished here, as I'm proud of you all. Thank you for everything. Please enjoy the free booze and food. It's Quincy's shout!"

A cheer rose up and Quincy made some good-natured, expected mutters of disapproval about them having no restraint, earning more laughter.

Alex returned to her seat.

Sam gave her an admiring look. "Nice speech."

"So what did you think of my film? Well, what you saw of it."

"Loved the music."

"Of course you did." Alex snorted. "Just the music?"

"And the stunt work. That scene with Chloe running, was that all her or Kiri, too?"

"A bit of both."

"Cool."

"So you liked the music and the stunts." Alex prodded her in the ribs. "That's it, woman?"

"I *really* liked the dead puma."

"The hell? It was a card saying 'dead puma here!'"

Sam snickered at her outrage. "Sorry, I'll stop teasing. Okay, from what I saw, it looks beautifully shot and really exciting. And, I may have enjoyed

Shezan making all those lovesick doe eyes at Jennifer—although I'll deny it if anyone asks."

"Well." Alex smiled in relief, heart lifting at the praise. "Booyah."

"That's not a word," Sam murmured fondly. "At least not this century."

Alex laughed.

The after-party was thumping. A buffet spread had been laid out on trestle tables, and lanterns hung from trees and nearby trailers, giving a warm glow. Against the backdrop of the dark green Kaimai Ranges, with the stars above, it was easily the prettiest party Alex had ever attended.

Skye was burbling with excitement as she gave Chloe four pairs of matching socks with the word "Hollywood" knitted up the side. "For your family," she was saying. "I can't wait to meet them next week. I've made matching suspenders, too." She beamed proudly and held a pair up.

"Choice." Chloe took them. "Um, are these bells on the suspenders?"

Alex chuckled and turned back to Gina, who looked like she'd died and gone to heaven, with exciting new food to try and a whole crowd to gossip with.

"Did you like what you saw of *Shezan*?" Alex asked. "Bear in mind it'll be way better with all the effects in place and, well, all the rest of the scenes."

"Oh, I'm not one for fantasy films, so I'm probably the worst person to ask. Although I admit I loved the romance side. How beautiful that was. Those lovely lesbian ladies finding each other." She became a little dewy eyed. "I really wanted them to be together."

"*Lesbian ladies*?"

They turned to find Melody staring at them, an inquisitive eyebrow lifted.

"Oh yes," Gina said enthusiastically. "You and Chloe did a fine job. I truly believed you were in love."

Oh shit. Alex had really hoped not to be around the moment Melody worked out the ninety-eight-percent gay content of her movie.

"Oh." Melody shrugged. "Yeah. That."

Alex blinked. "Wait, you *knew*?"

"Course." She rolled her eyes. "How come you didn't level with me that you were making a down-low lesbian romance?"

"I wasn't sure you'd take it well."

"Why?" She flicked her hair. "Does my neck look that red to you?"

Wait, what? "I didn't want to risk your chemistry with Chloe by making you self-conscious if you weren't aware. Besides," she said delicately, "you do have a fondness for Bible quotes and large crucifixes."

Melody snorted softly. "Hey, my crucifix is costume jewelry my best friend makes. I wear it to support her business. My Bible quotes are actually hilarious and ironic, thank you very much. And I don't support the oppression of minorities, *ever*. I'm only biased against ugly people." She shuddered. "That's different. Their stupid faces annoy me."

"That's ridiculous," Gina interrupted. "How can ugly people help how they look?"

"Not my problem."

"*Hamuti,*" Gina muttered under her breath, then pursed her lips.

Alex had no idea what that meant and wasn't about to ask in front of Melody. She cleared her throat to get the actress's attention. "Well, anyway, you did a great job on my film. You'll get offers from it, I have no doubt."

"Christ, I hope not." Melody screwed up her face.

"What? You don't want to be successful?"

"Eww, no. Look, I'll be honest. I only took *Shezan* cos I thought it'd be a stinker."

Alex peered at her. "Why?"

"Dad's the one who wants me to be a star. That's *his* dream. I want to study political science. So we did a deal: He'd pay for college if I agreed to do one studio movie. He thought I'd catch the acting bug and wouldn't want to do school after that. Anyway, I turned down any decent script that he sent my way. Then *Shezan* came up, and it was perfect. How utterly shit was the first draft?"

"It wasn't…ideal," Alex acknowledged.

"So I took the job and figured I'd do the bare minimum, no point being noticed, or worse, becoming an *acting sensation*." She looked appalled at the thought. "So it was all going to plan, then Chloe started hitting on me. At first I thought she was, like, a total lez." Melody glanced around, seeking out the actress in question, and inclined her head Chloe's way. "Boy was I wrong. She's only got eyes for one person." She snickered.

At that moment, Chloe was kissing Sid like she needed his air.

"Oh!" Sid gasped, loud enough for everyone to hear as he broke away, looking genuinely amazed. "You like me? *Like*-like me?"

"Christ, that man is slow," Melody muttered. "I think even the grips knew she was into him."

"Excuse me, that's my son you're mocking," Gina said, voice steely.

Melody snorted. "Did *you* know Chloe liked him?"

Gina said nothing.

"And did you?" Melody looked at Alex.

Alex coughed.

"See? Everyone did. So anyway, when I worked out Chloe was doing a professional seduction, not a personal one, I figured you guys had to be *Ben-Hur*ing me. At first I was annoyed. Shit, rude much? But then I thought about it. How many hero movies are there for queer kids?" She looked thoughtful. "That's the thing about growing up in LA. Half your friends are gay or bi or pan or whatever. So, I decided to *really* act and try to make it good for them. I *am* an ally, after all." She tossed her hair again.

"You are full of surprises," Alex murmured. "So what's next then?"

Melody's smile turned evil. "Next Dad's gonna be coughing up my college money. I love to win." She paused. "But I swear to God if you've made some big sleeper hit out of this thing, some *Brokeback Mountain* dealio, I'll be so pissed." She glared at Alex for having the temerity to produce unexpected excellence.

"Uh…"

"I wanted the movie to be good, but not *too* good, y'know? I admit I'm a little worried after that highlights reel. And did you *have* to create cinema's most gorgeous opening? Was that *absolutely* freaking necessary?"

Alex simply stared at her, totally blindsided by the whole conversation.

"Okay then," Melody said breezily, and it was like flipping a switch. "It's been an education. Cool working with you."

"Well, you, too. It was…um…nice."

"I'm sure it wasn't." Melody grinned. "But no hard feelings." She whipped out her phone. "I'm gonna bail on this lame-orama party and convene with my followers. 'Kay?" She was already moving away when she glanced back to Alex. "By the way? I was only joking about hating ugly people. God, you're easy." She cackled and wandered off.

Gina watched her leave, looking baffled. "That girl doesn't seem right to me. Was any part of that conversation normal where you come from?"

"No," Alex said, dazed. "And I can't believe she knew. She must have been laughing at us the whole time. Turns out I was the oblivious one."

"Does it matter? Your film seems real good, and a lot of that's due to her. And if some battered, old, beer-pulling *wāhine* like me enjoys a film way out of her usual comfort zone, I think that young woman might have a point. *Shezan* could really catch on. Be a big hit even."

"From worst film ever to a hit?" Alex shook her head. "Crazy. But don't jinx it. The wider world might still hate it."

"I doubt it, but fine, I'll be quiet about it." Gina took her measure. "You know, you film people certainly brightened up my pub. I'll miss you when you're gone."

"You'll also probably have a lot fewer headaches."

"True." She laughed.

"We'll miss you, too. And Sam will miss you like crazy."

"I suspect so," Gina said quietly. "And I'll miss her in the worst way. But a mother's job's to help her baby birds fly, not hang onto 'em and choke 'em to death."

"Sam will come back often, no matter what happens with me and her. Don't worry."

"A few visits here and there just won't be the same. But that's the thing about life, isn't it? It's not meant to stay the same. If it does, you're not doin' it right."

"That's profound."

"I have my moments." Gina smiled.

Sam approached, slid an arm around Alex's waist, and pecked her cheek in greeting. "Hi."

"Time for me to go try those pastry things," Gina announced. "Maybe get the recipe out of your cook." She glanced at Sam. "And bub, I trust you'll come and see me before you disappear with Ms. Trouble, here."

"Sure," Sam promised. "As if I would just sneak off to LA."

"Okay then. Good." Gina bustled away.

"So where have you been?" Alex asked.

"Judging a limbo competition for the Amazons. I'm still not sure how I got roped into it."

Alex blinked. "Limbo? Who won?"

"It was a three-way tie." Sam took a sip of beer.

"How many were in it?"

"Three."

"Then you're a terrible judge." Alex laughed.

"Nah, actually the infrastructure collapsed. The mop's handle snapped in half when the chairs fell over."

"Oh no."

"Because Sid tripped over the chairs. Because Chloe finally asked him out."

"Hooray."

"He said yes. And all that romantic stuff somehow inspired the Amazons, who insisted they get to kiss the judge because those are apparently 'limbo rules.' They might have been kidding but, just to be sure, that's when I decided that it was high time to declare a tie and vacate the vicinity."

"So much restraint. Those girls are very kissable." Alex suppressed her smile at Sam's discomfort.

"I told you once before: When I'm with someone, they're all I think about. I'm not interested in anyone but you."

Alex saw the sincerity in her eyes. She was still getting used to that. Being someone's number one. She swallowed. "Thank you."

Sam smiled. "By the way, Sid brought his guitar. You're in for a treat. Man has a voice like honey. Want to listen?"

"Lead on."

Sid was sitting a little away from everyone else, singing a beautiful, traditional Maori song that sounded as old as the mountain behind Ika Whenu. Chloe was sitting in front of him, humming along.

Alex and Sam dropped to the grass near them. Sam wrapped herself around Alex, who was sitting in front of her.

The hairs on the back of Alex's arms raised at the melody. "It's so beautiful."

"That's *Hine e Hine* I was telling you about," Sam said quietly against her ear, wrapping her arms around her from behind. "Maori women would often sing this at the wharves as they watched their men depart on troop ships for war."

"War? But didn't you say it was an old lullaby, written by a Maori princess?"

"It is. It's about stopping sadness and being held in love."

Held in love. How apt. Alex leaned back deeper into Sam's arms.

As Sid's rich voice melted into the darkness, the stars shone, glasses clinked behind them, and the laughter and love of a cast and crew that had bonded over many months filled Alex with warmth.

Wrap parties varied. Some films were awful miseries, so everyone bolted as soon as they could find the exits. Others morphed into boozy, loud raves and lots of regrettable sex and hangovers. But every now and then, if you were very lucky, you experienced this: the bond.

Alex's heart grew at the affection she felt for the people she'd been through so much with these past months. The sense of closeness made them feel like family. That feeling would fade, of course, when they were all back to their normal lives, stuck in traffic jams, arguing with managers, and being hurled into their next productions. But right here, in this single moment frozen in time at the ends of the earth, the sensation was special.

How surreal it all seemed. Alex had come to New Zealand to pay a tax bill and had found her heart in the process. With eyes wet with tears, she took Sam's hand and squeezed it tight.

For almost an hour, they listened to Sid's beautiful rich voice filling the night air.

"You were right," Sam whispered in her ear. "In your speech. I *will* remember this moment forever."

Alex leaned into her and closed her eyes. "Me, too. Now and always."

Chapter 31

Purple Patch

PFEIFFER BEACH WAS EXACTLY LIKE the postcard. Purple sands, a blasting keyhole arch, and endless blue water.

Sam sat on her striped blue-and-yellow beach towel, staring at the startling blue of the waves, and wondered if this was all a dream.

Dreams didn't give you sunburn, though. She reached for her sunscreen and reapplied it to her limbs. Glancing to the woman under the beach umbrella beside her, she smiled. "Any good?" Sam asked.

"Not yet," Alex glanced at her over the top of the script she was reading. "But I'm deciding whether I could make it worthwhile. I've had quite the stack offered to me since *Shezan* came out."

"Not surprising. Hitting top twenty and making critics eat their words is phenomenal. That review that began '*It's not often I'm wrong about a movie, but in my defense, indie director Alex Levitin hadn't been assigned to* Shezan *when I called it the foulest creation in cinematic history*' was my favorite. I liked how he somehow all at once backpedaled, ass-covered, and gave you credit."

"Yeah, well, that's showbiz." Alex shrugged. "Meanwhile, I've been watching Caroline Bassett, one of the studio execs, doing victory laps all over the media, claiming credit for *Shezan*. Every now and then she even remembers to mention me." She laughed.

Sam returned her gaze to the sea. California was a strange place in many ways, fast and frantic, shallow yet upbeat, but somehow every day she spent here felt better than the last. Even after eight months, she was constantly discovering something new.

She'd been training with a professional motorcycle stunt rider and a martial artist to broaden her skillset. She'd met stunt coordinator Brock Hayes. The man's pale blue eyes had stared right through her and seemed to grill her like a lamb chop. Then he'd he put her through her paces. For two grueling days.

His low-key enthusiasm for her riding skills had left her on a high. She *could* maybe do this.

Brock had found her a small but key gig on one of his upcoming blockbuster movies and had been pivotal in getting her a work visa. He'd somehow convinced the movie's studio to sponsor her, citing her "extraordinary ability," claiming Sam was "integral and irreplaceable" to performing the stunt work needed for the film—both now and down the track. With a trilogy in the works for the character Sam would be stunt-doubling, that had swung it.

For whatever reason Brock had done this for a near stranger—although she strongly suspected Skye's hand in it—Sam was incredibly grateful.

Getting used to Hollywood itself had been an adjustment. People worked fast, talked faster, and everyone seemed to be on the make. They were constantly looking for something, running from something, afraid to be themselves while somehow pretending that's *all* they were. She understood now why Alex, when not networking, preferred to spend time with her former Cambridge friends, who'd known her when she was starting out and treated her exactly the same.

Meeting the famous Elizabeth "Bess" Thornton had been the biggest challenge. There was something truly weird about meeting your girlfriend's ex. Not just because she was Alex's first love, but because she was breathtakingly beautiful.

Any insecurities or doubts had been erased the moment Summer Hayes entered the room. Bess didn't smile much, but her face lit up, her eyes brightened, and her tone went from polite to a lower register. It was as if no one but Summer had existed for her at that moment.

Speak of the devil.

Summer and Bess were making their way along the shoreline, walking slowly and leaning into each other.

"Ah, there they are," Alex murmured. "I'm glad they're here. And not just for the fancy hotel rooms." She snorted.

Before they headed to England for work, Bess and Summer had decided to wave off California in style by staying in one of Big Sur's five-star hotels a few miles up the road. Bess had wanted to see the beach that had captivated Sam all the way from New Zealand. And Summer seemed to be using the few days away to try and store as much sunshine in her pores as she could before she landed in London.

They were putting their friends up at their hotel, too, as part of their grand farewell. Sam would have been just as happy staying in a tent, but there was no denying the sheer luxury of silken sheets. Besides, she had wicked plans to test out those sheets with Alex later tonight.

There was a small party planned for this evening at Summer and Bess's panoramic cliff-top suite, and more friends would be arriving for it later. The party included an infamous Shakespeare trivia night, the first Sam would attend.

By now, Sam had met all of Alex's friends and heard tales of how these events went: a bunch of English ex-drama students feeding off each other, challenging each other, performing for everyone's amusement.

Sam had been told—repeatedly—not to worry if she didn't know anything about the bard, that no one would care. And while she was looking forward to seeing Alex in her element, immersed in her favorite passion, surrounded by the friends she loved, there was another reason for the nervous ball of excitement curling in Sam's guts.

Summer had been Sam's partner in crime of late, secretly tutoring her, and Sam had come up with quite a few squirrelly questions for tonight. She tried to picture Alex's shock at her sudden expertise on the topic and grinned.

Her eye fell again to Bess and Summer, lost in each other, their languid steps in sync. Those two just seemed to lock into place at each other's side like they belonged there.

Sam wondered if that's how she and Alex looked around each other these days. She felt Alex's pull often now, always sensing when she was near.

"They're really something together, aren't they?" Alex said, following her gaze.

"Yes," Sam murmured. "But so are we."

That earned a soft, warm smile. "We are." Silence fell for a moment, and Alex's eyes returned to the page. She laughed. "Ha! This scriptwriter has a soft-butch cop falling for a lesbian director. Secondary characters, but still! Sly bastard."

That was the other thing about living in LA. Everyone knew everyone's business and status. It just existed in this who-cares state of awareness, like, "Here, meet Alex Levitin, the gifted indie filmmaker, and her girlfriend, Sam."

The first time it had happened, she'd been taken aback. Sam was still getting used to being part of a couple that was "known" in certain circles. Hollywood thrived on connections and knowing everyone's secrets. Something it had in common with Ika Whenu.

"Slick bastard's even written in a small motorcycle stunt that needs a woman to do it. Do you think he's brown-nosing?" Alex asked, not looking up. "He so is."

Sam smiled, knowing Alex's little outbursts at the universe didn't require responses. She regarded her lover fondly. Being a pale-skinned redhead, Alex was covered, top to toe, in cool white cotton, a wide hat, sunscreen, and thick black sunglasses that made her look like an elusive movie star.

Sam, with her light NZ skin, baggy blue shorts, and white T-shirt, looked exactly like a tourist.

She joined Alex under the shade of the umbrella. A life lived under the soft skies of home had not prepared her for the relentless California sun. Gratefully ensconced in shadow, she leaned back, mesmerized by the whoosh of the ocean smashing the rock arch.

"How's Sid?" Alex glanced up at her. "Any gossip from home?"

"He emailed a new bunch of photos." Sam passed over her phone, cued up at the latest pictures. In the first, Sid stood tall and straight, grinning madly, chest puffed out in his new AO police uniform, comprising a dark gray polo shirt and black police vest, pants, and hat.

"Aw, love how proud he is. He's like a pig in mud. In a good way." Alex said hastily. "No dodgy cop joke intended."

Sam snorted. "Uh-huh."

Alex flicked to the next photo. Sid was leaning against the back of his ute, about to take Bruce and Killer out for rounds.

"Look at those mutts," Sam grinned. "Tongues hanging out, cheerful as can be."

"Did you just call Sid a mutt?" Alex teased. "And yes, they're a funny trio." She swiped to the next picture.

Chloe and Sid's beaming faces appeared. The pair wore matching beanies that Skye had knitted them—the glitter-thread stitching looking especially...er...fetching.

"They seem happy," Alex said, studying their expressions.

"They are, although now Chloe's back in LA again and pining."

"Hasn't she been home to New Zealand, like, three times lately?"

"Mmm. I think so."

"Sounds serious." Alex looked thoughtful. "Well, well. Summer might get her destination wedding after all."

"Her what?"

"Just something Bess said to me ages ago. Summer was teasing about how she'd love to go to New Zealand for a friend's wedding."

Sam's eyebrow lifted, seeking more.

"Forget it. My friends are so random." Alex scrolled to the next image. "What's this a photo of?"

Sam leaned over and inspected the screen. It was her postcard corkboard, which now lived at the police station under Sid's careful curation. "The Ika Whenu escapees board. And my brother's sent a photo of the newest postcard to arrive. The one right in the middle." She pointed.

Alex zoomed in on the screen. "It's...Pfeiffer Beach."

"Yeah." Warmth filled Sam's chest. "He's binned Nicole's postcard and now mine's pride of place."

Alex glanced at her. "Must feel good to finally be on your board."

Sam couldn't even begin to explain how it felt. *Good* didn't even touch the sides.

Alex passed her phone back and dropped a kiss on her cheek.

Sam smiled and ran her hand through the grains of purple sand. Even though this wasn't her first trip to the beach of her dreams, each visit felt like a win. She'd proved herself. Stared down her fears. Clawed her way out of her rut.

She felt free.

Alex rummaged around in her bag. "Here." She passed over a glossy postcard. "To start a new collection."

Sam stared at the image of California's coastline.

"I thought it might be nice to collect one for everywhere we go together. Be nice to have memories of where you've been, not reminders of where you never got to."

"That's…" Sam smiled. Thoughtful. Romantic…

"I mean, you don't have to," Alex rushed on. "But I thought it'd be a good way to make new memories."

"It's a great idea."

"Turn it over."

Sam flipped the card and read the note in Alex's handwriting.

Tonight, after the party, let's go universe watching, then make love till dawn. When we wake, we'll sit in bath robes on our hotel balcony for breakfast like some fabulous romance movie cliché, and talk about all the things that matter and all the things that don't. I love you. You own my heart.

— Alex.

A ripple of delight went through Sam. Well, they'd been shuffling toward this, saying it in every other way but out loud. The confirmation was everything, though. Laying the card down reverently on her towel, Sam met Alex's eyes. "That's beautiful."

Alex's cheeks turned pink. Her expression searched Sam's.

Sam leaned closer. "You know, in hindsight, I think I fell in love with you the day I watched you boss everyone around about that missing lamp."

"You like bossy women then?" Alex said lightly, but relief and joy lit her eyes.

"In-charge, determined women who know their own minds have a certain appeal." Sam allowed a faint smile. "Especially one in particular. You are so… God, you're beautiful, smart, and I can't imagine life without you. These days I wake up and I can't wait for *more*. Trying more things, more interesting food, and more new places. Seeing more of the world. All of it. Everything." Her cheeks flooded with heat, and she wondered if she'd gone too far. It was the most she'd ever revealed. Old fears and doubts rose up and clawed at her.

Alex smiled. "Well, yep. I'm down with that. All the way." She suddenly laughed. "God, loving you makes my vocabulary dry up. I sound like an idiot."

"Small price to pay." Sam joined in laughing.

"No valiant denial of my idiocy?" Alex's eyes sparkled with mirth. "Oh dear."

Sam kissed her. "No. None. Besides, it's mutual. I can't even think straight around you."

Alex leaned against the door frame, watching Bess Thornton prep nibbles to go with a delicious-smelling tasting plate ordered from the hotel's Italian restaurant downstairs.

"Hey, love, smells divine." Alex came to stand beside her friend, stealing a cheese cube from Bess's intricate arrangement, and popped it in her mouth.

Bess gave her a warning look. "Stop messing with art."

"So highly strung." Alex chewed contentedly. "Delicious."

"Mmm. Illicit gains always taste better." Bess looked over Alex's shoulder. "Where's your cute cop?"

"Balcony. Sam wants to soak in the five-star cliff-top view before the party starts."

Bess nodded. "So, you look happy. Don't tell me you finally did it?" She reached for the carrots and began to artfully arrange the sticks around the cheese.

"Are you trying to get that into MOMA?" Alex peered at her creative construction. "And what have I finally done?"

"Confessed undying love to your woman."

"You know, you don't get to say *finally* like that. You only told Summer you loved her a few months ago despite it being bleedingly obvious for a year to everyone with eyeballs—including Summer."

"Yes. Well. We're not talking about me being…" She sought the word.

"Cautious? Slow? Oblivious?"

Bess huffed out an exaggerated sigh. "I was going to say anal. I wanted it to be absolutely perfect. I had this whole dinner planned I'd been working on for months, reconstructing a beautiful meal we'd had. But after all that

I blurted it out early. Terrible impulse control." Bess gave a wry smile. "So was I right? You did it? You told Sam?"

"Yes." Alex beamed.

Bess smiled at her, then focused on putting a lone cherry tomato on top of her cheese construct. She stepped back and peered at it. "Too much?"

Alex snorted. "Don't ask questions you don't want to hear the answer to."

"I see." Bess glanced at her. "So what happened? When you told her?"

"What do you think happened?" Alex asked.

"Well, I'd say she definitely cares. But I also gather from our chats that Sam's not the greatest at being open about her feelings. A little...aloof usually?" Her eyes crinkled. "Goodness, Alex Levitin, I'm starting to think you have a type."

Alex rolled her eyes. "Don't start."

Bess chuckled. "Anyway, given how you practically floated in here, I'd say you got an 'I love you' back from your woman."

"Yes." A wash of pleasure flooded Alex at the thought of being someone's *one*. Sam's one. "It's...amazing" She snatched the cherry tomato and popped it in her mouth. "I'm celebrating tonight."

"I'm really pleased. And Sam's lovely." Bess added a new cherry tomato to the top of her cheese pyramid, then shot Alex a dire look when Alex's fingers inched toward it. "Of course, I have no idea how she's coping with LA—after all, the woman practically exudes decency, goodness, and loyalty. And LA can't easily digest any of those things."

"I think it's a mutual case of Sam and LA side-eying each other a lot and going, 'what *is* that?'" Alex said.

Bess laughed, then shook her head. "Hell, I'm going to miss this. Us. Party nights, friends. Being around to see Sam's movie debut. All of it."

"You're only gone for six months, though. While you're doing that Campion film, right?"

"True. Still. I'm re-evaluating a few things lately." She lowered her voice to a conspiratorial whisper. "Such as, I'm starting to think I might actually *like* LA."

Alex straightened in shock. "Who are you, and what have you done with Elizabeth Thornton?"

"I know, I know." Bess smiled. "I'm sure it'll pass."

"Yeah. It will. Now I should get Sam her drink and try to peel her anti-social bum away from the stunning views and back into the rosy bosom of humanity."

"Thanks for that mental picture," Bess said, lips curling. "Come back soon? I need a hand with prepping the charcuterie board. You always were a legend at meat slicing."

"Yes, chef." Alex grabbed a beer and a plate of snacks and headed for the balcony.

On the expansive wooden balcony outside Bess and Summer's suite, Sam sat in a deckchair and stared out toward the ocean far below. The azure sweep of water was occasionally crested by windswept tufts of white. What was mesmerizing was the orange hue everything took on as the sun slipped over the horizon. The grassy cliff seemed to glow from underneath.

The sounds of party preparations drifted out through the wide glass doors behind her. She could make out the rhythm of Bess's low, throaty tones and Alex's amused higher voice, although she couldn't hear the words. It was their time to reconnect, and she didn't want to interrupt that.

Alex popped out a minute later, handing her a beer and a plate of snacks. "Hey. You doing okay out here?"

"I'm fine." Sam tried the beer. *Nice.* "I've been just trying to wrap my head around a sunset at eight-thirty in *July*. Of course, the seasons here are all about-face, so it's making my brain melt a little. So now I'm just zoning out, admiring the colors."

Alex laughed. "Right. I won't be long. Just helping Bess in the kitchen. We learned long ago to let me operate the knives." She turned to leave, then stopped. "Hey, please don't stress about tonight," she said, looking stressed enough for both of them. "The trivia thing, I mean."

Sam chuckled, gave her a careless wave, and returned to her view. She jabbed a crunchy, low-fat, actress-friendly cracker into the beetroot-and-dill dip Alex had put in front of her and gave it a try. Not too terrible. Not as good as Gina's, of course. She chuckled at her staunch loyalty.

The remaining two guests arrived in a wash of laughter and actual cheek kisses—proof they hadn't been sucked into the Hollywood cult of air-kissing. Brian and Rowan burst through the French doors onto the balcony with a dramatic flourish, apparently debating the burning question of what color Pfeiffer Beach's sand actually was.

"Mulberry," Brian announced.

"It's plum," Rowan corrected, dropping to the chair beside Sam. "Definitely." He turned to her. "Hello again, Samantha darling. Just ignore my colorblind boyfriend. Playing mad scientists appears to have gone to his head."

She smiled, amused.

Brian dropped into the armchair on Sam's other side. "Sam, love, you look as dashing as ever." He glanced across her to Rowan. "Okay, it's mulberry with a dash of sangria. Speaking of drinks..." He pitched his voice toward the kitchen. "*I would give all my fame for a pot of ale and safety!*"

Sam started at the booming voice reverberating in her ears. *How does he do that?* He'd give even Gina a run for her money during the pub lunch rush.

"*Henry V*," Rowan noted dryly. "And what fame is this that you're giving up?"

"Harsh." Brian's hand thumped across his heart. He turned to Sam. "You see what I must endure?"

Sam opened her mouth to reply, but by then Rowan was busy citing Warhol. She settled back, content to enjoy their good-natured banter and soak in the evening skies.

The sun had slipped a little farther down the red-streaked sky when Summer emerged, her blonde hair slicked back, looking as sunny as her name. She handed out dark ales to Brian and Rowan.

"I heard you two arguing before," Summer said. "Pfeiffer Beach is plain old purple, guys. Do you always have to overthink everything?"

They glanced at each other, as though puzzled by the question.

"We're British," Brian finally said. "Of course we do."

Summer snorted and shook her head.

Rowan turned back to Sam. "Enough about our nonsense. You look extra perky with sprinkles on top. What's happening? Did Alex finally pop the question?" His bushy eyebrows gave a rakish waggle.

She wondered how to answer that. 'None of your business' seemed a little unfriendly to one of Alex's oldest friends, but she'd only met the man once before. He was astonishingly perceptive, though, she had to give him that.

"Rowan, behave, you impish cad," Brian interrupted. He turned back to Sam. "I'm sorry, he forgets you're not from LA, where the sharing of one's relationship status gets dished out as frequently as CVs. I'll spare you the inquisition and just say, we both think it's marvelous how you and Alex look so captivated lately, besotted even, and we're delighted for you both."

Besotted? The men were spared a good old-fashioned Kiwi eye roll when Alex reappeared, sliding into Sam's deckchair alongside her.

"That's enough out of you two," Alex said. "Stop trying to make Sam squirm and tell us about your new comedy show, Rowan. What's it called?"

Rowan virtually preened at his pet topic. *"Surviving Shezan—Inside the World's Worst Movie and Dining Out on My Director Friend's Name."*

Alex's mouth fell open. "Shit. Seriously?"

He snorted. "Lord, you're easy." He jabbed a carrot stick into the dip. "It's called *Life After Mum's Basement—The Unemployed Years.* What of you two? Anything new on the horizon?"

"I'm debating whether to do a film an up-and-coming indie writer penned for me," Alex said. "And I do mean *for me.*"

"Ahhh, Hollywood's sycophants, God love 'em. And Sam, darling?" Rowan turned to her. "What's new from New Zealand's finest import?"

Bess came out onto the balcony, looking her usual picture of elegance, wearing black jeans and a pale lavender blouse that whispered against her pale, long neck. Her beauty, as always, made Sam stare just a little. How did people like this exist in real life?

She turned back to Rowan. "I'm doing a small motorbike stunt in one of Brock's films. Well, the first of a few, actually, because the movie's part of a trilogy."

"Oooh." He gazed at her in awe. "So the rumors were true: Our Alex has found herself a daredevil."

"A Batgirl, actually." Alex grinned. "That's what I mentally called her the day we met."

Sam blinked. "You what?"

Alex turned to her. "You came flying out of a hole in some bushes on your black beast. So, yep, Batgirl."

Brian leaned forward and waved between Sam and Alex. "God, you two are so adorable together. They should make collectible dolls. Did you know Summer and Bess have them now? Some fans from their old TV show are making a killing on them on Etsy."

"Tell me you don't have them," Bess muttered. "People are just cashing in on the Hunter fandom."

"Absolutely I do," Brian said with a firm nod of satisfaction. "I have a mint pair of the two of you making heart-eyes at each other."

"We don't make heart-eyes." Bess sounded weary.

"Tell that to the dolls."

Bess cleared her throat. "Okay, deluded friends, come inside. Let's eat, drink, and see what our collective of bard lovers think they know."

"What *is* a collective of bard lovers actually called?" Rowan asked curiously.

"If it helps, a group of bards is a gallant," Brian said.

"It is?" Summer asked. "How do you know?"

He shrugged. "I was on an internet forum for discussing group nouns one day. They were debating earnestly whether to call it a 'bumwobble of cyclists.' Naturally, I voted yes."

Sam shook her head. Hanging around Alex's mentally agile friends was like being jabbed repeatedly by a livewire. Challenging, unexpected, and confounding. They were absurd. Funny, too.

"I'm sorry we're all nuts," Alex murmured against her ear. "I'd say it gets better, but once you add excessive alcohol, it's all downhill from here. Unfortunately, it only gets crazier when we toss in Shakespeare. Just be glad Amrit and Zara had to work, or you'd see a full spectrum of insanity." Her eyes sparkled.

"They don't seem especially insane," Sam said.

"Winner tonight gets to kick a football off the balcony," Brian suddenly announced from the lounge. "Don't worry, I brought mine."

"Oh." Sam froze. "I see I spoke too soon."

They headed inside just as Bess vowed to take a meat cleaver to the ball if he tried any such thing.

"Ho boy," Alex said. "They're in fine form already. Gird your loins."

That evening, long after everyone had gotten drunker, louder, and funnier, long after Sam's limited Shakespeare trivia had—very briefly—astounded the group, and long after Summer had trounced them all amid much laughter, Sam found herself staring up at the night sky.

She and Alex were wrapped around each other on one of the deckchairs on the private balcony outside their own room. Below them, now invisible in the darkness, came the crash of waves, soothing and peaceful.

A few balconies along, they could hear the faint sounds of music coming from Brian and Rowan's room, and a clink of glasses in the darkness.

In the other direction, where Bess and Summer's suite was, lay silence. Their hosts had kicked everyone out half an hour ago. Amid knowing looks, everyone had gotten the hint and wheeled off to their various rooms.

Sam was looking forward to gathering her own lover in her arms soon. But not quite yet. Right now, Alex's dreams came first: inspecting the universe, one star at a time.

Alex sighed with delight. "I've missed this. Thanks for indulging me. Not just with the stars, but with all of it. Everything."

"It's no hardship," Sam said.

"Any regrets?" Alex asked after a few moments. "About coming to the States with me? Now you've seen my life, my world, met my mad friends?"

"No." Sam held Alex closer. "I'm right where I want to be."

They lay in silence, soaking up the warmth of each other's bodies, and their closeness. Sam could feel the soft thudding of the pulse at Alex's neck against her lips.

"Your friends are mad, though," she added as an afterthought.

"I know." Alex started laughing before saying, "Shush, they might hear us."

"I'm not saying anything," Sam murmured. "I'm just laying here, thinking about you, and how beautiful you looked tonight."

"Good lighting."

"Mmm. That must be it." Sam chuckled.

Alex gave her arm a light slap.

"Hey! What was that for?"

"Pulling a con on me." Alex's tone contained laughter.

"Did you enjoy it?" Sam asked.

"You know that I loved it. The idea you'd go through all that for me. For my friends, too..."

"Why wouldn't I?" Sam pulled her closer. "You're worth a few hours' research. And Summer's pretty fun to hang out with. Besides, I wanted to see the look on your face. It was priceless. I've raided marijuana crops in the middle of the wop-wops and received less shocked looks from the drug lords than the one you gave me when I somehow knew that Shakespeare's father was a cop."

"You totally got me." Alex laughed softly, then gave a contented sigh. "Today has been so wonderful. I'd love to stay here all night. Wake up with the dawn, see what colors the sky turns. Rustic pinks maybe? Burnt ochre?"

"Well, that would foil our plans for tonight. I'm sure your postcard declared we would make love till dawn."

"Oh yes, quite right." Alex bobbed her head. "Promises were made. I should probably get right on that."

"Yes." Sam smiled. "You should. But not this minute. I want to soak you in a little bit first. All this ambience... I'm filing it away forever."

Alex's fingers curled around her ribs, stroking languidly. She nibbled under Sam's jaw, causing the hairs at the back of her neck to stand up.

Sam's breath hitched.

"I love your body," Alex said absently as her fingers slid up to Sam's shoulders, then down her arm. "It's sleek and powerful. Not just beautiful but strong. Why is it when I'm with you I feel so safe?"

Sam trailed her fingers across Alex's cheek. "Because you know you always will be."

"Yes." Alex exhaled. "I felt it in New Zealand, too. The day I realized how much you meant to me. I suddenly understood how different it felt being with you. Like I was someone who was important to you, someone you needed, not just wanted." She cupped Sam's neck and drew her in for a kiss.

Sam's lips were warm, yielding, and moved under hers, inviting more. Desire sparked, along with hunger, but it was infused with love. A delicious, heady combination.

Alex indulged herself for long, breathless minutes.

"You've always mattered to me," Sam whispered when they pulled apart, her voice so soft that her words almost disappeared into the night. "Even when you were driving me nuts. My crazy brother was right about that." Affection filled her tone.

"Yeah, Sid might have been onto something there," Alex agreed with a small laugh. "I'm pretty glad he was." Her roaming hands stilled. "I love you."

Sam's heart swelled at the words—so simple but containing everything that really mattered. "I know the feeling." Her voice cracked.

For a long time, they simply held each other and watched the stars. Sam memorized Alex's soft breathing and the steady heartbeat fluttering under her ear.

In the distance a bird called, its high-pitched tone slicing through the soothing sounds of waves somewhere far below. Sam's arms tightened around Alex, pulling her closer.

"This is perfect." Alex gave a contented sigh. "God, you know, this—*us*—is nuts given how we met, me nearly hitting you."

"It's funny how you keep telling everyone that's what happened," Sam murmured, a hint of a smile edging her lips. "But it's not true—not to mention being a terrible ending for a story." She lifted her head and offered Alex an arch look. "And to think you make movies for a living."

Alex blinked. "But…that's what happened."

"No, it wasn't. See, you *did* run me over after all." She leaned against Alex's ear and whispered, "And I never stood a chance."

"Ahhh." Amusement filled Alex's gleaming eyes and she leaned up and placed a kiss filled with promises on Sam's lips. "Yes," she breathed. "Quite right. How could I forget?" She smiled. "Now that's what I call an ending."

About Lee Winter

Lee Winter is an award-winning veteran newspaper journalist who has lived in almost every Australian state, covering courts, crime, news, features and humour writing. Now a full-time author and part-time editor, Lee is also a 2015 and 2016 Lambda Literary Award finalist and has won several Golden Crown Literary Awards. She lives in Western Australia with her long-time girlfriend, where she spends much time ruminating on her garden, US politics, and shiny, new gadgets.

CONNECT WITH LEE

Website: www.leewinterauthor.com

Other Books from Ylva Publishing

www.ylva-publishing.com

Breaking Character

Lee Winter

ISBN: 978-3-96324-113-0
Length: 315 pages (106,000 words)

Life becomes a farcical mess when icy British A-lister Elizabeth and bright LA star Summer try to persuade an eccentric director they're in love to win Elizabeth her dream role—while convincing a gossiping Hollywood they're not. Worse, they're closeted lesbians who don't even know the other is gay.

A lesbian celebrity romance about gaining love, losing masks, and trying to stick to the script.

A Curious Woman

Jess Lea

ISBN: 978-3-96324-160-4
Length: 283 pages (100,000 words)

Bess has moved to a coastal town where she has a job at a hip gallery, some territorial chickens, and a lot of self-help books. She's also at war with Margaret, who runs the local museum with an iron fist. When they're both implicated in a senseless murder, can they work together to expose the truth?

A funny, fabulous, cozy mystery filled with quirkiness and a sweet serve of lesbian romance.

A Heart This Big

Cheyenne Blue

ISBN: 978-3-96324-202-1
Length: 253 pages (89,000 words)

Country girl Nina loves to offer city kids a taste of rural life at Banksia Farm. When a lawsuit threatens, she needs help to avoid losing the farm.

Enter lawyer Leigh, who doesn't have time for small, unpaid cases or rural visits that wreck her cool—and her clothes. Still, warm-hearted Nina and her challenging daughter are awfully hard to say no to.

A captivating opposites-attract lesbian romance.

Food for Love

C. Fonseca

ISBN: 978-3-96324-082-9
Length: 276 pages (96,000 words)

When injured elite cyclist Jess flies to Australia to sort her late brother's estate, the last thing she wants is his stake in a rural eatery. She'd rather settle up, move on, and sidestep the restaurant's beautiful owner, Lili, and her child. Given her traumatic life, Jess isn't sure she'd survive letting her guard down.

A lesbian romance about how nourishment is much more than the food we eat.

Changing the Script

ISBN: 978-3-96324-296-0

Also available as e-book.

Published by Ylva Publishing, legal entity of Ylva Verlag, e.Kfr.

Ylva Verlag, e.Kfr.
Owner: Astrid Ohletz
Am Kirschgarten 2
65830 Kriftel
Germany

www.ylva-publishing.com

First edition: 2019

Credits
Edited by Alissa McGowan
Cover Design and Print Layout by Streetlight Graphics

Printed in Great Britain
by Amazon